This is the third volume of the Hittite trilogy, in which Ammuna, a disaffected senior Hittite General has had enough of the Hittite King's interference in his career and has sold himself to the Mittani Crown Prince Artatama for golden shekels. Worse, he's kidnapped King Tudhaliyas' 6 year old daughter, Princess Asmunikal, for those golden shekels.

It is now six years since the Battle of the Wide Plateau put Tudhaliyas on the throne (Vol 1—*Murder in Hattusas*), in the realm of the ancient Hittite Empire, and three years since Madduwatta's Rebellion was dismantled by Tudhaliyas, (Vol 2—*Madduwatta's Rebellion*), both times with Mokhat's help.

In this third volume of the Hittite trilogy, the reader is invited to participate in a seventeen-day pursuit from Hattusas to Nineveh, in a romp through the landscape of ancient Mesopotamia, when Mokhat's *special forces* chase rogue General Ammuna and his gang of mercenaries into the heart of Assyria, trying to rescue the kidnapped daughter of grief stricken King Tudhaliyas and his consort, Queen Nikal.

Tudhaliyas invades Mittani to force Artatama to release his daughter. The Kizzuwatna army is on the march, in support of the Hittite King, as is the Pharaoh, both allied to Hattusas by binding treaties. Cities allied to the Mittani come under attack one by one. There are catastrophic consequences for Artatama's father, King Saustatar of Mittani when a Hittite army appears on his doorstep. Has Artatama overstretched himself? Has his ambition become his downfall? Will the *special forces* rescue the princess? These are the questions this third volume proposes to answer.

Mittani Kidnapping

Sasha Garrydeb

Historical Novel

Volume 3 of the Hittite trilogy

London
2012

Published in Britain in 2012
by ABC Publishers
24 Treadgold Street London W11 4BP

e-mail: abcpublishers@ntlworld.com

A CIP catalogue record for this book
is available from the British Library.

ISBN 978-0954814489

Printed by
ABC Publishers,
Notting Dale,
London W11 4BP.

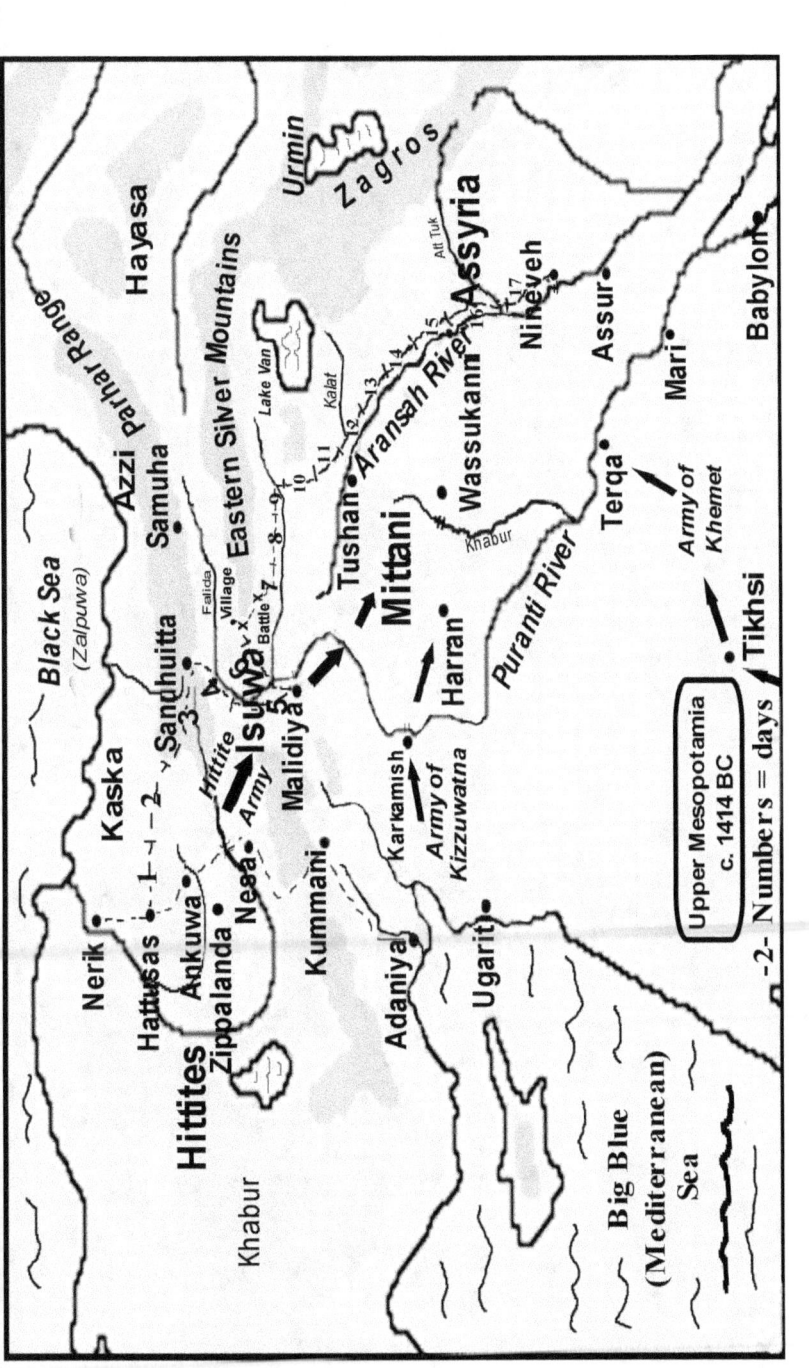

CHARACTER LIST (main characters in bold)

Mokhat—brother of the Kaska king, in charge of expedition
Palaiyas—ex Prince of Tiryns, companion to Mokhat
Onasiyas—Colonel and leader of the *Special Forces*
Neti—Captain and deputy to Onasiyas
Asmunikal—King Tudhaliya's 6 year old daughter

Ammuna—rogue Hittite General, leader of the kidnappers
Lawana—Colonel, Ammuna's deputy

Tudhaliyas—King of the Hittites
Nikal—Queen to King Tudhaliyas
Zidanta—General commanding Hittite army
Muttalu—General, deputy to Zidanta

Artatama—Crown Prince of Mittani
Napat—false Mittani merchant in Artatama's service
Tarkuni—Mittani spy master who switches to Artatama
Haratam—Artatama's agent for Ammuna in Assyria
Saustatar—King of Mittani, Artatama's father
Ratukani—Mittani Genral, army commander

Shunashura—King of Kizzuwatna
Talshura—Kizzuwatna Crown Prince
Tapalass—General, commander of the Kizzuwatna army

Malda—village head near the Zagros mountains

Pudil—Assyrian colonel of cavalry squadron
Musuri—Assyrian colonel on other side of river
Tarasina—vacillating King of Isuwa
Kanisa—General and then king of Isuwa
Aplahanda II—King of Karkamish
Muhar—General of Karkamish
Harupal—Karkamish town engineer
Tupkish—King of Harran

Ulurra—Mokhat's wife
Mahera—married to Palaiyas

Glossary

Cubit = 0.46m or 18 in. League = 5 km or 3 miles
The shekel was the state currency (named after the Babylonian shekel)
    40 mina = 1 shekel usually in copper or silver
    2 weight mina = 1 Kg

manes = spirits of the dead
Taru = Hittite storm god
Teshub = Hurrian storm god
Kaska Tribes centred round Nerik as its capital
Kizzuwatna = allied kingdom south of Hittites
Wassukkani = capital city of Mittani
Hayasa = Wild tribe east of the Azzi (poss. Armenians)
Puranti River = Hurrian name for the Euphrates
Aranzah River = Hurrian name for the Tigris
Big Blue Sea = Mediterranean Sea
Eastern Silver Mountains = Taurus Mountains

Khemet = the ancient Egyptian name for Egypt
Pharaoh Amenhotep II (1424-1401 BC)
Djat = First Minister to Pharaoh
Waset = Thebes
Iteru = Nile

Part of the Hittite King List

Old Kingdom
Muwatallis I (c.1422-1420 BC)
Muwas during the short Civil War
New Kingdom
Tudhaliyas I (1420-1400 BC)

The story is set in the tumultuous period of the Hittite Empire in what is now Turkey, at the beginning of the New Kingdom. The year is 1414 BC, six years after the civil war that brought King Tudhaliyas to power on the Hittite Lion Throne. The time is autumn. The kings are real.

Kidnapping
1
The Merchant

He'd thrown a dark cloak over his powerful frame to disguise his appearance—and he attempted to stay in the shadows as far as he possibly could, constantly looking round, checking to see if he was being followed. But he felt extremely uncomfortable in this role. As a senior general in the Hittite army, Ammuna tried hard to conceal himself, but it was difficult. He was used to pushing himself into the forefront, not slinking around in the darkness like some feral dog.

This was the second clandestine meeting he was going to with the bearded Mittani merchant, and if he were seen, it would be extremely difficult to explain what he was up to, if not outright fatal for him. On the other hand, if the Mittani agreed to his price, then he would be rich beyond his wildest dreams. The Mittani, in the form of this merchant, had brought a proposal to him and he'd named his price. Now he was about to find out if they'd agreed to the exorbitant fee—and if by some outrageous miracle they had, he would do his utmost to carry out the task they'd assigned him. It all depended on the bearded merchant and what he had to say tonight.

Ammuna skulked along the alleyways of Adaniya like some common thief, making his way down to the harbour. He looked for the Ugarit ship with the eye painted on the bow, the one where the Captain had been bought and paid for. He found the vessel berthed in the same place as last time, but this time it was low in the water, implying it had taken on its cargo and was ready to leave on the morning tide.

He heard the oncoming tramping of nearby feet and quickly hid behind a bale of wool on the quayside while the shore patrol went by. When they'd gone, Ammuna gingerly sneaked down the gangplank and onto the ship's deck, all the while peering at the stern of the vessel. In the shadows, he spied the burly outline of a figure waiting for him. A few quick silent strides across the deck and he reached the waiting merchant, who grabbed his cloak and pulled him into the shadows with him.

Ammuna furiously snatched his cloak back from the merchant's large hands, as if to say, *how dare you touch me?* 'Well?' he hissed at the glaring merchant. 'What did they say?'

'It's a high price…' began the merchant, his dark eyes twinkling with mischief.

Ammuna cut him off, 'I didn't come here to listen to twaddle. It was *you* who sought *me* out, not the other way round. I gave you a price—take it or leave it. What you're asking me to do is so outlandish and dangerous that the price is worth every shekel I'm demanding. Did they agree, or didn't they?' He didn't want to bandy words with this scoundrel any more than he had to.

The merchant stroked his black beard, still glaring at the general, and then said, 'They agreed. One million golden shekels on delivery of, *you know who,* to Wassukanni. Nothing if you fail!'

An inner sigh of relief shuddered through Ammuna's body. They'd *actually* agreed to his price. He'd managed to pull off the *outrageous miracle.* Admittedly, the hard part was yet to come, but the reward would be commensurate. 'And the other part; the royal seal…, to seal the bargain? Have you got it?'

The bearded merchant poked his hands into his dark cloak and rummaged around, pulling out a brown leather pouch and extracted something from it. He held it out to Ammuna. 'If this is lost, or it falls into the wrong hands, then the full weight of Mittani will hound you down to the underworld. I was instructed to tell you that.'

Ammuna took the proffered item, peered at it as best he could in the darkness, satisfying himself it was the royal seal of Mittani. Then he quickly hid it in his own pouch at his belt. 'Expect me with the merchandise in about a month's time. Alert your border guards to give me any assistance I may require. I don't expect to need it but alert them in case. I need to get through the border *fast* with no hold-ups. As for your spy network—I may need to use them, hence this seal. Notify them they should help me if I need help.' Ammuna gave one more stinging glare at the merchant, then turned on his heels, walking straight-backed along the deck as if he were the captain of the ship.

Halfway across the deck he remembered where he was and quickly hunched his shoulders, switching to a soft walk up the gangplank back to shore, again warily looking out for the shore patrol.

As he took the long stealthily hike back to his mansion near the main army barracks, his mind went back, as it did quite often, to what had led him to the path he'd just taken—that of treachery to the rightful king he served. Served, albeit with tongue in cheek.

Six years ago, Ammuna had been the top army commander of the then rightful monarch, King Muwas, who'd been challenged by another royal faction for the right to succeed his brother to the Lion Throne. A short but vicious civil war ensued which culminated in the battle of the Wide Plateau—a battle which Ammuna lost. He'd been allowed to stay in the army with a renewed oath of loyalty to the new king, yet over the years he'd served with a distinct lack of enthusiasm, until he'd been finally demoted to his current job.

It was the last straw. Ammuna felt insulted and knew without a shadow of doubt his days in the army were numbered. Soon, if he were lucky, he would be retired on a small pension and put out to pasture. Ammuna wasn't ready to retire, and certainly not on the miserly pension he was likely to be offered. As a man of action, he took matters in his own hands—and had induced the Mittani to make him an offer—an offer, which if to his liking, he would not refuse. The big question now was....could he deliver?

It took Ammuna almost until dawn to reach his mansion. Most of the time and effort was spent in having to stay in the shadows all the way back there. Even then, he had to go round the back of the house and climb over a wall into his own back garden, to avoid his own sentries. His head hit the pillow just before reveille. Reveille prompted his personal aide to come and rouse him for breakfast—as he normally did.

*   *   *

Adaniya castle was halfway up the precipice facing the river and backed on to sheer cliffs for protection. The sizeable town below the castle spread lazily downwards and then along the riverside and was a conduit for a huge trade with the other merchants operating their extensive trading network on the Big Blue Sea.

'Your highness, General Ammuna wishes to speak to you. Shall I have him shown in?' General Tapalass, the tall commander of the Kizzuwatna army, asked the young Crown Prince Talshura, in the audience chamber of the castle.

'I wonder what he wants?' the prince voiced aloud, his smooth forehead creasing in a frown. With his right hand he brushed back his dark long hair. 'He's been keeping a low profile to date—which suits us nicely. Have you been keeping an eye on him as the Hittite king asked us to do?'

'Yes your highness,' replied the imposing dark featured Tapalass. 'Although I have to tell you, he went missing in the middle of last night when our servant checked on him. However, he was back in his bed when his aide woke him this morning. We've instructed the servants to keep a closer watch on him.'

'Missing? I wonder where he disappeared to? Well, show him in, let's see what he wants.'

General Ammuna marched into the room as if he owned the place. He stopped before the prince and bowed slightly, almost arrogantly, dark eyes not on the floor as was customary but on the young prince. 'Your highness, I have been recalled to Hattusas for consultations and will be back here in about two weeks. Protocol demands I inform you of my leave-taking. With your permission I will depart in the afternoon.'

The prince nodded and said, 'Thank you for informing us. May you have a safe journey and give my fond regards to the King in Hattusas.'

Ammuna bowed almost imperceptibly and marched out of the audience room. Walking down the corridor, he scowled at the notion that this twenty three year old had been put in charge of the Kizzuwatna military; thus making him his nominal boss. That he should defer to this snotty nosed youngster made his bile rise.

General Ammuna was on attachment to the Kizzuwatna military to teach them some of the new chariot tactics his commander, General Zidanta, had invented, and was supposed to defer to the prince as his senior. He'd never been happy with the arrangement, feeling this young upstart was a novice in military matters. As he left the building, his mind nagged him regarding this predicament, and not for the first time.

For the last six years, he'd been on attachment to various overseas military postings. He'd spent three years in Kussara advising their military, making sure it didn't become too robust. Then after Madduwatta's disastrous episode three years ago, he'd been seconded to oversee the dismantling of that army and replacing it with an army committed to central Hittite oversight. He ensured Madduwatta's General Visanitti was removed and sent to a minor post in Hattusas. Then for the last year, he'd been seconded to the Kizzuwatna military, but he knew this was a ruse to get him out of the way, to get him away from Hattusas. In effect, all of his postings had been significant demotions—and he blamed the Hittite king for this relegation. He knew Tudhaliyas could never really trust him —and now he proposed to repay the king's lack of confidence with the worst betrayal he could manage. He'd been stewing and planning *some* outrage which would discomfort the king; but *now* he'd come up with a scheme that would top anything he'd previously thought up.

Ammuna was in clandestine contact with some of his former officers from his time with King Muwas, and had promised them untold riches if they would join him in an adventure—likely to be treacherous and perilous. As most had also lost out in the aftermath of the civil war, where they'd all been demoted, they were only too happy to throw their lot in with him, especially if they were to become rich. Before he was sent to Kizzuwatna, he'd hand-picked twenty officers and men from the old days, men he could rely on, and taken them down to Adaniya with him to his current posting.

When Ammuna returned to his mansion, he ordered his chariot brought round to the front, and for his special *loyal* troops to assemble for the long journey back to Hattusas. These were the very men who were to be the core of his new *loyal* band of mercenaries. The day before he'd asked them all if they wanted to become rich—and to a man, they'd agreed they did. He'd then sent riders to collect more of his *loyal* officers and men from the old days. They would meet up with him along the road at various points on the route up to Hattusas.

Ammuna headed his *loyal* band out of the river port of Adaniya, up the lush verdant valley following the river, which flowed down to the sea from its mountainous source. It was autumn and the weather was as soft and easy as the gods could make it, or the people might wish for; warm days and careless nights. The greens were gently giving way to yellows and browns, and clouds hung around the peaks high up in the mountains to their left.

It would take the group at least four days of hard riding to get to Hattusas, and they would arrive just in time for the autumnal equinox festival. They followed the benign valley system to Kummani, where they picked up fifty *loyal* men from the old days. Then they continued over the mountains to Nesa, the original capital of the Hittites, whose language was still called Nesi by the people. The city was the ancient hub of an Assyrian trading outpost for over a thousand years. It sat overlooking the mighty Marassantiya River on a small dusty plain surrounded by mountains.

There, Ammuna picked up more men, around a hundred to add to his *loyal* band of mercenaries. He was careful to meet them outside the city, and never went inside himself, in case he was recognised.

Recognised? It was a mere precaution, not a likelihood he mused. Out of the blue, his mind again wandered to a time six years ago, a time when he was on top of the world. Then a catastrophe had occurred—to him personally.

Six years ago, he'd been on the losing side of the civil conflict, and that had pitted Muwas and Tudhaliyas against each other for the right to sit on the Hittite Lion Throne. He'd been in command of King Muwas' army, and after the battle, when his forces were overwhelmed, he'd made a run for it. General Zidanta, the commander of the victorious army pursued him and caught him—then astonishingly, instead of putting him to the sword, the wily old soldier offered him the post of becoming his deputy, but that lasted only a month before the new king intervened. King Tudhaliyas didn't trust him, or any of the men on the opposing side in the war. He considered they'd made their choice at the outset, and they should be forced to live with their choice. He'd ordered Zidanta to find Ammuna another job, one where he had less control over the Hittite military. Ammuna shook his head, trying to clear the intrusive thoughts, yet they were never far away, churning away with their insidious poison, just under the mental horizon.

Led by Ammuna in his chariot, the band now consisted of some a hundred and seventy men and was beginning to be blatantly visible to all who saw them. They looked like a Hittite cavalry column heading up north. If he were challenged by another Hittite column, his story was to be just that; he'd been called up to Hattusas to report to the king.

After crossing the bridge spanning the mighty Marassantiya River, then sometime further on, its minor tributary, they came to Ankuwa. It was next on the list of cities the column was to nearly-visit. They could have bypassed it, but instead, they waited in a discreet gully about half a league outside of the city for another thirty *loyal* men to join their expanding convoy.

Mid-morning of the fourth day, they reached a thick leafy forest about two leagues outside Hattusas, where another twenty men led by his deputy, were waiting with seven covered wagons. Ammuna had prearranged this assignation a month earlier when he'd planned a very different outrage. There were now two hundred and twenty men, all *loyal* to Ammuna, and *not* to their rightful king. In the olden days, at least forty of them were part of his personal bodyguard, and the rest, former members of the Ininas Chariot Regiment Ammuna had previously commanded. All these men were now his *loyal* mercenaries, willing to carry out whatever dastardly deed he'd ask of them. All had been victimised for picking the losing side of the civil war.

In the forest clearing, Ammuna stayed on his chariot and had his lanky deputy, Colonel Lawana; gather the men around him in a circle. This is where he belonged, mused Ammuna, on a stage with his men hanging on his every word, not skulking around in a cloak in an alleyway. This was the point at which he would outline the whole plan to them.

Ammuna set his strong dark features at them and began. 'Relax men, I'm about to tell you what I'm planning to ask of you—what I want you to do to earn all that lovely money I've promised you. Some of you already know what's in the wagons. They're filled with caskets of wine and beer some of us are going to use to get into Hattusas. Tomorrow is the Nuntarriyashas Autumn Festival and all the taverns are going to be overflowing with revellers.

Forty-two of us are going to enter through the western Lion Gate, hidden in the wagons; we're going to park the wagons outside the palace gate, and four officers will accompany me in to the castle. We're going to find the room where Asmunikal is lurking, and we're going to abduct her and take her to Wassukanni. My insiders reliably inform me that Tudhaliyas won't take his daughter with him to the Temple because it's too arduous. So, she'll be alone, apart from her minders. The job for the thirty-eight left in the wagons is to make sure the eastern King's Gate stays open for our escape. That's the job you signed up for.' He stopped and smiled, and watched their array of reactions.

Most of the men were awestruck; quite a few mouths dropped open at the immensity of what they were being asked to do. The surprise and shock silenced them. They peered at each other, mostly in astonishment. Then they looked at Ammuna. Had the general gone insane? Did he really think he could go into the Royal Castle and kidnap the king's daughter just like that? This wasn't just the ordinary soldiers—the officers were just as taken aback as the men were. The old man's gone doolally was in the minds of most of the men.

'Well, I can see that I've caused a bit of a stir.' He waited until they'd settled down. 'Look lads, if I didn't think we could pull it off, I wouldn't be standing here in front of you asking you to trust me. There's a lot going for us. The king and queen are with the high priest at the main temple, officiating in the festival. The castle will be minimally guarded, and the biggest element on our side is surprise. Nobody is expecting anyone to nab the king's daughter.

'We'll be in and out before they know what's hit them. I've thought this through carefully. If I had any doubt, I would drop this like I would a hot piece of metal. I'm not keen to get myself killed, or to get *you* killed for that matter. When we were asked to go into battle, it was for a lot less pay than I'm offering you now. Yes, there's an element of danger involved, but we're soldiers—that's our job. We thrive on danger. Only *this* time we're not fighting for some fancy notion of king and country, but for ourselves—so we can retire and live the life of wealthy men. True, it can't be in any of the Hittite lands, but money talks wherever we are.

'If you don't feel like doing this, I won't hold it against you. A hundred and seventy-eight of you will have to wait here anyway. All I ask is, those not wishing to take part, wait here until we get back, and then they can go about their normal business as if none of this ever happened. They won't be paid, that's all. So now, who's with me? You're welcome to discuss this as long as you need to—only I do need an answer sometime soon.'

There was silence—then people paired off and began talking. All of the officers came and stood clearly with Ammuna. They'd made their decision to support Ammuna a long time ago—come what may. When the soldiers formed once more round the chariot and the final count was made, not one of the ordinary soldiers defaulted. It was lunacy, but Ammuna was their General. They'd follow him into the netherworld, if he asked them to.

'Right lads, I'm most gratified by your confidence in me. I knew you wouldn't let me down. Now I suggest we open a couple of those casks of wine and drink to our success. What do you say?'

A hushed roar of approval met that suggestion, the enthusiasm creeping through the forest like a blast of blustery weather; and a number of men went off to open the casks of wine for an extended toast to their success.

'Make sure they don't get too drunk,' Ammuna told Lawana. 'We need clear heads in the morning. I want you to pick the forty men who are coming tomorrow in the wagons right now, and make sure they stay sober. Pick the smartest fighters. You and I will be on the first wagon. No fires tonight. You'll find cold rations in the wagons. Let the men have some fun, but make sure there's latrines dug downwind, and the horses are fed. Set the normal sentries around the camp throughout the night. Make sure they're sober and stay awake.'

'Yes sir,' replied Colonel Lawana.

'When you've done, Colonel, come and join the fun. I want to be as one with the men tonight.'

2
ABDUCTION

The next day, seven covered wagons set off around mid-morning, with Ammuna once again donning a dark cloak, as did his deputy, Lawana. They sat in the lead wagon, followed by the other six wagons, and drove the two leagues all the way up to the western Lion Gate of Hattusas. Ammuna waited a little distance off from the gate, and then followed a grain supply convoy in, to create some congestion. As they approached the gate, Ammuna put on a good show, acting the part of the tough boss of the booze convoy coming in from Zippalanda to resupply one of the taverns in the city during the festival rush.

The officer at the gate had orders to check each wagon to see they contained what the boss of the convoy said it contained. The very same officer was somewhat irritated at the workload imposed on him that day. Convoys had begun coming in at dawn and been continuing throughout the morning and the officer was tired and snappy with the drivers of the convoys. This suited Ammuna for his purpose; he'd calculated his arrival just as the gate sentries were getting flustered and short-tempered, so they would do a sloppy check of the wagon's contents. Two barrels in the third wagon contained swords, knives, and such.

Ammuna had a couple of large flagons of beer ready for the ordinary sentries and a skin of wine readied for the captain of the gate. He traded jokes with the captain of the gate, knowing how to deal with the army men.

'You've got a rotten job there, son, especially on this festive day,' he told the young captain at the gate, trying to encourage his irritation.

'Tell me about it,' replied the captain. 'It's been murder from the time we opened the gate at dawn. Don't know where they're all coming from.'

'All we've got is wine and beer for *The Pride of the Citadel* tavern in the Upper City,' Ammuna told the captain. 'Look here, you've been run off your feet; why don't you stop for a moment and have a taste.' Ammuna offered the readied wineskin to the captain.

'I shouldn't, really,' said the officer, eyeing the wineskin, while contemplating his dry mouth.

'Go on, nobody will notice. In fact, here...take the whole skin. You can nip at it when you've a chance.' Ammuna thrust the wineskin at the captain. 'There's a couple of flagons of beer for your men in the next wagon. I know how thirsty this work can get. Enjoy the festival.'

The captain looked around and took the wineskin, surreptitiously, hiding it under his cloak. Instead of having his men search the booze convoy thoroughly as he should have done, he waved it through the gate without checking it at all, telling his men to grab the unexpected gift of beer. Ammuna waved merrily at the sentries as he entered the capital of the Hittite Empire, having successfully accomplished the first part of his plan.

Ammuna named a tavern close to the castle gate. He knew the city like the back of his hand. He'd lived in the castle with King Muwas before the Battle of the Wide Plateau six years ago. Now he drove the convoy slowly through the crowded Upper City towards the citadel gates, parking the wagons near *The Pride of the Citadel* public house. Ammuna had one of his officers arrange with the inn landlord to supply him with booze at half price. The tavern keeper was overjoyed at the prospect of making a large profit on the transaction. Now the thirty-eight men who were to wait outside the citadel, unloaded all the wine and beer and stacked it neatly in the tavern's cellar for the landlord. The officer in charge took the agreed payment from the proprietor and everything was transacted as if it were a legitimate business deal.

The weapons from the barrels were distributed and Ammuna's wagon would stay behind, while the other six would move on to the King's Gate and wait there discretely for Ammuna. They were to ensure the gate remained open at all costs. It was Ammuna's only way out of the city.

Ammuna removed his cloak and threw it into the back of the wagon, as did the four who were to accompany him into the citadel. Under the cloaks, the five officers wore their neat yellow army tunics, and Ammuna led them through the familiar narrow corbelled arches of the citadel gates.

'We're here to see Prince Katuzzuli,' Ammuna told the sentries; and on seeing it was the general, they saluted him smartly and didn't question his announcement in any way.

The arches opened into the lower paved courtyard holding stables, an armoury, and various guardrooms. Ammuna marched on further with his officers in tow, to the official access of the palace. On this festive day the quadrangle was empty, two sentries stood guard at the doorway. Again, the approaching group were saluted smartly as they marched past heading for the main staircase. When they were up the staircase and had turned left, instead of right, into the main corridor, they began to walk quietly on tiptoes. Ammuna led them down the corridor to the sovereign's living quarters; an area he was intimately familiar with from six years ago, having spent many hours listening to the outrageous claims of King Muwas, while sitting and drinking his wine.

He heard laughter coming from one room and made his way towards it. Ammuna knocked on the door so as to have someone to grab when they opened it.

'*Come!*' shouted a woman's voice from inside.

Ammuna held his men back. 'You two stay here and guard the door; let no one enter.' He knocked again.

'*Come!*' came the louder exasperated response.

Still they waited for the door to be physically opened. When finally, they heard footsteps coming and the door opened, Ammuna walked in dagger drawn, and he thrust it into the elderly woman's stomach—as she stood there looking down in shock, staring aghast at her own demise.

A young girl played with some dolls in the middle of the room, oblivious to what was happening. Lawana caught the dead woman and sat her in a chair near the door. Ammuna looked around the room to see if anybody else was with her—nobody. He quickly walked over to the little girl and picked her up, putting his big hand over her mouth. She scratched and bit him like a disturbed polecat that'd been interrupted in the middle of her game, but Ammuna kept his iron grip tightly on her mouth to prevent her from screaming.

The two accompanying officers quickly put a cloth in her mouth and tied her up, and in the middle of all this, the girl went limp, having fainted from the shock of being so roughly manhandled.

'Thank the gods she did that,' scowled Ammuna. 'I was on the verge of hitting her to knock her out,' he snarled. 'What a spoiled brat. Colonel, grab that small carpet over there—we'll roll her up in it. Make sure she's able to breathe, but not able to make any noise,' he ordered his second. Ammuna then removed a clay tablet from his leather pouch and placed it prominently on a side table to be found by whomever came looking for the girl.

Just as they were about to leave with the bundled up girl, the two officers he'd left outside, hurried in through the door and closed it gently behind them. One of them put his finger to his lips, telling them to be quiet. Then they heard footsteps approaching down the corridor. They stood on either side of the door waiting. The door swung open without any knocks, and a tall old man entered, looking round the room for its occupants.

'*Asmunikal*,' called the old man; then he saw Ammuna and his cronies. He attempted to back out and close the door but Ammuna grabbed the old man and quickly stuck his dagger in his chest. The old man crumpled to the floor with a snarl on his face.

'By the great god Taru, I've wanted to do that for a long time,' sighed Ammuna, smiling and looking down at the corpse of the old man.

'Who was he sir?' asked a lieutenant, one of the younger officers.

'That, my boy, was the last surviving cause of my downfall. Him, and his brother Himuili, had King Muwatalli assassinated; and that started the civil war six years ago. That, my son, *was* Prince Katuzzuli, the uncle of the king. Secretly, I'd hoped I'd come across the old scoundrel, but this is better than in my wildest dreams. May the gods curse him in the netherworld for causing me so much misery. Now, quickly, let's get out of here. We've been lucky so far.'

Two of the captains carried the rolled up carpet with the princess inside, and they marched stealthily back down the corridor to the top of the stairs. Everything was quiet as they descended the ornate staircase to the bottom. Ammuna led the group outside, past the sentries, and into the quadrangle. They marched through the courtyard towards the narrow corbelled arches of the citadel gates, and past the sentries, who again saluted them smartly. They disappeared round the corner of the tavern to the waiting wagon. No sound came from the carpet as they placed it gently inside the covered wagon.

Ammuna recovered his dark cloak and reclaimed his disguise as the leader of the convoy by smearing a little dirt on his face. His four officers donned their cloaks. The three got inside the wagon out of sight and Lawana joined Ammuna on the driver's seat; then they began their leisurely ride down to the eastern King's Gate. Any attempt at speed would only arouse suspicion.

In a measured pace the wagon reached the King's Gate where the other six wagons waited for them. The driver-come-officer in charge of the six wagons was talking to the gate captain, laughing and clearly having a good old chin-wag. They broke off their talk as Ammuna's wagon was seen to arrive.

'Well, nice to have had this chat with you; must go now,' said the disguised non-com, climbing onto the wagon. 'My boss has just arrived and I've got to go. Enjoy the festival.'

Ammuna's wagon stopped in front of the other six wagons and the captain of the gate looked at Ammuna, furrowed his eyebrows, then said, 'Don't I know you from somewhere?' still looking at Ammuna quizzically.

'Probably,' replied Ammuna. 'I've been through here many a time with my wagons.'

'No, I mean from somewhere else? I'm sure I do, but I can't place it just yet. Oh, never mind, it'll come to me. Off with you then. See you next time.' The captain stood there watching the convoy go through the gate, scratching his head trying to remember where he'd come across the big old convoy boss. His face looked familiar but out of context to this present setting.

'Damn that captain!' snarled Ammuna to Lawana, when they exited the gate and were far enough not to be overheard. 'I remember him well. I had to reprimand him one time for being late on returning to barracks. That was four years ago when he was a junior lieutenant. Strange he remembered me? If he puts my face and rank together, the king will know for sure who snatched his daughter. Let's hope it takes some time for him to do that.' Ammuna led the wagons south to disguise his real intent of going east. He was leading them back to the thick forest where the rest of the *loyal* band waited for him.

'Can't be helped,' responded Lawana, referring to the gate captain. He was almost euphoric. 'We've pulled it off. *I can't believe we've pulled this off.* When I heard what you had in mind, sir, I was sceptical, I must admit. But here we are with the king's daughter in the back of our wagon.' Lawana turned round and shouted into the back. 'Make sure she's still breathing. You can unroll the carpet but keep her tied up. Make sure she can't scream.'

'We're not clear yet, Colonel,' Ammuna told him. 'We've a long way to go to get to Wassukanni. Once we've left the wagons, we'll head east to Samuha. We can't go south-east, as I'd like to, because Tudhaliyas will send the whole army after us. First place he'll close off is the south-eastern route to Mittani. So, we're going round that problem. They think, or at least I hope they think, we've gone south-east. That's why we're heading down south right now. Once we've got rid of these wagons we can put some speed on.

The wagon convoy finally arrived in the forest hideout. Once the waiting men laid eyes on Asmunikal, they went wild in praise of their general. They gave Ammuna a hero's welcome. To a man, they'd been sceptical something like this could be pulled off, but here she was, their endorsement to riches yet to come. Quickly the horses were unhitched from the wagons and turned back into mounts.

Ammuna stood on his beloved chariot and faced them once again. 'I promised you success—and I keep my promises.' He had the scowling Asmunikal on the chariot with him, being held in place by two soldiers.

She was no longer screaming or yelling, as she had been when they'd removed her gag, having assessed her predicament, she now relied on her father, the king, to rescue her. As a royal princess, she'd been well taught how to cope in difficult situations. Only six years old, and she was behaving like a woman of three times her age.

'We are now heading east to the Upper Lands, to the holy city of Samuha,' Ammuna told his listeners. 'We should be there in four or five days. After, we'll head down to the Puranti River and on to Tushan, where we'll cross the great Aransah River. Once we've crossed the Isuwan border, we ought to be safe for the time being. The Isuwan king is not happy with Tudhaliyas and has asked to join the Mittani confederation. I would even go so far as to say, our job should have been over once we reach Tushan, but unfortunately, my bargain with the Mittani is to deliver the princess to Wassukanni; only then will we get paid.'

The mercenary column of two hundred and twenty *loyal* cavalry, having abandoned all their heavy wagons, set out east from the thick forest for the holy city of Samuha, home to the goddess Istar, led by Ammuna's chariot. They intended travelling fast and putting as much distance as they could between them and the menace now emanating from the Hittite capital.

3
Ammuna Unmasked

The king's palace was in turmoil with the chamberlain wringing his hands and shaking his head in denial. The king stomped around shouting at all his officials. From next door the queen could be heard wailing, grief-stricken at the loss of her only child.

The sentries on duty that day, were lined up at one end of the room, being questioned by senior officers as to the identity of the strange general who'd been and gone—presumably the culprit of the despicable deed. In a third room lay the shrouded body of Prince Katuzzuli, while on a sideboard lay the shrouded body of the old woman nurse, who'd been killed, just for being there. Priests from the now abandoned autumnal festival were looking after the bodies. The festival was supposed to have lasted forty days, but now was forsaken due to the terrible events that had taken place in the palace.

Queen Nikal, sallow and tearful, her dark hair tussled, was inconsolable and kept insisting Tudhaliyas send for Mokhat to rescue her daughter. 'I don't trust any of these minions to rescue my child,' she cried, waving her hand at the people in the room, 'When I was kidnapped by that hoodlum Harep six years ago, it was only Mokhat and Palaiyas who managed to rescue me,' she wailed. 'Even *you* told me you didn't think I would have survived if it weren't for them. You must ask them, *please*, for our child's sake... Don't you care what happens to your daughter?' she screamed for the umpteenth time.

On hearing her accusation, Tudhaliyas stormed out, and had taken it out on his generals. Even poor old General Zidanta's tall dark muscular features cringed when he was given a mouthful of oaths, before the king abruptly ceased, realising it wasn't the general's fault.

'I'm sorry, I shouldn't have said that,' he told the general. 'I'm just overwrought at what's happened. And we still don't have this strange general's identity. Who would dare carry out such a thing? Surly he can't have been a real General in our army? Must be some blackguard posing as a General. Who'd do such a thing?'

It was late in the afternoon and the rumour-mill had started throughout Hattusas, spreading something terrible had happened at the palace. Why else would the king and queen cancel the Autumn Festival? Only then did the Captain at the King's Gate remember who the wagon boss reminded him of. He rushed off to the citadel and reported the peculiar episode to a colonel, who had sense enough to pass it on immediately upwards to Zidanta.

'Sire, I think we've found the identity of our rogue General. When you told me to dismiss him six years ago, I thought you were wrong. Now I admit your instincts are better than mine. It was Ammuna—he's the one who's got your daughter. I'm sure of it. They're descriptions,' he pointed at the sentries at the far end, who'd been on duty, 'now tally with the description of the Captain at the King's Gate. He had a convoy of wagons go through the gate around noon, which is when we think all this occurred. He didn't recognise him then, but he's been trying hard to remember where he'd seen the wagon master before. News of this outrage jolted his memory. It's definitely Ammuna. And I'm afraid the news that your daughter's gone missing has gone through the capital like a brushfire. The high priest has already got people praying for her safe return.'

'*Ammuna*? That no good scoundrel. That's why I sent him down to Adaniya, to get him out of the way. What with the clay tablet we found in Asmunikal's playroom, I have to assume he's working for the Mittani.' Tudhaliyas was fiddling with the clay tablet in his hand.

'May I see that again, your majesty,' requested Zidanta.

The king handed the disreputable tablet to the general. General Zidanta was still the most capable general in the Hittite army, which is why he was its overall commander. He was trying to squeeze the last bit of information from the piece of clay. The message was clear and unambiguous. "*Withdraw from Kizzuwatna and return the suzerainty back to its previous owners—or else Asmunikal dies.*" The Mittani had ordered the kidnapping in order to demand Tudhaliyas retreat from Kizzuwatna. There could be no other interpretation. Finally, Zidanta said, 'Sire, I think Artatama is behind this. I feel it in my bones.'

'My conclusion as well,' replied the king. 'He tried to cause trouble for me with Madduwatta three years ago—it failed. Now he's sunk even lower and gone after my daughter. Well, I've come to one decision. Within weeks, I want my army at our eastern border ready to invade Mittani, whatever the outcome of my daughter's rescue. Also, we must let Kizzuwatna know what's happened. I want their army with me at the Mittani border. I will not have *that* young monster causing me this amount of suffering. I'll invoke the mutual aid treaty we have with Khemet and ask them to send their army to join ours. I want to put paid to Artatama once and for all. This stunt was the last straw. I'll teach him where his antics have led him.'

'I think you're wise to follow this course. It's one exploit that's gone too far. I will have the army ready. May I suggest I send our eastern forces to the Mittani border right now? It may cut off Ammuna's getaway. He must be heading down to the Mittani border as we speak. If I can block the border, we may have a chance of wrestling your daughter from him.' Zidanta was eager to do something, and all this talk didn't achieve much except hot air.

'Do that. But also put out a call to the other cities of the empire to send their regiments to the capital for a campaign. I will destroy Wassukanni no matter what happens. If Saustatar won't rein in his son, then I'll do it for him. This situation must be brought to an end.' The king stopped with a sudden thought. 'Wait one moment. What if King Saustatar has no idea what his son is up to? I want to send a strong message to Saustatar demanding he return my daughter; otherwise, we destroy Wassukanni. Have we got pigeon contact with Wassukanni?'

'I think so,' answered the general. 'I'll check.'

'Then send a pigeon message demanding the release of my daughter. Follow up with the swiftest messenger we have. Let's see what his response is. Maybe *we* can get *him* to rescue Asmunikal. That's assuming he's unaware of his son's actions. We still must have our army at his border in two week's time.' Just then, the wailing got louder from the next room where the queen was. 'Excuse me, I must see to my wife. She's devastated. It's breaking her heart having her daughter kidnapped.'

Tudhaliyas went next door and saw his wife spread on the couch, pounding her fists into the cushions. 'I want Mokhat....I want Mokhat....' She sobbed loudly.

The king went to her and put his arms round her, lifting her to his chest. 'Al-right, I've sent for him. Calm down. If he's able to, I'm sure he'll come.'

'I'm sorry, but I can't see any other way out,' she cried into his shoulder. 'He must come. My daughter's life is at stake. If he can't rescue her, nobody can.'

'There, there, calm yourself. I've really sent for him.' In fact, as soon as he'd heard of the catastrophe, Tudhaliyas had sent a general and some soldiers to Nerik to try to talk Mokhat into coming to his aid. Trouble was, he didn't think Mokhat would be interested. He had his own family to think of. To put added pressure on Mokhat, he'd sent the request on behalf of the queen, not himself. Mokhat was more likely to do it for the queen, having saved her in similar circumstances once already.

*   *   *

General Labamulis led a squadron of a hundred cavalry all through the night, into Kaska territory, heading towards Nerik. He was as nervous as could be, knowing there were Kaska scouts on either side of his squadron trailing his every move. It was a whole day's journey and they were now nearing the capital late in the afternoon.

Despite the current friendly relations between the Hittite king and the Kaska tribes, both sides were weary of each other and tended to stay clear of any military contacts. They had been at war with each other throughout Muwatallis' reign, with the Kaska ousting the Hittites from their holy city of Nerik. It now served as the Kaska capital with the Hittites being forced to make use of Arinna as their alternative pilgrimage site.

But the general had been specifically ordered by the king himself, to go to Nerik and ask Mokhat to come back with him to Hattusas. He had a clay tablet written on Queen Nikal's behalf, pleading for Mokhat's help in rescuing her kidnapped daughter. The general was ordered to carry out this mission even if he had to fight his way into Nerik; that was how the king had put it to him. The small squadron would not have stood a chance against the Kaska, but it was a poignant phrase underlining the urgency of the mission.

At the bridge leading into Nerik, they were met by a powerfully built Kaska General who politely asked them if they were lost. On hearing of their assignment, the Kaska General asked the squadron to remain on the far side of the tributary river, while Labamulis with a couple of officers were escorted across the bridge to the citadel, where Prince Mokhat would receive them.

All of Nerik had become aware a Hittite squadron was approaching the capital, and a large Kaska crowd turned out this early in the morning, waiting on the other side of the stone bridge, curious to know what was going on. However, some were armed just in case. Labamulis and his two officers had trouble getting through the hostile crowd to the castle that stood on the hill. Mokhat, Palaiyas and King Kasalliwa waited impatiently for the Hittite General in the audience chamber.

The general had his two officers wait by the door as he strode into the hall towards the king. 'Your majesty, I bring you greetings from King Tudhaliyas and a message from the Queen for Prince Mokhat. 'I've ridden hard through the night to get here.' Labamulis bowed deeply to King Kasalliwa, extracting the clay tablet and handing it to the king.

'My thanks to the King of the Hittites and I return his greeting. What brings you all the way up here into the lion's den?' The king was smiling, and handed the clay tablet to Mokhat. Mokhat's sharp bearded face poured over the tablet, and his tall, medium build, shrugged, while his long dark hair fell over his face as he listened and read.

'Sire, we are in the middle of a tragedy unfolding in Hattusas,' replied the Hittite general. 'The king's daughter, Princess Asmunikal, has been kidnapped by people disguised as army officers. We had no idea who they were when I left Hattusas, only that they impersonated a Hittite General, leading four officers. Prince Katuzzuli has been murdered and the queen is utterly distraught. The king has beseeched I implore Prince Mokhat to come and see our grieving queen at his earliest convenience.'

Mokhat understood that as double speak for *come urgently*. He'd read the tablet:

"The queen sends her dearest wish Prince Mokhat come to Hattusas with speed. The Mittani have kidnapped my daughter, Princess Asmunikal, and have made off with her to the gods know where. You have children of your own —you must know how I feel. Please, please, come and help. Queen Nikal."

Then another piece had been added on behalf of the king:

"You managed to rescue her mother, Nikal, six years ago when I'd given up hope of ever seeing her again. You discovered the culprits behind the murder of my chief spy, Satipilli. You are my only hope of seeing my daughter alive. I beg of you not to resist my request for help. My Sun, Tudhaliyas."

Mokhat handed the tablet to Palaiyas who cast his sharp eyes over the tablet. This would undoubtedly concern him as well if he were to get involved with the Hittite king again. Three years of blissful peace had gone by since the last time with the Satipilli business. He'd raised a family with Ulurra, who'd given him a son and daughter in that time. Palaiyas' daughter was Asmunikal's age and his son was three years old. The idea of leaving them to go on this outlandish adventure was not to be taken lightly. That's assuming Palaiyas would accompany him if he were to go to Hattusas. As these ideas were running through his mind, Mokhat noticed his brother looking quizzically at him.

'Well? I can almost hear your brain working overtime, brother,' said King Kasalliwa. 'What have you decided? Will you answer the call, or will you let the girl die?'

'That's not fair! How can you put it like that?' Mokhat protested. 'There's no guarantee even if I did get involved, that we'd be able to get her back.'

Palaiyas was grinning quietly, his tall muscular frame rocking gently from side to side. 'Oh, come now?' He told Mokhat. 'You know what *we* are going to do, surely. After all, it is Nikal's daughter we're talking of. Your godchild.

She's my Sophia's age. What if it were *your* own daughter? If nothing else, we must at least go down to Hattusas and see what we can do. If you decide not to follow this up, we can at least commiserate with our poor distressed *friend* Nikal.'

Mokhat glared at Palaiyas for coercing him with those persuasive phrases. He sighed and grinned back at Palaiyas. 'General, give us an hour, so we can say farewell to our families. Then we'll join you on the other side of the bridge. We should make it back to Hattusas by tomorrow morning if we ride through the night.

4
Return to Hattusas

Once again, they were riding into the Hittite capital to help the king get out of a dire circumstance. Admittedly, it was a situation not of the king's own making, but it didn't make it any less dangerous. The autumnal night had been warm and they had ridden persistently throughout the hours of darkness, but taking it gently so as not to tire the horses unduly. Dawn had seen them coming into sight of the capital, with the grey granite walls in the distance just as forbidding as Mokhat remembered them.

The military column climbed the northern hillock towards the small plateau on which Hattusas stood, veering right towards the gate on its western side. The column cautiously approached the sealed Northern Gate leading into the Lower City. General Labamulis ordered one of his officers to call out to the guards up on the crenelated tower to open the gate, which they unsealed and threw open after the night's password was given.

They rode through the gates and further on, passing by the huge temple of the Storm God Taru, situated to the right of them, from where they could hear loud chanting even this early in the morning.

'The high priest is keeping an all night vigil for the safe return of the crown princess,' Labamulis told Mokhat, to explain the unusual activity inside the holy building.

They continued through the slumbering capital, past the grain silos, to the well-fortified citadel standing on a hill on the far eastern side of the city. Once through the familiar narrow corbelled arches of the citadel gates, and into the lower paved courtyard holding stables, they dismounted and left their horses for the grooms to deal with. They walked the short distance to the official access of the palace, up the steps and through the entrance to the grand staircase.

The chamberlain waited at the top of the stairs, greeting Mokhat with, 'Your highness, his majesty is most anxious to speak with you before you see the queen.'

Mokhat looked at Palaiyas and shrugged. General Labamulis excused himself and went to see his superior to report the success of his mission. The chamberlain led them into a quiet room at the back of the throne room where they found an exhausted Tudhaliyas, sitting at the table with his head leaning on his elbow.

When he heard them come in, he lifted his tired head, composed himself, and rose from the chair to his tall full extent. 'I'm relieved to see you Prince Mokhat—and you Prince Palaiyas. I'm not sure what you can do in these circumstances, but the Queen is besides herself in wanting to see you. I think she's expecting a miracle from you. She believes simply by you coming here, her daughter is going to be saved. I'm under no such delusion. I think we'll have to hunt that scoundrel Ammuna down and remove my daughter from his greedy grasp—and if she survives, by some miracle, I will build another temple to the gods in gratitude for that phenomenon. But unlike the case with Madduwatta, this time I intend to have that scoundrel Artatama's head on a platter.' It was a long speech by a tired man, getting a load off his chest, but it gave them new information.

'Do you know for sure it was Ammuna who grabbed your daughter?' Palaiyas asked before Mokhat could speak.

The king invited them to sit, and sat down heavily himself. 'Yes, it's been confirmed. He came up from Kizzuwatna when he knew I'd be away at the festival, kidnapped my daughter and took her away rolled up in a carpet....*in a carpet*. When I get my hands on him, *I'll burn him alive in a carpet.*' The venom of his words was scorching.

Mokhat believed the words of the king. 'My condolences to you and the queen on this awful tragedy,' said Mokhat. 'Believe me, if there's anything we can do to help, we will.' Mokhat looked at Palaiyas for confirmation of his offer.

Palaiyas nodded in agreement, then added, 'Your majesty, we badly need some facts to work on. When exactly did this happen; how many people were involved; and where do you believe they are right now as we speak?'

The king handed the infamous clay tablet left by Ammuna to Mokhat, and then turned his attention to Palaiyas' questions. 'We think Ammuna took my daughter sometime noon two days ago. There were four of them who entered this castle, all dressed up as Hittite officers. The captain of the King's Gate tells us Ammuna was in charge of a convoy of seven wagons leaving through his gate some time later. We estimate there must be at least fifty men with him in the convoy that we know of. Remember who he was. I should think that he could gather at least five hundred disaffected individuals to this venture, assuming the Mittani are paying them.

'As for where he is, that has to be pure speculation. We have sent out messages throughout the eastern and southern provinces asking for our spies and army posts to keep a sharp lookout for anybody answering his description. This is one time that the speed of the pigeon messages will come in very handy. We've had nothing in so far, but the wagons were seen heading south. I'm assuming that to be a ruse, knowing the former General—and Zidanta agrees with me. General Zidanta is of the opinion Ammuna will head due east to bypass the border blockade we've imposed on the Mittani. That means he's probably heading for either Samuha, Malidiya, or Karkamish. Karkamish is too obvious as a direct route to Wassukanni, so Zidanta believes it's more likely that Ammuna, having ditched the wagons, is going east as far as Samuha as fast as whatever he's using can carry him. We found the abandoned wagons late last night in a forest south of here. Zidanta's then of the opinion he's likely to turn south heading directly for Wassukanni, to Artatama. With this route, he's hoping to bypass our military attempts to block him, and although it's a lot longer, he may think it's a lot safer. He's probably on his fancy chariot, which he's known to be over fond of. Anybody with him is on fast horses. That's our estimation of his transport and whereabouts.'

Mokhat stroked his beard, having read the clay tablet and asked, 'So now, what do you propose to do about this? More to the point, what do you expect two simple individuals like us to do when you've the whole country at your disposal to deal with the matter—the whole army?'

Palaiyas looked at Mokhat as if he'd flipped. This was a most insulting approach to a request for help from an old friend and ally.

The king stopped and looked as if he'd been slapped in the face by someone he trusted. Tudhaliyas got up and walked out of the room.

The two friends tended to speak Kaska to each other now Palaiyas had learnt the language; he'd been living in Nerik for some three years. 'What's got into you?' asked Palaiyas in Kaska. 'You've never been so blunt or rude as long as I've known you? You must have a good reason for riling the king.'

Mokhat responded in Kaska, 'I'm trying to lower expectations. I'm going to ask you the same question. What can *we* two do a whole army cannot? What does the king expect of *us*?' Mokhat looked squarely into Palaiyas' eyes, waiting for an answer. Inwardly, Mokhat had no desire to go chasing after some lunatic rogue General. He wanted to go back to Nerik and be with his family. Ulurra awaited him, as did his children. To add to the problem, these adventures were never without risk. What if he were killed or injured—what would happen to his family? In the last mission, three years ago, he was single; now things had changed.

'Put so candidly, what can I say?' There was the undertone of anger in Palaiyas' voice. 'But let me *pose* you a question in return. Three years ago, we were asked to help with Satipilli's disappearance, and you could have said the same thing then. *What could two men do when the king had all the resources of the whole state to call upon?* Nevertheless, you didn't. We undertook that mission and it almost cost you your life, *twice*. Did we or didn't we *successfully* conclude that business—just us two poor individuals?'

There was no answer to that argument. Mokhat just shrugged his shoulders as if to say, *so?* 'I assume then, you propose we follow Ammuna and await our chance to rescue Asmunikal, is that what you have in mind?'

'That's exactly what I have in mind—even if I've to do so by myself.'

That last remark wounded Mokhat deeply. They had been close friends for a long time and shared many dangerous situations. The idea that his friend would go on without him was not a situation that Mokhat would contemplate. 'That's *not* going to happen,' Mokhat said loudly. 'Come what may, we stick together.'

Palaiyas stood there and smiled, then burst out laughing. He shook his head and grabbed Mokhat by the shoulders. 'You had me going there. For a moment I thought you were really going to let me go on alone.'

Just then, the king returned with the queen. He led her to a chair and gently helped her to sit down. The once tall beautiful regal woman, who Mokhat had known, was now reduced to a shadow of herself. Mokhat was shocked how frail she looked and how badly she'd taken her daughter's kidnapping.

'Your majesty,' Mokhat walked over and took her hand, 'I'm so sorry for your loss. I've been talking with Prince Palaiyas, and we will of course do everything we can to help get Asmunikal back for you.'

At hearing those words, the king's face relaxed and he breathed deeply. The king watched his wife's face and saw part of the burden lift from her.

The Queen sighed and said, 'Thank you Prince Mokhat for those kind worlds; you don't know what it means to me to hear you say that.' Nikal's demeanour changed from despair—to a small glimmer of hope. Her eyes brightened and she looked up at Mokhat. 'I *know* you will get her back for me. I thought I was lost when that monster Harep took me prisoner, but against all odds, you managed to rescue me. I know you won't let me down this time. You have children of your own; you know what I'm going through. May the gods speed you—thank you.' She suddenly looked very tired and the king helped her to stand and took her to the doorway where he put her into the care of her handmaidens with orders for her to be taken to her bed.

Tudhaliyas came back, stood in front of the two princes, and stared perplexedly at them. 'I thank you most profoundly for those kind and encouraging words to the queen—but were you being sincere?'

'Palaiyas and I have talked it over and we will make our utmost effort on behalf of your daughter.' Mokhat's voice and body language made it clear he was speaking the truth.

'Then I'm doubly grateful,' replied the king. 'Back there for a moment I had the impression you were about to refuse me. But let that instance flutter into the past. What I have for you is the support of the army—and a *special unit* that has been formed within the army for such a contingency as this. It is led by an officer with whom you might be familiar, Colonel Onasiyas. He has trained a group of a hundred men, a *special force* chosen for their superior fighting skills, adepts at sword, dagger, spear, bow and arrow; trained in survival and able to deal with water, mountains, or desert. They are mounted on horses chosen for their stamina, tenacity, and speed. They were initially formed to be used on the Ahhiyawan border, which is why they have Onasiyas as their commander.

'I brought them back to the capital a month ago for final assessment by General Zidanta and myself, before passing them out and assigning them back into the west for duty. It was fortuitous that they were here at this time. These men will now include people who know the eastern area you're going into, there will be men who can speak Mittani and Assyrian. I'm putting them under your orders Prince Mokhat. It's the best I can do in the circumstances.'

The king put his hand in his pouch that hung from his waist, and pulled out a couple of items. 'Prince Mokhat, here are the royal seals of Hatti and Khemet you returned to me three years ago. I'm now restoring them to you to use as you see fit.' Tudhaliyas held out the two seals and Mokhat took them and put them in his pouch.

The king continued, 'I'm also giving both you and Prince Palaiyas the rank of a General in the Hittite armed forces—since your going to be chasing after a former general whose disgraced himself. I think it might be of some use to you. There are a couple of uniforms ready for you over on the side couch over there.' The king indicated near the wall.

Mokhat thought the king must have taken it for granted he and Palaiyas would be coming to his aid, and this rankled with him.

'Now my good friends,' concluded the king, 'I've been up all night and I must get some rest. I've ordered a large breakfast for you and I hope you do it justice. When you leave, no matter what the time, come and say goodbye to me and the queen. Oh, and I've sent for Colonel

Onasiyas. He should be here shortly.' With a long statement out of the way, the king left the room.

Palaiyas was beaming with pleasure. 'Good old Onasiyas; he seems to be coming up in the world. I'll be pleased to renew my acquaintance with him.' Mokhat and Palaiyas went to the couch near the wall and got into their generals uniforms, then returned to the table.

The servants brought in their breakfast and they got stuck into it with gusto. Their last meal had been biscuits while riding through the forest in the middle of the night. Here, they were tucking into hot slices of lamb and goat, pancakes laced with honey, and fresh fruit. Near the end of their meal, General Zidanta's dark muscular frame walked through the door as the servants were clearing the remnants of the breakfast. He had a tall muscular officer with him, Onasiyas, dressed in some strange navy blue outfit.

'Greetings, your highnesses,' said General Zidanta. 'I see you've joined the higher echelon of the Hittite army.' He smiled at the generals uniforms the two princes wore. 'Has the king informed you of the little group we've gathered together for you,' Zidanta asked of Mokhat.

Mokhat looked up from the table, 'Yes General, just now. Some kind of *special force* with our respected Colonel here as its commander. Please join us and tell us all about them,' invited Mokhat.

Zidanta and Onasiyas joined Palaiyas and Mokhat at the table and they sat facing each other. Palaiyas winked at Onasiyas, instead of saying hello, and Onasiyas winked back at him. Zidanta left it to Onasiyas to explain the details, which tallied with what the king had told Mokhat and Palaiyas. Having finished the explanation, Onasiyas added, 'It only remains to determine what time we leave. I must say, the sooner the better. The enemy has a good start on us.'

'Are the troops ready to leave now?' asked Palaiyas in surprise. He'd assumed they were going to stay in the capital overnight. After the night's ride, he was hoping for a warm bed to rest his weary bones.

'They're down in the citadel stable yard right now, waiting to mount their steeds. Your horses are ready and we have another extra set of mounts each, which we will interchange, every twenty leagues. That will mean we will be travelling *fast* with no rest until well into the night. That's two hundred horses with a hundred and three men— oh, and forty pack horses. Both I and the General think it best if we try to overtake Ammuna while he's still on Hittite territory. We go to Sanuhuitta with as much speed as we can muster. Then we'll turn south and try to cut Ammuna off before he reaches the lower Puranti River.' He looked expectantly at the duo.

Mokhat stood up as if ready to go, while Palaiyas rose reluctantly, still thinking of the warm bed waiting for him somewhere in the capital.

'Apologise to his majesty for us,' Mokhat told General Zidanta, 'for not saying goodbye to him, but say we were thinking of his daughter in not doing so.'

The old general wished them good speed and invoked the gods to aid them in their task.

Onasiyas, Mokhat and Palaiyas walked back down the way they had entered and out into the fresh air of the quadrangle. In the stable yard, they found the hundred soldiers dressed in navy blue outfits such as Onasiyas wore, waiting impatiently to mount their black horses. Onasiyas yelled, '*Mount!*' and they jumped onto their horses backs.

'I notice all the men are wearing beards like mine. How did you know we would meet again?' Mokhat asked Onasiyas when they had mounted, curious at this seeming coincidence.

'Your highness, no offence was meant,' Onasiyas was quick to explain. 'I thought if they all looked alike, but differed from the ordinary clean shaven Hittite soldier, that would create a bond between them, they would look after each other better which would improve their fighting abilities.

Then Mokhat switched his interests. 'What are those?' he asked, pointing at the strange pack horses, as he adjusted the harness on his horse. 'They remind me somewhat of the ponies the Gemirri had when we came across them three years ago.'

Onasiyas smiled, 'Those, your highness, are steppe ponies from the plains beyond the north-eastern mountains. We discovered them when we were looking for exceptionally hardy pack animals. They were being sold by the Hayasa.'

On hearing the word *Hayasa*, Mokhat spat out, '*The Hayasa?* Those curs are in league with the Azzi, and you know we're still at war with them, do you?'

'I hope you're not at war with these poor ponies, your highness?' Onasiyas joked.

Mokhat saw how ridiculous his outburst had been and laughed at himself. 'No, the ponies are safe from my wrath; but only barely, as you've just noticed. But if they creep up on me during the night—who knows what I may do?' he chuckled.

Even Palaiyas joined in the laughter. 'You know well, my dear Onasiyas, the Prince is ferocious when he's aroused.'

The mounted column rode out through the corbelled arch and into the Upper city heading for the King's Gate, through a crowd waiting just outside the palace gates. The crowd was there holding a vigil in sympathy with the royal family and their loss. They passed through the King's Gate and out into the hot sunshine of an autumnal mid-morning, picking up speed, riding fast through fields' now emptied of the harvested barley, heading for the holy city of Samuha some eighty leagues to the east; a five days journey at the breakneck speed they were travelling. With Ammuna two days ahead, they had a lot of catching up to do.

5
Pursuit Begins

On the morning of the third day as Mokhat's *special forces* left through the King's Gate, Ammuna's column was almost two days ride from the eastern city of Sanuhuitta. They were riding along the bottom of a dried out riverbed emanating from the eastern Parhar Mountain Range, the direction they were headed. The southward facing city of Sanuhuitta nestled snugly in the mouth of a valley protected by the crags and cliffs of the Parhar Mountains.

All day they continued along the lengthy dried out riverbed at a steady trot, getting ever closer to the high mountains. By twilight, the imposing Parhars with their densely covering of conifers towered over the column and they had finally arrived at its scree-sloped weather-beaten base.

'What do you think,' asked Ammuna of his deputy, as Lawana rode by the general's chariot, 'shall we go over the forest shrouded mountains and save time, or go round its base and save the horses?'

Colonel Lawana, staring at the chariot, said, 'Sir, if we didn't have your form of transport, I would counsel going over the mountains, but I fear it could prove impossible in the chariot.'

'Yes, I'd come to the same conclusion,' smiled the general. 'I'm too fond of this vehicle to have it damaged. Ah well, so it's the easy way round, then. We'll follow the base until we come to a secluded spot for the night.'

Some time later, as the light began to give out; Ammuna ordered the night stop in a sparse deciduous forest clearing by a small stream trickling down from a mountain brook. The packhorses were relieved of their burden, and all the horses hobbled and left to feed; logs were chopped and a couple of fires started with latrines being dug downwind. The assigned cooks unpacked the rations, water filled pots hung over the two large fires and a number of logs were placed round the blazes for the men to sit on. The food would include dried meat and barley porridge. As a result of fatigue, the morale of this *loyal* band was subdued.

Ammuna told Lawana, 'Get the men bedded down as soon as you can; we have an early start tomorrow. Rotate the sentries throughout the night.'

A soldier came up to Lawana and said, 'Sir, the girl won't eat anything—just sits there and pouts.'

'All right I'm coming,' said the colonel. 'Excuse me, sir, I'll be right back.' He got up and went to where the unhitched chariot stood, followed by Ammuna, whose face was grim with suppressed anger.

The chariot floor had a cloth laid on it and a log facing it. It was supposed to act in place of a table and a bowl of barley porridge sat on the cloth with a wooden spoon. Asmunikal sat staring at the porridge stubbornly refusing to eat.

Since the general had decided to join him, Lawana thought he ought to leave it to Ammuna to deal with the princess.

'Now what's all this,' began Ammuna when they reached Asmunikal. 'You must eat, your highness, to keep your strength up,' he stroked her head lightly to cajole her.

Asmunikal suddenly turned and grabbed the left wrist of the arm he was stroking her with and bit into his wrist as hard as she could.

'*Argh!* You nasty vixen,' Ammuna swore at her, and slapped her hard across her forehead with his right hand. The six year old fell backwards to the ground, her face full of hate as she glared up at her kidnapper. Ammuna was just about to kick her when he checked himself, having glanced at his deputy's horrified face. 'If she keeps this up, our erstwhile Artatama will only get a corpse,' he spat out in anger at Lawana as he barged past him. 'Let her starve,' he added over his shoulder, being his solution to the brat's refusal to eat. He stomped off angrily back to the fire.

Lawana was shocked at the scene he'd just witnessed. This was not the general he knew and respected. Hitting a child of six should have been below his dignity as a Hittite General. Hitting the king's daughter outraged his mind. Lawana was on the point of intervening when he saw Ammuna about to kick the princess. Lucky for the both of them, Ammuna stopped himself.

Outwardly, he was grim, but inside he was furious with Ammuna for debasing his professional standards. He thought, *this whole enterprise may not have been my finest moment—but more to the point, if this type of thuggery happens again, I'm leaving this lot to their covetous fate. I don't need the money that badly—at least I hope I don't. Look at what it's done to my general? I used to look up to him with respect.*

Colonel Lawana had been relatively comfortable at his posting in Ullama when he'd received the message from his former commander, asking him if he wanted to join him in a venture which would make him rich. Previously, he'd accepted his fate of being left out of the promotion stakes, of never climbing higher than a Colonel, having been on the wrong side in the civil war, but it still irked him. Unmarried, and yet married to the army he'd loved; he had decided to throw in his lot with his former commander just to do something other than stay in mediocre Ullama. Now with this dubious behaviour by his general, he wasn't so sure he'd made the right choice.

Lawana called for two fresh soldiers to replace the ones guarding the girl, and told the ones currently guarding her to go and get some food, then he returned to the fire and parked himself by Ammuna, sitting silently listening to the other soldiers talking of their plans; what they were going to do with their share of the loot. Lawana sat in a thoughtful mood, not one Ammuna would have approved of had he known what was running through his deputy's head.

The dawn chorus woke those still asleep. A light mist permeated through the forest clearing as the cooks stoked up the fires in preparation for breakfast. Another fine day was emerging from the quiet of a congenial autumnal night.

Lawana was giving orders to speed things up while Ammuna sat with his head back as his orderly scraped his chin with a razor sharp knife.

'Come on you lazy lot,' shouted Lawana at the whole encampment. 'I want your backsides on your horses, not on those logs. Let's get this jamboree on the road.' It produced the desired effect and soldiers were gulping their breakfast down as fast as possible.

A little while later, the column sped in full gallop besides the Parhars with Ammuna in his chariot leading the way. Asmunikal was seated on cushions in Ammuna's chariot with the general at the reins whipping his horses ever onwards. He had two trusted soldiers in the chariot with him to keep an eye out on the brat so she didn't cause him any more trouble.

All day they rode in the merciless heat of the autumn sun, only stopping for a short while to rest the horses while they ate a dry meal in the middle of the afternoon. By late afternoon, Ammuna's column passed alongside a sheer cliff on their left, which had an overhang protruding from the high mountains, a jutting sculptured by nature and time. On noticing it, Ammuna raised his arm, bringing his men to a abrupt halt. Turning to his deputy, he said loudly, 'See that overhang up there; might it not be a good place to put a few volunteers up there so they could roll and throw boulders at anyone foolish enough to follow us?'

Lawana followed Ammuna's gaze and smiled. 'Yes, I see where you mean. So you think, sir, we'll be followed along this very route?'

'This is the usual route to Sanuhuitta, isn't it? Ammuna asked him. 'I'd be surprised if they didn't follow us along here. In fact, I would consider it a dereliction of duty if they didn't come along this very track.' Ammuna's obduracy would have it no other way. 'It's only prudent to assume they will—and so when they arrive, we should have a convivial welcome for them. See if you can rustle up a few volunteers. Tell them there'll be a little extra in it for them.'

With the promise of *a little extra,* Lawana had no trouble getting five men to volunteer to scale the cliff and arm themselves with stones and boulders at the top. They would be entirely safe from attack in their little redoubt. Lawana told the ambushers they should head for Tushan afterwards, where they would meet up with the rest of the group. Lawana personally felt this ambush was a waste of time since he assumed the pursuers would take the shorter mountain route to save time. After the tricky scene with Ammuna and Asmunikal the previous night, he didn't want to argue with the general, so he'd agreed to this useless ambush.

Having prepared the undersized ambush, the column moved on along the side of the mountains towards the mouth of the valley containing the city of Sanuhuitta, leaving the five ambushers behind, who were climbing up to the overhang with their rations. Ammuna's intention was to slow down whomever the king sent after them, nothing more. He wanted to let them know he was aware of their intentions to stop him, and to instil a little caution in any followers. People who are cautious are always more wary and slower in their pursuit. The journey to Wassukanni, at top speed, would take at least two weeks; anything could go wrong during such a long pursuit.

They continued for the rest of the day amid the yellow browns of autumn. By evening, they were half a league outside the city of Sanuhuitta, trying to be unobtrusive and entirely failing to be so. There were fields heavy with summer's abundance still being harvested by many of the local folk, and flocks of skittish goats roamed the vicinity, tended by shepherds, who stared with curiosity at this Hittite column nearing their city. Ammuna had sent out scouts to look for a small forest he could hide in for the night, and they had now returned, and guided the column to a wood not far away. Over in the west, the golden disc was lowering gently over the horizon. In the fading light, Ammuna sent out two groups of three soldiers to buy barley flour to restock their supplies, and ordered them to drop hints to the locals the column was heading for Samuha.

'I thought Samuha *was* our destination,' enquired Lawana, when he heard what Ammuna was telling the two groups.

'I'm changing our plans,' replied Ammuna. 'I've a feeling our followers are closing in on us, so we're heading directly for Malidiya. King Tarasina of Isuwa is in his rebellious mood again and is flouting all orders emanating from Hattusas. I've heard on the grapevine he's in talks with the Mittani. I think he might give us a welcome and we would then be safer from our pursuers. Besides, Wassukanni is closer that way and we'll be finished with this whole thing the sooner. Any objections?'

'No sir, I think it's a good move,' replied his deputy. 'The sooner we're paid, the happier I'll be.'

'My sentiments precisely,' Ammuna confirmed.

Inside the small wood, the general ordered two subdued campfires to be built.

'We'll rest for a little while so our mounts get some water and grazing. I want to be on our way well before dawn,' Ammuna informed his deputy.

'Yes sir,' Lawana replied. He gave orders for the food to be rapidly prepared and eaten. They did without the usual log sitting banter and turned in quickly after their meal.

In the dark before dawn, people were ordered out of their blankets and invited to help themselves to cold rations. Then quietly, everybody collected their mounts and walked their horses southwards, hoping this way, they would mislead any followers as to the real direction they were heading, and to surreptitiously allow the column to disappear from the landscape by staying within the shade of trees and hedges as much as possible.

'It's two days down to Malidiya,' Ammuna said to Lawana, 'so we'll keep this walking up for another five leagues and then we're back on the horses in full gallop. Let the men know,' he informed his deputy.

*   *   *

About the same time Ammuna was walking south through the woods near Sanuhuitta, Mokhat's *special forces* were half way across the Parhar Mountain Range, having chosen the quicker route to the city.

At the outset, his force had been two days behind Ammuna, but using their extra horses, they were catching up and had gained half a day, all thanks to the strategy Onasiyas adopted of continually changing their mounts every twenty leagues. They had also ridden well into the night, and stopped only for short breaks. Coupled with the stamina of the forty hardy steppe pack-ponies carrying their supplies, Onasiyas' system had given them a distinct advantage.

The company of a hundred men had entered the Parhars via an upward leading valley and now crossed the forest-covered mountains as fast as the terrain would allow them, avoiding the ambush set by Ammuna, as Lawana had predicted. They were likely to reach Sanuhuitta around evening of that day, only one and a half a days behind Ammuna, according to Onasiyas.

For Mokhat and Palaiyas it had been the most difficult three days in their riding careers. The *special forces* had been in training for months for this type of task but Mokhat and Palaiyas had been leading a leisurely family life for three years, and were a little our of condition. The short stop on the first night was a blessing but by dawn, they felt muscle pains where muscles should not have been. The next night was marginally easier, just as they'd reached sight of the Parhar Mountains. The third night saw them in the mountains sitting around a campfire, when Onasiyas told them of the death of his fellow officer, Captain Feliyas. He'd been a friend to Mokhat and Palaiyas from their days in Ivalanda three years earlier during Madduwatta's Rebellion. Feliyas, according to Onasiyas, had fallen in a battle near the Ahhiyawan border a year before. It was an unnecessary death in a skirmish, where Feliyas had been cut off and his entire company slaughtered by overwhelming numbers. The tragic incident prompted Onasiyas to suggest the establishment of the *special forces*.

Now these same *special forces* had developed a superior travelling tactic enabling Mokhat to anticipate catching up with Ammuna sometime soon. They'd set out two days behind Ammuna and, according to Onasiyas, they'd gained half a day by shortening their two night's rests and staying in the saddle longer than usual, albeit switching mounts every twenty leagues. At this rate, Onasiyas estimated, they would be outside Sanuhuitta by nightfall and he proposed to rest there and allow the horses to recover from their punishing ride. However, what puzzled Onasiyas, and he voiced this during their rest period, that contrary to expectations, he'd not come across any Hittite forces trying to block Ammuna's escape as the king had ordered. He'd expected the eastern area to be crawling with Hittite patrols looking for the culprits who had kidnapped the king's daughter.

The rough, dense terrain they were crossing, forced Mokhat's company to lead their horses on foot through the conifers, avoiding the patches of sharp stones in a scree-laden valley leading further up into the high Parhar Mountains. The bracing mountain air seared the lungs of the heavily breathing soldiers striving to maintain the punishing pace, yet it cut the journey to Sanuhuitta by at least a third of a day. It was a series of up and down journeys; up one side of a mountain and down the other side.

At one point while the *special forces* walked their horses along a narrow ridge, one of the pack ponies, for no reason they could fathom, suddenly began to kick. It bucked and kicked eventually dislodging its burden, which one of the men tried to cut loose, but only managed to cut one side so the pack slid sideways. This unbalanced the load, impelling the animal to fall down a long steep incline, from which it could not possibly survive.

'Damn, what could have caused the animal to do that?' demanded Palaiyas angrily of the heavens above.

The man in charge of the packhorses suggested it was probably a stone caught in its hooves, and the poor animal tried to kick it free. At least that was the only explanation he could come up with.

The scouts in front knew the mountain route and led Mokhat's group confidently across the mountains towards the mouth of the fertile valley containing the city of Sanuhuitta. They arrived at the western outskirts of the city just as the light was fading. The scouts advised they camp in a wood to the south of the city by a small stream, giving them a plentiful supply of water. There was a harvest moon that night lighting up the clearing by the stream. Men were sent out to gather wood for a large fire. The exhausted horses were taken to drink and then hobbled, and left to graze on the lush grass near the water's edge.

A short time later, a non-com came hurrying back full of excitement and reported to Onasiyas, 'Sir, I've found some interesting tracks in another clearing not far from here while I was gathering some wood. I think you should come and have a look.'

Leaving the cooks to begin the food, Onasiyas led Mokhat and Palaiyas in a small procession, following the soldier to where the interesting tracks were to be found.

'There sir, what do you make of them? I think it's the tracks a chariot makes, and they're heading south, can you see?' enthused the non-com.

They were in a large clearing lit up by the strong moonlight and soon noticed the disguised remains of two large fires someone had attempted to obliterate from the landscape.

'Yes, I see what you mean. They must have camped here the previous night.' The Colonel walked all round the edges of the clearing looking for signs. 'Look there, a mass of horse's hooves leading away from here,' Onasiyas agreed. 'Good work soldier,' he told the non-com. 'Well spotted!'

'I would estimate well over a hundred horses,' added Palaiyas, examining the fresh tracks.

On closer examination, Mokhat added, 'More like two hundred. And this is definitely a chariot track. I would say whoever it was, were walking their horses away from this camp down south. What seems clear to me is, they're not heading for Samuha. But the good news is, they seem to be moving slower than we thought. We've gained a day on them. That's not bad, considering they're moving fast. All that's down to our colonel's system.'

'It would seem we're catching up with them. But I have to agree with you, your highness,' ventured Onasiyas. 'If these are last night's tracks then we're a whole day behind them. At this rate, if we keep up this pace, we should catch up with them sometime soon. Mind you, the only large city in a southward direction is Malidiya. King Tarasina of Isuwa is being a right pain at the moment rejecting any orders coming from Hattusas, and has let it be known he wants closer ties with Wassukanni. Ammuna might see this king as his salvation.'

Mokhat looked at Onasiyas and said, 'I think you're going to suggest we turn south towards Malidiya in the morning.'

'You've read my mind, your highness. I think we should follow the trail.' Onasiyas was scratching his beard and trying to think ahead. 'I want to send out some scouts at dawn and confirm from the local population Ammuna was here. I'm recommending our column follow this trail south in the morning. If the locals confirm they've *not* been seen going to Samuha, then the scouts can catch us up and we'll continue—otherwise, they can chase us and we can change course towards Samuha. This way we won't waste precious time. It's two days to Malidiya from here and I want us to try to overtake them before they reach the protection of the Isuwan army. That'll mean hard riding tomorrow.'

'I agree with you,' replied Mokhat. 'Now let's get back, have our food and get some rest. We've got a hard day tomorrow.'

6
Fall of Artatama

Wassukanni resided thirty leagues due east of Karkamish and was the capital of the Hurrian kingdom of Mittani. It was situated a hundred and twenty leagues south-east of Hattusas, the capital of the Hittite Empire. The Mittani were an Indo-European aristocracy, whilst the majority of the population were poor Amorite tribe's people. This Hurrian Empire had its heartland in the Khabur River region, where Wassukanni was located, and it lay west of Assyria, with whom they had an overbearing big-brother relationship. At this time, the Mittani considered Assyria a vassal state.

The Mittani king, Saustatar, was engrossed in looking at the plans for a new extension to his palace his architect laid before him. 'That is excellent work my fine friend, but why isn't it finished?'

The architect looked worried. 'Your majesty, I've not had any financing for over a month now. How can I to pay for the material? How am I to pay the workmen? If only I could have some shekels, we could continue this fine work and we'd soon finish it for you.' He stood quietly with his head bowed, waiting for his king to reach a decision on funding.

'I don't understand. I released a large amount of money to my accountants for this project—yet you say you haven't been paid? How is it possible?' The tall and muscular king turned to his aide and demanded the chief accountant be brought before him. Work on the new palace extension had slowed due to a shortage of funds and the king was now insistent on discovering where the funds had gone.

In a short time, the old chief accountant appeared at the doorway and approached the king with his head on his chest. If the king had been able to see his eyes, he would have seen a terrified man, yet there was a measure of resignation in his eyes as well. He had known this moment would come and feared his days were numbered. Threats from the crown prince—and now from the father—he was caught between two blocks of granite. He stood before the king and dropped to his knees.

'What's all this?' asked the king, seeing his chief accountant trembling in front of him. 'What have you done that warrants such fear?'

'Y..y..your majesty. I'm at my wit's end. I am torn asunder by threats and I'm in fear of my life. Forgive me your majesty.' The man was almost in tears.

The king's face became angry at what he perceived as foul mischief in his trusted accountant. His dark eyes blazed, he swished his long locks of dark curly hair, and tugged angrily at his curled dark beard. 'Speak, you dog, what have you done with the money I released to you?' The king's voice came out in a controlled hiss, and all the more dangerous for it. 'You were given two million shekels from the royal treasury to finish my new palace. 'You need to explain how it all could disappear before I send for the torturer.'

A shudder went through the senior accountant. 'I was threatened with death if I didn't make the money available to you son. Last week he demanded I hand over that amount to him and insisted I keep my mouth shut or I would end up in the river.'

'Are you accusing Prince Artatama of taking the money? Is that your story?' The king had suddenly calmed down as he saw where his questioning was leading. He couldn't afford to be in a temper when he dealt with his cunning son.

'Yes sire....I mean no sire. I'm not accusing anyone, your majesty. I'm just stating the facts, sire. Prince Artatama demanded the money—and to save my life, I gave it to him. He is the Crown Prince, sire.'

'So according to you, my son appropriated two million shekels intended for my new palace? Is that correct?' King Saustatar said this loudly so the whole room could hear. He knew his son had spies in his court and this scenario would be swiftly related to him.

'Yes, sire. I had no choice if I were to stay alive.'

'I want the Crown Prince found and sent to me instantly,' shouted the king to the General in charge of his bodyguards. 'Do not come back with excuses. If need be, bring him here by force.'

Just then, another aide came into the audience hall, hurrying towards the king. 'Sire, a pigeon message has arrived from Hattusas. I thought it urgent enough to interrupt.' He held out a wax tablet for the king. 'Sire, we translated the numbers of the encrypted message and the result is on the wax tablet before you.'

Saustatar read; '*You have kidnapped my daughter, Asmunikal. If she is not released and returned to me, expect my army at Wassukanni shortly. Reply! My Sun.*' As the king read this message, his brows raised perceptibly as he got to the end. '*What in Teshub's name is going on?*' He shouted loudly.

His aide coughed and said, 'Sire, a rider-messenger is expected within a week to follow up this short message.'

The king waved the aide away from him and his fury turned his face crimson. 'If this is another one of my son's schemes, I will disown him,' he said through clenched teeth to his counsellor standing behind him.

Artatama was brought in between the king's bodyguard, and as he entered the hall, he pushed the guards out of the way and angrily marched up to his father. Then he noticed the king's crimson face and the chief accountant there on his knees. He stood before his father with his fists clenched, his dark eyes full of fury. 'Why am I brought here like this?' he demanded, but not as loudly as he'd originally intended. He knew his theft had been uncovered and this foul deed had come to the king's notice.

The king looked down on his son and said angrily, 'How dare you rob the royal treasury? Don't deny it,' the king pointed at the chief accountant still there on his knees. 'And I've received a message from Hattusas that the king's daughter has been kidnapped. He's accusing me and threatens to bring his army down here. Have you completely lost your senses?'

Artatama had his mouth open and was about to say something in his defence.

The king cut him off with, 'Ever since the Hittite Civil War, you've been obsessed with getting your revenge on the Hittite king. I told you six years ago, it was a mistake taking sides in *any* civil war—but I let you have your way. Then three years ago, you nearly caused a war with the Hittites when you encouraged that megalomaniac Madduwatta to rebel against the Hittite King. Now this recent escapade; and look at the results of your obsession. You've ended up with theft and kidnapping. This fixation must stop. I assume you are behind the kidnapping in Hattusas? Oh, don't bother trying to deny it. It would simply add lying to your litany of misdeeds. You, my boy, are going to be taught a lesson on behaviour to you rightful sovereign. You will either toe the line or I will disown you. Now I will teach you your first lesson in good conduct to your king.' Saustatar called to the General in charge of his bodyguards, 'Take this scoundrel down to the dungeons and he stays there a whole week on dry bread and water. There's to be *NO* contact between him and his cronies. This is solitary confinement. Is that clear?'

'Yes, your majesty, quite clear.' Four of the bodyguards surrounded the shocked Artatama. Just as suddenly, the shock turned to rage—but Artatama had the good sense to suppress it.

'Wait,' commanded the king. 'What have you done with the money? I want that back right now.' The king probed his son with his dark eyes, expectantly, waiting for an answer.

Artatama stood there sullenly avoiding his father's gaze, his fists still clenched. He remembered clearly six years ago, it was his father who had ordered him to take the army north to cement the alliance with the then King Muwas. Now his father claimed he had counselled against Mittani involvement in the Hittite civil war. He resented his father for having such a selective memory.

'Right, you will stay in the dungeons until I get an answer from you on the two million shekels you've stolen; that means indefinitely.' The king began to look sad at what he had to do, but resolved to break the arrogance of his son. 'Take him away,' he commanded. Out loud, he said to the audience chamber, 'If anyone tries to contact this wretch,' throwing his hand at the back of his departing son, 'he'll end up in the cell next to him.' Saustatar looked tired but determined.

He then turned to his senior counsellor and said, 'I want a general proclamation issued to all the towns which hold fealty to me. *If they come across a group of men holding a six-year-old girl prisoner, they are to to release her and detain the men. By order of King Saustatar of Mittani.* Make sure it goes out to the towns in the west as a matter of urgency. If they have taken the Hittite King's daughter hostage, that's the direction they'll be travelling. Next, send commiserations to the Hittite king and tell him I had nothing to do with the taking of his daughter. Send a copy of the proclamation to him as my sign of good faith. Tie the coded message to one leg of the pigeon and the copy of the proclamation to the other leg. Now send for General Ratukani.'

Ratukani, his army commander, presented himself in front of the king.

Saustatar said, 'I want a quiet mobilisation of the armed forces and I want them facing west and south. Put out a call for the other vassal cities to send their regiments to the western border. Assyria will stay out of this but Khemet has a defence treaty with the Hittites and I suspect Tudhaliyas will invoke it. Expect a Khemet army from the south and a Hittite army from the west. They may not attack if they take notice of what I've told them, but let's be prepared. Is that clear, General?'

'Yes your majesty. When are we expecting them?' asked the general.

'Let's be ready for them in a week, but I estimate in about two weeks—unless I hear otherwise. Be prepared and never underestimate your opponents,' Saustatar advised the general unnecessarily, the king's dark eyes flashing in anger. 'That way lies disaster! Take note, Isuwa is now *our* ally so put the army about five leagues south of Malidiya.'

Saustatar sighed deeply at all his troubles, then shook his head in despair at his son's antics. The day had started badly and seemed intent on continuing in that vein. The king clapped his hands to indicate the audience was over for the day and he went in search of his consort, seeking some solace in her kindness. He found the tall Kiluhepa, sitting back erect in all her finery in the middle of her boudoir, being groomed by her maids. He shooed them out of the room and came and sat in front of his consort, looking into Kiluhepa's kohl-painted eyes, and as always, found what he sought in those dark pools of liquid.

*   *   *

That morning, word had finally reached Kizzuwatna their army should prepare for combat on the eastern front. The messenger who brought the news had ridden all night, urging his horse ever onward and had ridden it into the ground in the urgency of its delivery. The poor horse collapsed on him as he was pushing it up the access road to the citadel in Adaniya, throwing him to the ground, forcing him to walk the short distance to the gate. It was the third horse that died under him on his long punishing three-day journey down from Hattusas; he'd been ordered to push them hard.

The Hittite courier, covered with dust and tired from the road, was ushered into the morning audience chamber of King Shunashura, the gangly king of Kizzuwatna.

The courier bowed and said, 'Your majesty, I bring you an urgent message from the king in Hattusas.' He handed the king the sealed writing boards and took three paces back.

The sallow faced king with long auburn hair, broke the seals and read the message. Slowly his brow crinkled and a look of astonishment replaced his calm visage. 'But this is outrageous,' he shouted. 'Ammuna of all people.' Then he scowled, 'I never did like the man. Far too full of himself! They should've put him down after the end of the civil war, like the mad dog he is. *Send for General Tapalass and my son,*' he shouted at his senior aide. 'We have work to do!'

His son, Crown Prince Talshura, arrived first on the scene, walking with confidence into the audience chamber.

'We'll wait till Tapalass arrives,' the king told his son, as the young man placed himself by his father's side. 'I don't want to repeat myself.'

A few moments later, General Tapalass marched in and bowed deeply in front of the king. 'You sent for me, sire?'

'Now listen well. I've received an astounding message from King Tudhaliyas. He states his daughter has been kidnapped by....' the king paused for effect, 'General Ammuna and some of his pals.' He stopped and watched the shocked reactions of his listeners. 'I can see it's outraged you as much as it did me. Nevertheless, that is what's in the message. Remember this is my granddaughter we're talking of—and *your* niece,' the king looked at his son. 'He tells us he's certain the Mittani are behind the kidnapping and asks us to prepare to send an army to invest Karkamish. He is going himself through Isuwa to Malidiya and then on to Wassukanni. He says our army should be outside of Karkamish at the latest two weeks from now, and he'll meet us down there.

General Tapalass looked grim. 'I smelt a rotten medlar when Ammuna was down here; always avoiding his duties.'

'Wait, that's not all.' The king lowered his voice. 'Tudhaliyas included a copy of a tablet he found in his daughter's room. It says; "*Withdraw from Kizzuwatna and return the suzerainty back to its previous owners—or else Asmunikal dies.*" Now, Tudhaliyas also wrote we should take a critical look at all those who might not be as loyal to me as I would have hoped for. Unfortunately I have to agree with him, mainly because of the message left by Ammuna.'

The Crown Prince looked puzzled. 'I don't understand, father. Why should we suspect those around us because of a tablet left up in Hattusas?'

Shunashura looked kindly at his twenty-three year-old son and said, 'My boy, the implication is clear. The Mittani could not hope to take control of Kizzuwatna without inside help. If the Hittites say to the Mittani, "Right, go ahead, we won't stop you." Do the Mittani really think I would quietly submit to their control without a fight? No! But they seem to be confident of regaining control over us all the same. How? It must mean they've bought a number of my senior officials, both civilian and military, to feel so confident of overcoming my objections. Now do you see?'

Talshura was nodding his head, 'Yes father, I see what you've in mind. I'm sorry for being so slow.'

'So,' continued the king, 'one of the first things we must do is ensure the army is loyal to me. *That* I will leave in the capable hands of the General here. What ever it takes, clean the stable. I want anyone who may be dubious in their loyalty, to be exiled. Get a ship ready and send them to Alasiya. That will put them out of harms way. You my boy, will go and find my spymaster and check with him if he knows of any civilian traitors to the crown. They can go on the same ship. I want the ship out of here by this evening.'

'Yes father,' replied the king's son. 'That scoundrel Ammuna, told me he was being recalled to Hattusas a week ago, in a most arrogant manner,' Talshura told his father. 'I was glad to see the back of him, I must say.'

'Well now we know why he went back up to Hattusas,' the king told his audience. 'My son, General, I need not tell you how urgent all this is. We need to clean our stable and our army must be ready to march within two days at the latest. The first order of business is to get rid of the traitors in our midst. Then we will do as our good friend Tudhaliyas asks of us. I must send a messenger back to Hattusas to tell the king we'll meet him and General Zidanta outside Wassukanni after we've dealt with Karkamish and Harran as he requests. Instead of killing horses with messengers, I'll send a coded pigeon up north. That should get there in a day. Now we need to get to work.' He made it clear to his son and his general they should go about their urgent tasks.

'Any news of Asmunikal, father?' asked Talshura before going, a worried edge to his question.

'No, my son! He says no more than what I've told you.' The king turned to his aide and said, 'Take the messenger,' he nodded at the dusty Hittite soldier standing at attention, 'clean him up and make sure he's fed and rested.'

General Tapalass rushed out of the palace and mounted his horse, setting off to the main military barracks a short distance outside of the port town of Adaniya. There, he went straight to his HQ and waited for the arrival of all his senior officers. They'd been ordered to assemble for a war council of the Kizzuwatna army. He and his deputy made a list of any questionable officers and they both waited for them to appear. He would begin with the senior men, then get their accomplices from them.

The Crown Prince went from the audience hall with the general and parted from him on the ground floor. He left him to go down into the cellar looking for the spymaster to ascertain what he knew of the traitors within the civilian hierarchy of the king's administration. This was going to be an arduous day for both Crown Prince Talshura and General Tapalass.

7
Isuwan Border

The sun beat down pitilessly on the bunch of *loyal* mercenaries following Ammuna in his quest for riches. They'd left the cover of the forest and were riding hard, out in the open all through mid-morning, when they finally reached the shores of the Upper Puranti River. Remnants of the early morning mists hung lightly over the waters of the Upper Puranti imbuing it with an otherworldly atmosphere.

Ammuna's chariot swung south alongside the wide river heading towards Malidiya, the capital of Isuwa, and the *loyal* band of bought soldiers followed their leader. Around noon, Ammuna ordered a halt in a shallow brushwood ravine leading down to the river shore, halting his men to afford them a nibble at some dry rations. Asmunikal still wouldn't eat anything and she sat sullenly on the cushions in the chariot sipping some water from a small water skin. In the ravine, Ammuna was hopeful of staying out of sight.

They were almost ready to move on; when out of nowhere, a horse carrying a soldier in a yellow tunic appeared at the top of the ravine. The soldier looked down on the peaceful scene of a group of fellow soldiers finishing their meal and he gave them a friendly wave. He got a response he wasn't expecting; one of Ammuna's men grabbed his bow and loosened off an arrow at the waving soldier. Alarmed at such a reception, he again looked at them for an instant, then turned his horse and galloped off in a hurry.

'*Who fired the shot?*' yelled Ammuna, furious at being discovered.

One soldier rose sheepishly to his feet, still holding his bow. 'Sorry sir. It was a jerk reaction. My instinct...' he trailed off at seeing the fury on his general's face.

Ammuna rushed up to him and demanded in his face, 'What were you thinking of you stupid boy? Now he's rushed off to report to his commander he's seen us. Didn't you see he was waving in a friendly manner? He was totally unsuspecting of anything; we could have got him to come down here and then so easily have slit his throat. Then he couldn't report to anyone.' Ammuna turned to the rest of his men, 'The next time anyone pulls such a stunt, I will personally put my knife into him; do I make myself clear?' Silence greeted the statement, so Ammuna repeated, '*Do I make myself clear?*'

'Yes sir,' responded his soldiers in unison.

'Now we mount and ride like the furry. Who was riding point before we stopped?' Ammuna asked.

Two soldiers raised their hands.

'Right, you two; go up there and see in which direction the soldier rode off.' Ammuna turned to his deputy, and shook his head, 'What a disaster. Keep your eyes peeled for trouble. Now the enemy knows where we are.'

Lawana sighed, 'Yes sir, it *is* a disaster.'

The two scouts returned and reported, 'The man rode off into the west. We didn't see anyone else, sir.'

'We'll keep going along the river—but no stopping,' Ammuna told Lawana. 'Let's hope he's part of a small reconnaissance outfit, not a full blown squadron.'

Ammuna led his men at top speed alongside the river for a while until he noticed a large number of soldiers on the ridge of a hill to his right, outlined against the sky, paralleling his group a quarter of a league away. At this point in their journey, the river was in a valley flanked by low hills on either side and Ammuna kept his men going until it was clear those on the ridge were simply keeping his group in sight, shadowing them. Every time Ammuna stopped, so did those on the ridge; when Ammuna moved on, so did they. They made no attempt to intercept him or engage his group.

Ammuna brought his column to a halt and turned to Lawana, 'This won't do at all you know. I estimate we're a couple of leagues from the Isuwan border. There must be at least a hundred of them up there. If I'm right, they're shadowing us so as to tell a larger force where we are, so they can cut us off up ahead. We'll need a diversion. Let's get into those trees over there so they can't see us so easily.'

Ammuna on his chariot, led them into a small riverside coppice. Once under the small canopy of leaves, Ammuna continued, 'Look here Colonel, I want you to take fifty men and create a diversion. This late in the autumn with no rain, the soil is fairly dry, even on the riverbank. Pick the best horses and the best fighters. I want you to tie some small branches to the tails of the horses and strike out back the way we came. Put three or four riders out to your left to create a small dust cloud, it should cover the rest of the riders, then have the rest follow; oh, and make lots of noise as you leave.

'Head back a league and then strike out directly in to the west. You must make it look like we are all with you, so create a large dust trail. They won't attempt to intervene if they think we're all with you. Keep going west for a league then cut the branches loose and sneak round them. They'll be looking for around two hundred men, so your fifty, if they're quiet, might be able to outwit them.

'Meanwhile, I'll take the rest of the men down river after we see the enemy following you. Keep going until you lose them, then swing back south and east, and we'll meet up inside Isuwa tonight. Remember we're not far from the Isuwan border where we ought to find sanctuary. If all goes well, this should be our last hurdle. After this, we'll be travelling through Isuwa and Mittani, which I understand is friendly territory. When you reach the border, I'll arrange for you to be met by an Isuwan patrol. I'll leave word where you can find us. We'll be camped somewhere inside Isuwa tonight and we should be in Malidiya tomorrow night.'

Lawana picked out his fifty men and explained to them what they were about to do. The branches were tied to the horses tails and the fifty galloped out of the tree cover heading back north-west with the outriders on the left creating a covering dust cloud. They created enough noise and dust to be convincing, making it clear they were intent on circumventing those shadowing them. The Hittite group on the ridge spotted the breakout and immediately gave chase back up northwards after Lawana's small group. The ruse amused Ammuna, furnishing the rest of his men with a great deal of satisfaction at the cunning of their general.

Ammuna sent scouts out to make sure no other enemy patrols were around, and when they reported the way forward was clear, he resumed his journey south as fast as he could. As per his estimate, they reached the Isuwan border by mid afternoon and they soon came across an Isuwan patrol on the lookout for their Hittite opposite numbers. The meeting almost descended into an armed conflict until Ammuna managed to calm the Isuwan Captain of the patrol, who had to be convinced these hundred and sixty-five Hittite soldiers were not in fact Hittite soldiers, despite their Hittite uniforms. After a lengthy parley, the patrol captain politely requested Ammuna to follow him and shortly thereafter led them to a large force of Isuwan soldiers in their drab brown tunics, camped in an area near the river. An Isuwan general was in charge of the force.

Ammuna's group prompted many hostile stares from the encamped Isuwans, being dressed in their Hittite uniforms. The Isuwans, some six hundred of them, were in fact readying to repulse an expected Hittite attack on them at any moment, since their king had recently changed allegiances from Hattusas to Wassukanni. This was one of those periodical shifts their temperamental king, Tarasina, did every now and then.

Once inside the Isuwan encampment, Ammuna jumped off his chariot and said to his driver, 'Make sure you keep a close eye on the brat,' indicating Asmunikal. 'I want two men watching her at all times whilst we're here.' Then he was led to the tent of the Isuwan commander.

The Isuwan general was waiting for him with an outstretched hand. 'My name is General Satiniya, and you must be General Ammuna?'

'Yes, that's right. Good to meet you general,' replied Ammuna, taking the proffered hand.

'We've had instructions from Crown Prince Artatama to give you all the help you require. I assume you could do with being re-provisioned? We'll take care of that later, but right now I want your men to join ours and make yourselves at home.' Satiniya smiled warmly at Ammuna and invited him to sit.

'Could I ask a small favour of you right at the outset, General?' Ammuna asked as he sat down. 'I noticed quite a bit of hostility from your men towards mine as we entered the camp. I'm aware of the reasons, but could you give instructions to your officers to inform your men we are *not* the hostile Hittites they're here to fight. It would make our stay a little bit more comfortable. I'd appreciate that.' Ammuna smiled back at the Isuwan general.

'Why of course; be glad to.' Satiniya called to his deputy and gave the requested order, and also told him to have the Hittite horses looked after and Ammuna's men fed.

'One more thing,' Ammuna added. 'I've had to send my deputy with fifty men in a diversionary subterfuge to throw off a Hittite squadron following us. Could you give orders to have your patrols keep a sharp lookout for my deputy and his group of fifty soldiers. I'd like him to be told where I am and if possible, to be brought here to join me. Is that feasible?' Again, Ammuna smiled pleasantly at his opposite number.

'Why certainly. That's within my remit.' He gave the instructions to his deputy when he returned from carrying out the previous order.

'Now I would like to offer you the hospitality of my table,' and he clapped his hands for his orderlies to serve food and wine.

Ammuna looked at the food being brought to the table and his stomach gave a growl. His last meal was at breakfast and he was itching to get stuck in to this delayed sustenance but politeness forced him to take it easy.

Both generals were somewhat wary of each other, and Ammuna sensed it had to do with Isuwa's current antagonism with the Hittites. The Isuwan general was fixated on Ammuna's Hittite yellow tunic and couldn't dismiss it despite Artatama's instructions to help the rogue Hittite general. It all demonstrated itself in their false smiles to each other, and the picky nature of their eating; they took small portions, nibbled at the food without any real enthusiasm, and drank little of the excellent wine provided.

'If you'll allow me, I will take a look at how my men are settling in,' Ammuna asked Satiniya, trying to find an excuse to leave the table.

'Why of course, general. I've had a tent close-by made available for your personal use. When you're ready to retire just ask my orderlies.' General Satiniya rose from the table at the same time as Ammuna and escorted him to the exit, happy to see the back of this strange Hittite.

Ammuna heaved a sigh of relief when he'd exited the Isuwan marquee. *I don't trust that man*, he thought to himself as he wandered over to his own men sitting round the big fire, relaxing after a hard days riding.

'You were wise not to join us,' Ammuna said to a captain as he seated himself on a log next to his interim deputy. 'This general is a bit of a slithery type. Make sure you post secure sentries around our bivouac. I feel uncomfortable around this lot—it's as if they're waiting for orders to have a go at us. They can't seem to forget we're not part of the Hittite military any more.'

'Yes sir, I got a very uncomfortable feeling from the whole lot of them,' agreed the captain. 'I'll be glad to see the back of them tomorrow.'

'Any sign of Colonel Lawana and his group?' asked Ammuna.

'Not yet sir! He'll be all right, sir. The Colonel is smart; he'll get through them.'

'Yes your right. I'm going to turn in. How's the brat holding up? Still on her cushions?'

'Yes sir. She refuses to eat anything we give her—only takes the water. Insists on sleeping in the chariot on those cushions—I think she's using them as comfort cushions, sir.'

'Fine! Another week or so and we'll be rid of her. Just make sure she's alive when we deliver her.' Ammuna rose from the log and went to look for the orderly who was to show him which tent he'd been assigned.

In the middle of the night, a group of forty-two soldiers in yellow tunics walked quietly into the encampment leading their exhausted horses. They bedded their horses down and then managed to sit at the embers of a fire and eat some cold food before joining their comrades in sleep. It was Colonel Lawana's group. He'd evaded the squadron sent to intercept him but lost nine men later in a skirmish with another large patrol. That was the luck of the draw, as he saw it.

Ammuna awoke at dawn to the persistent sound of an owl hooting. It had taken umbrage at having its territory invaded. He noted he had company in his tent; Lawana was quietly snoring on another hammock on the other side of his quarters. He hadn't heard him come in during the night. He smiled, stretched and got dressed. *I'll wake him when breakfast is ready,* he thought as he left the tent. He sauntered through the dewy clearing, over to where the captain was ordering his cooks to look lively and get the food going.

'Sleep well?' Ammuna asked the captain.

'Yes sir, reasonably well,' the captain responded. 'I put the Colonel in your tent, I hope that was alright?'

'Fine, that's where he should be. I've let him sleep until we get the food ready. What time did his men get in?' Ammuna asked.

'Just a while ago; they were totally exhausted. They'd been in a fight with a large Hittite patrol. He told me he'd lost nine men.' The captain shrugged his shoulders as if to say, that's the army for you.

As the captain was relating this, Ammuna realised the captain must have been awake most of the night since he'd talked with Lawana. 'Make sure you don't over do it, Captain. Well done, but try and rest when you get the chance.'

'Yes sir,' replied the captain appreciatively.

The smell of food was getting stronger and Ammuna told the captain to wake everybody. Breakfast was ready.

'I hear you had a bit of trouble,' Ammuna asked Lawana when he appeared for his share of the food.

'They came out of nowhere just when I thought I'd managed to give them the slip. One moment we were riding along quietly; next moment we had to fight for our lives. Fifty of us against a hundred of them. Finally, I gave the order to run for it. I lost nine men in that skirmish. I simply couldn't avoid it. Sorry General, should have been more careful. All I salvaged was five of our horses.' Lawana seemed to have taken it personally.

'Don't blame yourself. Things like that happen in our line of work. It wasn't the first time and it won't be the last time. All the men who died knew exactly what they were in for when they signed up for this business. Anyway, glad to have you here,' Ammuna patted the colonel on the back gently, trying to connect with him. 'By the way, did you come across the large squadron we did all the fancy manoeuvring for?'

'Only in the far distance as we were crossing the Isuwan frontier,' Lawana told him. 'There must have been around three hundred of them. We did well to avoid them.'

After his men had eaten, Ammuna went to say farewell to his host, the Isuwan general. 'We're leaving now and I really appreciate the provisions and your hospitality,' Ammuna told Satiniya. 'It's a pity I won't be in a position to repay your generosity.'

'Think nothing of it. Happy to oblige a friend of Crown Prince Artatama. By the way, I'm sending ten of my men to the capital with a report for our king on the situation at the border. I was wondering whether you'd like to accompany them to Malidiya. I assume you don't know the route so they would be able to guide you, in case you get lost.' Satiniya grinned widely at making such a proposal.

'Why that's generous of you. Certainly, we'd be delighted to have them guide us. Thank you so much,' and Ammuna grinned right back at Satiniya for having these guards imposed on him.

Ammuna's chariot was brought to him, still bearing the brat, as he called the Hittite king's daughter. She was standing up in a haughty manner trying to look like she was above what was happening to her. Ammuna jumped onto the floor of the chariot and grabbed the reins from the driver, giving them a shake, forcing the brat to grab the rail. He shook the reins, telling the horses to get a move on. He waved to Satiniya as his column left the camp, followed by the ten Isuwan guides-come-guards.

On leaving the forest, they found a landscape shimmering in the early morning haze still clinging to the ground. There were mackerel clouds in the sky suggesting unsettled weather to come, with a temperate sun which would allow Ammuna's column to travel throughout the day without baking them as though they were in an oven.

'Go back and order those Isuwan curs to the front of the column,' Ammuna shouted at Lawana. 'They're supposed to be leading us to Malidiya, not following us.'

Colonel Lawana peeled off and rode back to carry out the order. He found the commander of the Isuwans in a foul mood as if he'd been given unpalatable orders.

'Captain, get your men to the front and lead the way to the capital,' Lawana shouted at the dour Isuwan officer.

The captain glared at Lawana but complied with the order, picking up speed and riding his ten men to the head of the column, with Lawana behind close behind.

8
First Blood

Mokhat's *special forces* had been following the chariot track south all the way to the mighty Puranti River where they finally came across a small Hittite patrol having a bite to eat, resting leisurely by the river. As Mokhat's men rounded a small bend in the river, there they were, all peacefully munching away—then abruptly the whole patrol dropped their food and grabbed for their weapons, seeing the unusual appearance of the dark tunics. They had no idea who they were dealing with having never come across such uniforms before. Mokhat rode forward, dressed in his Hittite general's uniform, raised his hand and shouted at them to stand down.

This Hittite patrol consisted of around a hundred men, enough to give a good account of themselves, but still small enough to be wary of these dark uniformed bearded men sitting on their horses and watching them. The captain of the patrol raised his hand to indicate to his men they shouldn't fire their bows yet. He focused on this Hittite General coming towards him, and he came forward on foot hesitantly shouting, '*Who are you*?' Finally, he picked up his courage and advanced on Mokhat's horse. Both stopped a small distance from each other.

'I'm on a secret mission for his majesty King Tudhaliyas. If you come closer I will show you his royal seal,' shouted Mokhat as he waited for the captain to come forward.

The captain came to Mokhat, still cautious. 'I'm sorry sir, but I don't recognise those uniforms.'

'Nor should you,' Mokhat told him. 'Our little select group was recently formed. I commend you. You have every right to be cautious; it would be a dereliction of duty to be otherwise.'

The captain peered at the royal seal and satisfied himself it was genuine. 'Captain Palanquin of the first Ullama regiment at your service sir,' he stood to attention. The captain's men lowered their weapons on seeing their captain at attention. They had concluded the Hittite General must be genuine.

Mokhat dismounted and waved at Onasiyas and Palaiyas to bring the rest of the group down to join him. 'At ease captain,' Mokhat ordered. 'I am General Mokhat four days out of Hattusas. Be so kind as to inform me the purpose of your patrol.'

'General sir, my colonel sent me to scout around and keep a sharp lookout for a group of Hittite soldiers led by a rogue general on a chariot who has kidnapped the king's daughter. We were not to engage him but shadow him and send for reinforcements.' The captain now visibly relaxed and stood at ease.

'There you have the reason for our strange uniforms,' Mokhat told him. 'We are after the same quarry.'

At this point Palaiyas and Onasiyas rode up and both dismounted, coming to join Mokhat. The captain began to feel nervous again at having two generals so close to him and was contemplating standing at attention again, when Palaiyas came and rested his hand on the captain's arm to reassure him.

Mokhat introduced his companions, 'This is General Palaiyas, and this, Colonel Onasiyas, commander of the *special forces* chasing *ex*-General Ammuna and his kidnapping bandits. We should go over and reassure your men. If we may, we'll join you and your men in your noonday meal. We have this dried meat and a little wine to contribute to your men—if that's acceptable?'

71

'Your most welcome, sirs,' and the captain led them all back to where his own men waited. All were curious to see who these strange dark-uniformed men were. The captain had a word with his senior non-com and explained the situation, then he gathered the other non-cons and told them. And thus it was the facts concerning this strange outfit were rapidly spread amongst the Hittite patrol.

'So now captain, have you any news for us about our common enemy?' Onasiyas asked the captain, who still seemed a little awed by this group of dark uniforms mingling with his own patrol.

'Yes sir. We chased them yesterday,' reported the captain. 'My scout came across them near the river relaxing in a shallow brushwood ravine a couple of leagues from the Isuwan border. They fired at him and he came back and reported to me. We sent off for reinforcements and then I shadowed them along a ridge for a while so as to be able to tell our larger force where they were. I suggested to my colonel he go south-east as quickly as possible so they could cut them off before they crossed the border.

'Then they pulled a fast one on me. They hid under some trees and suddenly came out of the trees riding back up river. I thought the whole lot were making a break for it so I followed them. It turned out they'd split up and sent half their force back the way they came to enable the rest to continue downriver. I lost them when they stopped making a dust trail.'

'Hmm!' Mokhat responded to the information. 'I was told Ammuna was tricky. You've just confirmed it. So you're telling me he's managed to cross the border into Isuwa.' Mokhat waited for a ratification.

'I'm afraid so sir,' the captain confirmed. 'We haven't followed him. My colonel is waiting for confirmation from Hattusas of what we should do next. We moved away from the border to avoid a clash. My colonel's been told if we venture into Isuwa, they're likely to attack us, the situation being what it is. We'll need at least four or five regiments to follow the rogue general across the border.'

Mokhat shrugged and looked at Palaiyas. 'From my information, our king is getting and army together to invade Mittani and he's likely to crush this King Tarasina in Malidiya along the way. I can't see him being allowed to continue to rebel and thumb his nose up at Hattusas. But that's at least a week away. In the mean time, I suggest you bide your time and await events. You'll be in Malidiya before you know it.'

The information seemed to relax the captain. 'I'll inform my colonel of this, if I may?'

'You have my permission to do so,' replied Mokhat. 'Tell him to keep his scouts out on patrol and make a note of where the Isuwans are concentrating. This will be of use to our army coming this way. One more thing; the Kizzuwatna are also sending an army and they'll probably be investing Karkamish; that's for your colonel's ears only. Now I'm afraid we're going to have to leave you and continue downriver.'

'But sir, there's a large Isuwan force down there,' warned the captain, 'guarding their border. You'll never get past them.'

'Ah, now don't underestimate my odd looking group,' Onasiyas butted in. 'We'll get past them; have no fear—one way or another. But you didn't say how large this force was?'

'My scouts tell me there are about five hundred of them in front of you.' The captain stood shaking his head and wondered how these men in dark uniforms were going to get past the massive Isuwan presence, and how was it possible for them to chase the rogue general through all of Isuwa?

Mokhat asked Onasiyas to get his men moving and they said goodbye to the patrol captain. The poor man looked on as they rode downriver, thinking it was the last he was ever going to see of them, still concerned at them riding into trouble.

When they'd gone out of sight, Mokhat called a halt and asked the men to gather round and listen carefully. 'I want two scouts well ahead of us, but they must try to blend in, and three scouts on the right flank to warn us of any problems from that direction. Remember you're all dressed in uniforms no one has seen before, so if you're in difficulties, don't run; try to talk your way out of trouble. You are hunters out to chase down some game for profit, boar, red deer and the like. What you're wearing isn't a uniform but simply dark dress—try to remember that. Also by the time you're in trouble, we're more likely to be nearby, so talk yourself blue in the face; try to waste their time to give *us* time. Right, that's all I have to say. Let's get moving.'

By mid-afternoon they'd managed to put themselves near the Isuwan border, when one of the scouts came galloping back to report. 'Sir,' he addressed Onasiyas, 'we came across an Isuwan patrol ahead, and the scout who was with me, he's talking to them as we speak.'

'Is it far?' Onasiyas asked urgently.

'No sir, just over that hill in a gully,' the scout informed him.

'Try and do this quietly,' he told his men. He trotted off towards where the other scout was, followed by his troops.

They came to the rise but stayed below the ridge of the hill, dismounting and creeping to look over into the gully. They saw their scout being held by a patrol of around a hundred men. They had him by the arms, and as Mokhat, Palaiyas and Onasiyas watched, they were shocked to see the scout thrust to the ground and held there spread-eagled by four Isuwan soldiers in their brown tunics. Then another one of the soldiers raised his spear and thrust it in their man's stomach.

Onasiyas jumped up and stood on top of the hill. 'I simply can't let this happen to my men without getting even,' he declaimed loudly to Mokhat and Palaiyas.

They both rose to their feet and stood next to him and nodded in agreement. 'I'll support whatever you want to do, my dear Colonel,' Mokhat told him.

The Isuwans in the gully suddenly noticed the three men in dark dress standing on the hill. Their leader pointed at the three strangers and swung his horse round towards the hill. Those who dismounted, jumped on their horses and the Isuwans began to gallop upwards towards the hilltop.

Onasiyas told Captain Neti, his deputy, to have four of the men stay with the spare horses and the pack ponies while they took care of this little problem.

Mokhat, Palaiyas and Onasiyas mounted their steeds and were joined by the rest of the *special forces* along the ridge. At the sight of so many darkly dressed men on horses above them, the Isuwans suddenly pulled their mounts to a halt, waiting to see if any more were going to appear. When no more appeared, they resumed the charge expecting those on the hill would turn tail and make a run from the group of soldiers coming at them. It didn't happen that way.

Those on the hill unsheathed their bows and fired a salvo of arrows at the oncoming charge, downing well over twenty of the Isuwans. Another quick volley reduced the numbers even further. Then Onasiyas gave the order to draw swords and led the charge at the oncoming Isuwans. The shock on the faces of those wearing the brown tunics was evident, but they were too close to abandon the charge and they clashed heavily. The months of strenuous training of the *special forces'* paid off handsomely. The Isuwans weren't prepared for the superior fighting skills of those they faced, or the intensity and ferocity of the fighting. They fell one after another until there were few of them left.

When the two opposing forces finally ceased fighting, there were around sixteen Isuwans remaining with their hands clutching the air, having abandoned their swords and eager to surrender. The others were lying on the ground either dead or injured.

'*Off your horses*,' shouted Onasiyas to the Isuwans.

The prisoners dismounted and sent their horses to join the other hundred horses who had began grazing on the lush grass a little distance from the battlefield.

'Right,' Onasiyas said jumping off his horse, still in a foul mood. He looked at his prisoners closely. 'You,' he pointed at one of the brown tunics. 'I recognise you as one of those holding my man down before he was killed. Why did your lot kill him? How could one harmless man menace a hundred? Tell me before I put a sword in *your* stomach.'

The Isuwan soldier was trembling with fear. 'I only did what I was ordered to do. I didn't kill him, I swear.'

'I want to know *WHY* he was killed, not who killed him,' growled Onasiyas at the quaking brown tunic.

'The colonel said he was a Hittite spy,' replied the soldier almost in tears. 'That's why he ordered the man's death.'

Others of the *special forces* had dismounted and come to stand by their prisoners. At a nod from Onasiyas, they used their daggers to execute all of the prisoners. 'We can't have them going off and reporting our whereabouts,' Onasiyas said to Mokhat as an explanation of this foul deed he'd ordered. 'By the way,' he motioned to Captain Neti, 'how many men did we lose? Have you counted them yet?'

'Just done that sir,' the captain responded. 'We lost one man and seven wounded. Not too bad considering.'

'That's one too many in my opinion,' Onasiyas glared at the captain. 'I didn't train you to lose any men.'

'Look here, don't be too hard on him,' Mokhat counselled Onasiyas when they'd moved away, and the captain had left to take care of the wounded. 'They fought with a skill and stamina I've never seen before, and let's face it; we only lost one man whilst the enemy lost all theirs. Now I know what to expect when we meet Ammuna —and I don't think much of his chances. Ease up one yourself, my friend.'

'Yes, we did alright, but we could have done better. We could have come out of this fight without any losses; that's what I've been aiming for in my training.' Onasiyas spread his arm out at all the dead bodies around them and continued, 'I think we'd better make a move away from here before more of the enemy arrive.'

'Let's move away from the river,' suggested Palaiyas, 'over the ridge of the valley. We'll have more manoeuvrability if we meet any sizeable patrol. They won't be able to hem us up against the river.' Then he turned to Onasiyas, 'We need to get out of these Hittite uniforms now we've crossed the Isuwan border. I suppose you have a pair of spare dark uniforms on the pack ponies?'

'But of course, your highness.' Onasiyas called to his deputy, 'Captain Neti, get one of the men to unpack two of our spare uniforms for the highnesses,' Onasiyas ordered his deputy.

When Mokhat and Palaiyas got into their dark outfits, they now looked no different from the rest of the soldiers and blended in perfectly with the other men.

Mokhat said to Onasiyas, 'We need to find out exactly where Ammuna is, and to do this we need to get through to the Hittite spy network. As I remember, General Zidanta told us to go to the crossroad tavern just outside Malidiya and wait for a contact there. That's where I propose we go next. Are we agreed?'

Onasiyas and Palaiyas both nodded their heads at the suggestion and the column swung away from the river over the hill, heading for the crossroad tavern.

9
Perfidious Trap

Another mild cloud covered autumn day brought Ammuna's *loyal* group of mercenaries galloping through into midday. They were riding amongst scenery suffused with a myriad of shades of green, deep greens to yellowish greens, primarily as a result of the water table being closer to the surface in this area and the proximity of the mighty Puranti River going down all the way to the Gulf of Erika far to the south. Ammuna deemed it a good time to stop by the riverbank for a bite of dry rations.

When they resumed their ride, the wind picked up, adding a rush of freshness to their ensuing strenuous exercises. By mid afternoon, they could see their destination; a large city perched on a flattened hill in the far distance sketched against an uncertain sky. On rounding a small hill they came across a large Isuwan patrol of two hundred men or more, and it was only as a result of having the ten Isuwan soldiers in their muddy brown tunics out in front, a skirmish was avoided. The gruff captain at the fore of Ammuna's column smiled suddenly at the sight of his fellow Isuwans and rode out quickly to meet them, followed by his ten men.

Ammuna halted his chariot to allow the Isuwan captain to convey the reason for the unusual appearance of this column of yellow tunics approaching their capital. It would seem the Isuwan captain's gruffness was to be explained by his anxiety in being outnumbered by what he considered to be the enemy, namely Ammuna's Hittites. He had been afraid of being butchered by those he escorted.

Despite being told these Hittites were friendly, he couldn't get past the uniforms and was in fear of his life.

The captain sent one of his men back to Ammuna and requested he come and have word with the Isuwan colonel commanding the large Isuwan patrol. Upon approaching the colonel in his chariot, Ammuna felt a distinct coolness if not outright hostility, yet the colonel was all smiles, much in the manner of General Satiniya. Ammuna put it down to the same dull reasoning which had worried his Isuwan captain.

Briefly, the colonel looked sharply at Asmunikal, standing in the chariot with a frozen face when Ammuna had joined him, then said, 'You must be General Ammuna,' he quipped.

'Well then, I must be,' retorted Ammuna frostily in answer to the false smiles. Then he remembered the million shekels and changed his tone to be more accommodating. 'I was led to understand I would be welcome in King Tarantula's territory now Isuwa is allied to Wassukanni. All we want is to travel to Wassukanni through Isuwa in safety and peace. If you could escort us to a campsite for the night, we will cause you no further difficulty.'

The Isuwan colonel sat with his thoughts for a moment then replied, 'I have the perfect spot for you. It's in the middle of a forest with a nearby spring. I'm thinking of your safety, what with those yellow tunics being so visible. Had I not seen our brown uniforms with you, I would have attacked you. Being inside the forest should keep you out of predicaments way.' The colonel had a quiet word with their gruff captain and then turned back to Ammuna. 'The captain knows the spot I'm referring to and will take you there. Good luck and fare well. You might want to think of changing your tunics to something more neutral—white for instance. It would be less of an incentive for our forces to have a go at you now you're in Mittani space.'

Ammuna thanked him for the offer of the campsite, and his suggestion on their tunics, smiled at him, and then swung his chariot to follow their Isuwan captain away from the colonel's patrol. His group was led away from the river into a deep forest to the west of Malidiya, well away from prying eyes. The light was beginning to go as the sun dipped down low in the sky, making the shadows eerie in this strange forest. They travelled deep into the cover of the forest canopy and eventually they came into a large clearing with a small pool coming from a deep underground spring. By this time, the moon had risen and it threw a white light into the clearing, bathing it in ghostly luminescence.

The Isuwan captain said his goodbyes to Ammuna and took his men swiftly out the way they came, saying someone would come in the morning to show them the way out and the route towards the Mittani capital.

'Good to be rid of them,' spat out Ammuna, as he watched them disappear. Work was then begun to dig a latrine pit downwind and have the horses watered and fed. A couple of large campfires were mapped out in the clearing and logs were collected by the men, leftover from the previous occupants of the glade.

'This is going to be the first night in a couple of weeks we can rest without fearing an attack,' Ammuna told Lawana when they'd settled down on a couple of the logs.

'I hope your right,' Lawana responded. 'The men could do with a good night's rest tonight.' A moment of silence erupted between them, then Lawana continued, 'Would it not be an idea to see if some of our men might rustle up a deer or two to put on the fire? We passed some game as we came deeper into the forest. I'm sure our men could hunt them down. It would boost morale no end.'

'Good idea,' agreed the general. 'Why don't you arrange it now? Maybe the smell of meat roasting might force the brat into eating something.'

Lawana went to find a junior officer to take out a small hunting party armed with bows and spears. 'Don't come back empty handed or I'll put you on the spit and roast you instead,' Lawana warned the lieutenant half seriously.

The cooks made spits out of old branches and put up an A-frame over the fire in readiness, however, in the meantime, they readied some pots of barley porridge to be getting on. A while later, the hunting party returned with the carcases of a large red deer and surprisingly, a wild boar. Both were rapidly de-gutted, skinned and slung over each of the two fires. Men watched, salivating, as the two animals roasted on their A-frames over the flames, joking and singing in the meantime with merriment.

'I must say you were perfectly right in saying it would improve morale. Look at them, happy as young kids on their first hunting trip. Well done Colonel!' Ammuna congratulated Lawana.

'"Give a soldier a good full stomach and he'll die happily for you." Remember who said that?' Lawana enquired of Ammuna.

'You have a splendid memory, colonel. You got any more of my saying to throw back at me?' laughed Ammuna.

Even with the two large kills, each man only managed to get a small plate of the roast meat—hence the barley porridge. There were two hundred and six men to feed, not counting Ammuna and Lawana. The brat still wouldn't touch the food offered to her, although her minder noted she looked at the roast meat proffered to her, longingly.

Just as the whole camp was settling down after the most enjoyable meal in ages, and they were readying for a small sing-song around the fires, Ammuna stood up and climbed up on the log he had been sitting on. He needed a platform to address the men. He raised his hand and asked them all for some quiet. He had something to tell them. 'Lads, we have just had a splendid feast, and I'm sure there will be many more like this.' That got a large nod of approval from the gathering. 'I've asked you all to put your lives in some danger in order to improve yourselves. Instead of dying for your country, you are now committed to going along with me and to enriching yourselves.

'What I haven't told you yet is by how much richer you are going to be at the end of this voyage. I see in front of me two hundred and six ordinary soldiers. I can tell you each and every one of you will get exactly two thousand four hundred and twenty-seven golden shekels to do what you want with. That's five hundred thousand shekels divided amongst two hundred and six men.' He paused while a laudable intake of breath was heard in the clearing. 'That is far more than anyone of you could make in a lifetime of toil either in or out of uniform. It is a fortune to any reasonable man. That is what I offer you. You will split around half a million golden shekels amongst yourselves no matter how many make it to Wassukanni with me.

'If you're sensible, you will be able to live comfortably like a rich man for the rest of your lives. With that sum, you could take a wife, bear children and be secure until your dying day. To those who don't make it—and I include the nine of our comrades who fell in the recent skirmish, and to any who fall by the wayside—I will personally take care of their families and they will get their share. To those families I will give three thousand golden shekels, the difference will come out of my share, which won't compensate for the loss of their loved one, but will make it possible for them not to starve.

'Now I want to include a word of warning to any of you who fall foul of the disease called greed. Should any of you fall in combat at the hands of your *own* comrades, in the false thought that the fewer of you there are, the more there will be for you to share at the end, then I'm going to have to disabuse you of this idea. As of now, I am going to investigate every death of each of you personally. If I should conclude that the death was not due to the enemy or an accident, then I will pursue the culprit until I find him, and be absolutely certain that I *will* find him; I will then personally slit the culprits throat, and furthermore, I will slit the throats of their families and relatives as well. This may sound harsh, but none of you have anything to worry about as long as you behave well towards each other.'

Ammuna then put his hand in his pouch and pulled out a golden image of a woman's face. Holding it up for all to see between his thumb and forefinger, he said, 'I swear by this sacred sign of Fishtail, what I have told you will come to pass, and if I offend the goddess by breaking this sacred vow, may my spirit wander in the fires of the netherworld for all eternity. Any questions?'

Ammuna stood on the log and waited while a small murmuring went round the whole clearing. No one raised their voice to question their good fortune. However, one non-com did get up and said, 'Three cheers for our general,' and the entire clearing erupted with three loud cheers.

'Thank you men, for your vote of confidence. From it, I gather you're not too unhappy with what I've told you.'

Lots of nodding heads responded to his last statement.

'Good, then I'll let you get on with your enjoyment.' Ammuna jumped down from the log and said to Lawana, 'Now it's time to have our little officer's conference—same topic. There's me, you, three captains and the lieutenant,' Ammuna told Lawana. 'Will you go round quietly and collect them and we'll meet at my chariot.'

When the officers had gathered round Ammuna's chariot, the general told the brats minder to take her off to the side so he could have a quiet chat with his officers. Then Ammuna said, 'You've just heard what I've told the ordinary soldiers. Now it's time for me to tell you what your share of the take is. What I haven't told you so far is how much I was offered to do the job by our worthy Crown Prince. He's offered one million golden shekels for that little brat over there.' Ammuna drifted his arm in Asmunikal's direction. 'As the man responsible for organising this whole thing, I've taken two hundred thousand shekels for myself. One hundred goes to Colonel Lawana here; and the rest of you will get fifty thousand golden shekels each.' The faces of the four officers, excepting Lawana beamed with delight. The senior captain said on their behalf, 'We much appreciate your generosity sir,' and all four abruptly jumped to attention and saluted Ammuna by thumping their left chest with their right fist. Ammuna returned the salute.

Ammuna turned to Lawana, who'd been standing quietly and listening to the exchange. 'Well, what do you say to all this?'

Lawana was grinning at Ammuna. 'What can I say? I'm happy you included me in your confidence. I don't feel I've deserved all that much but believe me; I won't be rejecting any of it. It's far more than I expected and it might last me some time. Thank you sir.' Lawana kept grinning at Ammuna.

As they were concluding their officer's meeting, Lawana noted on the other side of the clearing, a sentry was leading a dark cloaked figure into the camp clearing—the mysterious figure was holding on to his horse's bridle, and the horse was perspiring heavily. The sentry and figure stopped short of the fires. The officer of the watch, one of the captains, left Ammuna's little meeting and went to have a talk with the sentry.

Lawana kept an eye on this activity and finally went over to join the captain to investigate. Lawana listened to the strange interloper for a while and then he returned to Ammuna and told him, 'Sir, we have a problem. There's a fellow over there who says he must speak to you. He gave your name and says he comes from Artatama.'

Ammuna jumped at the name and walked swiftly to where the cloaked figure waited, followed by Lawana. Four more soldiers had left the fire and surrounded the figure in case there was a trick involved.

'So, what can I do for you? I gather you called me by my name,' Ammuna asked the man cautiously.

'General Ammuna, it's not what you can do for me, it's more of what I can do for you. I represent Crown Prince Artatama, *not* the king. I'm part of the Mittani spy network; only I report to the Crown Prince. Our network is now split in two. Some remain loyal to the king; others have joined with me in favouring the young Crown Prince. First, I must ask to see the seal you carry—it's just a formality, you understand.' The cloaked figure removed his dark hood and underneath it was a dark bearded man of medium size and build—in fact nothing remarkable about him at all, except for the air of mystery surrounding him.

Ammuna looked carefully at the strange fellow and finally put his hand in his pouch and retrieved the Mittani Royal Seal he'd been given in Adaniya. 'Is this what you wanted to see?' Ammuna held the seal out to the fellow.

'Yes General. Now we have that out of the way, I have come to warn you, you are being surrounded as we speak, and the encirclement is closing in on this encampment. The Isuwan King has ordered all of you are to be put to the sword with no exceptions. Supposedly, the orders come from King Saustatar of Mittani. Crown Prince Artatama has been thrown in the dungeon by his father and is now busily washing his hands of all of his son's intrigues —including this one. That's the bad news. The other news I bring is marginally better. I'm here to show you a way out of this forest—a path that avoids the encirclement. Also, to tell you, you should on no account go to Wassukanni. Artatama has re-arranged to meet you in two weeks time in Nineveh, in Assyria. That's on the banks of, what you call in Hittite, the mighty Aransah River.'

Ammuna stood listening to this, and his features hardened. 'You know of my deal with the Crown Prince?' he asked the spy grimly.

'Yes general. I'm aware you'll need paying. You'll have to take my word for it, once you've delivered the Hittite princess to Nineveh, you *will* be paid the agreed amount,' then the spy whispered in to Ammuna's ear, 'plus a discomfiture sum of another half a million golden shekels. That should be incentive enough for you to complete your task.'

Ammuna instantly decided to keep the extra payment for himself and didn't intend to tell his cronies what the spy had told him of the extra money.

'Now you must remove those yellow tunics and discard them,' continued the spy. 'They're a deadly give-away. Then we must douse the fires, and cease the noise. From here on, we have to be absolutely quiet. I have to inform you, according to my information, the Isuwan king has four thousand soldiers closing in on your camp as we speak. Oh, and general, the chariot over there,' the spy pointed at Ammuna's beloved vehicle, 'it will have to be left behind. Where we're going there's no room for a chariot. We will be travelling through the densest part of this forest and I'm not even sure the horses will make it through there, but we will have to try. We would be at a severe disadvantage if we had to leave the horses behind.'

Lawana nodded urgently to the captain and implied he join him. He'd heard enough to go and collect the rest of the officers, inform them what was being planned, and to rapidly go round the soldiers and tell them to quench the fires and collect their horses. They were to do this silently and rapidly. They were going to try and avoid an ambush tonight.

The whole camp was in a silent uproar with men removing their tunics, leaving them in their under-shirts, then rushing around collecting their personal things and finding their mounts. When the encampment was ready to move off, they stood waiting for Ammuna to lead them.

Ammuna ordered the brat gagged and tied and two men were to carry her and guard her with their lives. They were to stay close to him near the front of the escaping convoy. With one last look at his beloved chariot, Ammuna followed the Mittani spy in to the densest part of the forest, as quietly and as quickly as they could possibly manage. Thus the convoy set off tramping east throughout the night. What should have been the most restful night of the journey turned into a flight for their lives.

From time to time, they heard men's voices coming to them from the distant darkness, confirming what the Mittani spy had told them. There were people out there at this time of night up to no good. Finally, they came to a point in the escape where they had to break through the encircling line advancing through the forest. Ammuna and the Mittani spy both agreed, the best course of action was inaction. Ammuna's group stopped in the heavy darkness where the moonlight couldn't penetrate, then they listened, and heard the distant line approaching them. The men covered the horse's eyes and then they crouched in silence and urged their horses to lie still on the soft forest floor, all covered with branches, while the Isuwan military line walked around and past them unaware their quarry was hiding nearby. With such a large group trying to be stealthy, it had been difficult, but not impossible.

When the enemy line had passed by, Ammuna heaved a deep sigh of relief. 'That was too close for comfort,' he whispered to Lawana. 'They're going to be furious when they discover we've escaped and all they find is a pile of yellow tunics. We'd better move and get out of this forest as quickly as we can.'

The Mittani spy whispered to Ammuna, 'When we get out of the forest, I strongly suggest you head towards Malidiya; they won't be expecting that. Then circle round the northern side of the capital and follow the Puranti River back to the fork which splits it in two. Cross the Puranti above the fork, the river flow will be less violent. Anyway, in autumn, the river is low. Go to the eastern bank and then head north-east for at least two days until you come across the western end of the Eastern Silver Mountains. Follow an eastern route along the southern side of the Eastern Silver Mountains for four days. Then stop and cross the lower Puranti River again, but this time southbound. In roughly three days, you'll reach the mighty Aransah River. Follow it south along its bank for another eight days, which will get you to Nineveh. I will leave you when we get out of the forest and I wish you a safe journey. There is a wooden bridge crossing the Puranti just outside Malidiya, but it's guarded by a large squadron, at least it was when I crossed it yesterday, and I don't advise you trying it.'

Ammuna caught the spies arm and whispered close to his face, 'Thanks for you help, but before you go may I ask you to seek out some white tunics for me and my men and have them left somewhere along the route we're going to take? It would save me time and effort.'

The spy thought for a second and nodded, 'I'll see what I can do for you. In about two days from now look out for some one as you near the mountains. If this person doesn't have them, at least he will have more information for you as to where and when.'

Ammuna nodded and followed the spy along the path he'd selected in leading his group of *loyal* men to safety. The rest of the trek through the dense parts of the forest took some time but it was the safest route to avoid any other remnants of the Isuwan forces out to annihilate them. By the time dawn began to creep through the canopy, they had reached the edge of the forest, and the group halted whilst the spy went out to make sure the way was clear of Isuwan soldiers. He came back and reported he could see no threat to them.

'Well thanks once again,' Ammuna told the spy, 'and I will look for your man in two days.' He mounted his horse, as did the rest of his men, and rode off towards Malidiya.

The spy stayed behind and waved a farewell to them, then was seen to mount his horse and trot off towards the south.

Ammuna took his men carefully round the northern outskirts of Malidiya, following gullies and forest cover where they could shelter from prying eyes. His men were under strict instructions not to make a sound whilst scouts walked ahead making sure the way was clear up ahead. In this slow manner, the band of *loyal* mercenaries reached the part of the riverbank suggested by the Mittani spy as a good crossing point.

'Find me the two best swimmers,' Ammuna ordered Lawana. 'They're going to swim across the river with the brat on their backs.'

'One of them is going to be me,' Lawana told him. 'The other one is the senior non-com. I'll take the girl first and the non-com can swim by my side in case of any unexpected problems.'

'Good,' Ammuna quipped. 'I don't need to tell you to be careful with her. She's now worth one and a half million to us, you know. Lose her, and we've lost all this hard work we've put in.'

'Yes sir, I know.' Lawana quipped back. He was beginning to lose some of the respect he'd nurtured over the years for his commanding general. This venture had shown a side of Ammuna he'd not seen before and it didn't show him in a good light, at least not as far as Lawana was concerned. Raw callousness and far too much greed had come to the fore, and it turned Lawana's stomach. A certain amount of hunger to get ahead is essential to move up the ranks, but if one loses one's self-respect and replaces it with a callous disregard for inculcated values, it's a slippery road downwards to avarice and cruelty, then the road back to barbarity is assured. Lawana had no desire to degenerate to that level of bestiality.

'Get your non-com to take a rope across the river and tie it to the tree trunk over there,' Ammuna pointed at a thick tree on the far bank of the river.

The non-com swam the river easily, fastened the rope round the trunk and returned. Then each man took his horse into the river, and while it swam, he held onto the swing rope above him. It wasn't long before the whole group had crossed the slow flowing river. Lawana had tied Asmunikal onto his back and then swum the river almost nonchalantly.

They rested on the eastern banks of the river for a short while and then were galloping off towards the western part of the Eastern Silver Mountains clearly showing in the distance.

10
Hittite Agent

By the time the light began to fade, Mokhat had led the *special forces* into a small wood out of prying eyes. They camped overnight in this wood, using cold rations and avoided building a fire in case the Isuwans noticed the rising smoke.

The next day saw them heading south west for most of the day, trying to stay out of the way of the various Isuwan patrols they almost encountered. Every time their scouts spotted the Isuwan military, they returned to the column and Mokhat had them hide amongst the shadows of some nearby cover, be they bushes, woods or forest. In their dark uniforms and their black horses, they blended in well with the shadows and managed to avoid detection, but the extra horses were proving hard to hide. They played cat-and-mouse all day until late afternoon, when they came onto the road leading south to Karkamish. Mokhat paralleled the road southwards, following it a short distance away from the road. Travelling on the road itself would have invited trouble from the Isuwan military; it was their arterial highway. This way they managed to circumvent the Isuwan capital to the west and finally reach the sought after crossroad.

The crossroad led north to Sanuhuitta, west to Kummani, south to Karkamish, and east to Malidiya. Scouts brought back the news they'd spotted the tavern, and Mokhat stopped his group in between two low hills about half a league away from the tavern. A short way off the road there was the small tavern simply called, *The Crossroad*

Tavern, which was Mokhat's destination. There he hoped to make contact with a member of their own Hittite spy ring.

'I want you and Palaiyas,' he motioned to Onasiyas, 'to come inside the tavern with me. The rest of the men will stay here and stay out of sight. Avoid contact with the enemy if possible. If you're forced to move, send a man to inform us where you are,' Mokhat was giving orders to Captain Neti, who was staying behind with the group. 'We'll be back as soon as we've concluded our business there. Any questions? No! Then we'll see you later.'

Mokhat, Palaiyas and Onasiyas rode quietly near the road towards the tavern. As they neared it, they noted an Isuwan patrol of around twenty men were just mounting their horses and riding off towards Malidiya.

'We'll have to sit near a window so we can keep an eye out on the crossroads for more patrols. I don't want to be taken by surprise,' Onasiyas told Mokhat.

'How are we to recognise our man?' Mokhat asked Onasiyas.

'He'll know us. These dark outfits will inform him who we are. He's been told to look out for us,' Onasiyas informed him.

When they entered the tavern, they noted only three customers. One was an old man in a dirty cloak lolling around as if he were well into his cup. There was a middle-aged couple sitting at a table eating some bread and talking quietly.

'I don't think our man's here yet,' Mokhat whispered to Palaiyas.

They sat near the door and waited for the tavern keeper to serve them. The old drunk looked at them blearily and stood unsteadily on his feet. He fumbled in his pouch and threw some money on the table, then he wobbled past where Mokhat was sitting and bumped into Mokhat.

'S-s-sorry,' he mumbled at Mokhat and managed to steady himself before continuing to the door.

The tavern keeper appeared, and came over. 'What can I get you gentlemen,' he said obsequiously.

'Palaiyas,' said Mokhat, 'be a good fellow and see if the horses are alright,' and Mokhat winked at him.

Palaiyas understood he was to go outside, but he had no idea why. Still, he did as Mokhat requested.

'Now, we'd like a good flagon of your best wine, landlord,' Mokhat told the tavern keeper.

When the landlord went for the order, Mokhat opened his fist and showed Onasiyas a clay seal with the Hittite double-headed eagle on it. 'That came from our drunk as he passed me,' he informed Onasiyas. 'Stay here and wait for the wine. I'm going to find the drunk. He's probably with Palaiyas right now. I'll be back shortly.'

Mokhat went outside and looked around. Palaiyas was on the other side of their horses and Mokhat could see two pair of legs underneath the horse's belly. He wandered over to where the two were, and looked at the suddenly sober drunk.

'Well, that was quiet and act you put on in there. When I walked in, I dismissed you entirely.' It was a sort of compliment to the acting ability of their contact.

'I'm sorry, but it's best that way. People tend to leave me alone if they see I'm a drunk. Now, which of you gentlemen is General Mokhat?' he asked politely.

'That will be me,' Mokhat replied. 'This is General Palaiyas,' Mokhat nodded at his companion.

'I won't ask to see your seal, not with those outfits on. I can't see anyone who'd want to impersonate such uniforms. I was warned to keep a sharp lookout for you and to give you any assistance I can. So how can I help you General?'

'Since you've been informed of who I am,' Mokhat told him, 'you must also have been told of our mission. So my fine exponent of the dark arts, where is *ex*-General

Ammuna at this moment in time? I assume you've kept track of his whereabouts.'

The agent thought for a moment, and then said, 'I've tried my best to find out what's happened to him, and frankly our little group here has uncovered some interesting information. We managed to ensnare and catch a Mittani spy yesterday trying to head back to Wassukanni, and he's been a mine of information. Apparently, King Saustatar has thrown his son, Artatama, into the dungeon for kidnapping our king's daughter, at least that's what the Mittani spy tells us. There's the matter of some missing money involved as well. But the most outrageous news is, King Tarasina tried to surround Ammuna's entire group and intended to kill the lot of them. This was his interpretation of the orders he'd received from Wassukanni. What is despicable, is his orders included not leaving any one alive, and he applied it to mean our king's daughter as well. I've sent this information off to Hattusas and I expect them to act upon it when they come down here to sort this king out.'

At hearing the Isuwan king had thought nothing of killing Asmunikal, Mokhat and Palaiyas were utterly shocked. 'The scoundrel!' exclaimed Mokhat. 'That's well beyond the limit! I earnestly hope and expect King Tudhaliyas will bring him to account when he gets here. It's the same muddled thinking which keeps pushing this silly king to switching sides every now and then.'

Palaiyas added, 'He thinks he can squeeze more concessions out of each side if he plays one off against the other. He needs to be taught a severe lesson—one his house will remember for a long time.'

'Well, that as may be,' their agent continued. 'The Mittani spy also divulged that he rescued Ammuna on orders from Artatama. Apparently, there's a split in the loyalties of the Mittani spy community. Half are for Saustatar and the other half for Artatama. This one was working for Artatama. He says Artatama is planning to escape and head for Nineveh. He told Ammuna to head there. That's where they're going to meet and exchange the king's daughter for payment. The spy told Ammuna to cross the Puranti River and follow the lower Puranti for three or four days, then recross it and follow the Aransah River down to Nineveh. Oh, and just before I forget, Ammuna's been forced to ditch his chariot, so if you've been following those wheels, they've gone. The whole group's on horses, around two hundred of them. They've also ditched their yellow tunics.'

'Good work! This is really top class intelligence. Thank you. By the way, any chance of getting the spy to tell you what Ammuna had for breakfast in the morning?' Mokhat put a little levity into the exchange to break the tension.

'Sorry General,' their agent didn't see anything funny in what Mokhat had said. 'I'm afraid our Mittani friend didn't last the night. It took a lot of persuasion to get him to divulge such a lot of good information. It didn't come cheap.' The agent smiled apologetically.

'Do you know where Ammuna crossed the river?' Palaiyas asked.

'He couldn't go across the bridge outside Malidiya because it's heavily guarded, so they crossed half a league upriver from Malidiya, above the fork in the river,' the agent replied. 'At least that's what we got out of Artatama's spy.'

'Well, thank you. We'll head off after Ammuna now, unless you have anything more to tell us?' Mokhat told the agent.

The agent stood for a second then shook his head, 'No. I think I've told you everything. I suppose you're aware this whole area is going to be inundated with the Hittite army in a week's time. I expect us to be investing Malidiya by then and the Kizzuwatna are going for

Karkamish. Even the Pharaoh has an army coming up from Khemet. The whole place is about to get very messy.'

'So I understand,' replied Mokhat. 'Could you assist us a little further?'

'I'm yours to command, general,' the agent quipped.

'I want you to lead us to the spot where you think Ammuna might have crossed the river. You know this area better than we do. It would be quicker and safer that way,' Mokhat informed him.

'Happy to, general,' smiled the agent. 'I'll wait for you by the horses while you finish with the tavern.'

Mokhat waved as he and Palaiyas went back into the tavern to enjoy some of the wine.

The trio emptied the wine flagon between them and paid the proprietor, exiting into the fading light as the sun began to lower into the west.

On leaving, Palaiyas mentioned to Mokhat, 'I could probably have done without any drink. Water would have been better for thirst.'

'Fine, but it would have been suspicious for us not to have a drink in a tavern while we were in there, don't you think?' Mokhat replied.

'Oh, *I* enjoyed that,' Onasiyas contradicted Palaiyas. 'So now we head for the river, eh?'

'The light might be fading but I think we ought to keep going until we get to where we're to cross the Puranti in the morning. Our guide will lead the way. We should camp on this side for the night and we'll pick up his trail in the morning,' Mokhat said. 'I should think it's still a good distance to get to our night's camping ground.'

'How far do we have to go tonight?' Onasiyas asked their agent when they'd rejoined him.

'It's still a fair distance but we should make it by midnight,' he replied.

They found Captain Neti somewhat jittery when they reached the spot where they'd left him.

'Report,' Onasiyas ordered his deputy when he'd dismounted his horse.

'A few close calls, sir,' the captain reported. 'There's been a number of Isuwan patrols passing close by. One nearly came on top of us. I thought we might have to fight our way out. As you can see sir, we're all in one piece, so no problems, but I'd like us to leave this area. It's not too healthy staying around here.'

'You're in luck then. Mount your men and let's get moving,' Onasiyas told him.

The ninety-nine men of the *special forces* were led north-east around Malidiya by their agent. He seemed to know where the tight spots were, where the Isuwan military stamping grounds were. It took them well past midnight to get to their campsite and some of the men first hobbled their horses, then slumped onto their blankets and went to sleep without bothering with any food. Others ate their cold rations and then turned in.

Before daybreak, the dawn chorus made such a racket that it forced everyone awake. They were camped a little way from the river itself and Mokhat asked Onasiyas to send out scouts to see if there was anyone else near them. When the scouts came back and reported they couldn't find anyone nearby, Mokhat ordered a small fire to be made and hot porridge to be served to the men. The fire was to be put out as soon as possible. The men should eat as much as they could because they were going to travel a long distance that day.

'Oh, and a word of caution,' Onasiyas added to his men. 'Remember we're likely to have to swim the river shortly. Eat so you're comfortable enough to be able to swim.'

Their agent had been out already and came back full of confidence. 'I think I've found Ammuna's crossing point,' he told Mokhat while the cook handed him a bowl of hot barley porridge.

'Well done. How far is it?' Palaiyas asked him.

'The river forks about sixty cubits upriver from here. There's a lot of horses going into the river above the left fork. The tracks are a day old and the numbers seem to tally with the people Ammuna had with him,' the agent replied.

When the men had eaten and the campsite tidied, as per their usual practice of obliterating their traces, the agent led Mokhat and his men upriver to where he'd found the tracks. 'You've been a great help to us,' Mokhat told him. 'I'll be sure to mention it to the king when we get back to Hattusas.'

The agent seemed pleased but a little embarrassed at this idea. 'I'm only doing my job, general. You don't have to say anything, really.'

'Nevertheless, I always give due where it belongs,' Mokhat responded. 'By the way, when the crap start flying around here, be sure to keep your head down.'

'Oh, I intend to do just that,' replied the agent. 'I'm a survivor, general.'

'Take care of yourself and thanks again.' Mokhat, Palaiyas, and Onasiyas bade farewell to their agent.

The agent waved a farewell to them and walked quickly deep into the darkness of the forest canopy.

'Now, quickly let's get some rafts together,' Mokhat told Onasiyas. 'The horses can swim across with their rider but the pack ponies will need unloading and their packs ferrying across on the rafts.'

Men were sent out to keep a sharp eye out for the Isuwan military, whilst others set to chopping down the nearby trees and constructing rafts. These men had practised such skills in their training and four sizeable rafts were speedily assembled. One man was sent across with a rope tied round his waist, which he attached to a tree on the opposite side of the slow flowing Puranti.

Mokhat was looking at the river with dread, being reminded of his previous encounters with this innocuous looking liquid. 'It's lucky we're in late autumn and the river is low and slow at this time of year,' he confided to Palaiyas.

Palaiyas knew of Mokhat's aversion to water, having been almost drowned in it twice, so he put his hand on Mokhat's arm and tried to comfort him. 'It'll be alright. You know I'm a strong swimmer—and I'll stay close by you while you cross on the raft, just in case. '

Mokhat didn't show it, but he squeezed Palaiyas' arm in return. 'I know you will. I'll try not to disgrace us by cringing too much from the water,' he reassured Palaiyas. 'It's a bit like sticking your hand in the fire. Once you've been burnt, you shy away from fire as a normal reflex reaction without thinking. With me its water, and with the same good reason.'

Firstly, all the group's horses were loosely linked with rope, then half of the *special forces* led the horses into the water and encouraged them to swim across the river while a man clung to the back of each alternate horse, guiding them by holding onto the swing rope above him. This way all the riding horses were brought across the mighty Puranti River. Then came the turn of the thirty-nine pack ponies, with three men being ferried across on each raft; it took two journeys. It wasn't long before the whole group were standing on the other side of the river, having dismantled the rafts to hide their traces.

'Ammuna's trail leads back upriver,' commented Onasiyas. 'Surely that can't be right?'

'We'll soon find out,' Palaiyas answered. 'We'll have to go where the trail takes us.'

'Let's get started,' Mokhat suggested. 'We've lost enough time already.'

With that candid comment, the group mounted their steeds and galloped after Ammuna.

11
Artatama's Escape

Crown Prince Artatama walked stiffly, with his head held high, as the General in charge of the king's bodyguards escorted him to the dungeons. He was fuming inside at the craven imbecility of his father for refusing to support his actions against the Hittites. Led by their general, the four bodyguards tramped down into the bowels of the citadel, removing the angry Artatama to his solitary confinement.

The escort behaved respectfully to the Crown Prince, mainly as a result of the volatile politics of Mittani, where the tables could easily turn, and the prince would probably be in a position to have them put inside the dungeons within a month's time. As it was, Artatama made no effort to resist the escort. They were only carrying out the lawful orders of their king. Aspiring to be their ruler someday, he had a vested interest in them obeying the sovereign's orders to the letter.

Still, all the way down into the depths of the citadel, Artatama kept remembering his father's selective memory—whilst declining to acknowledge his own selective memory. For him, six years ago, it was his father who had ordered him to take the army north to cement the alliance with the then King Muwas. Now, to Artatama's amazement, his father claimed he had counselled against Mittani involvement in the Hittite Civil War. This went round and round obsessively in his head, while he conveniently and steadfastly refused to recognise his own misdemeanour of dipping into the state treasury, or of taking it upon himself to order the abduction of the Hittite king's daughter. The latter two were major decisions of state taken by him in an arrogant style, neither of which he'd advised the current head of state, namely his father.

He resented his father for not supporting him, for not taking a tough line with the Hittites. Six years ago, Artatama was optimistic of unifying the two states of Hittite and Mittani, into an Empire of his own making, with him taking a prominent role. He'd then dreamt of marrying his sister to Muwas and of being the power behind the throne, and even expanding the new empire into Khemet and decapitating that interfering old power once and for all.

Instead, six years on, and he was being led to a dungeon; incarcerated by a craven father who was only interested in appeasing the Hittite king. It was the latter that really made him grumpy. Artatama saw it as almost treasonous, although he noted the contradiction that a king can't really be a traitor to himself. Then there was the question of the future of Mittani—but more, from Artatama's point of view, what of *his* own future?

Even before the jailer closed the dungeon door, Artatama was planning on leaving as soon as his contacts could arrange it. As his sat on his bunk in the dungeon cell, his attention turned to his immediate future, and there the expectation was for a swift escape from this confinement. He wouldn't admit it, even to himself, but he was feeling claustrophobic for the first time in his life. In this tense frame of mind, he waited the rest of the day without anyone contacting him. Instead of reflecting on his past failures, he sat and fumed at his father for being such a weakling. At his henchmen for being so slow in getting to him, at the Hittite king for being on the throne he coveted, at Khemet for aiding this Hittite king, and at life in general for impeding his wishes at every turn.

Crown Prince Artatama, the child born with the silver spoon in his mouth, had just concluded that for himself, life wasn't being fair to him, as he saw it, and that he was being thwarted in his rightful desires, despite his devious and cunning ways. In short, he'd been spoilt for far too long and was now being denied what he wanted, even by his own father, and he would have thrown a tantrum if it were not for his inflated opinion of himself. It would never do for the Crown Prince to throw a tantrum, no matter how much he might want to. In this neurotic state of mind, Artatama spent the first night in the cells.

By mid-morning of the next day he heard feet approaching along the dungeon corridor. He'd been desperately listening out for footsteps as a sign that his henchmen were on the move. Instead, the jailer had brought unleavened bread and water, all ironically laid out on a silver platter. After all, he was still the Crown Prince and decorum was being observed.

'Good day to you, your royal highness,' said the jailer. 'Orders from his majesty,' announced the jailer as he opened the door and placed the platter on the wooden bench near his bunk. Then the jailer did something entirely unexpected. He winked at Artatama and quickly left the cell, closing the door behind him.

At this familiarity, Artatama's hackles began to rise— but he suddenly stopped himself. Maybe the jailer was trying to say something—but wasn't able to say it out loud.

The Crown Prince looked at the platter and noted a bulge in the unleavened bread; he opened it carefully and found a clay tablet inside. It said in the wedge script, *be ready in the afternoon*. The tension lifted from him as if a load had been taken from off his back. This is what he'd been waiting for. Instead of being grateful, all he could think was, *why had it taken a whole day to arrange this?*

Mid afternoon, two pairs of footsteps were heard to come down the dungeon corridor. Artatama was lying on his bunk and at the sound of the footsteps; he swung his legs outwards and sat up. The sight of the person who the jailer opened his dungeon door for, gave Artatama a start.

Standing in the doorway was Tarkuni, the Mittani chief spy. A small wiry man with a thick black beard.

'How is his royal highness faring,' he asked gently.

Suspicious of his intentions, Artatama shrugged and said, 'How would you expect me to fare in here? So, Tarkuni, what do you want. Has my father sent you down to wheedle out of me where I've hidden the money?'

'No your highness, no one sent me down here. I've come below to see if you'd like help in getting out of here, or are you happy to rot in here?' And in a show of impudence, or was it clumsy intimacy, the spymaster sat down on the only seat available, the wooden bench.

'Why would you want to help me?' Artatama couldn't decide whether to trust this man or not. He'd had little to do with the official spy network, preferring to build his own trusted circle of people.

'A number of us have taken the decision to switch our support and have decided you're a stronger investment for Mittani's future than your father. It is sincere. It would be foolish to reject our help, your highness. There are no strings attached I assure you, unless of course you're enjoying these palatial surroundings?'

Artatama accepted the latter irony, and equally the spymaster's help. 'Welcome on board master Tarkuni. So what did you have in mind for getting me out of here?'

'I've had to include the jailer into my plan, so we're going to have to take him with us when we go. The plan is somewhat simple; the jailer opens the dungeon door; you change into an ordinary soldier's outfit. We then walk out of here unchallenged. That is unless you want to complicate things. I'm afraid I'm finished as the head of the official Mittani spay network after this.' Tarkuni sat there with a wry smile and looked at the Crown Prince, head slightly held at an angle to the side, watching his new master.

Artatama was stunned at the simplicity of the plan. He burst out in a chuckle. 'Brilliant! Would you accept, if I offered you the job of running my spy network?'

'I'd be delighted to, your royal highness,' responded Tarkuni.

'So, when do you propose carrying out this daring rescue?' Artatama asked, raising his eyebrows.

'What's wrong with now?'

'This gets better and better,' chuckled Artatama. 'Well let's get on with it then.'

'*Jailer!*' shouted Tarkuni.

When the jailer appeared, Tarkuni said to him, 'As we discussed. Have you got the sack I gave you?'

'Yes sir, right here,' he opened the dungeon door, then bent to the side in the corridor and handed Tarkuni a medium sized sack.

'You'll find the uniform in there, your highness. Please put it on and we'll be on our way.' Tarkuni popped his head out into the corridor to make sure there were no prying eyes. He asked the jailer, 'Is the way clear further up there?'

'Yes sir. Am I coming with you like you promised?' the jailer asked.

'Unless you want to stay and face the consequences?' Tarkuni threw at him.

'No sir. I'm coming with you,' the jailer muttered. 'They'll skin me alive for letting him go.'

Once inside the uniform of an ordinary soldier, nominally, Artatama disappeared into the background with the rest of the other invisible soldiers.

'Your highness, you still stand out like a sore thumb,' complained Tarkuni. 'Bend your back a little and lower the helmet over your forehead more. Try to show less of your noble bearing and more of a soldier's humility. Endeavour to act like an *ordinary* soldier and less like the Crown Prince in an ordinary soldier's outfit.' Tarkuni said all this softly so as not to irritate Artatama. He had often seen Artatama strutting around the palace and feared others would recognise the strutting soldier despite his ordinary uniform before they got out of the city.

Artatama was fighting the urge to take a strip off of his new spymaster, but then again saw the sense of what he was being advised to do. He attempted to emulate an ordinary Mittani soldier and found it very difficult. He walked up and down inside his cell and couldn't stop himself strutting.

'Walk up and down,' he commanded the jailer.

The jailer walked up and down while Artatama studied him. He then made a better attempt at emulating the walk.

'Ah, now that's an improvement,' said the spymaster. 'I think we're ready to go. Lead on,' he told the jailer.

The jailer led the way out of the bowels of the dungeons, followed by Tarkuni with Artatama bringing up the rear, as befits an ordinary soldier. As they came out of the citadel's front entrance, Tarkuni stopped suddenly. In front of them in the courtyard stood King Saustatar, talking to three generals and surrounded by his aides.

The jailer threw a cloth over his head to cover his face, as he had no business being in the courtyard. Artatama's reaction was to pull his helmet further down over his forehead.

'Be calm,' hissed Tarkuni to both of his companions. 'I'll deal with this.'

The king finished with the generals and came towards them.

'Ah, just the man I wanted to see,' said the king as he approached Tarkuni.

'Your majesty,' Tarkuni acknowledged.

'Come and see me later in the afternoon,' the king commanded, looking behind him directly at his own son. 'I've a job that requires your special talents.'

'As you command, your majesty,' responded Tarkuni as the king continued on his way. He'd stared at his son but took absolutely no notice of the soldier standing behind Tarkuni, or the individual with his face covered, presuming him to be something to do with Tarkuni's spy network.

The king marched through the entrance heading back into the citadel, leaving the three escapees smiling quietly to themselves with relief at going unnoticed.

'The king looked straight at you, didn't he?' Tarkuni asked Artatama. 'I told you no one notices ordinary soldiers. They're simply invisible.'

Artatama simply shrugged his shoulders at the improbable situation.

The trio headed for the far part of the courtyard near the citadel gates where the stables were. Tarkuni took the lead from thereon and picked out three of the horses normally allotted to his spies. Within a short period, they were trotting through the busy streets of Wassukanni, heading for the main gate out of the city. Tarkuni waved to the captain of the gate in a nonchalant manner, implying he was off on one of his usual excursions with a couple of helpers in disguise. This was such a usual occurrence that the captain didn't even look twice at the party leaving his gate.

Once through the enormous city gate, the trio swung left around the city walls eventually heading east. Artatama dug in his horse's side and galloped off in sheer exuberance at having got free and of outwitting his father's stupid restrictions. He was master of his destiny once again, and he'd acquired a most useful ally in Tarkuni. He slowed and waited for them to catch up.

'Now I need to get in touch with my people in the city so they can bring the money out of there for me—then I head for Nineveh,' Artatama confided in Tarkuni when the spymaster caught up with him. 'I've business to transact there. Do you want to come with me or have you things to do in the capital?'

'I'll accompany you for a short part of the journey,' Tarkuni suggested, 'and you can fill me in on what I should do with your spy network. Who I should contact and so forth, and who's currently in charge of it. You might want to write an order transferring control of the network officially to me, with your seal on it, so there's no question of whose now in charge. Then we need to talk of future directions.'

'Good point,' Artatama agreed. 'Stay with me for today and we'll come to a few conclusions as we ride. If you have to go back to Wassukanni, you'll have to sneak back in. Once it becomes known you've helped me escape and abandoned the king, your life will be forfeit if you're caught.'

'Yes, your highness, I *was* aware of that.'

12
Hayasa Attack

Artatama's spy had been able to rescue Ammuna's *loyal* group from a massacre just in time and then counselled Ammuna to take his men north to the Eastern Silver Mountains to circumvent Mittani territory altogether.

Following their frantic escape from the forest ambush by the perfidious Isuwan king, Ammuna made his *loyal* group of mercenaries gallop speedily towards the distant mountains. After a short mid-morning rest, Ammuna ordered Lawana to get them back on their horses and then led them forward as fast as they could travel away from the river towards the western end of the Eastern Silver Mountains, which were clearly visible in the distance.

By noon, a small Isuwan patrol of about twenty managed to spot them, and from thereon, kept them in their sights. They trailed them all the while, but could do little to hinder their journey, as they were too few of them. The patrol sent riders back to Malidiya to notify the king the fugitive general was being tracked, but they needed a larger force if they were to give chase and deal with him. As the Isuwan patrol was merely an irritant and could do nothing, Ammuna simply ignored them and presumed within a day or so when his group re-crossed the Isuwan border, they would give up the chase and fall back.

By nightfall, the Isuwan patrol had given up the chase; the patrol had come to the limits of its boundaries, stopped and watched Ammuna gallop off into the vastness beyond their borders. The general then led his group another league further into the wilderness and as the light failed, he finally gave the order to make camp for the night on the banks of a small stream running from the Eastern Silver Mountains into the Puranti River.

Lawana and Ammuna were sharing a boulder while eating a hot meal of porridge and rehydrated meat.

'It just shows no one is to be trusted,' Ammuna told Lawana as they discussed their narrow escape of the previous night.

Lawana spat to the side in contempt. 'It's the duplicity that sticks in my throat. Why not tell us to go to the netherworld, if he didn't want to help us. No, instead he shows us to a campsite in the forest and waits till we're asleep before trying to kill us all. Tarasina has always been the worst miserable scoundrel. Someone should get rid of him,' judged Lawana in disgust.

'According to the spy, he was simply carrying out King Saustatar's orders,' Ammuna retorted. 'What we have to keep in mind is, Saustatar's thrown Artatama into the dungeons. The father and son are at odds over this matter, so from now on, we must steer clear of all Mittani, unless they're clearly from Artatama. I have a feeling this business is going to end badly for the Mittani. If I were Tudhaliyas, I would take an army to Wassukanni and teach the Mittani a lesson they would never forget.'

'For all we know, that's exactly what our king is doing right now,' Lawana replied.

'He's not *our* king any more. Try to remember Colonel, otherwise it might muddy your thinking and your loyalty.' Ammuna was watching Lawana closely. He'd sensed an increasing distance between them over the last few days and he couldn't work out what the reason was. Lawana had always been fiercely loyal to him, as well as being fair and tenacious; which is what made him a good officer. But recently there'd been a subtle change in his demeanour towards him, and it worried Ammuna.

'I'll try to remember,' said Lawana. 'But general, we have a much more pressing problem which is going to effect us all. We're running short on provisions. We're going to have to find a way of restocking our larder.'

'Hmm, now that's more serious, I agree. How long have we got before we run out?'

'Another couple of days, then we'll have to forage. The next settlement we come across, we're going to have stop and see if we can buy some more food, assuming they'll sell us some,' Lawana answered.

'Well I've got some golden shekels, so we're not short of money. I'm sure we'll manage to buy food with the gold.' Ammuna put down his bowl and stood up to stretch himself. 'It'll be alright, Colonel. Warn the scouts to keep an eye out for any habitation tomorrow. If they find a village, we'll head straight for it and see if we can replenish.' Ammuna sat rubbing his chin for a while, then said, 'When we stopped, I went and had a look at our brat. I tried to pat her on the head and in return, she tried to bite me again. When it didn't work, she had a go at kicking me in the groin. Who's been teaching her these tricks? She's totally wild,' Ammuna complained.

'We've not really treated her as she's used to, general. You can't expect her to let you pat her on the head as if she were a pet dog. We've not tried to gain her confidence, so we mustn't expect her to like us.' Lawana said this in an offhand way, which irritated Ammuna.

'I suppose you're right, but she's still a snotty nosed brat who needs to be taught some manners,' Ammuna said angrily.

'I hadn't notices any snot on her nose,' mumbled Lawana. 'She's angry, that's all. Wouldn't you be in her situation?'

'Colonel, you're not feeling sorry for her, are you?' Ammuna was looking at his colonel in a quizzical way, trying to fathom his thoughts.

'Not sorry, no. But I can see how she must feel, given the circumstances,' said Lawana. 'General, you're being too severe with her. She's only six years old, and she probably misses her mother.'

Now Ammuna began to understand the peculiar changes he'd noticed in Lawana. His trusted Colonel had begun to have second thoughts about this whole venture. The brat had got to him somehow. He promised himself to keep an eye on his colonel so he didn't undermine the enterprise. He decided to warn the brat's minder not to allow Lawana near their prize. If Lawana tried to approach the brat, the minder was to bring her directly to Ammuna and he would sort things out. Ammuna reminded himself this snotty little girl was worth one and a half million golden shekels to him—and he intended to collect all of it. To Lawana he said, 'Fine, let her miss her mother—how's she holding out otherwise?'

'Seems to be alright. She's a tough little lady. She's taken a liking to one of the non-coms who took her across the river on his shoulders. He feeds her and is looking after her. She's riding with him at the moment,' Lawana informed him.

'Good! Keep it going the way it is. Anything to keep her quiet,' said Ammuna. 'Now it might be useful if we turned in and had an early night.'

'I'll tell the men,' responded Lawana.

The next morning, clouds hovered in the sky threatening to turn the weather nasty. The mood of the camp was subdued and in tune with the atmospheric conditions.

'*Let's get this breakfast over with. We're losing travelling time,*' yelled the senior captain at the non-coms

'*You heard the officer,*' yelled the non-coms in their turn at the men, still gulping gruel down their throats.

Men packed their belongings, unhobbled their steeds, threw blankets over their horses and made ready to depart.

'*Mount and move out,*' shouted Lawana at the gathering.

By mid-morning, the mountains loomed larger as the column of two hundred and six men closed in on them. The surrounding countryside was flooded with undulating hills and the grass here was burnt dry by the unrelenting sun this late in the autumn, although the threatening sky might change all that. The skyline was dominated by the mountains and the clouds were coming over them from the north. The landscape was peppered with trees and brushes but as far as they could see, there was no sign of any habitation.

By noon, one of the scouts reported they'd come across a hamlet nestling on the near side of a hill half a league away from their position at the base of the mighty mountains. As the group rode out of a dip and cantered over a rise, the hamlet lay before them in the lee of the opposing hillside facing them.

Ammuna lifted his hand above his head and pointed at the hamlet; the hand signal told the rest of the column they should follow him and aim for the village.

It was a small rural village of scrub farmers and communal shepherds herding their village goats and cattle under the shadows of the mountains. The chief of the community had seen the column approaching the village and had come out to welcome the new arrivals with a hospitality committee of five elders. As Ammuna's column neared, more of the villagers were coming out of their houses to see what all the fuss was about. Children ran back and forth playing games while the adults satisfied their curiosity. Dogs did a lot of barking as they sensed the presence of strangers.

'Captain,' Ammuna called for the senior captain to come near. 'Listen carefully. I want you to take the brat to the back of the column. I want the four men guarding her to make sure nobody in the village sees her. Gag her and bind her—make sure she's quiet. Take her to the stables and keep her there out of sight. There must be a stable in the village. Keep her there until we leave. If you have to, put a sack over her head, but keep her out of sight. Am I clear?' Ammuna glared at his senior captain.

'Yes sir, quite clear.' The captain rode to the back, taking the brat with him.

Lawana listened with silent fury at the way Ammuna treated the king's daughter, but there was nothing he could do, and he wasn't sure he wanted to. There was a lot of money at stake.

When Ammuna's men reached the chief and his group, one of the village men came forward with a platter held on a decorated woven cloth; the platter contained a loaf of bread and a saucer of salt, a sign of welcome to an esteemed guest. Abruptly, a spark of lightning flashed up high in the mountains, startling the proceedings, followed by a loud clap of thunder rumbling across the sky from that direction. It was as if the mountains were announcing Ammuna's arrival.

Ammuna stopped his column a few cubits from the welcoming villagers. He and Lawana got off their horses and approached the man holding the bread and salt.

The village elders were all smiles, 'We welcome you to the village of Falida,' intoned the man with the platter.

The chief of the village added, 'My name is Malda, I'm the headman of this village. We would be pleased if you would join us in a small communal meal we have arranged for you and your men.'

'Thank you Malda for your kindness. If I didn't know better, I would say you were expecting us,' Ammuna said to the tall dark senior elder.

'But of course we were. Yesterday we received a visit from someone who works for a friend of ours, someone who we do a lot of business with. He sent us his messenger from Tushan, who happened to be in our area, and told us to expect friends of his and for us to treat these people as close friends, as if our friend was here with us himself.' He pointed at one of his group, a middle-aged man standing by his left side. 'This is the messenger. He will explain when we sit down to our meal. I'm sure you and your men could do with some food after your long journey.'

Lawana said to Ammuna as an aside, 'My guess is, this might be the handiwork of Artatama's spy.'

'I'm thinking the same thing,' whispered Ammuna back to his deputy.

Malda watched the whispering between his guests with a smile of tolerance and acceptance.

Then the general took the bread from the platter, broke off a piece, dipped the small piece in the salt, and popped it into his mouth. Lawana followed Ammuna and did the same thing. Hospitality protocol satisfied, Malda led Ammuna and his men, now surrounded by some of the curious villagers and their children, into the village proper.

'We will take you to our meeting place where the meal is laid out.' Malda called for two of his men to take the general's and Lawana's horses into a stable, then led the way to a large village hall in the centre of the village. Ammuna's men followed the two villagers leading the two horses and found a corral close to the stable where they left their two hundred odd horses, the captain asking the workers in the stable to feed their steeds. That done, they all, barring the four guarding the brat, joined their general at the village meeting hall. Asmunikal was led, her head covered with a cloth, into the back of the stable and kept there until the next day.

The spy's messenger didn't wait for the meal and had gently pushed his way to Ammuna's side, 'General, may I introduce myself. My name is Salis. You met my boss a couple of days ago when he helped you evade the ambush. He's asked me to bring you two hundred and fifty white tunics which you asked for.'

Although Ammuna knew this was the messenger's purpose in his meeting with them, he was still surprised by the speed of this episode. 'How did he manage to be so efficient?' he asked the subordinate. 'It was only one and a half days ago we last saw your master. How did he get in touch with you?' Ammuna felt such atypical efficiency was almost unnatural.

'I was coming here as part of my routine travels and yesterday I got a pigeon message sent to me in the last village I was in. They had some undyed Isuwan uniforms getting ready for the brown dyeing vat. I took two hundred and fifty of those uniforms off their hands as per instructions and brought them here for you. I hope I did right?'

'Well yes, of course; that's what I asked for,' Ammuna told the messenger. 'Thank you for the tunics. I have another question for you. I suppose you couldn't arrange for us to buy some provisions from these people, seeing you know them so well? We're running out of supplies. We need supplies to last us for a couple of weeks.'

'I'm sure I can arrange it for you,' replied the spy's messenger. 'You will need to pay for them; have you got money?'

'Will golden shekels do?' Ammuna asked the man.

'You must know, general, gold will *always* do,' the messenger smiled a crooked smile.

'I will pay them for the provisions, for the food we are about to eat and for the fodder for our horses, plus a little extra. Can you tell them, so they know they won't be out of pocket for all their generous hospitality,' Ammuna told the messenger.

The messenger smiled and nodded his agreement.

The circular meeting hall had enough room to house all of the villagers, some three hundred inhabitants, and the tables bearing the bountiful food were now laid out in rows along the hall's length. A long top table was situated diametrically opposite the entrance, and Malda invited Ammuna and his party to sit. Various prominent villagers took their places at the table amongst Ammuna's men, and then Malda stood up and called for silence while he offered a few words of welcome to their honoured guests. Malda didn't speak for long and when he'd finished, Ammuna rose and thanked the headman and the village for their generous hospitality—then the meal began in earnest.

Ammuna leaned over to Malda and said, 'Out of interest, which city do you owe your allegiance to? Are you part of Isuwa? Who collects your taxes? I ask, because you're so out of the way, I should think it difficult for any city to claim you.'

Malda laughed at Ammuna's question. 'You're very astute, general. You're right; they do find it difficult to collect our taxes. Isuwa has tried for many a year; as soon as they appear, we retire to the mountains and leave the village empty. They've burned it and flattened it, but we find it more profitable to rebuild than to pay. So, in answer to your question—we have no allegiance to anybody but ourselves. We deal with the Mittani merchants out of Tushan; mainly because they're further away than Malidiya and don't expect anything from us other than payment for their goods. Everything necessary to life, we make ourselves. We grow our own food, manufacture our own implements.' Malda nodded to one of his fellow villagers down the table, who got up, came over, and put a dagger down in front of Ammuna. 'Let me show you something. Consider it a small gift from our village to you, general. Please, tell me what you think of this metal this dagger is made from?'

Ammuna picked up the dagger and examined it. It was a fine piece of work. 'Good forging; fine craftsmanship. It's not bronze.' Ammuna pulled out his own bronze dagger and clashed the two as it would be clashed in a fight, edge against edge. His bronze dagger was damaged while the other didn't suffer any damage at all. He did this again and got the same result. 'I've come across this metal before, but it's rare. We have a few examples of it in Hattusas. The king has a sword made from it. Did you make this dagger here in the village?' he asked in amazement.

'Our blacksmith is a wizard with metal,' Malda told him. 'This dagger came from a rock which fell from the sky. We keep a sharp lookout for such rocks coming from the sky because it delivers such strong metal.'

Ammuna held out his hand to Lawana, 'Colonel, your dagger please.'

Lawana gave him his dagger and he showed it to Malda. 'This is of the same metal, but it's expensive and hard to get.'

'Yes, nice bit of work. Now you've got two; one for you and one for your friend,' smiled Malda.

Ammuna returned Lawana's dagger back to him and put Malda's gift in his sheath in place of his bronze dagger, leaving his bronze dagger discarded on the table. Ammuna's senior captain sitting nearby, reached out, with the intent of taking it, but he looked for approval from Ammuna. Ammuna nodded and the captain took it for himself, being ever the opportunist.

The same senior captain leaned over to Lawana and said, 'I've been talking to my neighbour here, one of the goat herdsmen from the village. When we were stabling our horses, I noticed a couple of strange looking horses, small and wild looking. I've just asked him what they were and where they came from. He tells me they come from the steppes in the far north, beyond the mountains. He traded them with the Hayasa for some goats. The Hayasa have crossed the Eastern Silver Mountains and are said to be roaming in the east.'

'Is it relevant captain?' Lawana asked, getting irritated at the lengthy narrative.

'That's what I'm trying to tell you, colonel. There's a large group of wild men to the east of us. From what my neighbour tells me, there might be anything between hundreds or even a thousand in our way if we keep going eastwards.' The senior captain was being insistent. 'They could be a danger to us colonel. I think we need to warn the general.'

At the last statement, Lawana suddenly took an interest in the captain's news. 'Now that's different. You're right; if they might be a threat to us then we need to tell the general. Remind me again when we've finished this feasting business just in case I forget.'

Following the meal, and to round off the greeting, Malda had organised a few folk dances performed by the villagers for his honoured guests. The meal and dance show lasted well into late afternoon and when it was finally concluded, both villagers and soldiers were well satisfied with the hospitalities given, and received.

Ammuna had specified, his men were to behave with propriety and sobriety, although the latter went against their soldierly nature. Wine and beer had been flowing in abundance and a number of Ammuna's men had forgotten the strictures and lapsed into rowdy inebriation—Lawana had a small squad placed at the tables near the door for those eventualities. Their duty was to gather the rowdies discreetly but with as much force as was necessary and confine them in a room at the back of the hall to sober up.

This was much appreciated by the village chief. 'I see you keep good discipline in your outfit, and may I say it's to my liking,' Malda said to Ammuna as he watched one of the soldiers being carted off to temporary confinement.

'It would be simply bad manners to allow one of my men to cause a nuisance of himself at such a time, don't you think?' Ammuna responded.

Salis, the messenger, whispered into Ammuna's other ear, 'General, when this dancing business is over, I want to show you your new white uniforms which I've stored in this hall over there in the corner.' He pointed directly behind him.

Ammuna nodded, he'd heard Salis over the music.

The last dance was a harvest dance with lots of reaping innuendoes executed by the villagers—then the music ceased.

Malda stood up and said, 'General, I invite you and your officers to my humble home. I hope it won't be too cramped for you. Your men, I think, might be more comfortable in the stables; there's too many to accommodate otherwise.'

Salis nudged Ammuna and pointed to the uniforms at the back of the hall to remind Ammuna they were there.

'Malda, could we collect our new tunics and then we'll be with you,' Ammuna looked at Lawana and pointed to the uniforms, 'See to those, will you colonel,' telling him to go over there and deal with their distribution. Ammuna followed Malda outside, breathing deeply the fresh air coming from the mountains, then both headed for Malda's home as per his invitation.

Throughout the day, there had been intermittent bellowing from the thunder god in the heavens, and now, just as they were crossing the street, another loud rumble of thunder echoed from the mountains.

'Teshub has been talking to the people all day, but I wish I knew what he was saying,' Malda said to Ammuna, referring to the Hurrian god of thunder.

'Yes, it is unusual to have so much rumbling without the rain following,' replied Ammuna. 'It's as if the earth was complaining about something; an itch it can't scratch.'

'I'm sure He'll get round to explaining whatever he's saying to us; he usually does,' Malda said as he reached his front door. 'Now please come in to my humble home. My woman will make us something hot to drink; a herb brew to relax us.'

It was then, Lawana caught up with them wearing his new white tunic, following them through the door into the medium sized room. 'I've put the officers in charge of distributing the new uniforms,' he told the general. 'When they're finished they'll join us here,' he added, handing Ammuna his own fresh tunic.

'Are they any good?' Ammuna asked, feeling the cloth.

'Standard Isuwan army issue, only without the brown muck they steep it in,' replied Lawana.

Inside the room, they found four young men standing patiently. 'General, these are my sons,' Malda said, pointing at the men. 'They will give room and board to your five officers. I only have room for you general, and the messenger.'

'I'm most grateful,' replied Ammuna, looking at Lawana to sort things out.

Lawana nodded and went back outside, followed by Malda's sons, to find his officers and pass on the good news, they had a bed for the night.

The next morning at dawn, Ammuna's men were standing by their horses, waiting for the order to mount. There were ten extra packhorses loaded with the supplies bought from Malda, and Ammuna was saying his goodbyes to the village chief.

'Sure you're happy with the payment?' Ammuna asked his host.

'It's more than generous, general. We are delighted to have been of service to you,' replied Malda. 'We're sorry there was so much thunder during the night. It made sleeping difficult. I assure you it wasn't our fault.' He chuckled at his own wit.

He's got double what it's worth, thought Lawana. *Of course, it's generous. Wily old farmer*, Lawana concluded to himself.

'*Mount!*' Ammuna commanded, and with a last look at the village, the column departed to the east following the southern base of the Eastern Silver Mountains.

'*Captain!*' Ammuna shouted for his senior captain. 'Did everything go well with the brat?' he asked grimly.

'Yes sir. She's alright and still under guard at the back of the column.'

'Good man. That's all.' Ammuna dismissed him.

By mid afternoon, two scouts were seen by Lawana to be furiously heading back towards them. One was gesturing at his rear with his hand in the air while the other seemed slumped over his horse. As they neared, the one slumped over his horse was seen to have an arrow in his back.

Ammuna raised his hand and brought the column to a halt.

'*Enemy....following us...massive..,*' shouted the gesturing scout as he came close to the column.

'You two,' ordered Ammuna at the couple of soldiers behind him. 'Look after the wounded man.'

'Now, take a deep breath soldier,' commanded Lawana of the upright scout. 'Then start again. What enemy?'

The scout did as he was ordered, took a deep breath and said, 'We were just coming over a small ridge when we came across about twenty men on small ponies. First sign of us, and they started firing their arrows at us. We turned and made a run for it back here to warn you sir. I looked around while we were running for it and I saw a large mass of ponies behind those, chasing us. I think there's really large numbers of them sir.'

As he was making his report, from the distance, a rumbling of horse's hooves could be heard heading towards them.

Ammuna's ears pricked up and he peered into the east. *'Right, listen up. We're heading for the mountains. We'll use them to guard our backs. Move it right now.'*

The column swung left towards the Silver Mountains, galloping towards them as fast as their horses would carry them. In the distance, the rumbling of sound grew louder and a huge number of horses came towards Ammuna's retreating men.

As the *loyal* mercenaries came close to the mountains, Ammuna picked a sheer face and headed there to make a stand. He ordered his men to form a tight half circle with the horses tightly side by side. Asmunikal was placed near the sheer cliff face with the four men guarding her, screening the princess with their own bodies, their own shields up. All those carrying bows notched their arrows.

'Wait until they get close,' yelled Lawana at his men. *'Make every arrow count. It'll be one less man you have to fight. Make sure you use your shields.'*

They were going to have a fight on their hands, which might put paid all their well-laid plans. Ammuna could not believe his eyes; there were at least a thousand of the enemy charging them. He shook his head and mentally prepared himself for his journey to the underworld. With so many arrayed against his small force, he could only see one outcome. His total annihilation.

*'Fire your arrows, **now**,'* Ammuna shouted at his *loyal* soldiers. *'Who are these men?'* he shouted at Lawana.

'I think they're called Hayasa,' Lawana shouted back as the first fusillade of enemy arrows hit them.

A number of his *loyal* men fell off their horses struck by the enemy arrows which had managed to find exposed bodies. Horses were hit and some buckled under the impact of the incoming missiles. Then suddenly, the first tremor began to shake the ground. It lasted for a few eye blinks but it spooked all the horses. They reared and threw their riders. This happened to the charging enemy as well. Their charge abruptly came to a halt as their horses became unmanageable and began bucking and kicking. The enemy tried to regain momentum and resume the charge, but then another stronger tremor shook the ground—this time it was longer, and the mountains began to tremble, dislodging boulders and stones, hurling them outwards and downwards on the charging enemy.

Ammuna shouted, '*Dismount and get closer to the rock face—hurry.*'

Another big tremor shook the ground under them, terrifying the animals further. Those who could, got control of their steeds and pulled them closer to the sheer cliff to avoid the falling boulders. Pressed against the cliffs they watched, frozen with fear, as their world collapsed around them.

The enemy was in disarray with horses rearing, throwing their riders, and fleeing in panic. The attack was over; nature had won the day. An earthquake had interrupted man's violent games and interposed itself in their midst. Any members of the Hayasa who were still mounted after the first initial shocks, turned their mounts around and headed back east in complete terror. The gods had intervened in their rapacious enterprise and they were now heeding the pronouncement to head back north towards their own home.

13
Earth Tremor

Mokhat and his *special forces* left the Puranti, after crossing it in pursuit of Ammuna, and headed east for the distant Eastern Silver Mountains. His scouts insisted the enemy had gone in that direction. This puzzled Mokhat since it made no sense. Ammuna was going away from Nineveh, but his agent back in Isuwa had been adamant Ammuna had been told to go there by his spy, so he had no choice but to follow in Ammuna's footsteps.

Due to various delays, such as meeting their agent, and the care they needed to take on Isuwan territory, the gains Mokhat made in catching up with Ammuna had now been eroded. They were again a whole day behind the rogue general and his band of mercenaries, concluded Palaiyas and Onasiyas, after consulting with their expert scouts. There was nothing to do but pick up the pace and try to make up for the loss along the trail.

They rode like the furry until afternoon, all the time swapping horses, enveloped with the thought of the poor young girl they were attempting to rescue. As the days of her captivity increased, so it spurred and motivated them to increase their efforts.

However, running both sets of horses into the ground was not in their interests, so they stopped mid afternoon for a rest and a bite of food.

Onasiyas finally voiced his anxiety in regards to their ensuing chase. 'Is there nothing we can do to get ahead of Ammuna? I'm feeling frustrated at merely dogging his tracks. I'd like to get these two hands on the scoundrel.' He clenched his fists in the air and shook them at the heavens.

'I've been trying to think of a way to outmanoeuvre the rogue myself, but I've not come up with anything,' responded Mokhat. 'Any ideas, Palaiyas?'

'We could head for Nineveh directly from here and wait on the outskirts for his arrival, now we know he's going there for certain,' he suggested to Mokhat.

'The problem is, as we've just experienced outside Malidiya, something can go wrong with Ammuna's plans and force him in a different direction,' bemoaned Mokhat. 'We could end up waiting for him outside Nineveh, whereas changed circumstance would put him in Assur, Mari or even Babylon. We simply can't predict his next move with any accuracy. Remember, we're trying to rescue the king's daughter, and it's my assessment, her life's in danger, more so than ever before. I've no doubt Ammuna would have no qualms about ending her life if it suited his purpose.

'I'm assuming Artatama is paying him a large sum to do this horrific abduction. Where money is involved, people will do the most outrageous deeds, and Ammuna is outrageous and devious. No! We must conclude, we have to stay on his trail and try to catch up with him as swiftly as we can manage. Are we agreed?' Mokhat looked at their faces, seeking an answer.

Palaiyas nodded after a short hesitation, and Onasiyas followed his lead but more reluctantly.

'If we've finished, I suggest we remount and continue the pursuit.' Mokhat ended the discussion and got to his feet.

The *special forces* followed Ammuna's tracks through the undulating hills and the sun burnt grass till nightfall, and rather than lose them in the dark, they camped in the shadows of the Eastern Silver Mountains on the banks of a small stream running from the mountains into the Puranti River.

Onasiyas told them to make a fire and cook some hot food. This was when the rigorous training told; nobody grumbled at the tiring day on horseback as they sat around the fire; they simply got on with what had to be done.

In the dewy dawn chorus of a balmy Autumn, the camp stirred and the embers were soon rekindled; breakfast was hurriedly put together and wolfed down. The men packed their belongings, unhobbled their horses, threw blankets over their mounts and made ready to depart.

'*Mount and move out*,' shouted Onasiyas at his men.

The skyline was dominated by the looming mountains as they rode on towards the east. Patchy clouds were coming over them from the north. When the sun finally broke through the clouds, it blinded them, forcing them to squint as they galloped through a landscape sparsely scattered with trees and brushes.

By noon, a scout came galloping back to report they'd come across a village huddled up against the near side of a hill half a league away from their location at the base of the mighty mountains. As the scout was making his report, a flock of birds flew over screeching their heads off and the scout's horse suddenly reared up and threw its rider. Other horses began to neigh and prance around as though something was frightening them. A deep grumble came from the earth below. Mokhat was thrown as was Palaiyas, but Onasiyas steadied his mount, managing to calm her.

Then the first tremor hit and shook the landscape, vibrating the ground, shaking it like a rag doll. It felt as if the solid ground had turned into quicksand—there followed a massive roar of noise from deep under, giving the impression the ground was ripping apart and the heavens were falling in on them. More riders were thrown from their horses as the animals became unmanageable in their panic. Others jumped off their mounts and tried to hold on to the reins when the animals reared and kicked. Those who managed to control their horses, watched with apprehension as large boulders broke off from the distant mountains and came crashing down to earth a league from where they were. Then it all stopped as suddenly as it had begun. The dismounted stood dazed, and shook their heads. Those still on their horses tried to quieten their animals.

The second tremor was more prolonged, and the earth buckled like a wave on the ocean with a lot of booming noise coming from deep underground. Although the second tremor was longer, it also stopped as abruptly as it had begun. The group held onto their mounts as best they could, waiting for the earth to calm itself. Then came the big tremor, shaking the ground and ripping it asunder. A distance south of them, a long chasm formed, running from east to west, from the directions of the mountains to somewhere behind them towards the Puranti. It was only stubborn willpower and discipline which drove the *special forces* to hang onto their horse's reins. Others of the group grimly held fast to the terrified pack ponies, trying to save their provisions. The ground shook, rippled and then buckled, but eventually it quietened down, leaving the specks of life on its surface to regain their composure.

'*Is everyone alright?*' yelled Mokhat in the following stillness.

'It looks like it's over,' Palaiyas said hesitantly, not wishing to tempt fate. He craned his neck to look at all the men around him. 'The men look like they've survived intact,' he told Mokhat.

Both prince-generals stood side by side holding on to their horses; the animals still had wide panicky eyes and flared nostrils, showing they would bolt given half the chance.

Mokhat said all at once, scratching the back of his head in the process, 'Wherever Ammuna is, it must have hit him as well. I pray and hope the king's daughter is safe.'

Palaiyas added, 'But *I* also hope a big boulder has squashed that no good traitor.' He spat to the side in contempt, still unnerved by the tremor.

Onasiyas, having given his reins to his deputy, was casually strolling amongst his men patting them on the shoulders, reassuring them. For others, he had a few words of comfort from their commander. After a time, when they'd reassured themselves that the earthquake was over, they remounted their steeds and warily resumed their journey towards the village the scouts had discovered earlier. In fact, they were on the northern side of the rift which appeared during the earthquake. It seemed to be leading them towards their goal. A scout went to look down into the rift to fathom its depth.

'Well?' demanded Onasiyas when the scout returned.

'I can just see the bottom sir. It's about thirty cubits deep,' he reported.

'And the width? What's your estimate?' Onasiyas demanded.

'Widest, I estimate around ten cubits and the narrowest about six cubits,' said the scout.

'Let's hope we can cross it when the time comes,' observed Onasiyas to his scout. 'The men could probably manage it, but I'm not sure the horses would jump it. Then there's the twenty pack ponies; I'm sure they can't get across no matter what we do. We'll have to find a way. We're on the northern side of this rift and we'll need to get to the southern side if we're going to Nineveh. Anyway, we'll get to the problem when we need to—in the mean time we'd better get moving—see if we can find the village you mentioned.' He added to the scout, 'Keep your eyes peeled for any variations on the width of the rift. Let me know later on the narrowest spot you find.'

'Yes sir,' said the scout and jumped on his horse.

When the *special forces* rode over a fractured ridge, the village, or what was left of it, lay before them in the rubble of the opposing hillside facing them. Running through the middle of the village was the chasm created by the enormous upheaval. Miraculously the rift ran right down the middle of the main street, leaving houses on either side with a few hanging on the edge of the deep fissure. On either side of the new crevice, people were standing amongst the wreckage of their houses staring in shock at what happened to their lives.

Mokhat and his men were on the northern side of the crevice, and they stopped to asses what to do next. 'One way or another, we're going to have to find a way across this thing,' he pointed at the chasm, talking to Palaiyas.

'If we follow it to the mountains, that's where it'll terminate,' replied Palaiyas. 'We should be able to cross it there.'

'You may be right. I don't think we've much choice,' sighed Mokhat. 'But first, let's see if we can give these poor villagers a hand to sort out their calamity.' He turned to Onasiyas, 'Get your men to give the villagers a hand. Rescue those you can, help the injured, and see if we can help rebuild a few shelters before nightfall. Get the cooks to brew up hot drinks and get the hot food going. Looks like we're staying here for a while. We can't leave them like this.'

Both Palaiyas and Onasiyas nodded in agreement. They set the men to work, pulling out those buried inside their collapsed homes. Handling the children's bodies was the worst job for all involved. At least a third of the villagers on this side of the crevasse were dead or injured; the other two thirds seemed to be in shock, wandering around the ruins plaintively calling their loved one's names. It was the last tremor which had done the worst damage. The southern side of the village seemed to have faired marginally better, and on the other side, people were standing on the edge of the ravine shouting for people they were seeking in the northern half of the village.

129

A lieutenant arrived with an elderly dishevelled man in tow. 'General sir,' he addressed Mokhat. 'We dug this man out of his house. He claims to be the village elder. He would like a word with you.'

The man's eyes were a bit wild, and sad at the same time. Dust covered his whole body. 'General?' said the old man slowly with a pained expression. 'You're the second general I've met today. I'm sorry; my name is Malda, I'm the head of this village. This village was....' A tear rolled down his face. 'I'm sorry. I've just lost my wife. I'm still a little lost.'

Mokhat's ears pricked up as he heard of a second general. 'My condolences on your loss. My men will stay and help your village as best we can. But you say I'm the second general you've met today. Tell me about the first one.' Mokhat called to one of the men to bring some water, while he waited for a reply. He needed information.

'Yes, the other general was General Ammuna. That's what he called himself. Do you know him?' Malda's chest heaved with the effort to control himself.

'Yes I know him. He's a very bad man. Tell me, did you see a young girl with him, about six years old?' Mokhat was eager to hear news of Asmunikal.

'No, sorry. We saw no girl in his group. I didn't look, of course, but no, I can't remember any girl with them.' The distraction of the conversation allowed Malda to recover his composure.

'How many men did he have? What was your impression of them?' Mokhat was seeking any bits of intelligence on the men with Ammuna, which might be invaluable in a future fight.

Malda thought for a moment then said, 'There were about two hundred soldiers with the general. They looked like professional soldiers to me, but I'm no expert. What can I say? We sold him supplies and he paid generously for them. He arrived yesterday to meet up with one of our traders who supplied him with new tunics. Then we did the business, had some food. They stayed the night and left early this morning. Then about noon this happened,' Malda swept his arm in a wide arc encompassing his ruined village. 'What *are* we going to do?'

'Malda, you've been most helpful. As I said before, we'll stay and help you sort yourselves out, but tomorrow we must go after Ammuna again.' Mokhat put his hand on Malda's shoulder to reassure him. 'Look, have you got anything long enough to bridge the gap?' Mokhat pointed at the nearby rift.

Malda thought—and then looked to the end of the torn street. Malda's face lit up. 'We've some long beams in the stable which we're getting ready to build another barn with. They'll probably reach the other side.'

More villagers were beginning to appear as they were talking, straggling in, looking to Malda to give them a lead. Men, women and children. There were around thirty of them. All were a bit shocked while a few were lightly injured.

'Show my men where the beams are. We might be able to use them to cross over there,' he indicated the other half of the village. 'At least we could go over and see if they need any help,' Mokhat told him.

Malda pointed at a couple of men and told them to take the soldiers to the old stable and show them where the roof beams for the new barn were stored.

More people were arriving and crowding around Malda, asking questions, comforting each other, asking if people had seen their missing relatives.

Mokhat thought it high time he had a word with the crowd before it got out of hand. 'I'm going to have a word with them,' he told Malda.

Mokhat climbed on his horse and shouted over their heads. '*Hallo! Give me your attention please.* As you can see, I have some men working hard to rescue as many of you as we can. We need you to go and help them. Standing around here won't get anything done. My cooks are preparing hot food and drinks. Others are helping the injured. I need you all to go and help those still trapped. We need to recover the bodies and put them in one place. We also need you to assess the damage and see what can be repaired before nightfall. I know some of you are in shock, but we have to get on with life no matter what it throws at us. So, please, go and give a hand to help with those still trapped.'

People looked at the man on his dark horse in his dark uniform, and it got people thinking. Finally, they all began to go about with a renewed vigour, searching amongst the houses, trying to salvage what was left of their lives.

Twenty of Onasiyas men were carrying a long beam towards Mokhat. Onasiyas was leading them.

'This will easily span the chasm, I'm sure of it,' Onasiyas told Mokhat. 'There's another one like this coming behind this one.

Suddenly the dogs began to frantically yelp, barking as if they were mad. Mokhat remembered the animals seemed to sense trouble before it occurred, so he yelled as loud as he could, '*Grab your horses now; there's another shock coming.*' Just as he finished saying this, the ground shuddered with an after shock and all the men of the *special forces* grabbed the reins of their animals and held on tight, while the twenty men carrying the long heavy beam dropped it as if it somehow had turned red hot.

It was a short after shock and caused more panic than damage. People dropped to the ground and tried to hug it. Children were crying with fear and the women wailed to the gods to spare them.

Malda lifted his hands to heaven and moaned, 'Not again, please not again. What have we done to deserve this? How have we angered the gods?' The village chief was close to tears with anger and grief.

Mokhat put his arm around Malda's shoulders to steady him and offer moral support in the form of physical human contact. 'Fear not my friend,' he said softly. 'There may be a few small shocks yet to come but the big ones are over. I have experience of this type of thing. What is important is for you to stay calm and give an example to your people—and to decide what is to be done.'

Malda looked with wonder at this general in his dark uniform. He seemed almost calm. More importantly, he claimed to know what was going on. The village chief straightened his back and composed himself. 'I'm grateful for your support, general. You came to our aid when we needed you the most. I won't forget this in a hurry; nor will my people. But please, pardon the rudeness—I don't recognise those dark uniforms. Which army do you represent? I would like to know which nation to thank for sending you to us in our hour of need.'

'I'm from Hattusas, as are all my men. We are a special unit of the Hittite army. As I said before; we're hunting a rogue Hittite general who's done something bad.' Mokhat cleared his throat. 'So, the next thing to decide is which side of the rift you're going to rebuild your village on? That must depend on where the land is most fertile. Up north with the mountains or south towards the river and the trade routes? I'm only guessing the trade route is to the south, mind you?'

With decisions to be made, Malda became more decisive. 'Yes, I think we're going to have to rebuild on the southern side.'

Mokhat spied Onasiyas coming towards them. 'Colonel, if you would join us for a while, we could do with your expertise.'

Onasiyas strode up beaming, 'Yes general, how can I help you? By the way, I think we've enough timber to build a good bridge across the chasm,' he aimed his hand at the rift.

'You've just answered the very question I was going to pose to you,' Mokhat responded. 'Have you got someone who's a good bridge builder?'

'I've got an expert at it. He's surveying the wood in the barn as we speak.' Onasiyas looked pleased with himself for pre-empting Mokhat's request. 'I estimated it would probably be quicker to build a proper bridge than us taking the animals all the way up to the mountains looking for a way to cross the chasm—which might not be there. It would also go a long way to help this village recover from the earthquake.'

'Well done colonel. Let's build them a permanent structure—that's a priority. They've decided to rebuild their village on the southern side of the rift, so the sooner the bridge is built, the quicker we can begin to cross, and start with the shelters.' Mokhat turned to Malda. 'Get a few of your people to help carry the timber for the bridge. If the village blacksmith is still alive, we need to get him to work producing long nails for the bridge. He might even have them already made. You also need to get all your possession out of the damaged houses and bring them here, so when the bridge is built, it'll be easier to get the stuff across.'

Malda called some of his villagers together and assigned them to help Onasiyas' bridge builder. Others he sent to help with the rescue of their possessions. More of the village was coming to him for direction, looking lost in the aftershock. He gave them orders as to what to do and they left feeling they had some purpose restored to their lives.

When Malda came back, Mokhat told him someone was calling for him from over the other side of the rift.

Malda went to see, and came back smiling. 'I've just found one of my sons. He was on the other side of the village when the chasm formed.'

'I'm happy for you,' Mokhat said solicitously. 'However, I must remind you that this is autumn and winter is not far behind. If the winter is severe near these mountains, as I suspect it is, then you'll need to make sure all your food is gathered and collected here, near your possessions, ready to cross the bridge. Shout to the others on the other side what your plan is, so they can get to work over there and begin to rebuild your shelters—your son is already over there so get him give a lead to those involved in the work. It'll give him something to do. We'll help you today and tomorrow, but we're on a mission and we can't stay any later, so I suggest we all get to work right now.'

Mokhat spied Palaiyas coming back at the head of a bedraggled group of villagers. Palaiyas' navy blue uniform was covered with dirt, dust and sweat, and he was thoroughly dishevelled.

'We've laid out all the dead and dug out all those we could find buried in the rubble,' he told Mokhat as he came up.

'You look a sight,' Mokhat grinned at him, 'but you also look like you've been extra busy. So now, can we say the majority of the people on this side of the rift are safe; either rescued or being looked after?'

Palaiyas nodded quietly in response to the question. He seemed subdued and tired. 'I need some food and a short rest,' he told Mokhat. 'And so do they,' he added, meaning the bedraggled group of villagers he was leading.

'The cooks are doling out food,' Mokhat pointed to a large fire further up the broken street.

Palaiyas led his shabby sad group towards where the food was being dished out.

Onasiyas and the bridge building expert were hard at it, calculating the abutment loads at either end, the materials and labour that would be needed to build the bridge, and the time it would take.

By late afternoon, a temporary bridge had been put across the chasm, while they excavated and prepared the chasm banks for the building of the main structure on either side of the rift. Palaiyas was now in charge of work on the southern side—Onasiyas was busy with building the permanent bridge, and Mokhat had taken to organising the northern portion of the village. Malda managed to be reunited with all his sons, and they buried his wife and their mother. By nightfall, a semblance of a permanent arched bridge with rails was taking shape. The decking still needed to be laid. The entire village was now on the southern side of the rift and large fires were burning to keep the huddling population warm. Soldiers and villagers mingled around the fires in a friendly camaraderie, united in a common underlying principle, that in the face of death, they had all survived the disaster nature had thrown at them.

14
Storm God's Salvation

As Ammuna watched the Hayasa break off their attack after the earthquake and stampede back east in terror; a wisp of a smile crossed his face in bemusement. There were still a number of the enemy chasing their small horses after being thrown during the tremors. Ammuna watched the panicked mounts head east, chased by their shocked riders. He guessed why they were fleeing away from their quarry, and thanked the non-existent gods for their naïve behaviour.

Ammuna was one of the few educated men of the period who put no faith in religion—assuming it to be an enterprise run to benefit the priesthood. What *he* could not see with his own two eyes, he refused to take seriously, and to date he'd seen no physical sign of any gods, other than the stories told by the priests, who he knew, had a vested interest in promoting such nonsense. So now these phantom gods had intervened in saving his skin from certain death, he was happy to make a mental nod in their direction—and he proposed to take a leaf out of the priest's book, and use the situation to bolster his enterprise.

Ammuna turned his attention to his own casualties, when another tremor shook the ground. Another round of panic ensued, with horses rearing up, kicking the empty air.

'Steady there,' Ammuna told his horse, holding him tight. '*It's only an aftershock*,' he yelled at his men. 'Nothing to worry about. Keep hold of your horses.'

Many of his *loyal* men had fallen under the fusillade of arrows fired by the Hayasa, prior to the tremors.

'*Colonel*,' he shouted at Lawana, 'see to the men.' But as he said this, he saw his shout was unnecessary; the colonel was already going to help the wounded on his own initiative, as did the other men of his group who were still unhurt.

Those horses beyond help, being far too badly injured, were dispatched quickly as a mercy. A few of the men were pulled out from under their own horses. As the enemy's arrows struck, these horses had bucked and buckled, falling on to their own riders.

All in all the final casualty count was twenty-three dead and seventeen wounded. They also lost eleven horses. Evening was coming and Ammuna decided to move a league south before setting up camp for the night. As a matter of urgency, he sought out the non-com who'd been looking after Asmunikal. To his relief, he found the king's daughter very frightened and clinging to the non-com, but otherwise safe. He discarded the idea of going any further east just in case the Hayasa had abandoned their flight and had stopped. Better safe than sorry, was one of his mottoes when making a decision which didn't involve a fight—thus erring on the side of caution.

He gathered his three remaining officers, one of the captains was no more having been hit by an arrow in the chest, and told them to bury the dead and get the men ready to move south. Ammuna said a small hurried eulogy over the communal grave of his *loyal* departed, and told his listeners that he would compensate their families as previous promised. Ammuna didn't want to stay in the vicinity of his near demise any longer than he had to.

The horses were still a bit skittish and so men walked, leading them by their bridles in a sombre procession. All of the ponies carrying their provisions were intact and Ammuna thanked the non-existent gods for small mercies.

On their way, another small tremor caused a little havoc but being on foot, they managed to contain the horses, which were easily panicked.

Once they'd travelled south a league, the group camped by a small stream they came across flowing down from the mountains, and the men saw to their horses and then tended to the wounded. Of the seventeen wounded, ten had relatively light wounds where the arrows had hit an arm or torn the flesh, three had medium walking type wounds where no vital organs had been punctured; two were in critical condition where one died on the way to the campsite. All were being tended by the allotted medical men. They were made as comfortable as possible and Ammuna came to see them as soon as he had dealt with his horse.

'Well, what's the news? How are they?' he asked the captain-doctor in charge.

'One of the wounded died on the way down here sir— the other, I'm afraid, won't survive the night. He had an arrow through the neck. I don't know how he's lasted this long. The rest will probably pull through. Ten are just simple bandage cases with flesh wounds. I'm not going to bother much with them except to change their bandages. Of the three with medium wounds, one of them is giving me concern because there may be an infection, but he's strong and should survive. Basically general, considering the number of arrows we had coming at us, we got off lightly.'

'Thank you for the report captain. You're doing a remarkable job here—I and the men appreciate it.' Ammuna left the captain in good humour and rejoined Lawana, who was sitting on a log near one of the fires.

'We came out with barely a scratch, if you think of what was being thrown at us,' Ammuna said to Lawana as he sat down. 'Those barbarians outnumbered us ten to one, or worse. Had it not been for the earthquake, we'd not be sitting here.'

'I can't argue with that,' answered Lawana. 'When I saw their numbers, I thought our enterprise had come to a premature end.'

'Have you managed to count up our losses yet?' Ammuna asked.

'Twenty three dead; seventeen wounded, and we lost eleven horses,' the colonel replied.

'Make it twenty four dead—one of the wounded died on the way down here, and the captain tells me the other one won't last the night.' Ammuna told him sadly.

'It'll leave a hundred and eighty and us two,' Lawana concluded. 'We started with two hundred and twenty; we've lost forty men so far. It's a heavy attrition rate, don't you think?

'What about the brat? Is she alright?' Ammuna asked, ignoring Lawana's last question.

'Yes she's fine. Still as abrasive as ever. The men protecting her did a good job. She's somewhat over friendly with her non-com—and is currently hungry and demanding food from him. I've just checked on her,' Lawana told him.

The cooks got to work producing a hot meal made of barley and reconstituted dried meat and the smell was drifting towards them as they talked. Hot herbal drinks were being handed out.

'Good! As for the attrition rate you mentioned earlier,' Ammuna stared at his colonel, 'every soldier who joined us knew the risks involved. I made that plain at the outset. You can't do something as outrageous as we did and not expect some comeback. We've been lucky so far. Don't forget the forest incident. Had Artatama's spy not shown up, those Isuwans would have massacred us without any compunction. It's no use griping about the dangerous profession we've chosen.'

Lawana stared into the fire, not looking at Ammuna. He might not have liked what was said, but he knew the general was right. Soldiering was a dangerous business, and now more so—yes they had come off relatively lightly so far. 'I suppose your right sir. I was thinking of the poor soldiers.'

'All soldiers are poor colonel, that's why they are ordinary soldiers and not officers. It's die of starvation without the army or die in it, and live well within it while your alive. I commend your concern for the men, but we senior men must keep a sense of proportion. Anyway, I'm going to try to ease their mental plight. After the meal, I'm going to give the men a pep talk, considering the trauma they've just been through—it might ease their poor befuddled minds.' Ammuna informed Lawana. 'Pass it on to the other three officers so they're prepared.'

The cook brought them a bowl of food and a cup of herbal brew. The two men sat and munched meditatively, each buried in his own thoughts.

'We'll head for the Lower Puranti in the morning and follow its course for a couple of days until we find a suitable crossing point,' Ammuna told Lawana as he finished his meal.

'Yes general, I thought it might be your idea. I agree entirely. Let's hope we can find a bridge this time, otherwise we'll have to swim for it again.' Lawana put his bowl down and emptied his cup.

'Now for the pep talk.' Ammuna stood as did Lawana.

Men, listen up. The general has something to say to you all, so pay attention,' Lawana said loudly, then he sat down.

Ammuna stepped up on to the log, balancing on it, using it as a platform so they all could see him. 'My dear *loyal* men, earlier today we went through an experience which was violent—and deadly for a number of us. I want you to remember with kindness those who are no longer with us. They were your brothers-in-arms. We are all sitting here tonight mainly due to those divinities on high who are guarding us in our enterprise. Without their intervention earlier today, we would all be full of arrows and residing in the Dark Earth. When the gods sent the earthquake to protect us, it saved us and sent the barbarian horde intent on our murder, back to where they came from; some Isarra hole back in the north-east.

'I do believe the gods sent the earthquake to protect us and they're looking after us in what we're doing—in our enterprise to better ourselves. I can't find any other explanation for what's happened. For their beneficence, we will give thanks to them at the end of my speech. I want you men to take heart from this episode and feel comforted the gods are looking kindly upon us—and are on our side.

'Tomorrow we'll head for the river down south and follow it for a couple of days—then we'll find a suitable crossing point and make for the other side. We'll then head for the Aransah River and follow that down to Nineveh, where our journey ends, and we get paid. I'm guessing, but it might be safer if we all stick together when we're in Nineveh, until we decide what we're going to do. When we get there, we'll settle on what to do and where we're going.

'I hope what I've just told you eases your minds and gives you some hope for the future. Now I ask you all to stand, and I will lead you in a prayer to our Lord the great Storm God in the great Kuntarra who we thank for sending us the earthquake.

'Hear me oh Storm God of the Hittites, hear these words of gratitude from one of your most devoted followers. We gathered here, thank you for protecting us from the barbarians who tried to destroy your servants, and we thank you for sending the earth-shaker to vanquish our attackers.' Ammuna bowed his head, stepped down from the log, and resumed his seat. All his *loyal* men resumed their activities, but were more subdued in doing so.

Lawana was looking at him with a twinkle in his eye. 'It was a good and noble speech general. But as I remember, you're not one of the most enthusiastic followers of the priesthood.'

'Colonel, may I remind you we have a mission to fulfil, or had you forgotten? The speech was nothing to do with my beliefs or me—it was not about me. It was for the men and their mental comfort. Why must you try to pull everything apart? Today the men have been through a traumatic experience and as their nominal commander; it is my duty to make sure they are in a fit state to continue to function so we can finish this journey in good order.

'If my speech helped, then how can you criticise it? Anyway, we'll know in the morning if it did any good. We'll see how they react, how they behave. If the spring is back in their steps, then I will have done my work.' Ammuna stood and stretched. 'And now I think it's time to turn in. Good night to you colonel.' Ammuna went to where his blankets were spread and climbed in. The rest of the camp followed shortly and also climbed into their blankets, with only the sentries wide-awake.

15
Surgery

Another loud dawn chorus woke everyone and the fires were rekindled to cook the group's breakfast. The horses unhobbled and taken down to the stream to drink their morning fill. A ground mist hung throughout the entire encampment, clinging to the earth, making it look as if the earth was sweating. Men washed themselves in the cold waters of the nearby stream and the sun peered over the horizon in the east.

'*Come on you lazy louts, get yourselves moving.* This isn't an easy civy camp you can lay around in all day.' The non-coms were going around and chiding the men to greater effort so they could get the food down quickly and get back on to their long trek.

Ammuna was already up and looking at his investment from a distance, namely the brat. He was watching her friendly non-com help her with her ablutions down at the stream and then fetch her hot barley porridge.

My little non-com has turned into her personal servant, he thought with amusement and contempt, but he was sensible enough to leave well alone. The brat was into a routine which fitted in with the group's travelling schedule and he knew better than to disrupt it. His contempt for the daughter of the king had an ulterior motive—it was masking the possible need to dispose of the brat at a point in the future. He had to steel himself for the potential deed and he couldn't afford to have any kind feeling for her—which is why he'd called her a brat in the first place.

Ammuna noted the medical officer was intent on having a word with him. Ammuna pre-empted, 'Yes what can I do for you captain?'

'Sir, I have to report the wounded man I mentioned to you yesterday, the one with the arrow in his neck, has just died. Also, the man I mentioned as being wounded but likely to recover; he seems to be getting worse. I note he's got a touch of the blackening at the infection site. When we camp tonight, I may have to try to remove his leg—although I've no idea how I'm to do it in the present circumstances.' The captain seemed unhappy about the prospect.

'Thank you captain. Keep me posted. If you decide to operate tonight, let me know. I might be able to help. I've seen a few amputations in my time.'

'Yes sir, thank you.' The captain went back to tend to his wounded.

As the journey resumed, it turned out, they were only about two leagues away from the Lower Puranti and they reached its northern shore by mid-morning. Sitting on their horses looking at the mighty river, it was as if the whole column gave a deep sigh. This was the point of catharsis when the horrors of the previous day, the ground shaking, the near deaths which almost consumed them, seemed to leave them and enter the river, to be washed away in the flow of the water going all the way down to the southern sea.

The column's mood changed as it swung left along the riverbank, continuing in a gentle canter with the autumn sunshine warming their faces. The bird life along the shores, with its gullies and inlets, was loud and reassuring, where ducks, plover, snipe, pelicans, storks, and even gulls, all loudly vied for what the river had to offer. Had they been able to ask the locals, they would have informed them the Upper Puranti was on a major route for migrating birds.

It was thus, the journey went on along the rugged shoreline until well past mid day, when Ammuna called for a halt so the men and horses could have a short rest and down a bit of food. The day was mild and it felt more as if they were having a picnic rather than an army stopover.

The medical captain strolled over to where Ammuna and Lawana were sitting. 'Sir, is there any chance of a longer stopover. The soldier I mentioned earlier, the one with the blackening; I'm sure he's got poisoning in his blood. I'd like to try to take the leg off before it kills him. I've seen this before and it is deadly if I don't act speedily.'

'Can't it wait till we make camp this evening?' Ammuna asked.

'I'm not sure he'd survive if we leave it any longer. Every bit of time matters when there's a fever of this sort. As it is, the leg below the knee needs to be removed. If we leave it any more, then the whole leg will have to come of to the thigh and I don't think I could do this out here. That will mean the infection gets closer to the head and I don't think he would make it through the operation. Also, there's the daylight; we could see better what we're doing right now. That increases our chances of success.' The captain finished and waited while Ammuna gave it some thought.

'What do you think?' the general asked Lawana. 'Can we stay here and make camp?'

'I can't see what difference it would make if we went on further,' Lawana advised. 'We'd still have to deal with this problem tonight. Let's get it out of the way right now— as the captain wants.'

'Fine. We'll make early camp right here by the river. You'll have fresh water if you need it,' Ammuna said to the captain. 'And when you're ready to amputate; give me a shout. I've picked up a few tricks that may be useful to you.'

'Thank you sir. You may have just saved this man's life.' The captain walked away briskly to tend to his patient who was lying on a frame slung between trailing poles pulled by a horse.

Lawana went off to give the necessary orders to set up camp in situ. Two large fires were lit and the horses all hobbled and left to feed on the grass. Latrines were dug downwind and sentries nominated and posted. A complete miniature army camp was set-up in no time.

Ammuna went to find the medical captain. He wanted to have a word with him and see how bad the injured man was. He found him in a tent preparing for the operation. Ammuna ducked his head and went inside; took one look at the bared left leg of the patient lying on a blanket, and left the tent with the captain following him out.

Ammuna stopped outside and began shaking his head. 'I see what you mean,' he said to the captain. 'If the blackening isn't stopped now, the man will surely die. I've also seen this before. You'll have to make sure you cut high enough to be clear of the blackening. How do you propose to go about this?'

'Sir, I would normally cut quickly round the flesh of the leg and then saw through the bone, but I have a big problem there; I have no saw. I've looked everywhere for it and I can't find it. I'd welcome any suggestions, sir.' The captain made a grimace, which emphasised the worried look on his face.

Ammuna called for Lawana, who happened to be soaking his tired feet in the nearby river. Lawana but his boots back on and went to see what the general wanted.

'Colonel, I want you to turn this camp upside down and find the missing saw.' Ammuna looked grim. He was getting angry at a vital piece of equipment going astray. Some fool had probably used it to saw wood or some other tomfoolery. He told Lawana what the medical captain had told him; for Lawana that was sufficient. Lawana called all the officers and non-coms together and told them the problem of the missing saw and how it was threatening the success of the operation, and he demanded they find the missing saw.

147

The search was thorough and the camp minutely turned over, but the saw remained missing.

'This is despicable. How can a saw go missing?' Ammuna demanded after being informed of the fruitless search. 'What else can we do?' He stood near the tent and scratched his head. Then a small smile lit his face. 'Find me the best expert sharpener we have,' he ordered Lawana.

Lawana came back with a non-com. 'This man claims to be our best sharpener,' he told Ammuna.

Ammuna looked at the non-com and said, 'Listen, find me the largest axe we have and sharpen it until you can shave with it. You're about to save a soldier's life. Oh, and colonel, I want all the officers to attend me here. They have work to do,' Ammuna told Lawana.

When the officers and non-coms arrived, Ammuna explained to them, 'I want a tree stump cleared of bark; I want it pristine clean. I want it here in front of me. I also want two soldiers to put two swords into the fire until they're white hot. Anybody who's stomach heaves at the sight of blood, I don't want them near me right now—and while I'm at it, they shouldn't have joined the army in the first place. I want a bucket of clean boiling water readied to clean the stump.' As Ammuna was giving these orders to the assembled officers and non-coms, gathered round him near the medical tent, the medical captain was listening to all this quiet bemused. It would seem his commanding officer was hijacking his operation.

When everybody had gone to obey the orders, the medical captain asked Ammuna, 'Sir, can I ask what you have in mind?'

'We've searched the campsite; turned it upside down and the saw hasn't turned up, so we must improvise. I'm determined to save this man. Now listen carefully. I've only seen this done once in my whole career. I intend to swing the axe myself onto a point we'll mark on his leg, which is going to be placed on the clean log with no bark. If all goes well, I will hit the mark and the leg will come off in one quick go. The two men with the swords will quickly cauterise the stump and stop the bleeding; then the bucket of hot water will be used to clean the stump and you'll put a bandage on it. Anything to add?' Ammuna stood waiting for the protest.

The captain raised his eyebrows, then said, 'He'll die one way or another—but this might be the solution. One suggestion—get as much alcohol as we can find and pour it down the man's throat. Have him so drunk the shock of the axe taking his leg off won't be felt by him.'

'Good idea,' Ammuna agreed. 'Go and see to it. Tell the quartermaster you have my permission to sequester all the alcohol you can find.'

It was well into mid-afternoon when everything was ready for the operation. The injured man was singing away merrily after being drowned in alcohol, oblivious of what was going on around him. Ammuna was holding the sharpened axe, testing its blade with his finger. A small log had been prepared for the man's leg, stripped of its bark. The log was brought and gently placed under the leg. Two soldiers were standing by a fire outside the tent tending to two swords, which were red hot. The medical captain marked the point on the leg where Ammuna should strike with a cinder.

'Two soldiers on each hand, if you please,' ordered Ammuna. 'Two soldiers on his right leg. Captain, will you hold his head. One soldier is to hold his injured ankle—and when you see me bringing the axe down, I want you to pull the ankle. If all goes well, the foul leg will be in your hands so careful falling backwards. Right, are we ready?'

The injured man was all smiles in his inebriated state.

Ammuna swung the axe and hit the cinder mark with precision. The soldier holding the ankle pulled and tumbled backwards. The injured drunk screamed loudly. Ammuna removed the embedded axe from the log and the two soldiers with the red-hot swords ran them over the flesh of the cut where the veins and arteries were spouting blood. The medical captain lifted the bucket with the now tepid clean water and poured some over the cauterised wound. The injured man fainted and was out of it.

Ammuna said to the man who'd held the ankle, 'Take that out and bury it.' Instead, he stared in disgust at the amputated leg lying near him. Then the general turned to the captain, 'I think we've done it—is he breathing?' he asked the medical captain.

'Yes sir. Out like an oil lamp, but breathing. He's going to be hurting like the demons when he come to—but I think he'll live.'

'You,' Ammuna shouted at the soldier with the amputated leg, 'Don't just stand there. I said take the leg and dispose of it. Are you deaf?'

'General—thank you. I don't think I could have done it,' said the doctor. 'That was a most accurate swing of the axe, and a real nice cut. I was worried the bone might shatter, but as it turned out—it didn't.'

'It would have if the axe hadn't been sharp.' Ammuna seemed pleased things had turned out successfully. He looked at the bloody scene and said to the captain, 'When we depart from this place in the morning, leave this bloodied log just as it is. Don't clean this area up. If anyone is following us, and they happen to come across this site, I want them to get the wrong idea.' Ammuna smiled to himself at the deception he intended to perpetrate. Part of warfare was mind games played on the enemy to put them off their stride. While the supposed followers were wondering what went on here, they weren't chasing him, and that was his intention.

16
Second Blood

The previous evening, Mokhat's small group of ninety-nine specially picked soldiers had crossed the newly constructed bridge thrown over the rift running through the middle of the village, and at dawn the next day, began following the hoof-prints of Ammuna's column the specialist trackers were ordered to pursue. By mid afternoon, the tracks had led them to the base of the Eastern Silver Mountains, the scene of Ammuna's near annihilation.

'Spread out,' Onasiyas ordered his men. 'I want to know in detail what happened here. You've all been taught how to analyse a battle scene and to deduce what occurred. Let's see you put some of the knowledge into practice.'

Mokhat and Palaiyas were constantly being surprised at what this newly formed *special forces* of the Hittite army had been put through in their training. They were proving to be adept at a variety of tasks, not least in rescue work, for which the village headman had made sure they were overstocked with various luxury supplies in gratitude for their help.

'From what you can see, what do you think happened here?' Mokhat asked Onasiyas playfully, climbing off his horse, putting him in the same spot he'd put his own men.

'I think Ammuna got ambushed by those Hayasa Malda told us about. From what I can see, I would say the earthquake interrupted the engagement and the Hayasa fled in panic.' Onasiyas jumped from his horse and looked squarely at Mokhat.

'And what may I ask colonel, do you base the assumption on?' Palaiyas chipped in playfully, having joined them on the ground.

'Over there I see a mound, which might be a mass grave, although I've no idea how many are in it. I can't see any of Ammuna's soldiers lying around the way I see the bodies of the numerous Hayasa corpses; which suggests Ammuna buried his dead after the Hayasa had fled. The number of Hayasa dead suggests there were a great deal of them and Ammuna was probably getting the worst of it, until the earth tremors interrupted the battle. The Hayasa corpses with Hittite arrows in them mostly lie in a semicircle backing onto the sheer cliff, which is where Ammuna was making his last stand. Some of the boulders have crushed quite a number of the Hayasa, confirming the earthquake happened while they were engaged in battle. The only thing I can't gauge from here is Ammuna's casualties, not without getting closer and examining the mound over there. If I've left anything out, maybe you'd care to add your own thoughts?' Onasiyas had switched the playful probing around and put it back on Mokhat and Palaiyas. He was smiling, knowing he'd made a good job of his preliminary assessment.

'Excellent colonel,' praised Mokhat. 'I must say this special training has set a new standard of soldiering and I'm glad I'm on your side, not fighting against you. I saw what your men did to those Isuwans a number of days back, and I was greatly impressed. Now I see that the same attention to detail has been done in observation training.

'I agree with Prince Mokhat,' added Palaiyas. 'When I get back to Nerik, I'm going to suggest to the king the Kaska set up a similar small specialist force to fight the Azzi.'

'Or the Hittites, if it ever comes to that again,' quizzed Onasiyas.

Palaiyas shrugged his shoulders at the suggestion. He knew it might come to it yet again. The two had been at war many times and were only now in a peaceful phase thanks to Mokhat's close relations with the Hittite king and his consort.

'Not a current problem. Here comes your captain with the report,' Mokhat told Onasiyas. 'Let's see if he agrees with your assessment of what's happened here.'

To Onasiyas' pleasure, the captain parodied Onasiyas' description of the battle almost word for word, only adding he thought the size of the mound indicated to him there were around twenty to fifty corpses inside; no more.

'Thank you captain, that will be all. By the way, you did a good job. Get the men ready to pull out. I want us back on Ammuna's tracks as soon as possible.' Onasiyas was quietly smug at his captain's report.

'How many people did we say Ammuna had with him?' Mokhat asked Palaiyas.

'About two hundred, according to our agent back in Malidiya, and our trackers. Why?' Palaiyas responded.

'If he's lost around fifty, it would make a significant difference to us if we ever catch up with him and have to fight it out with his lot,' Mokhat told him.

Onasiyas remounted his steed and made a gesture with his raised hand in the air, which indicated to his men to reform their column.

Mokhat and Palaiyas mounted their horses and joined Onasiyas at the head of their small column and the scouts continued tracking Ammuna's men down south towards the Lower Puranti River.

As the light faded and the evening loomed up, Mokhat called a halt by the same small stream Ammuna had used as a campsite the previous evening. No matter how well Ammuna had cleaned the site and covered his traces,

Onasiyas' trackers had uncovered evidence of their presence at this spot.

'My men have reopened the hole where they dumped their rubbish, and it seems from their contents, they've got casualties. My man estimates over ten wounded; that's from the dressings he found,' Onasiyas informed Mokhat as they were sitting on a log round the large campfire eating rehydrated fish and fresh bread, baked only yesterday by Malda's villagers.

'That could be a bit of good news for us,' Mokhat replied.

'How so?' enquired Palaiyas, listening from the other side of the log.

'It might slow him down a bit,' answered Mokhat.

'I doubt it,' Onasiyas put in. 'I don't think the general would allow it.'

'Anyway, I want us on our way before dawn tomorrow.' Mokhat had a serious frown on him. 'I want to put on speed on during the whole day. You never know, we might get a sight of him and his rabble. I'm assuming he's heading south to the Puranti to avoid any further possible contact with the roaming Hayasa.'

'It will be done your highness,' responded Onasiyas.

'For the last time colonel, while we're on this mission, please refer to me as *General*. The less information we give out to others who may be listening, the better,' Mokhat told him.

'Yes sir, *general*,' said Onasiyas with the hint of a smile. 'And general, may I recommend we turn in if we're to start early tomorrow.'

'Good idea, colonel. Give the order.'

Even as dawn was breaking, the camp was bustling with activity. Breakfast was being dished out and the horses made ready for a hard days riding.

'Morning generals,' Onasiyas greeted Mokhat and Palaiyas as he sat down to his meal. 'I sent a scout out early before dawn, and he reports we're about two leagues from the Lower Puranti River.'

'Splendid. We should make it in no time,' Mokhat announced. 'Then we'll follow the river and find where Ammuna crossed. He'll head for the Aransah and follow it down to Nineveh. This time, if we push hard, I have high hopes of catching up with him.'

Shortly thereafter, the *special forces* were at full gallop on their mounts, heading the short distance, according to their scout, for the Lower Puranti River. A little later, the two generals and a colonel veered their column leftwards and paralleled the mighty river, still speeding along the rugged shoreline in an attempt to shorten the distance between chasers and chased.

Around mid-morning, scouts came back and reported a strange scene up ahead. When the column reached the spot, the scout showed Onasiyas a bloodied log and the remnants of what looked like a campsite.

Onasiyas looked down at the scene and seemed puzzled; then got off his horse and looked around further; then turned to Mokhat and asked, 'General, what do you make of this?'

Mokhat jumped off his horse and studied the area. 'Could be human or it could be animal; the blood I mean. My problem is, Ammuna is usually so careful to clean his site up before he leaves, to eliminate all traces of his presence. So why leave this mess unless it was intentional. If he did this deliberately, then he's sending a message, albeit a violent one. *I want everyone to search this site*,' he said loudly so everyone could hear. 'See what you can find —report back to the colonel when you've done. Do it quickly so we don't waste too much time here.'

'Colonel, I've been meaning to ask you but I keep forgetting,' said Palaiyas; 'Is Ammuna aware of your *special forces*?'

'No, I'm sure he isn't. Not many people have been told of their existence for obvious reasons. We, the king and a few select individuals, including General Zidanta of course, want them to be a surprise if they ever come across them. Why do you ask?' Onasiyas raised his eyebrows.

Palaiyas waved his hand at the bloodied log, 'I'm wondering why Ammuna would bother to play silly games with us. It doesn't matter whether this blood is animal or human—what matters is that he left it there for us to find.'

'Not us specifically,' replied Onasiyas. 'He's left it there to put off *anyone* following him. I mean he's warning anyone following, if they continue to chase him there will be a bloody ending in store for them. Surely that's the import of this message.'

'Yes, I agree with you there colonel,' said Mokhat. 'That's how I read this message.'

Then, those sent out to scrutinise the campsite, came back to report. The captain approached Onasiyas. 'Sir, beg your pardon, but as far as we can determine, the log is the only salient item here. Everything else seems to have been tidied up.'

'Thank you captain. Get your men mounted and ready to continue the journey,' Onasiyas told him.

'There you go, it's confirmed,' Palaiyas said. 'It's a simple message and we've read it right. I mean we knew before we started we intended to kill the lot of them if we ever got the chance, didn't we?'

'Right, let's get mounted and get on with the chase,' agreed Mokhat. 'I'd like to send the same message to Ammuna if I could. Blood for blood—I'm happy to oblige the rogue.' Mokhat mounted his horse and led the group back out to continue the chase along the shoreline.

By noon, Mokhat's column had made good distance and he stopped the group in a gully for a bite to eat.

Everybody had dismounted and begun to relax, when two scouts came riding back yelling, '*Alarm, alarm, we're being pursued.*'

Everybody grabbed their weapons. Arrows were notched into bows and readied in the direction where the scouts were coming from.

'*Wait for it,*' shouted Onasiyas. '*Let's see who it is first.*'

They didn't have to wait too long as a large group of ponies came thundering at them. The mounted warriors riding them began firing arrows at the *special forces*, who obliged by returning fire far more accurately than their aggressors did. Many fell as the *special forces* arrows brought them down. As their attackers realised a lot more were facing them than the two opponents they had begun to chase, they veered the ponies away in an arc, still firing arrows as they turned and rode back the way they came.

'*Listen to me,*' shouted Onasiyas. 'Get behind anything you can find which might protect you.' Then he shouted at the returning scout, '*Over here you two, report.*'

The scouts came riding over, still grim from their encounter. One of them said, 'Sir, we came across the barbarians as they were heading up north away from the river. Unfortunately their rearguard managed to spot us and we hurried back to warn you.'

'You did right. Now tell me, how many were there?' ordered Onasiyas.

'We estimate, from what we saw, there might be as many as three hundred or more,' said the same scout. 'They must have sent a small bunch after us. They've probably gone back to get more of their pals. If the whole lot comes after us, we might have trouble, sir.'

'Let me worry about that. You both did good, now rejoin your group,' enjoined Onasiyas. He turned to

157

Mokhat, 'Lets mount up and get away from the river. I want to set up an ambush, but in a place of my choosing. I'm fairly certain they're a band of Hayasa; probably part of the mob which had a go at Ammuna.' Not waiting for Mokhat's reply, he shouted to his men, '*Mount up. We're moving inland.*' Then he continued to Mokhat. 'I don't want them to find us where they're expecting to find us. We'll head towards them but a little way inland. I want to find a spot where we have cover and they don't. I want their arrows hitting trees and branches while ours knock them off their horses. We'd better move fast.'

The column sped away from the river but in an arc towards where their attackers were coming from. A little further on, Onasiyas spied a thicket of small trees with bushes; a copse suitable to hide his hundred men. It was a small distance off the route along the river where he expected the enemy to come. His men dismounted and found cover behind the trees, then readied their arrows. Everybody heard them before they could see them, shouting and whooping to frighten their opponents.

'Wait until they're parallel to us, then let them have it. I want rapid fire, volley after volley. If anyone lets them get close to us, I'll have you all on charges at the end of the battle.' Onasiyas smiled at his little joke. '*Here they come. Get ready to fire.*'

The Hayasa warriors came galloping furiously along the shoreline of the Puranti, and as they came parallel to the ambush, they encountered a sudden volley of arrows followed by another volley in short succession, knocking many off their ponies. The little horde came to an abrupt halt, and turned to face where the arrows had come from, sending their own volley of arrows in return. Then they began charging towards where the *special forces* were hiding, firing as they rode, but they encountered a barrage of arrows raining down on their own heads, decimating their numbers. Volley after volley took a heavy toll of the Hayasa horde until fewer than a hundred were left. As their numbers dwindled, their charge floundered and suddenly came to an abrupt halt. They looked bewildered at the ferocity of the fusillade of arrows hailing down on them. Then came more shouting by the remaining Hayasa. A mere fifty survived, and they turned their ponies around and scurried back the way they'd come, leaving their dead, wounded, and dying, to fend for themselves.

Onasiyas came out from behind his tree with a big grin on his face, still holding his bow. 'Well, short and sweet, eh?' he exclaimed loudly. 'I don't think they'll be back.' He turned to his men, who were appearing from behind their trees, and told them, 'Go and finish off the wounded, men and horses. We can't afford to take them with us, and it's not right to leave them in agony.'

'Did we suffer any casualties?' asked Mokhat, joining Onasiyas.

'*Captain!*' shouted Onasiyas. '*Report!*'

His captain and deputy came running up, 'Sir, two wounded; no fatalities….ehm, well no human fatalities. One of our horses got spooked and exposed himself. He was riddled with arrows. Dead I'm afraid.'

'Get our cooks to butcher our dead horse. We might as well have fresh roast meat tonight…save on our rations. What about our men, badly wounded or what?' Onasiyas demanded.

'No sir, a few flesh wounds. An arrow in a calf and a few arrows in arms. Nothing to worry about, they'll mend,' the captain told him.

'Good, gather the men when they've finished despatching the enemy wounded and we'll continue on our way.'

Mokhat, Palaiyas and Onasiyas remounted their horses and went over to have a look at the carnage they'd caused to the Hayasa.

'Poor fools,' said Onasiyas as he looked at the scene. 'They didn't really know what hit them. It'll teach them to tangle with *my* men.' He was looking at over two hundred bodies and a large number of dead ponies strewing the small area of the battle.

'I must say colonel, this is the best evidence of your men's training,' Mokhat told him. 'I've never seen such a devastating shower of arrows thrown at anybody. It's the rapid fire which amazed me—and I dare say, the poor Hayasa as well. Your men fired three for every one fired by the enemy, and believe me the Hayasa are no slouches when it comes to bow and arrow. They're fighting style is similar to the Azzi, with which I'm familiar. Both are masters of the bow and arrow, especially from a horse. Your men are far superior to them. Congratulations colonel, you're right to be proud of them—and I'm honoured to lead them.'

'Thank you general,' Onasiyas answered quietly, but the pride showed on his face.

'What were they doing down here...the Hayasa, I mean,' asked Palaiyas.

Mokhat scowled, 'Probably following Ammuna—trying to have another go at him....then they must have got fed up and abandoned their pursuit...turning up north, heading for home, that's before they spotted our scouts. They thought they'd have a go at an easier prey...and found out to their cost the prey wasn't so easy after all.'

'Hah, you can say that again.' Palaiyas was smiling broadly. 'It'll teach them to mess with our *special forces*.'

'You know what it means?' Mokhat asked of his two companions. 'Ammuna can't be that far ahead. If we hurry, we might catch him up.'

They continued the short journey back to the river and then rode hurriedly along its gullies and inlets into mid-afternoon, still a bit physically hyped, but otherwise subdued after all the fighting.

17
Fishermen

Ammuna and his *loyal* group spent a subdued night at the campsite where he'd used an axe to severe the gangrenous leg of one of his men. On a glorious autumnal morning, as dawn broke the next day, the assemblage quickly breakfasted and were ordered to continue their journey along the gullies and inlets of the right bank of the Upper Puranti River. Around mid-morning on the tenth day of their escape from Hattusas, scouts came hurrying back to report they'd comes across fishermen in boats dragging fishnets in the bountiful Puranti.

'Here's our chance to pick up a ride across the river,' Ammuna told Lawana. 'I thought we'd have to build rafts to get our provisions across, but if we do this right, we'll be able to use these fishermen instead.' Ammuna had told the scouts to be on the lookout for boats he could use to cross the mighty river, and it would seem luck had provided these fishermen.

'If they see our large column sir, I suspect they won't come anywhere near us in case we try to steal their boats,' Lawana responded.

Ammuna smiled at his deputy, 'I had it at the back of my mind, so here's what we'll do. If we hide the main column in the trees, and wait until one of the boats comes close to this side of the river, we may yet outwit these suspicious fishermen. I'll go down and see if I can talk them round, but in case it fails, I'll take two men with bows and arrows to encourage a fisherman to come to me and land on this side of the river. It'll give me a chance to convince him with shekels.

'I'll ask him to pass on a message to his friends, we're not a threat to them. If I dangle a few gold shekels in front of him and ask him to tell all the others, I'll pay handsomely if they'll take my men and provisions across the river on their boats. I'm sure I'll win them over. The horses will have to swim across, but it's the provisions I want to take across in the boats. It'll keep them dry. Anything to add to this course of action?' Ammuna asked Lawana.

'Seems sound enough to me,' agreed his deputy.

'Good, then let's go and execute this little plan of ours.'

Ammuna's column left the shore of the Puranti, veered inland towards the trees to their left, and began to move surreptitiously within the tree line aiming to get parallel to where the boats were casting their nets. The woodland leaves were still on the trees, although at various stages of turning ochre as autumn began to make itself felt on the landscape.

After a short while, the scouts crept back and reported they were now almost parallel with the spot where the boats were drifting their nets in the river. Ammuna left his column and took the two archers he'd selected for their accuracy and went down to the shoreline. The three of them hid behind bushes near to a boat closest to them and waited until it approached their shore.

Shouting at the fisherman in the boat, Ammuna came out of hiding, 'Hey you there, come closer, I want to pay you a few golden shekels to ferry me to the other shore.'

The elderly fisherman was startled by the shouting and looked suspiciously at the lone figure standing on the edge of the river. He stood up and peered along the shoreline to see if others might be hiding so as to steal his boat.

'How do I know you're alone?' asked the cautious fellow, still anxiously casting his eyes along the shoreline.

Ammuna was holding a golden shekel between his thumb and forefinger and letting the fisherman see its glint in the sun.

The fellow in the boat slowly sat down, scratched his greying hair, then picked up his oars and began gently rowing towards Ammuna, but seemingly in no great hurry to get there. He was obviously mesmerised by the glint of gold in Ammuna's outstretched hand. If it was a golden shekel, then it was likely to be more money than he'd see in a while, and all he had to do was ferry the holder of the coin across the river? It was too good an opportunity—if there wasn't a trick involved. The golden shekel would be worth more than his entire fish catch for the whole day.

Ammuna stepped down to the water line as the boat pulled on to the shingles and then gave a sharp whistle through his teeth. The smile vanished from the fisherman as he watched the two archers come into view.

'Damn, I knew it was too good to be true,' he burst out, grabbing his straggly beard, as if it was going to save him.

'Don't mind them,' Ammuna told the angry fisherman. 'They're my insurance you do as I ask of you,' and he threw the golden shekel at the fisherman, who caught it deftly in his right hand. He raised his grey bushy eyebrows, looked to see if it was genuine, then slowly smiled. Maybe he could come out of this with a profit *and* keep his head intact.

'Listen to me carefully,' Ammuna said as he climbed into the boat. 'I have a lot more gold where this came from, and a few might even come *your* way, and to your friends over there,' Ammuna gestured at the other boats further away. 'All I want from you and your friends is for you to ferry some men and bundles across from this shore to the other side.'

163

The fisherman slowly sat down still holding the gold coin possessively, listening to this imposing man, still stroking his grey beard with his free brawny hand. The fisherman had scrutinised Ammuna carefully, and concluded he was military. Taking his age into account, probably a senior officer. The appearance of the two archers confirmed his suspicion. His mind was working overtime, trying to find the downside to this proposition. If it was a trap, it was a weird one. 'How many men are we talking about,' he finally asked.

'Around a hundred and eighty.' Ammuna thought he might as well lay it out for the man.

'And you want me to ask my friends to help ferry them over there,' he cast his head at the other shore.

'That's it. Simple job, but it might take a number of crossings—and likely to take time, maybe the whole day. What I can promise you is, you'll all be well paid for the service.' Ammuna could see the man wasn't convinced. 'Look, when all the boats are lined up on this shore, I'll give you the money in advance—three golden shekels per boat. You have my word on it as a general.'

'You're not invading anybody are you?' asked the fisherman. 'I wouldn't want to help an invader, even if it costs me my life.'

'No, we're not invaders. We're travellers. We're on our way to Wassukanni to see the king, and we need your help to cross this river so I can keep our provisions and ourselves dry.' Ammuna said this as gently as possible and with a smile. He could see it was going to be difficult to allay the man's fears.

Just then, Lawana appeared from behind a bush, clambering down the embankment towards Ammuna, to find out why it was taking so long for Ammuna to return.

'You might as well bring the men down here,' Ammuna told him. 'I'm going to go in this man's boat over to talk to his friends to make them an offer, if you'll take me to them?' Ammuna looked at the fisherman to see if he would comply.

The old fisherman slowly nodded and picked up his oars and began rowing into the middle of the river towards the other fishermen. Whatever happened now, he'd be safer with his friends. The other fishermen had stopped fishing and were peering in Ammuna's direction from their boats, trying to fathom what was going on in the distance, keeping a close eye on their fellow fisherman. There were nine boats spread out in a loose formation along the river, mostly upstream from Ammuna. Now they were all pulling their nets in. They had seen Ammuna's other men arriving at the far riverbank and sensing something disruptive was happening which might pose a danger to them, they began to pull their nets in for safety.

As Ammuna's boat came within hailing distance, the fisherman in his boat began to shout to his friends and companions, all this man wanted was to hire their boats for the day. He'd convinced himself this might be on the level and he could earn a nice bit of gold if he played this game out to the end. He'd concluded, if this military man had wanted to rob him, or kill him, he'd have done it by now and taken his boat. Since he hadn't, surely it meant it was probably alright.

Curious boats finished pulling in their fishing nets and began to arrive one by one, meeting, and bumping each other; and then more boats joined them until all but one was gathered around Ammuna's boat. Raised voices were asking questions, creating a din in the middle of the river. *Was this on the level? How much should they charge? How many were to be ferried? How long would it take? Would they have to lose the day's fishing?*

In the middle of this small flotilla, Ammuna finally stood up in his boat and ask to be heard. '*Quiet!*' he had to shout at them to get their attention. 'Now, that's better. Good fishing folk—I'm here to help your finances *NOT* to rob you or do you any harm. If I wanted to do you harm, I could have got my archers do away with the lot of you and then had my men swim out and take your boats for free. But that's not how I want to do this. I'm an honourable general and I have no quarrel with you—all I want to do is cross this fine river of yours while remaining dry. You have the boats and I have the money.' At this point, he put his hand to his pouch at his belt and jingled the gold coins. 'I'm willing to pay each one of you three golden shekels for the hire of you boats for the day. That's my offer—what say you? Do we have a deal?' he sat down and waited for the noise to start, and when it didn't—he was surprised. The final boat arrived with a bump, having finally resolved to join his friends.

After watching their astounded faces, and seeing them nod their heads, his own boatman cleared his throat and began, '...Ahem!...Sir, I'm speaking for all of us gathered here now. The offer you have just made is far more than we could make if we fished for a whole week. There's no point in us discussing this or trying to bargain with you. We accept you offer without reservations.'

Ammuna knew his offer was generous and he'd expected this reaction. He knew men and most of their foibles and weaknesses. Becoming a general in the tough Hittite army had been two educations rolled into one, how to make war, and of knowing your men and how they would react. Motivation and incentive were his unspoken maxims, and the use of both had made him commander of the Hittite army—until the disaster of the civil war six years ago.

'Right then, let's get over to where my men are waiting and we'll begin ferrying my men across the river. As a sign of good will, I'll pay you your money in advance, but a word of warning. Should any of you try to make a run for it down river, I'll order my archers to bring you down. That's so we understand each other. Now, head for the spot I indicate.' Ammuna pointed at the spot where he'd boarded his boat.

Lawana stood on the shore with a broad grin on his face as the little flotilla arrived. His deputy greeted him when Ammuna jumped from the boat to dry land, 'I knew you'd do it, sir. If anyone could convince them it would be you.'

'Thank you kindly for those words.' There was a hint of sarcasm in his tone. 'But now could you organise our men and the provisions for the crossing. And while you're at it, make sure we fill up on water.' Ammuna turned and waited for the fishermen to come ashore and surround the general.

Lawana hadn't mean to be sarcastic in congratulating his general, but he could see Ammuna had taken it as such. 'Oh well...' he muttered to himself, and went to organise the ferry crossing.

Meanwhile, Ammuna was handing out the three golden shekels per boatman. When he'd finished with the payments, he raised his hands and said, 'If we put five of my men in each boat per crossing, then with nine boats we should make four crossings back and forth. Add two more crossing per boat for the provisions and it'll make six crossing in total per boat. We're at noon right now and I estimate it'll take us the rest of the afternoon to finish the job. Any questions?'

His own boatman, who'd turned into the spokesman for the group responded, 'Yes, I can see you are indeed a general, sir. You've worked all this out with military precision. I don't think there are any problems with what you've laid out. We ought to get started as soon as possible. The sooner we start, the sooner we finish.'

Lawana came back leading the dismounted men, who in turn were leading their horses. He was saying loudly so all could hear, 'Take your blankets and possessions with you on the boat. Five men per boat. Line up—I want nine orderly queues along the shoreline. Put nine equally distributed lots of provisions at the end of each line—they can go last. Get your horses ready—they'll swim with your boat. That way they won't get too frightened. One man will stay behind with the provisions and he'll accompany the provisions across and make sure the pack horses swim alongside the provision boats. Now let's get to it.'

Ammuna was standing alone on the riverbank watching Lawana organise the ferry crossings. 'Colonel, a moment,' Ammuna shouted at his deputy.

Lawana tuned and walked to his commander, 'Yes sir?'

'Colonel, make sure the brat and her non-com friend goes in your boat. I want *you* to keep an eye on her while we're crossing this river. This is our most valuable cargo—I don't want anything to happen to her, not now we're so close to our goal.' Ammuna tried to soften the order with a smile.

Lawana looked puzzled momentarily at this new order, but then replied, 'Yes sir. I'll look after the princess personally.' He's afraid we'll lose our cash cow, thought Lawana.

Ammuna returned to watching the crossings, a smile playing on his face while the wind tousled his hair. Then he turned his attention to the east as he realised the wind had picked up. Over a short period, as Ammuna watched the sky, the weather had become somewhat ominous as swift moving clouds came in from the north-east, blotting out the sun. The wind began to blow up more and Ammuna went down to his own boatman to seek his advice. He'd beached his boat back on this shore from his first ferry trip. Since he was local, he would be familiar with the weather conditions around this area.

'What do you think? Is this thing going to get worse?' he cast his arm in the direction of the clouds.

'It could,' replied the old man, scratching at his beard. 'It's autumn and the weather turns about this time. If there is a storm, then it'll only be a small one. Later on, they get much worse.'

'So....there shouldn't be any problems with the crossings? We can go ahead as planned?' Ammuna was scrutinising the old man's face carefully.

'If it blows up to a point where it endangers the crossing, I'll let you know, and we'll call it off until it blows over. My guess is it will be all right. Let's keep going and see what happens. I won't put your men in any danger, or my people's boats, I can assure you. What bothers me is the storm's swift moving. Probably alright though.'

Ammuna seemed somewhat relieved. 'Well, good. I'll rely on you to keep an eye out for the weather. As soon as you think there might be a problem, give me a shout and I'll stop the operation until it calms down.'

In the middle of the afternoon when half of the men had been ferried across the river, the old fisherman called to Ammuna to halt the operation. The wind had picked up further and was now blowing quite hard, making it difficult to row. Some of the boats had been forced a considerable distance downriver, although they'd landed on the other shore as they'd intended—then had to drag the boats back to where they should have landed. The crossing had gotten dangerous.

18
Across the River

'We're going to have to wait until it quietens down, sir,' the old fisherman man told Ammuna. 'I'm thinking maybe we should get under the trees. My nose tells me rain is coming. From the looks of it, it'll be pouring down soon.'

'*Colonel!*' Ammuna yelled for his deputy, having to shout over the rising wind. When Lawana came, Ammuna told him, 'Get the men and the provisions left on this side of the river, back under the trees. My local adviser tells me it's going to rain hard. Signal the people on the other shore they should find shelter and we'll resume the ferrying later on. For now, let's batten down. Oh, and make sure the horses are hobbled. Don't want them running off in a panic if the thunder begins.'

'Yes sir.' Lawana hurried off to carry out the orders.

The soldiers who'd already been transferred to the far side, understood immediately when they saw Lawana's signals. It didn't take a lot of brainpower to see that a storm was brewing and they needed to find shelter.

Those waiting to cross were instructed to head for the trees. There they tried to build some sort of cover from the tents in the nearby pile of provisions.

When the first droplets splattered the ochre leaves, many of the autumn leaves simply slipped from the trees and fluttered damply down to the forest floor. They were ready to drop off anyway, and the rain merely accelerated the process. As the rain increased, so did the denuding of the branches, leaving little or no cover. Those under the cover of the leather tents had to make room for those who had felt the leaf canopy would be sufficient against a little rainfall.

The rain turned into a deluge, which proceeded to flow down into the mighty Puranti, creating a torrent. This surged downstream, making any further crossings absolutely impossible.

Ammuna sat the deluge out inside his tent in the company of his officers and the old fisherman, all nice and dry.

Abruptly the old man went out into the downpour to inspect the river flow, and came back soaked, shaking his head. As he resumed his seat, he groaned, 'I'm sorry general, as I said earlier, from what I can see, there'll be no more crossings today. We'll have to wait for the river to quieten down and it mean suspending everything till tomorrow morning at the earliest.'

'One of the things I've learnt in my lifetime is, it's no use fighting Mother Nature,' Ammuna philosophised to his local advisor. 'If the river is refusing to allow us to cross, then so be it—we'll wait till tomorrow.' Ammuna turned to his officers and said, 'Go and tell our men on this side of the river to make camp for the night. Send a signal to the people on the other side of the river to do the same. Those on the other side will have to make the best of it without their equipment. It won't be the first time they've had to sleep out in the open. Oh, and make sure the brat is safe. By the way, where is she?'

'She's safe and dry—she's in the non-com's tent being looked after by the non-com she's taken a fancy to,' responded Lawana. Then he looked at the two captains and one lieutenant and nodded towards the tent exit flap. 'Right men, let's move it,' he said to the three officers. 'We're not finished yet.'

Ammuna put an affable hand on the old fisherman's shoulder and said, 'You and your friends are welcome to join us in our meagre food rations, and you'll have a dry place in our tents till the morning, if you wish.'

'Thank you general,' replied the old man. 'I think you'll find we can supply better food than you can. The fish we caught before you arrived, we can't take them to market now, so we might as well share them with you—if you're allowed to eat fish, that is.'

Ammuna beamed at this suggestion. 'That's just the kind of good news I like to hear. I personally love a good fish done on a stick around a campfire. I'm sure my men will jump at the chance of fresh fish. In addition, to reinforce our good intentions to you, I'm prepare to pay you for the whole catch so you don't lose out monetarily. Would it suite you?'

The old fisherman looked surprised—then seemed to feel hurt his gift had been transformed into a transaction. Finally, he smiled and said, 'I meant the fish as a gift, but being only poor fishermen, I'm not in a position to refuse payment. My old woman, back home, would tongue-lash me if I did.' He spread out his hands as if to say, I'm at your mercy, and smiled broadly.

'Then it's agreed. I thank you for your offer of a gift, but I insist you take *my* payment offer as being the more sensible one. Would ten golden shekels cover the catch?' Ammuna reached into his pouch and counted out the sum. He'd began to feel as if the payment for the little brat was only a small ride away, and the large sum Artatama was going to pay him was almost within his grasp, so he was feeling somewhat beneficent. Also, he hadn't shared with anyone the extra half a million promised by the agent in the forest—and he intended no one should know about it, ever.

'It is most generous—and yes, it will more than cover the fish catch.' The old man took the proffered coins and put them in his waist pouch. 'Let me go get the fish right now. I'll share the money out with my friends in the morning.' With that, he rose and went out to get the fish from the nets.

The captain came back to report, 'As you can see sir, the rain has eased and looks like stopping soon. I've got people trying to get a couple of fires going down by the river. I thought you might want to join us.'

'Good,' said Ammuna. 'Save me a seat and I'll be down soon. Oh captain...., make sure latrines are dug and the horses are looked after. And get the men to put up the tents properly and in an orderly military fashion.'

'Yes sir,' the captain replied and left.

The rain finally ceased and they were all comfortably ensconced around a couple of roaring campfires drying themselves out, and roasting their gutted fish on spit-sticks. Lawana pointed to the far bank on the other side of the river and said to Ammuna sitting by his side, 'Looks like our other men are having a bit of a sing song over there, trying to keep their spirits up.'

'Did they get their share of the fish? Have you been over there?' Ammuna asked ignoring Lawana's other comment.

'No I haven't crossed the river yet,' Lawana told him, 'but one of the captains is over there. We managed to get a couple of the fishermen to row across with some fish and tents. They were pulled downriver a fair distance, but they eventually got to our men. The captain's organised everything, as it should be. They've now got food and shelter for the night.'

'Well done! But....I've been meaning to ask—what news of the seventeen wounded? How are they progressing?' Ammuna asked his deputy. He'd refused the cooks offer to roast his fish for him and was concentrating on turning the vertical spit himself. This modest activity was one of those little memories which took him back to his younger carefree days as a junior officer when he was first stationed in Nesa on the lower Marassantiya River.

'They all seem to be recovering nicely, according to the captain treating them,' responded Lawana. 'They're over there at the other fire.'

'Good! I'm glad to hear that. What about the fellow whose leg I chopped off?' Ammuna took a bite out of his fish.

'Him too, general. He's still worried, I'm told, he won't manage to get by without his leg, but the captains working on him to allay his fears. And a couple of his pals are making a wooden leg for him, but he swears he's never going to use it.' Lawana was gently picking at his fish, taking the skin off and nibbling at the flesh, watching out for the bones—he hated the bones in a fish but enjoyed the taste of the flesh of the fish. 'Changing the subject sir, how far do you estimate we've more to travel?' asked Lawana.

'Once we've crossed this river, I would guess another eight days or so. It's about two days down to the Aransah River, and then all we do is follow the river down to Nineveh. Why do you ask?'

'No specific reason—just to get an idea of how long this thing's going to take,' responded Lawana. 'I'm trying to gauge how the men will last out. It's a strain on them you know.'

'Of course it's a strain on them. If they were civilians, I might be concerned, but as such, they're soldiers and expect this sort of thing as usual in their lives—lots of hardship....uncertainty. It goes with the job. But it shows the mark of a good officer you're concerned for their welfare. That's why you're my deputy, colonel. That's why I picked you. You're hard when you have to be, and concerned when things are a bit tough.' Ammuna sat munching his fish with a satisfied smile playing on his rugged features.

Lawana sat by his side picking at the roasted fish, thinking, *that's easy for him to say*. On the other side of Ammuna, the old fisherman was licking his fingers, cleaning them of the fish oil. 'I think it's time for me to turn in,' said the old man stifling a yawn. 'I'm not as young as you military men and we have work to do tomorrow. If I could be shown where I'm to sleep, I will say goodnight.' He stood and stretched himself.

'Go over to our sergeant over there; you're sleeping in his tent—he'll show you which one it is,' Lawana told the old man pointing at the non-com in question. 'See you in the morning, and sleep well.'

'Thanks for all your help,' added Ammuna, 'and goodnight.'

Yawning, the old man made his way to the non-com, who led him away to the tent.

Early the next day, the dawn cacophony from the riverside-feathered fauna woke the camp, and after breakfast, the soldiers began to gather at the river, reforming the nine lines as before, ready to board the fishermen's boats for the ride across. The river had lost most of its torrential violence overnight, the result of the storm, but was still running a bit faster than the previous day.

It took most of the morning to complete the ferrying, and for the final boat to reach the other side carrying the provisions. There had been only one mishap, when a boat was swamped carrying five men and the accompanying rowing fisherman. It happened when a horse begun to tug at its rein while it was swimming by the boat containing its rider. The horse decided it didn't want to be pulled by the rein and then panicked when the soldier wouldn't let go. It jerked back on the rein; as a result, the soldier was pulled over the stern into the river, capsizing the boat. Other boats rushed to the rescue and the capsized boat was pulled to shore and set to rights. The outcome was five wet soldiers and one dripping fisherman. Ammuna gave the man an extra golden shekel, which seemed to please him no end. He offered to do it again, in jest. This prompted the other fishermen to ask jokingly, if they could capsize their boats for an extra shekel.

Finally, Lawana came and reported all the men and provisions were across.

'How's the brat?' Ammuna asked him.

'She's quiet. No problem at all,' his deputy responded.

'Tell the non-com looking after her he's due for a large bonus if he gets her to Nineveh in one piece,' Ammuna told Lawana.

'Yes sir,' Lawana replied.

Ammuna then turned to the old fisherman and asked him, 'Well, it's mid morning now and we're off. Are your people satisfied with our little business?' He was watching his *loyal* mercenaries mount their horses and reform for the next phase of the journey south. 'By the way, you do have a name, do you?' he added.

'Yes general, I'm called Harmi—and yes, all my people are more than satisfied. You've been very generous. If you're coming back this way, look us up and we'll take you across the other way.' The old man smiled with hope he and his friends might earn more easy money. 'By the way, let me give you a friendly warning in my turn. Be careful and steer clear of any nomads you see between the Puranti and the Aransah as they're likely to try to rob you of everything, and probably try to kill you.'

'I think we can deal with any nomads, but if we come back this way, we'll take you up on your offer. In the mean time, you could do me a favour. If any others come after us in the next few days asking to be ferried across—don't do it. There's a bunch of criminals following us hoping to pick us off one by one. If you want our business again, you would do well to avoid these thugs. They'll rob you if they can. Do I make myself clear?' Ammuna put on his serious face, before breaking into a smile. 'Well goodbye and good fishing.' He climbed on his horse and wheeled the column off to the south, heading for the Aransah River.

'*Goodbye general,*' shouted Harmi.

Ammuna gave one last farewell wave to the fishermen and then led his *loyal mercenaries* south-east at a rapid pace into the noonday scrubland of a near desert.

'*Goodbye general,*' shouted Harmi again exuberantly, still surrounded by his friends, all frantically waving farewell to the disappearing column. It had been a most profitable encounter for the boatmen.

19
Mokhat and Harmi

Following the deadly encounter with the Hayasa warriors when Onasiyas' *special forces* acquitted themselves excellently in battle, the little column was hit by a drenching storm, which caught Mokhat's men entirely unawares. It was the same rainstorm which had interrupted Ammuna's river crossing.

In the afternoon, the *special forces* were congratulating themselves with the brilliant display of soldiery, and the lack of casualties they'd incurred, so the select band of men hardly noticed the clouds, or the dulling of the sky. They'd thought nothing of the fading light, until the first drops of rain fell–and then it turned into a deluge.

They quickly unbundled their greased leather sheets from the packhorses, tied their single ropes between two trees, throwing the leather sheets over the ropes and deploying their quick tents for shelters. They sat under their tents still grinning over their victory even though most of them were soaking wet.

'Where did that come from?' Palaiyas demanded of Mokhat, as if he were somehow able to give a sensible answer to a dim-witted question. Without waiting for a response, he continued, 'One moment we're dry; the next moment we're swimming.'

Mokhat sat in between Onasiyas and Palaiyas but was looking at Onasiyas with a smile. 'I'm nominally in charge of this column, but I'm *not* in charge of the weather,' he told Onasiyas, pointing at Palaiyas. 'Next he'll have me blamed for putting rivers in the wrong place so we're forced to cross them.'

Onasiyas shrugged at this bit of playfulness. 'I'm a mere colonel, and as such outranked by your wit. However, your complaints ought to be directed to the Lord Taru; I'm not sure he'd find your comments as amusing.'

This sudden turn of seriousness took Palaiyas by surprise and he put his hand up to Mokhat as a sign they should stop their humorous exchange. 'I'm sorry colonel; I meant no disrespect to our Lord. You're right; we shouldn't be complaining after our recent victory.' Palaiyas quickly changed the subject to take the conversation in a different direction.

'How far ahead is Ammuna right now?' Mokhat asked Onasiyas, taking the talk to practical matters.

'Well, I'm still working on the assumption we're one day behind, so I would guess he's crossed the river by now. Probably built a couple of rafts and used them to ferry the provisions across. The men and horses would of course swim for it. If we could find the rafts, it would make our crossing easier; but knowing Ammuna, he'll have destroyed them.' Onasiyas relaxed and looked outside, noticing the rain had ceased. He got to his feet and walked out beyond the tent flaps. 'Better get going, the rain has stopped.'

'We're going to lose the light in a little while,' commented Palaiyas. 'This time of year, it begins to get darker more quickly. Maybe we should get closer to the river and make camp for the night.'

'What do you think, colonel?' Mokhat asked Onasiyas.

'Yes, now you mention it, I agree. No point in fouling ourselves in the gullies in the dark—not with hostiles in the vicinity.'

'Oh, I think the Hayasa are well gone,' Palaiyas ventured. 'I'd guess they'll avoid us like the underworld deities we seem to be to them.'

'If I see any more of these wild men, I will send them to the underworld, I promise you…,' added Onasiyas.

'I've had a thought,' intervened Palaiyas. 'Those Hayasa; I'll wager they were following Ammuna when our scouts came across them. If that's the case, then we might have saved Ammuna from getting another hammering from them. What do you think?' Palaiyas looked at Mokhat to confirm his idea.

'No, I think the scouts reported them as heading up north, away from the river. They must have followed Ammuna till then, and finally abandoned him. Mind you, don't forget that Ammuna has the King's daughter,' Mokhat reminded Palaiyas. 'Her safety is our main concern. If we saved Ammuna's skin by taking on the Hayasa, then we did a good job, despite the fact that I'd like to see Ammuna rot in the deepest dungeon. But as for your earlier suggestion of getting us closer to the river; will we find such sturdy trees down there for our tent ropes?' Mokhat asked Palaiyas. 'Why not stay where we are? That way we don't have to put the tents up twice. I mean, we're already set up for the night. All we need is the campfires.' Mokhat looked at Onasiyas for corroboration.

Palaiyas shrugged, 'Suits me fine. So, we'll camp where we are then. I'll get the non-coms to dig the latrines and bed the horses down for the night,' Palaiyas added, getting to his feet and going out to give the orders.

Onasiyas joined Palaiyas. 'I'll come with you and get them to start a couple of fires going.'

Mokhat was left by himself in the tent, looking out at the sky, trying to divine the next move the weather was going to make. A little while later Mokhat got up and stood outside looking at the improvised campsite.

Palaiyas came up and told him, 'I've organised the sentries for the night. Three in depth all round the camp in three shifts. I don't want those Hayasa sneaking up on us during the night, looking for revenge.'

'Good idea. I've been thinking it might be an idea to send out scouts during the night. If there's more of these wild men, and I suspect there are, they might be planning to return the favour—I mean trying to ambush us tomorrow, the way we did to them today. What do you think?' Mokhat asked his friend.

'I don't think they'll be back, but I suppose we'd better play safe,' replied Palaiyas.

Just then, Onasiyas joined them. 'We'll have hot food in a short while,' he told them both.

'Colonel,' Mokhat began, '...can you arrange for four scouts to go out during the night and make sure the way to the east is clear of hostiles. I don't want those wild men setting *us* an ambush.'

'No problem—let them eat first and then I'll talk to my best scouts. I must say that if I were the Hayasa, I'd be tempted to set a trap for us—especially if their band is bigger than the lot we picked off earlier. There must be more of them from what I saw of the battle site where they attacked Ammuna and his cronies the other day.'

'Well, we'll soon find out when morning comes,' responded Mokhat.

At dawn, the *special forces* camp stirred vigorously and cooks rapidly made breakfast so they could quickly get on with chasing Ammuna and his gang. The scouts reported they saw large fires on both sides of the river during the early part of the night—which tended to reinforce Mokhat's belief that the Hayasa were still in the neighbourhood. Unbeknown to him, they were Ammuna's fires on either side of the river. Had Mokhat had any inkling Ammuna was within striking distance, he would have pushed his horses through the night to get to grips with his enemy.

'The scouts estimate the fires were somewhere around eight leagues to the east,' Onasiyas told Mokhat and

Palaiyas. 'Much further than any threat of ambush might pose. What do you think, general?'

'Nevertheless, I want to go cautiously this morning,' Mokhat told him. 'Send scouts out well ahead and have them dig out any threat of an ambush. I don't want the wild men catching us unawares.'

So it was, the column began the pursuit again, but the pace was at a canter, and by mid-morning, they found themselves only four leagues further east along the riverbank.

'Can't we go any faster?' complained Palaiyas. 'I feel like we're on a morning outing rather than a serious chase.'

'What do you think, colonel?' Mokhat asked Onasiyas. 'Can we pick up the pace?'

'The scouts haven't found anything so far. No sign of the Hayasa. However, I would urge caution for the next few leagues.' Onasiyas pointed at the horse-trampled path in front of them. 'There's recent signs of many horses travelling along the river bank and I believe something is going on here which warrants us to be on our guard. Until we cross the river, I advise we move at this pace.'

'There's your answer,' Mokhat told Palaiyas. 'I'm minded to follow the expert in this matter.'

Palaiyas shrugged and resigned himself to the slow pace. He was bored and fancied getting to grips with another enemy—*any* enemy. The excitement of the previous day's battle had roused his fighting instinct, and he was ready for another round of invigorating belligerency. It was the latent Mycenaean in him who was never far from the surface. Mycenaeans were trained from childhood to fight and fight until they *won*.

By late noon, they had travelled five leagues alongside the river shore, skirting around the various gullies protruding from the riverbank, until Mokhat called a food halt. While they were munching on dried rations, Mokhat took the opportunity to tell Onasiyas, sitting by him, to pick out ten of his best men. 'Colonel, when we manage to catch Ammuna, as I'm sure we will, I want you and your ten picked men to ignore everything happening around you and cut your way through to where the king's daughter is being held—and make it your priority to rescue her at *all* costs. It would be a disaster if they didn't succeed in freeing Asmunikal. You're to prevent any harm coming to her. Palaiyas and myself will deal with Ammuna and his men, with the help of the rest of your people, of course. Your top priority is to safeguard the king's daughter. Is that understood?'

Onasiyas nodded and said, 'Understood, sir. I had the same plan in mind from the outset, but it's best now you've made it an official order. I would consider our trip a disaster if any harm came to the Princess. Just then, Palaiyas returned to camp ahead of the scouts.

Palaiyas was in a constant frown and kept riding out in front of the scouts, returning with them each time, shaking his head. This had got on Onasiyas' nerves and he now mentioned it to Mokhat.

'What's the matter with him,' Onasiyas asked, pointing to the once again returning Palaiyas. 'Why's he so fidgety today?'

'For that, my dear colonel, you have to know the nature of the Ahhiyawans.' Then Mokhat laughed, as he noticed Onasiyas' scowl. 'Excuse me colonel, I keep forgetting your Ahhiyawan yourself. Well, then you must understand better than most how General Palaiyas feels. The battle with the Hayasa yesterday heated up his blood and he's itching for another fight—but surely I don't need to tell you this.'

'Is that it? As simple as that, heh? Sorry general, ...I thought it might be something I'd missed. I was afraid General Palaiyas had noticed something awry in what we were doing, and would come back and question my competence.'

'Oh, I see....well rest assured all's as it should be,' Mokhat pacified the worried colonel. 'As for your competence....let me be the judge. From what I've seen so far, I judge I've seldom come across a more competent colonel of the Hittite Army than yourself. Putting this special group together was a stroke of genius—and I congratulate you once again for doing so. Let me ask you, though....why are you feeling this insecure? It's the first time I've seen you agitated like this.'

Onasiyas scratched his beard and rode on silently for a short time before replying. 'You know general, I may be suffering from what General Palaiyas is suffering from, and I've only just noticed it.....thanks to you.' He smiled sheepishly and continued, 'My boys have been in two serious fights. Once with the Isuwans—and now with the Hayasa. Both times, they've acquitted themselves in a manner which makes me proud of them. I suppose after yesterday's fight, I'm itching for another fight just like General Palaiyas.' He burst out in a broad chuckle and gestured his hands in an outward motion as if to say, sorry but that's how it was.

Mokhat smiled and accepted the explanation. He'd guessed as much. Sometimes his former training as a priest became a useful tool. He'd spent years learning the nature of how people thought, how they acted and reacted to various calamities or joys in their lives. It had given him an enormous advantage when dealing with all sorts of individuals. Now he'd seen his two colleagues behave in a heightened state of agitation following their battle with the wild men. He knew it was a natural reaction following a fight, yet he was continually amazed how little people knew of themselves—how automatic their behaviour was without any self-analysis.

'If we've finished here, I suggest we move on. We can't be far from where Ammuna's crossed the river. I'm curious to see if he's left the rafts for us to use.' Mokhat made to mount his horse, followed by Onasiyas and the other men. He raised his voice so he could be heard, '*Let's move out!*'

Mokhat led, picking up the pace, speeding them into a strong canter and then a gallop.

Not a league further, Palaiyas came riding back alone, waving to Mokhat, and he joined him, both slowing to a canter. 'I think we've found Ammuna's crossing point. It's a couple of leagues further up river. I've left the scouts up there watching a group of fishermen on the far bank sitting round a fire, roasting fish. From what I could see of this side of the riverbank, there's been a lot of recent activity involving horses and men. It looks to me as if Ammuna's got the fishermen to help him cross the river. They must have used the fishermen's boats—sure saves on building rafts I suppose.'

'Good man!' exclaimed Mokhat. 'Finally, we're closing in on him. This is the closest we've been to Ammuna and his gang. Any idea when this happened? Yesterday? Today?'

'Sorry, the tracks are fresh—that's all I can say. But we should do the same, get the fishermen to ferry us across. If we do this right now, we might catch up with Ammuna. What do you think?'

'I agree,' said Mokhat. He raised his hand and ordered the column back to a full gallop, following Palaiyas, who'd swung his horse round in his eagerness had spurred it on ahead.

A while further on, they came across one of their scouts, and Mokhat halted the column near the man so he could be briefed.

'The fishermen are on the far bank round the bend in the river, sir,' the scout reported to Mokhat and Onasiyas.

'How many are there?' Onasiyas asked the scout.

'I counted nine boats lined up on the far shore,' replied the scout. 'There's nine men sitting round the camp fire.'

'Good!' Mokhat turned to Onasiyas, 'Colonel, can you get four or five men to swim the river and have a talk to those fishermen. Ask them nicely, but make sure they all end up on this side of the river.'

'No problem.' Onasiyas moved his horse over closer to his men and had a chat with them.

Five men dismounted and handed their reins over to their fellow soldiers, then went quietly down to the river and slid into the water, breast stroking quickly into the middle of the fast flowing river. The rest of the column dismounted and walked their horses stealthily a little distance inland away from the riverbank, then continued until they came opposite the fishermen. There they watched as the five men sneaked out of the water and climbed surreptitiously up the far bank then circled round to come on the fishermen from the south.

The fishermen were trapped against the river and looked on nervously as the wet darkly dressed men came towards them, fingering their daggers. They had their bows over their shoulders and smiled menacingly at the group round the fire.

'Now kind sirs,' said the non-com leading his group. 'Don't be alarmed....we simply want a little chat with you.'

'Who are you....sneaking up on simple fishermen?' voiced an old man hesitantly, clearly the spokesman for the group.

'Someone who means you no harm, unless we're provoked. We simply need a few answers to our questions....and maybe the use of your boats.'

The old man shrugged at this and gave in to the inevitable. 'I can see you're in a position to bully us....so we have little choice but to go along with what you've in mind, although I do protest at the style of your approach.'

'I apologise on behalf of my general, but we've reason to believe you've just ferried a gang of renegade soldiers across this river. Am I right?'

'Renegades? What do you mean renegades? They looked less of a group of renegades than you do. At least they had proper uniforms on.....not the bandit appearance you seem to present.' The old man finished the sentence more subdued than the bravado with which he'd started speaking. There was still the remnant boldness of Ammuna's golden shekels in his thoughts and he was half-afraid these *bandits* might rob them of their good fortune. He'd never had so much money in a whole lifetime of hard toil...and he was mightily afraid he might lose it.

'I think you'd better have a word with my commanding officer. Come along now, into your boats. We're going across to the other side of the river. My general will explain everything to you. Come along, get moving,' the five tough young men ushered the older fishermen into their boats—the non-com going with the old man in his. The two leading boats had a *special* soldier as a passenger and the three trailing boats also contained a soldier each to ensure they all stayed together till they got to the other shore.

Having beached on the northern side, the old fisherman was met by Mokhat, who nodded at the old man. 'I'm sorry we had to do it this way, but if I know Ammuna, he'll have told you a bunch of lies about not helping anybody following him...am I right?'

'What's all this about?' asked the old man. 'Why have you treated us like this?' he blustered indignantly, but with an undertone of caution now he saw all the rest of Mokhat's men. They looked extremely intimidating in their dark blue outfits.

'Come over here,' Mokhat invited the old man. 'Let's sit and I'll explain my men's behaviour. Your friends can listen in and make up their own minds.'

Mokhat sat on the embankment, as did the rest of the fishermen, loosely surrounded by Onasiyas' men. Mokhat got on his feet and faced the fishermen. 'Let me introduce myself. I'm General Mokhat of the Hittite army. These are my men, General Palaiyas and Colonel Onasiyas and his men. We're chasing the kidnappers of the king's daughter, abducted from the royal palace by the renegade General Ammuna and his gang of cut-throats.'

The look on the fishermen's faces showed incredulity and disbelief.

'I see you have a hard time grasping what I'm saying. Tell me—was there a young girl with the lot you ferried across the river?' Mokhat waited for a response.

'Who said we ferried anyone across the river?' asked the old man.

'Let me put it to you bluntly...since you want to play games. My men are all experienced trackers—we're an élite outfit from the Hittite army, hence our dress, but it's clear as if they were standing here in front of me; you ferried around two hundred men across this river recently, either yesterday or early today. It's pointless denying it. So, let me ask you again. Was there a young girl amongst the gang you ferried across—you could hardly miss a young girl?' Now there was an angry frown on Mokhat's face as he waited for an answer.

Hesitantly the old man said, 'What if there was? Is it a crime to take a general's daughter across?'

'So that's how they passed her off, did they? Ammuna's daughter. Let me tell you, and you'd better listen well. Yes, Ammuna *was* a general in the Hittite army, but the young girl was the kidnapped daughter of the king in Hattusas—*not* Ammuna's child. Turn out your pouches— lets have a look at why you're protecting him.'

That order caught all the fishermen's attention. 'I knew you were all robbers,' blurted out the old fisherman angrily.

Taken aback, Mokhat shouted, 'I don't want you stupid money. All I want is to see how much he paid you to side with him.' Mokhat indicated to his men to collect their pouches and empty them on the ground in front of each of their owners.

Eventually he stood looking at the little piles of three golden shekels before each fisherman. 'So that's what it takes to buy your loyalty?' Mokhat spat out with contempt. 'Well don't just stare at it. I said I didn't want your stupid money. Pick it up and put them back in your pouches. They're yours. Now we've established there was a young girl with Ammuna—how long ago was it you ferried them across?'

The fishermen were stunned into silence at having their shekels restored to them. They didn't know what to believe.

'Ammuna told us not to pick up anyone following them as they will probably slit our throats and steal our money *and* the fish. So, let me get this straight,' blurted out the old man. 'You're saying Ammuna's daughter wasn't his daughter, but the king's daughter—and that he kidnapped her?' He sat there with his eyebrows raised in astonishment.

'Ah, I do believe you're catching on.' Mokhat said sardonically. 'The king's daughter was kidnapped ten days ago and we've been chasing Ammuna ever since. We think he's heading to Wassukanni to get paid. So, how long ago was it you ferried them across?'

'Only this morning. You just missed them. I'm sorry but how were we to know?' complained the old man. He looked abashed at his fellow fishermen and shrugged his shoulders, as if to say, we're innocent.

Mokhat stamped away and began pacing up and down on the riverbank cursing and swearing. 'Damn... damn... damn—we almost had him. If I'd thrown caution to the wind and pushed us on, we'd have caught up with the filthy excuse for a general.' He stomped along the shoreline cursing and kicking pebbles into the river. But it didn't satisfy him, so he picked up more pebbles and threw them with some force into the middle of the river. Finally, he came back and faced the old fisherman. 'How soon can you ferry us across?'

'Right now if you wish, sir. By the way, I'm called Harmi.' The old man had decided this general was being straight with him, and it was Ammuna who was the out-and-out scoundrel.

'Well, let's get started,' ordered Mokhat. 'Will three golden shekels be enough, Harmi—per boat of course, since it would seem to be the current tariff,' Mokhat said in an offhand manner.

Startled at their second good fortune, all the fishermen swiftly ran to their boats, holding them so the dark clad men could climb into them while holding their horse's reins.

There were three men plus the allocated provisions, per boat, while the horses swam beside the craft; it took four crossings to get everyone to the other side.

It was getting late when Mokhat paid off the grateful fishermen with the agreed shekels and he was mulling over the idea of setting up night camp somewhere further on from the fishermen and the river. The light was fast disappearing, and so a league south of the river he told Onasiyas to set up camp and feed the men. They would continue their journey in the morning.

Kidnapping's Consequences
20
Invoking the Treaty

Four days after the abduction of the Hittite king's daughter, a somewhat exhausted pigeon arrived in Waset, the Pharaoh's capital in Upper Khemet, bearing a prearranged coded message. When the code was transcribed, it was found to invoke a section of the peace treaty between the two kingdoms regarding mutual defence —and coming to the assistance of each other when the section was invoked. Tied to the other leg of the pigeon was another note accusing the Mittani of the abduction of the king's daughter.

Pharaoh Amenhotep II conferred with his Djat to determine the validity of invoking the treaty since the Hittites weren't under direct attack.

'I'm of the opinion, my pharaoh, we are under no obligation to assist the Hittite king. The section of the treaty only applies if either of us comes under direct attack from a third party, which seems not to be the case in the current circumstances. I advise acknowledging the receipt of the message and ignoring it.' The Djat, as his First Minister, had always given wise counsel and the pharaoh invariably had taken his advice.

'You're aware of my desire to teach the Mittani some manners?' the pharaoh asked his Djat.

'Yes my pharaoh, I'm aware you've been itching to have a go at them, but is *this* the right time? Maybe a more suitable moment will present itself at a time in the near future,' prevaricated the Djat.

'Should I wait for my daughter to be abducted next by those scoundrels in Wassukanni? Would that be a more suitable time?' the pharaoh asked rhetorically of his first minister. 'And if kidnapping the king's daughter is *not a direct attack*, I'm not sure I know *what* constitutes a direct attack.'

The sarcasm bit hard into the thick skin of the wily politician. 'I take your point, my pharaoh. If it is your will, then I think we can stretch this situation of the message so the treaty's meaning includes this circumstance. I'm now forced to conclude the Hittites invoking their mutual defence treaty was entirely in order and as such we are duty bound to honour Tudhaliyas' request for assistance to deal with the bothersome Mittani.'

'I was hoping you would see it my way,' smiled the pharaoh at his minister for coming so swiftly into line with his own wishes.

'Just one more possible problem, my pharaoh. It will take you at least a month to get up to the Mittani border. By the time you get there, you may find everything's been settled one way or another. You may be too late to have any impact on this quarrel. I would be remiss if I didn't point this out to you.' The Djat made one last attempt to divert the course of pharaoh's intended action, and added, 'I assume you will be going to Mittani yourself?'

'But of course, and you forget the Tikhsi, my dear minister. They are my vassals and yet where is their tribute for the past year? I shan't have wasted the journey I assure you.' Pharaoh looked to see if his minister had been won over.

'My pharaoh, I wish you would reconsider leading the army yourself. You have any number of capable generals to take the risk on your behalf, men who are only too eager to put themselves in peril for you. That's what they're there for. Why must you put yourself in danger?' The Djat made this plea each time the pharaoh insisted on leading the army himself.

'You're a good counsellor my old friend, but you've grown too fond of your creature comforts. It's good for a man to get to grips with the hard face of the stone he's going to carve. My stone is this nation and I must share the hardship of my men, as well as being the head of the nation and their spiritual father, I'm also the commander in chief. I'm half-tempted to take you with me on this expedition. You would come back a changed man—and I suspect a better man.' The pharaoh saw the look of shock and distaste on his first minister's face and laughed out aloud. 'Well, maybe not this time then—but it might yet happen. You should be prepared.'

The Djat hurriedly changed the subject, 'Shall I call for the commanders of your divisions?' He'd acquiesced to the pharaoh's intent and would now smooth out all the wrinkles in his path.

'Yes, call the commanders. I'm taking four divisions. I want the three infantry divisions on the march in two days time—with the usual one thousand chariots as escort. They're to go through Sinai as per normal. I'll take the other chariots to the Red Sea in a week's time. I want two hundred transport ships to take the two thousand troops across to the Gulf of Aila and up past the Sinai Peninsula. I'll catch up with the rest of the army at the eastern end of the Salt Sea.

'Then we'll go all out for Tikhsi and sort them out as a first step; might as well deal with those bothersome kings on the way. Then we'll invest the Mittani city of Terqa on the Puranti River. The whole journey will take the better part of four weeks to accomplish even at double time, but it can't be helped. Send a confirmation to Hattusas we are coming up to assist them.'

The pharaoh was never happier than when he was planning a military campaign. It endowed him with esteem from those in his inner circle, since he would be putting his life on the line in every battle. Clearly, his bodyguards would lay down their lives for him, but should they fail to protect him, there would have to be a new pharaoh. That was the frisson of terror and excitement for those élites left behind in Khemet, when the pharaoh led his army out to battle.

The priesthood of Amun began an intense week of prayers for the pharaoh's victories and for his safe return. They had more to gain than anyone from this campaign, as one third of all the booty the pharaoh would bring back was always deposited in their underground treasury in the main temple of Amun. The innumerable enslaved captives would be put to expanding and building more temples and it would enrich the priesthood immensely.

It was four days after the main army departed, Pharaoh Amenhotep II took the rest of the chariot regiment from Waset, directly to the Red Sea, and then crossed it by ship, going up the Gulf of Aila to bypass the Sinai Desert. Even so, it was to be a long journey up to Mittani for twenty thousand men, 16,000 infantry, and 4,000 men with 2,000 chariots.

*   *   *

After the *clearing out of the proverbial stable*, as the king had so picturesquely put it in his initial conversation on the subject of traitors, there settled a subdued atmosphere up in the citadel of the port town of Adaniya for couple of days following the event. The chief minister and a number of generals had been tried for treason and then speedily executed. The king's son, Crown Prince Talshura had argued for clemency, until it was made clear to him by his father, after long arguments from both the king and the senior generals, sending traitors into exile was storing up trouble for the future. Consequently, the ship to Alasiya with the traitorous exiles never set sail, mainly due to a lack of passengers.

'What hurts me the most is my chief minister, someone in whom I placed the trust of my kingdom, was at the heart of the plot to enslave Kizzuwatna again,' lamented King Shunashura to General Tapalass. 'The Mittani promised him my crown. Artatama had the cheek to tell him he would replace me on the throne. If I get my hands on that snotty young prince of Mittani, I will chastise him onto death.'

It was in this manner of severity, the turncoats were rounded up and questioned to determine why they felt the need to reject their rightful king and support the return of the subjugating Mittani. The point was to get to the core of the troublemakers, those who induced others to turn against their lawful sovereign. These senior officials, both civilian and lower military, were then given to the soldiers for them to practice their sword skills on.

Within three days, the blood-letting had finished and around six hundred hardcore rebellious activists had been dispatched to the netherworld. It had been an excruciating time with many friends torn apart and even families ending in dispute; but it had to be done for the sake of unity and sovereignty.

After the stable had been so methodically cleaned, the Kizzuwatna army was exhaustively equipped and hurriedly made to march to the east, followed by its baggage train. It was led by General Tapalass and Crown Prince Talshura, heading towards the first Mittani city in order to repay in kind, the recent attention the Mittani had attempted to lavish on them. If the Mittani wanted to subjugate Kizzuwatna, then it was high time they found out the price of such an ambition.

General Tapalass was in no mood to listen to any excuses or to parley with the people in Karkamish; his intent was to invest the city and take it by storm. He wanted to battle harden his army, to clearly illustrate in blood, what the Kizzuwatna thought of their Mittani would-be-subjugators. That Karkamish had nothing whatsoever to do with the recent attempt at subverting Kizzuwatna made no impression on the tough skin of General Tapalass. It was a Mittani vassal state and he had every intention of venting his anger on it despite a plea of moderation from Crown Prince Talshura.

On the morning that ex-general Ammuna was preparing to cross the Puranti River to escape the Isuwan army, the fifteen thousand strong Kizzuwatna army was approaching Karkamish and preparing to invest it. The army had been putting together battering rams and ladders while still on the march through the forests where wood was in plentiful supply. It was amplifying its state of preparedness so as not to waste any time once they were at the walls of the city.

In the back of General Tapalass' mind, he was secretly nurturing the notion of putting the entire city to the sword and obliterating it from the face of this earth, and this was directly due to the displaced anger he carried at being forced to put so many of his friends to the sword back in Adaniya. The mere mention of the name *Mittani* put him into an unreasonable rage and the people in Karkamish were going to have to suffer the consequences of it.

On the following day, as Mokhat's group were beginning to cross the Puranti River where Ammuna had crossed it previously, the Kizzuwatna army had hemmed the army of Karkamish within the city walls and prevented them from fanning out to face General Tapalass' troops. Every sortie out of Karkamish's main gate of was thwarted and the city's troops were pushed back, finally being forced to withdraw back inside the city walls.

The two sides were relatively equal in numbers of troops they were able to put into the field, but the inability of the city's troops to exit outside their walls meant the fighting was limited to the vicinity of the main gate, and in close quarter fighting, the Kizzuwatna proved to be far superior. The same problem existed at all the postern gates out of the city, which General Tapalass had blocked.

Karkamish sat on an upraised bit of land facing the Puranti River and had it been built entirely of stone, it would have been virtually impregnable. As it was, there was a city building programme in progress which was intended to replace all the mud-brick walls with stone but it had only been completed to half its perimeter. The other half on the southern side of the city was still vulnerable. This is where General Tapalass now concentrated his siege engines.

Three hide covered battering rams with immense horizontal beams, one end covered with a bronze ram, had been constructed and readied—one for the main city gate and two for the southern wall. Each battering ram was suspended from another beam like a balance arm by cables around its middle, and this in turn was supported at both ends on a mobile platform on wheels. It was drawn back by a huge number of men who then push it forward in unison with all their might so that it hits the gate, or the wall, with its bronze head.

The battering ram was suspended in a mobile shelter, which provided protection against missiles and incendiary devices for the men underneath. The shelter was constructed from a framework of strong timbers with planks and wicker hurdles on the sides and then covered with a fireproof material such as uncured hides. A large number of Γ-shaped wooden barricades were fashioned to safeguard the besiegers from arrows and stones shot or thrown from the walls by those besieged.

Both sides were preparing for a lengthy siege which might take weeks, but the expectation proved to be false.

21
Malidiya Surrenders

On the first day of the kidnapping, General Zidanta sent the call to the various Hittite cities for them to dispatch their regiments to the proximity of Isuwa. He'd already presumed the king would want to send an army into Mittani, just for the insult caused, no matter what the outcome of the kidnapping. He'd read Tudhaliyas' mind and knew what needed to be done. As soon as humanly possible, the Hittite army had been readied and prepared for battle with the Mittani. Logistics and equipment were the only hold-ups. On the second day, these snags had been ironed out with Zidanta's forcefulness and the army was on the march on the same evening of the day Mokhat left with his band of *special forces*.

On the morning of the day Mokhat's group were preparing to cross the Puranti River at the spot Ammuna had crossed, the Hittite army swept across the Isuwan border and was approaching Malidiya. It was only two thirds of a day away from the city, with Tudhaliyas being intent on bringing King Tarasina to order. He'd had enough of the vacillating antics of the Isuwan king. If he wanted to join the Mittani, then he would have to take what the Hittites intended to dish out to the Mittani and their allies.

As soon as the Hittite army had crossed his border, King Tarasina had sent out a "peace" delegation with the specific purpose of prevaricating and delaying any action against him. Tudhaliyas brushed the delegation aside as if they were some kind of foul smelling irritation—which is exactly what they were to him.

'Tell your vacillating king, he made his choice when he refused to carry out my injunctions on dealing with the Mittani two weeks ago. He's allowed passage to a rogue Hittite general, simply to accommodate those in Wassukanni, and I'm afraid that can't go unpunished. Now, I don't really want to speak to his lackeys. If he wishes to prevent me from investing Malidiya, he should appear before me outside his citadel gates no later than tomorrow at noon. After noon I begin my siege of his city, and I promise you, I will lay waste to it. Go back and give this message to your dithering king.' Tudhaliyas then dismissed the quivering delegation and had them escorted out of his sight back to where they came from.

The king was continuously angry due to his missing daughter, and was only too happy to take it out on anyone and everyone who was in the slightest way connected to her kidnappers. The Isuwan delegation was lucky to get away so easily.

True to his word, by dawn of the next day Tudhaliyas was camped outside Malidiya with the city entirely surrounded by Hittite troops getting ready to lay siege to the Isuwan capital. Soon after sun-up, the high walls were infested with people coming to stare in horror at the belligerents who had surrounded their city and were intent on slaughtering them, and laying waste to their homes.

General Zidanta made his preparations clearly visible to the besieged, that he intended to undermine the cities foundations by having his miners dig under the walls of the massive fortifications. In preparation for building the siege engines, wood was chopped and stacked in clear sight of those watching on the walls. The engines would take the huge wooden gate down. That the enormous army would succeed in investing the city, there was little doubt, since it outnumbered the inhabitants by two to one. There could be only one outcome to this siege, and both sides knew it.

When noon arrived, the gates of the city remained stubbornly closed and shortly thereafter, Tudhaliyas gave the order for the siege to begin. Some while later as the slingers and archers began taking a toll of the defenders on the wall, the gates suddenly began to open amidst the flying stones and arrows, and a procession came out of the city led by King Tarasina.

As Tudhaliyas and General Zidanta watched the approaching pageant with wry humour and cynical smiles, the order was given by the general for the Hittite besiegers to stand down and cease all siege activity.

'It seems Tarasina has been induced to come to his senses,' observed General Zidanta to his king.

'Yes, your right. My guess is, he was pushed out of the gate by his own people,' Tudhaliyas replied to Zidanta's comment. 'I'm intrigued what he's got to say for himself.'

King Tarasina held his head high as if he were desperately trying to pretend he was in control and entirely above this sort of behaviour, but Tudhaliyas saw the glint of fear in his eyes as he drew near.

Tudhaliyas' bodyguards surrounded him to create a shield just in case there was one last trick in this sly Isuwan king, while General Zidanta was searching out the faces in the entourage for the Isuwan military commander. The Isuwan king's cortège stopped about twenty cubits from the Hittite king and then Tarasina came towards Tudhaliyas alone. Tarasina stood before Tudhaliyas and waited, as did Tudhaliyas. Tarasina couldn't force himself to do the one last thing expected of him—to kneel in front of his liege. As a vassal king, it was his duty to show respect for his sovereign, and yet in his fantasy, his arrogance simply resisted this final obligation. He didn't even bow his head. Only now did Tudhaliyas understand what had been happening in Malidiya with all these numerous changes in allegiances.

The general in charge of Tudhaliyas' bodyguards nodded, and a squad of ten broke away and surrounded Tarasina, grabbing him by his arms and forcing him to his knees. King Tarasina tried to resist, but was unable to, and sank to the ground, the stubbornness being driven out of him by force.

No one in the Isuwan cortège moved to help their king. Nobody on the walls of the city, witnessing the humiliation of their ruler, felt outraged or sought to protest at his treatment. They all felt he'd overstepped the mark by a long way and put them all at risk of annihilation.

'You are one stupid king,' Tudhaliyas spat out at him. 'Instead of looking to the welfare of your people, you have got tangled up in your own conceit. You would have sat inside your wall and watched your own people being slaughtered rather than alleviate their plight.'

Tarasina still tried to hold his head up as a last act of defiance, but his eyes were defeated and he expected no mercy.

Tudhaliyas nodded to the general of his bodyguards, who removed the dagger from his sheath and plunged it into Tarasina's chest. Tarasina showed no surprise at this action, and gave one final smile as his last act of defiance on this earth, then slumped to the ground.

General Zidanta led the Isuwan military commander towards Tudhaliyas. 'Sire, may I present a worthy successor to the fallen king—General Kanisa. I'm assured by him there will be no more vacillating from Malidiya and that we can rely on her loyalty as of now.'

'Welcome King Kanisa.' Tudhaliyas lifted Kanisa's right hand into the air for all those watching, so all could see the hostility was at an end.

An almighty roar rose from the city walls. Cries of *hail King Kanisa,* resounded from Malidiya.

'My lord,' said the new king, 'May I invite you into your city to join me in a feast.'

'It will be my pleasure,' Tudhaliyas responded. 'General Zidanta, bivouac the troops and let them have their fill from the baggage wagons. We have averted a lot of bloodshed this day. Let the men relax, eat, drink and be merry for tonight. All the senior officers to join me and King Kanisa inside the palace for the feast. Noon tomorrow, we move on to Wassukanni.'

'Yes, your majesty,' Zidanta replied

Tudhaliyas and Kanisa rejoined the Isuwan regal procession, which reformed and about faced to return through the gates back into the city, this time with Tudhaliyas slightly ahead and Kanisa almost by his side. The Isuwans were followed by the senior officers of the Hittite army led by General Zidanta.

When they entered the city, the population erupted with shouts of praise, joy and relief at having been spared the inevitable slaughter of a short time ago. Enthusiastically the populace hailed their new king through the city streets all the way to the king's palace, paying particular homage to the Hittite king who'd spared the city.

The brown shirts of the Isuwan military were on parade both inside and outside the citadel as befitted them honouring their previous military commander, and now their new sovereign. Kanisa had a word with his deputy commander and appointed him the new commander of the Isuwan army, asking him to join the cortège. The procession went up the stairs and into the audience hall, where all waited for a few word from their new sovereign.

Kanisa took Tudhaliyas up to the throne and bade him sit on the throne while he stood by his side. General Zidanta stood on Tudhaliyas' left side while the newly appointed commander of the Isuwan army stood on Kanisa's right. The new power structure stood facing the audience.

'I see you're waiting for me to say something,' the new king said to those in the hall. 'I welcome my liege to his city and urge everyone in this city to remember where our allegiances lie as of now. As for who will, and who will not remain in his posts—that will be sorted out after our visitors have left. For now, I want you all to concentrate on providing a fitting feast for our guests, with an open heart; and be thankful to them for their generous mercy. Get the banqueting hall ready and immediately get the kitchens to work. That's all, dismissed.'

His entourage went about his orders energetically and quickly dispersed to do the new king's bidding.

'I would consider it an honour if you would let me resupply your wagon train with all the necessities and provisions you've used up to date,' Kanisa offered to Tudhaliyas.

Tudhaliyas rose and said, 'Is there somewhere more comfortable where we can have a private chat?'

Kanisa led the way to a chamber at the rear of the throne room, spreading his arms, inviting them to sit. He shouted at the servants to provide his guests with wine.

Tudhaliyas responded to Kanisa's previous offer, 'It is most gracious of you—I naturally accept your kind offer of fresh supplies. We certainly could use them.'

They relaxed on couches in the private room with Zidanta and the Isuwan army commander present, an informal atmosphere permeating the room as the wine was served.

Kanisa confided in Tudhaliyas, 'I vow to you now there will be no more of the silly wavering that occurred under Tarasina. In me, you will have a staunch ally and vassal city. Tarasina was unbalanced and vain far beyond his powers to support such egotism. I know what we can and can't achieve and intend to behave accordingly. I'm a simple soldier and ruthlessly pragmatic according to military doctrine.

'It would have saved us both a lot of trouble if you'd taken control of Tarasina in the first place,' replied

Tudhaliyas. 'What stopped you? You must have seen this coming.'

Kanisa sighed deeply and said, 'Yes, I saw it coming. It was inevitable, your majesty. Every time our vain king changed sides, I expected to see your army outside the city walls. What stopped me getting rid of him each time was Tarasina had a large fanatical bodyguard loyal only to him. Until your external threat was visible, I wasn't able to get my military to act against him.

'Once our military became convinced they were to be annihilated, I was able to persuade them we should get rid of Tarasina. When our conceited king refused to open the gate to meet you, we moved on him and managed to disarm his bodyguard, after convincing some of them to change sides. We had to force the issue and I lost a lot of men doing so, but now we have them all locked up. Then we pushed him out of the gate in that procession you witnessed.'

'I see; yes that would explain it,' Tudhaliyas said rubbing his black beard.

'Look sire,' said Kanisa, 'I'd like to make it up to you for my inaction with our former king, by offering to join you on your march.' The new king looked as if he was pleading to make amends for Tarasina's bad behaviour. 'I can add ten thousand Isuwan soldiers to your army. As of now, we're ready to fight. We have an expert slinger's regiment, which I've been readying, and they can be effective. We know Wassukanni better than you, and can show you its weakest points. Will you accept this offer of reconciliation between out two nations?'

Tudhaliyas looked at Zidanta, who nodded encouragingly to him. 'I accept,' he said with a smile and took Kanisa's outstretched hand. 'Welcome on board. The larger the force we have outside the Mittani capital, the more convincing our presence will be, and the stronger our argument for the release of my daughter.'

22
Siege of Karkamish

Karkamish sat on an upraised bit of land facing the Puranti River. General Tapalass' and the Kizzuwatna forces had the city under siege and it was completely surrounded. The main siege engines were concentrated at the vulnerable southern side of the city where the walls were still made of mud-brick. They were due to have been replaced by solid stone walls but events had overtaken the building project. General Tapalass was intent on pummelling and breaching this section of the city wall. He took charge of the operation and set up his vantage point and HQ about a hundred cubits back, directly behind the two battering rams. The front gate battering ram was left to the Crown Prince.

The Kizzuwatna slingers and archers were taking a heavy toll of those light blue tunics on the battlements, desperately attempting to stave off the concentrated attack on their wall. The two hide covered battering rams pummelling the southern mud-brick wall had immense horizontal beams; the third ram under the command of Crown Prince Talshura was hard at work battering at the main city gate. The battering rams were suspended in mobile shelters underneath, providing the men working the rams protection against missiles and incendiary devices from above.

Each battering ram was suspended from another beam like a balance arm by cables around its middle, and this in turn was supported at both ends on a mobile platform on wheels. The ram was drawn back by a huge number of men in scarlet tunics, who then push it forward in unison with all their might so it hits the wall, or the gate, with its bronze ram. Slowly but surely, both wall and gate were being damaged and both would eventually give. It was simply a matter of time—and those on the wall and in the city were keenly aware of it. The assault made their activity the more frenetic.

The rest of the city was surrounded by a large number of wide Γ-shaped wooden barricades which were moving ever forward, behind which the besiegers in their scarlet uniforms, hid from arrows and stones shot or thrown from the walls by those wearing the light blue tunics of the defenders.

Both sides were preparing for a lengthy siege which could last for over a month, but in the event, the expectation proved erroneous. By the end of the first day, mostly due to the nature of the mud-brick wall, the southern wall was beginning to crumble.

General Tapalass went to see how his protégé was coming along at the main gate, but he found an ominous silence coming from this part of the siege. The Crown Prince had decided to give his besiegers a rest, and the place was pregnant with the sound of silence. The prince's men were resting and he was intent on giving them a respite until dawn.

The general was furious at this lack of activity but had to go gently as the Crown Prince was in nominal command of the army. 'Your highness,' Tapalass said as he approached the prince, 'this is no way to conduct a siege. While your men are resting, the defenders are working hard at reinforcing the gate. Every moment you let your men rest, the longer the siege will last and more lives will be lost.'

The ram at the main gate had made progress but the gate was a long way from being breached.

The Crown Prince looked at the general quizzically. 'Why the hurry?' asked the prince. 'We'll get through it. They can't escape—but my men have been hard at it all day and I thought a good night's rest would invigorate them for the next day.'

'Your highness, it will also invigorate the enemy. They will have rested and strengthened their position. We cannot conduct a war like this. The enemy *must* be destroyed, the sooner the better.' Anger was beginning to become visible on the general's face.

'General, why are you pushing so hard? What is your intention in this siege? When we breach the city's defences, how do you propose to proceed?' The prince was calm and studying his mentor.

'The quicker we take the city, the sooner we move on. It's a matter of expediency—I taught you that. When the walls are penetrated I intend to stand back and let the men do their jobs,' Tapalass replied. The prince noted an evasive undertone to the general's answer.

'By which you mean, the soldiers can do as they like —slaughter and pillage freely?' The prince's voice had risen a tone.

'I'm not going to stand in their way if that's what they want to do,' the general responded. 'Besides, it will be good practice for them when we reach Wassukanni.'

'General, you didn't teach me to slaughter unnecessarily. The Kizzuwatna army is not a butchering rabble. Tell me general—and I respect your opinion as you well know—what has this population done to deserve being massacred like this?' The prince had a hard stare on his face, not of stubbornness, but of moral conviction.

The general had trouble containing his anger, and bottling it up was turning his face red, yet he was unable to vent it on his nominal commander, the Crown Prince. 'They support the Mittani scoundrels,' he finally spat out.

'That general, for the ordinary populace, is not a crime worthy of annihilation,' the prince pointed out. This was a serious dispute by two of the top leaders of the siege.

'Your highness, have you forgotten what the Mittani tried to do to us a short while ago? The friends I lost because of their scheming? As far as I'm concerned, anyone supporting the Mittani deserves everything they are about to receive—and it includes being slaughtered.' Tapalass seemed to get great satisfaction from the last word.

'General Tapalass, I'm sorry to have to do this, but you leave me no option. You're letting your displaced anger cloud your judgement. I cannot permit this slaughter of the population of Karkamish to occur—and neither should you. It's immoral and you would undoubtedly regret it later on. My father the king, gave the command of the army to me. I've let you run the operation as you see fit because of my limited military experience. I've been content for you to run this command—up to this point. Now I'm afraid, I'll be taking full command of the army. You know I'm right. I'll take command until this siege is over and we're back on the road to Wassukanni. As I said, I'm sorry to have to do this, but your plans to lay waste to this city cannot be allowed to go forward. When we get to Wassukanni, and you still feel angry and want to sack the city, I will not stand in your way —I will support you to the hilt; but it would be immoral to execute all the inhabitants of this innocent city, merely for supporting the Mittani.'

The anger in Tapalass was subsiding as he listened to the tongue lashing from his protégé, feeling a little embarrassed at being berated by the younger man. Deep inside, he knew the young Crown Prince was right. He himself would never have advised such a course of action back in Officer's Training School. 'You are right, your highness, you *are* the commander of this army and I bow to your father's judgement in giving you the command. I will order my men to stop the pounding of the wall until dawn. I will also order them to be merciful. If the enemy shows a willingness to surrender—I will order them to accept it and stop the battle—taking all due precautions.'

'I'm pleased to hear you say this,' responded Prince Talshura. 'You'll see general, if the roles had been reversed and I was in a state of bloodlust, you would have done the same for me—made me think again as to what I was doing.'

All General Tapalass said was, 'Yes your highness, I hope your right. Now I will return to my mud-brick wall and give my men the orders to cease operations for the night till dawn. By your leave,' and the general marched off back they way he'd come. He was in a contemplative mood on his return journey and as the lust for vengeance was leaving him, it made him remember his dead friends with more kindness—the happier times before their betrayal.

After a fitful night, in the light of dawn, the general had his men renew the attack on the mud-brick wall with greater vigour. Tapalass sent in the miners under cover of darkness to weaken the wall's foundations just above where they were pounding. Mines were to be dug at this point under the foundations of the city wall to weaken the wall. Once the mine was dug, sappers would underpin the wall with wood supports and then cause the walls to collapse by firing the supports with resin, sulphur and other incendiary materials.

Halfway through the day they had to cease operations when the defenders began lobbing exceptionally heavy boulders down on the roofs of the battering rams. Those boulders shattered the roofs and killed many underneath. To follow the boulders, the defenders tipped hot oil down on the men below, taking advantage of the holes made by the boulders, and it made it impossible to continue without losing many of the men.

'General,' his deputy approached him and asked to be heard. 'The officer in charge of the battering rams informs me he's broken through the mud-brick, only to be confronted by compacted earth. He thinks the people on the other side of the wall have been busy piling soil up against that part of the wall we're pounding. The next stage will have to be left to the sappers. They'll have to dig through the soil.'

'Where in the name of the netherworld did they find those heavy boulders to lob down on us? And where did they get all the soil?' They were rhetorical questions and didn't require an answer. The general didn't like the devastation the boulders had caused to his battering rams, damaging their roofs. 'As for the sappers, good thinking colonel. Make sure we rebuild the roofs of both battering rams, and remove the swinging rams for now. Lets use them as cover for feeding in the sappers. I can't afford to wait for nightfall.'

'Yes general,' snapped the deputy and rushed off to carry out his orders.

The sappers waited until they could shelter under the renewed roofs of the old battering rams and then they proceeded to the holes in the wall to dig through the compacted earth; both enlarged holes were going to have tunnels, one going upwards, and further on, going horizontal. The dig upwards, with sappers positioned on ladders, was the more important since the commanders needed to know how much soil had been dumped against the wall, and what was waiting for them when they came out of the horizontal tunnels. With their own soldiers surveying their surroundings from the top of the mound, they could give them that information. The two tunnels were begun about fourteen cubits apart.

A messenger came from the prince bringing news from the front gate; it had almost been breached and the fighting there was getting desperate. The defenders were throwing everything they could get their hands on, down on to the besiegers. There had also been boulders and hot oil. There were many casualties.

Tapalass had his deputy call for reports from the other commanders as to what stage the siege was in around the entire circumference of the wall of the city. Were defenders trying to climb down and escape? Was there any activity at the postern gates? Was the siege secure? Did we have the enemy properly hemmed in? Tapalass was demanding information on how the battle was developing.

Meanwhile, the sappers standing on top of ladders in one of the up tunnels had broken through the top layer, only to have a couple of Mittani soldiers tumble in past them down to the floor of the tunnel. They must have been standing on the holes; the men in the tunnels below dispatched them viciously and speedily as they tumbled down on them.

The other up tunnel broke through the ceiling shortly after. The Mittani above, having realised what had happened, soon fired spears and arrows at the emerging Kizzuwatna soldiers in rapid succession as soon as they showed their heads. The scarlet uniforms had to fight their way out and crept onwards into the open behind the protection of their shields battling every step of the way. What gave them extra enthusiasm was their foe wore the dark blue of the Mittani. They had come across their *real* enemy, not the light blue tunics of the Karkamish soldiers. More Kizzuwatna soldiers climbed the ladders, pouring out of the holes in the ceiling of the earth mound, all eager to get at the Mittani.

News travelled down the line that they had come across Mittani soldiers and the scarlet clad Kizzuwatna were pushing impatiently upward into both tunnels to get at their Mittani enemy. The horizontal tunnels had a chain-line of soldiers passing baskets of soil back to the entrance to be offloaded, pushing the digging speedily ahead towards an ultimate breakthrough.

The colonel leading the assault in the tunnels sent his deputy, a major, to tell the general the mound was enormous and the horizontal tunnels needed to be at least fifteen cubits in length before they could come out to an opening. Facing them would be a half-circle barricade manned by at least five hundred Mittani, backed by more Karkamish soldiers. The messenger told the general the battle would be vicious and protracted. He readied his heavy infantry regiment, his one and a half thousand shock troops, to push into the tunnels. The horizontal tunnels were widened to allow for the wide Γ-shaped wooden barricades which would be used to protect the emerging soldiers; this would act as their counter to the barricade facing them.

Inside the horizontal tunnels, the soldiers were told what to expect when they broke through into the open, but they were only to break through the last section when their topside brethren had reached the bottom of the mound. It would then be a simultaneous assault from both horizontal tunnels and the two topside tunnels, on the barricade facing them. The Kizzuwatna poured out of the tunnels as fast as they could until many hundreds were in a line behind the Γ-shaped wooden barricades, ever moving forward towards the Mittani half circle barricade. When eventually the two sides were close enough, the Kizzuwatna abandoned their wooden barricades and threw themselves at the Mittani.

By this time, nine hundred scarlet uniforms were facing the Mittani dark blue, and more scarlet were joining them; and the battle raged on. The colonel in command was at the forefront of the battle, exhorting his men by example, to *get stuck in*. He was one of the first to leap over the Mittani barricade, which to his surprise, cost him a severe flesh wound to his left shoulder on his shield arm from a javelin thrust. It didn't deter him for a moment; he kept slashing and cutting at the foe in front of him until the enemy was crushed.

More scarlet uniforms rushed through the tunnels to join their comrades until the whole regiment had come through, and with this force of numbers, they eventually overwhelmed the Mittani line. Unexpectedly, once the Mittani had been eliminated, the Karkamish soldiers were eager to lay down their arms and surrender. The battlements were secured and the threat from above quickly neutralised. According to the general's orders, there was no slaughter and those who wanted to surrender were allowed to do so.

In the meantime, at the front gate, the men with the hatchets had enlarged the breach so the Γ-shaped wooden barricades could be pushed through the gap and used to protect them inside the city gate. Against all advice, the prince was insisting on being at the sharp edge of the fighting. He wanted to lead the first charge through the breached gate. He was finally convinced to go with the second wave, only after a number of senior officers refused to continue with the battle, if the Crown Prince risked his life in the first wave of the attack. It was a mutiny and inexcusable disobedience, but for a cause—that of protecting the Crown Prince from danger; and the Crown Prince eventually appreciated their action and backed down.

The cost in lives had been enormous and two hundred Kizzuwatna soldiers had perished in this battle, just to make a hole in the main gate, and the battle was far from over. Again, what made the fight so fierce was they were facing seasoned Mittani soldiers in their dark blue tunics. It was unthinkable for those wearing the scarlet uniforms they should give way to the dark blue Mittani scoundrels—so a few Kizzuwatna had become reckless in their eagerness and had paid the ultimate price. Their bodies were strewn all around the hole in the main gate.

Once through the hole and inside the main gate, the Kizzuwatna soldiers faced the half-circle barricade manned by their Mittani foes. Both sides fired fusillade after fusillade of missiles at each other; arrows, sling shots, and javelins sailed through the air in opposite directions, some striking their targets, but mostly they hit the barricades behind which the soldiers hid.

Cubit by cubit the Kizzuwatna scarlet uniforms pushed their Γ-shaped barricades closer to the Mittani half-circle barricade until a mere ten cubits separated them.

The prince's patience gave way and he pushed his way through in the second wave surrounded by his bodyguards. To the surprise of the prince's bodyguards, Talshura charged forward and pushed aside his own barricade holding his shield out in front, and then with a great leap hurled himself over the Mittani barricade into the enemy's frontline, closely followed by his bodyguard. As his foot landed on top of the barricade, he parried a hack from one Mittani soldier to his right, and thrust his sword into another in front of him as he landed. Then he fought ferociously for his life.

Seeing their commander perform such a heroic deed, his mass of soldiers threw caution to the wind and followed him *en masse*. The Mittani weren't expecting this sort of rapid robust assault and their line crumbled. The fighting was fierce and to the finish—until no Mittani was left alive. The ramparts were rapidly secured and the defenders removed from the walls; then soldiers fanned out into the city.

'Your highness,' a captain came running up to the prince, saluting smartly and said, 'there's a peculiar procession coming towards you carrying a large statue. It will be here shortly. We've came across it as we were moving into the city proper. I don't think it poses any danger to you.'

'Thank you captain.' The prince's curiosity was aroused. He stood and waited, but his bodyguard took no chances and formed a protective ring around him.

Firstly, Talshura heard the sound of drums coming from down a street; it was a gentle drumming creating a hypnotic rhythm. Then into the area littered with the bodies of the recent battle came senior officers of the Karkamish army carrying their own sword out in front of them with the handle outwards and the blade pointing to themselves. It was a sign of submission.

Then came a line of priests with their drums. There followed more priests, a few helping an old man dressed in finery, to walk. This was followed by a large retinue of priests with their acolytes carrying a massive platform bearing a statue of the goddess Kubaba seated on a chair, holding a mirror up to her face.

Priests rushed forward to clear the way for the procession, removing the bodies of the fallen and piling them up into two mounds, one for the Mittani and one for the victorious Kizzuwatna. The latter bodies were treated with more respect than their Mittani allies.

The old man who was being held up with the aid of his priests was the aged king of Karkamish. At the sound of a roll of drums the procession stopped halfway into the middle of the large plaza in front of the main gate. The chief priest stepped forward and faced Crown Prince Talshura, holding out a splendid looking sword with the hilt towards the prince.

'In the name of my king, Aplahanda II, king of Karkamish, I wish to surrender the city to the victorious Kizzuwatna army. We ask you spare the city any further destruction.'

General Tapalass appeared from another side street to the right, followed by a large number of soldiers in scarlet uniforms. The prince ignored the chief priest and went to meet his army commander. They embraced and complimented each other on being inside the enemy stronghold. Only then did the prince come over to the chief priest with Tapalass by his side.

Talshura had his shoulders back with pride of the victory and he stretched out his hand to take the proffered sword. 'Convey my thanks to the king and tell him that we accept the unconditional surrender. You can reassure him that we have no intention of sacking his city.'

'My king wishes me to inform you that we would have opened the gates to you at the outset, but we were prevented from doing so by the Mittani regiment that was quartered here.' The priest waved his hand at the mound of dead Mittani bodies. 'We have no argument with our Kizzuwatna friends and the king wishes that you and your people be treated as his guests while you are here.'

At hearing the latter statement, Crown Prince Talshura looked poignantly at General Tapalass, and the general understood the look; it said to him, *did I not tell you these people were innocent?*

23
Siege of Tikhsi

The day previous, the two parts of the Khemetian army met up at the northern end of the Salt Sea as prearranged by the Pharaoh. The larger part having gone through the normal Sinai route, while Pharaoh Amenhotep II had taken his two thousand troops with him the quicker course and crossed by ship to the Gulf of Aila and up past the Sinai Peninsula.

The twenty thousand strong standing army was now many leagues north-east of the River Jordan, having skirted the Golan heights and Mount Hermon, and was going across the vast empty desert into the land of the Tikhsi, having just crossed its borders, according to their scouts. These were a troublesome people who the Pharaoh had been forced to chastise earlier. He had a nominal claim to the city's suzerainty and this was a good opportunity to enforce it by making clear to the Tikhsi king, he was within easy reach of the Pharaoh's power. Should the Tikhsi king think of prevaricating in his allegiance, as he'd done on occasions in the past, then here was the Pharaoh on his doorstep once again, to teach him a lesson he would not easily forget.

The Pharaoh's spies had recently informed him King Atalshen of Tikhsi had been flirting with his Mittani neighbours and had concluded secret provisions with them. It was one of the reasons he'd agreed to this expedition to help the Hittite king in his war with the Mittani. It gave the Pharaoh a chance to have a word with this recalcitrant king in person, and ask him forcibly to mend his ways, and offer him an opportunity to provide him with the missing tribute for the previous year.

The general of his army, General Hatupt, rejoined the Pharaoh, travelling in his war chariot. 'Sire, scouts have just reported they came across a sizeable detachment of Tikhsi cavalry. When they approached and hailed them, the Tikhsi turned and ran for it in the direction of their capital,' the general reported leaning over his horse towards Amenhotep II. 'An unpromising reception, wouldn't you agree sire?'

'Most ungracious of them, I would say. It seems our king has forgotten his manners. How long before we reach the city?' The Pharaoh removed his Blue Crown war helmet and wiped the inside with a cloth, then replaced the helmet on his head.

'We should be there by mid afternoon, sire,' replied the general.

'I'm assuming the gates of the city will be closed to us, if the reaction of their detachment is anything to go by. General, make preparations to invest the city. It's time to teach this king how he ought to properly conduct himself when his liege comes for a visit.'

'Yes sire,' snapped the general, then rode off to consult with his senior staff and prepare a plan for the siege of Tikhsi.

A little while later the Pharaoh called over the chief officer of his bodyguard. 'Can you ask the senior priest of Amun to join me,' he commanded.

'Immediately sire,' the officer replied, and rode off to fetch him.

A while later, when the chief priest of the army arrived, the Pharaoh indicated he should join him on the deck of his chariot.

To which the priest said, 'My magnificent Pharaoh; you sent for me?' and jumped on board the chariot.

'Yes! Now listen carefully. When we get to Tikhsi, I want you to say the prayers to Onuris in front of the main gates before we begin the siege. If the men see you offer prayers to the Khemetian god of war, it will strengthen their resolve and increase their desire to fight,' the Pharaoh told the priest. 'Am I clear?'

'Yes your magnificence. It will be done as you say.' The priest was always reverential to his secular master since he controlled the purse strings. One third of any booty always went to the priestly coffers so the Pharaoh's wishes were always carried out without question.

'You can go,' said the Pharaoh.

The chief priest waved to the bodyguard who had brought him, to come and take him off the chariot. This the bodyguard accomplished by bending over the vehicle and grabbing the priest around his waist and lifting him off the chariot and over his horse's main. He then rode to the side and popped him gently on the desert floor, where the priest would find his own way back to his wagon on foot.

The journey to Tikhsi took longer than expected and the army finally approached the walled city late in the afternoon.

'As I surmised earlier,' exclaimed the Pharaoh. 'Those damned gates *are* closed to us.' He was shaking his fist at the gates while talking to General Hatupt, his army commander, who was riding by his chariot. 'They saw us approaching from a long way off and slammed the gates shut. This is outrageous; they will pay for this insult. General, prepare for the siege. And you,' he motioned to his bodyguard commander with his still raised fist, 'go get the chief priest. Tell him he's wanted at the main gate. He'll know why.'

Those on the battlements watched with alarm and horror as the whole city was surrounded by professional soldiers, led by seasoned and experienced officers. They watched the huge battering ram being put together in front of the main gate. The specialized companies who were experts in the use of the throwing axe were ready at the

220

front gate to protect the battering ram, as were the numerous archers and sling throwers. A large number of long siege ladders were built for the shock troops, who would lead the infantry in their assault on the cities walls.

The chief priest arrived and set up an altar facing the main gates and began intoning his prayers to Onuris, the Khemetian god of war. At this piece of magic, wailing was heard from inside the city and a lot of movement occurred on the battlement walls. The people inside the city walls were afraid the potent magic of the enemy priests would destabilise their sturdy walls and make them crumble to the ground.

As the chief priest was finishing his last prayer, the huge gates of the city began to open slowly. Tikhsi soldiers with their bared torsos began emerging, but without their weapons; they lined the sides of the road leaving the city as a guard of honour for an emerging Tikhsi priest, followed by the Tikhsi monarch, King Atalshen.

A huge smile spread across the Pharaoh's face at this turnaround in events. He looked at his general and nodded with satisfaction at the approaching Tikhsi king. King Atalshen of Tikhsi, as he drew near the Pharaoh, looked tired and drawn as if he hadn't slept for many a day.

Atalshen stopped short of the Pharaoh and bowed deeply, and nearly toppled over; he was quickly steadied by two aides to prevent an embarrassing fall.

'My liege,' the king said in a somewhat hoarse tired voice, 'I humbly apologise for the way you have been welcomed to my city. I can only say I wasn't in command of the gates when you arrived. There's been an upsetting problem with a few of my more impetuous advisers, who have taken it into their heads to hold me captive in my own palace, while they negotiated an accommodation with the Mittani. My army chief was the leader of this rebellion.

'I was totally against this move to accommodate my greedy neighbour, and the culprits knew it; so they insisted I didn't interfere. The Mittani would not have left it there, and would have incorporated my city into their empire. They prevented me from acting against them by holding me captive—until a short time ago. Only when you arrived in front of the gates did people loyal to me overthrow the usurpers. It was they who released me from my captivity in the palace, making it possible for me to open the gates to you. The usurpers are now in my dungeons thinking things over and awaiting my pleasure. Once again I apologise for your reception, which would have been entirely different had I been in command of the situation.'

It was a long speech, and an explanation of the drama which had overtaken King Atalshen of Tikhsi, in his own city.

The Pharaoh listened patiently and finally said, 'My dear king, I am deeply concerned at this news. If there's anything I can do to help you get rid of your troubles, don't hesitate to ask. I was angry at you, but now I see non of this was your fault. Are you sure you've everything under control?'

'Yes my Pharaoh, I am back in full control; and to show you this is so, I invite you into my city and into my modest home. My home is your home, and. I am your humble servant. My I offer you refreshments; your journey here must have been quite arduous across the desert.'

The general in command of Pharaoh's forces had already given the order to cease all hostile activities towards Tikhsi and the Khemetian army switched to setting up their peaceful bivouac outside the walls with many a soldier breathing a huge sigh of relief for his salvation.

The procession, with the Pharaoh out in front, followed by the Tikhsi king, went from the front gate to the king's palace, which turned out not to be so modest as the king had claimed. The city had only around thirty-five thousand inhabitants and the palace was sumptuous for such a small place—however, the Pharaoh found it overly modest compared to his own palace.

As the procession entered the palace grounds, one of the king's officers approached from the left gate as if to welcome the entourage, but as he got to within two cubits, he drew his sword and charged the Pharaoh, his face full of rage, intending to kill the ruler of the invading Khemetians. The Pharaoh's bodyguards threw themselves speedily in between the charging assassin and their monarch, and three of the bodyguards soon cut the man down, still with a shriek of hatred in his throat and his sword raised. The Pharaoh looked nonplussed at this assault on his life, but King Atalshen was scandalised.

'My Pharaoh, I most humbly apologise for this outrage.'

More of Atalshen's men came running, which caused the Pharaoh's bodyguards to surround him in defence. However, non of the Tikhsi soldiers were hostile and only came out of curiosity or to welcome their king back to the palace. It was a muddle which cleared itself, as it became evident nobody was looking for a fight.

'I'm so sorry my Pharaoh. That man must have been loyal to the commander of my army, and not to *me*. I should have done this immediately. I'll order a complete review of those people who were overeager to serve my army general.' Atalshen called over his aide, accompanied by a senior officer, and gave instructions for the army to be cleansed of traitors.

'If you need any of my men to help you in your task, I'd be only happy to supply them,' smiled the Pharaoh. 'It was a futile gesture of defiance,' commented the Pharaoh to the king, regarding the attack. 'Better make sure you leave no more of those amongst your people or you will store trouble for the future.'

The king smiled weakly in embarrassment. 'If you would allow a hundred of your men to help mine, I would be grateful.'

The Pharaoh nodded and told his commander to supply the troops to help the king's men.

So, while the procession entered the banqueting hall, a bloody suppression ensued swiftly throughout the palace with help from the Pharaoh's troops, in a pitiless attempt to weed out the pro Mittani faction.

In the banqueting hall, food was quickly served with a variety of mild alcoholic and fruit drinks. The court musicians provided background music to the refreshments —and peaceful civilised relations were resumed—but only in the banqueting Hall.

The Pharaoh said to the king, 'I've dealt with a few palace intrigues in my time and I know how it goes. Think nothing of this minor incident earlier; nobody got hurt. Now we're friends again, let's deal with the important things. May I inquire as to the whereabouts of your last year's tribute to me? I'm informed non arrived from you.'

Atalshen raised his eyebrows in surprise. 'What's this?' he burst out. 'My tribute didn't arrive? Why this is outrageous. I was informed it had been sent at the appropriate time—you should have received it long time ago.' Atalshen clapped his hands for his aides to attend him. When they arrived he shouted, 'Who was in charge of sending the tribute to our good friend the Pharaoh?'

One aide looked flustered at the shouting and said, 'Your majesty, the chief minister entrusted the task to the army, and so it would be down to the commander of the army.'

'You mean that scoundrel, my ex-commander, the one I've locked up in my dungeon?' Atalshen was getting angry.

His aide became fearful, 'Yes sire, the very same.'

'And where's the chief minister?' the king enquired.

'He's with your former army commander. They're in adjoining cells. The new commander of the army, the one you appointed today, locked the minister in the dungeon because he was too close to the general. Was that wrong?'

'No, he's absolutely right. My former chief minister should have seen the rebellion coming and warned me about it. He did nothing—implying he was conspiring with the general. Let him rot! I'll deal with them later.' The king turned to the Pharaoh and said, 'You see what I have to put up with. I swear I'll have those traitors put into holes in the desert and let the vultures peck their eyes out. As for the tribute I owe you, I will have another tribute made up immediately and I'll add this year's tribute in as well. You can either take it with you wherever you're going, or you can pick it up on your way back–whichever is the easiest.'

Listening to the king's woes and his attempt to remedy the problems besetting him, Pharaoh Amenhotep II was minded to be generous to his vassal and said, 'My dear king, I thank you for your offer, but I will only accept that which you can afford—not a handful more. And it might make more sense if we picked it up on our way back from our destination. As to where we are going—that I will answer with my next question. What can you tell me of Terqa? Size of the city, defences, and size of its army; anything which might be useful in taking the city.'

The king had guessed right; the Pharaoh was going to attack the Mittani. 'My Pharaoh, you have made me so happy. Since you're after those Mittani scum, and bearing in mind what they tried to do to me, I will help you in any way I can.' The king clapped for his aide, and when he arrived, he ordered the aide to bring all the maps of Terqa that were lodged in the archives. 'Bring any other information about Terqa you can find there. Find me our expert on the city, and hurry up.' Atalshen smiled conspiratorially at the Pharaoh, implying that all the information he had would be at the Pharaoh's disposal.

'You call them Mittani *scum*, and after what they have put you through I can't blame you, yet there seems to be something not quite right there. I can't believe King Saustatar would be so stupid as to antagonise all his neighbours. He's got the Hittites after him, there's rumblings of discontent with his vassals on his other side, the Assyrians. And with what he did to you, he's pushing into my sphere of influence. What has come over Saustatar? Why can't he see his folly?' The Pharaoh looked at Atalshen as if he expected an explanation.

'My Pharaoh, it's *not* King Saustatar who's at the bottom of all these intrigues. It's his overly ambitious son, Prince Artatama. Before my army commander usurped my throne, I had good intelligence of Artatama's objectives and his dream to rule the other kingdoms; hence my desire to keep my distance from the Mittani. Either Artatama's completely out of control and insane, or he's the most ambitiously sinister member of a ruling family to be born into our times since Sargon or Hammurabi. However, I doubt he's half of their abilities or their brains if his current antics are anything to go by.

'I would encourage you and the Hittites to bring this overly ambitious pushy prince under control, since his father seems unable to do so; and to show you my encouragement, I would like to accompany you with a part of my army to Terqa, if you will permit. I have good knowledge of the terrain and my additional forces will bolster yours.' This time it was Atalshen's turn to look at his guest expectantly.

The Pharaoh was taken aback by the offer, but not in an unreceptive way. 'I must say my dear king, I shan't refuse your offer. Welcome on board our great enterprise. I'll confide in you, when I thought of Tikhsi, I was mainly thinking in terms of a problem; but as things have turned out, you may be the solution to Terqa. This is a turning point in our relationship. If you come with me, and we succeed in Terqa, I will absolve you of your need to send tribute for the next five years and cancel what you currently owe me. Does that suite you, my dear king?'

Atalshen smiled and nodded in satisfaction at the Pharaoh's proposal. He'd half expected such a reaction, which is partly why he'd made the offer in the first place. It would make his treasury's coffers a lot healthier than it would otherwise have been. For the first time in a long while, Atalshen felt a sense of contentment spreading inside of him, and it wasn't the wine.

24
Attempted Ambush

Following the vanquishing of the vacillating King of Isuwa and replacing him with a new Hittite friendly king, Tudhaliyas' army continued its march on the Mittani capital, still intent on teaching their king a salutary lesson for kidnapping his daughter. He may not have been directly responsible for the kidnapping, but it *was* the king's son who was responsible for the foul deed. It was up to him to have controlled his wayward son.

Now he would have to take the consequences for not bringing his son in line earlier. This course of action had to be pursued for the sake of long term Hittite security, otherwise Tudhaliyas would be seen as weak, and who knows what his enemies would try the next time round.

King Tudhaliyas was riding on the right side of the newly appointed King of Isuwa, King Kanisa, chatting amiably with him on military matters to do with the ensuing campaign. General Zidanta meanwhile, was riding on Tudhaliyas' right, listening politely to the chit-chat, keeping a keen watch on anything coming from the east.

The combined Hittite and Isuwan armies had crossed the Puranti Bridge outside Malidiya, which was the main crossing point this far north, and were on the main route to Wassukanni from the west, now travelling in hostile Mittani territory.

Both sides had sent large numbers of scouts out to determine the whereabouts of their opponents, their strengths and routes of march. Reports had come back to Tudhaliyas the Mittani had concentrated their forces about five leagues downstream, seemingly waiting for the Hittites to appear there. This amused both kings and General Zidanta. It was true they'd intended to cross at this point before they'd taken Malidiya, and it meant there was a leak in the General Staff, for a Mittani spy must have passed on the information. However, all had changed once Malidiya was in Hittite hands.

General Zidanta made a proposal to Tudhaliyas as he rode by his side, 'If we follow the river till we get to the westward bend, then push on hard into the desert for Wassukanni, we might beat Saustatar back to his capital...'

'...and that way we may not have to fight Saustatar at all. Caught out in the open, he'd have to bring his son in line and hand over my daughter,' the king finished for the general.

'That's assuming he's in a position to do such a thing, sire,' added Zidanta.

King Tudhaliyas winced at that idea. He'd been under the impression his daughter was kidnapped for a purpose— but what if something had gone wrong and she was....' he couldn't finish the thought. He shook his head and thought of his queen back in Hattusas. She was barely holding together. He'd brought out the army in a desperate attempt to force the issue—one way or another. For the sake of the nation, this situation had to be resolved....hopefully with the rescue of Asmunikal....but he was prepared for the worst.

The general had a good inkling of what was going through the king's mind and said, 'Your majesty, we will get your daughter back alive, I promise. I have placed high hopes in Prince Mokhat's expedition. The people he's leading are the best we have—if anyone can bring this to a successful conclusion, then he and Colonel Onasiyas' *special forces* will.'

'Yes, I hope your right,' answered the king, '...for the queen's sake, more than anything.'

*　　*　　*

Waiting five leagues further downstream on the eastern side of the Puranti was the Mittani army, which had been joined by the Tushan army. The Tushans had been called to readiness by King Saustatar of Mittani, to come to his aid as rapidly as they could join him—it was for the coming battle with the invading Hittites. Saustatar had convinced himself, Tudhaliyas would cross the Puranti further down from Malidiya and gathered his army at the spot to oppose the invader. He'd assumed the Isuwans would destroy the bridge outside of Malidiya when the Hittites attacked.

Saustatar had expected to stop Tudhaliyas at *his* chosen spot on the Puranti, where he now waited, and was shocked to learn the Hittite army had already crossed the river.

Saustatar turned to his commanding general, General Ratukani and said, 'Remind me now, *why* are waiting down here when the Hittites have already crossed the river?'

'Sire, it was your initial contention the Hittite army would be forced to skirt Malidiya due to Isuwan resistance. You also insisted the Isuwans would destroy the bridge. This area was the likely spot where they would then be forced to cross the Puranti.' The general now saw the weakness of the plan, but a week ago, it had made military sense. 'I agreed with your contention—and so this is why we're here, sire. It might be advisable to revise the plan in view of developments.'

'Revise the plan.....revise the plan? That's an understatement, my dear general. How was I to know the Isuwans would capitulate so easily? My spies tell me Tudhaliyas replaced the Isuwan king and the Isuwan army has joined him in his invasion of my lands. Revise the plan, heh? In your opinion, even if we move up to face him, can we hope to win?' The king scowled, but he knew it wasn't the general's fault. He was so frustrated his own son was the cause of all this mayhem. His own son....his flesh and blood....would be the likely cause of the downfall of his dynasty. Instead of strengthening his house, he was destroying it.

'Sire, the spies warn us Tudhaliyas has amassed a large army, some sixty thousand strong. If we add another ten thousand or so of Isuwans—then we cannot hope to stand against such a force. There's also news the Kizzuwatna have taken Karkamish and are now crossing the Puranti further downstream. I'm informed they are heading for Harran. If we stay here, we'll be caught between the two armies. I wouldn't advise going to meet the Hittites with the Kizzuwatna at our rear.

'I counsel a return to Wassukanni as quickly as we can. The city walls can withstand such an onslaught—out in the open we would be slaughtered. Send the Tushans back to their city sire, and let's make haste and return to the capital. We should then send out a call to all our friends to come to our aid as quickly as the messengers can be sent. I believe Assyria might help us. Certainly the Tushans will come back and help us—but only as a larger contingent.' General Ratukani stood by his sovereign and waited for his decision.

'I don't think we have much of a choice. Give the orders—we'll head back to Wassukanni,' commanded the king, continuing to scowl at his predicament, trying to find a way of extricating himself from this dilemma. The king stared at his general, 'Look, I want to try one last thing; maybe it'll work and save our necks. Instead of sending the Tushans back home, have them head up north and then halt half way. We'll head a little south of the road back to the capital, and halt about the same distance east as the Tushans. I'm thinking of ambushing the Hittites. Surprise is a good tactic and if we hit the Hittites from two sides, north and south, we might force them to turn back. If we find we're getting the worst of it, we can always disengage and still head back to Wassukanni at speed, as can the Tushans. Explain it to them. If we're getting the worst of it, the Tushans should break off and go back to their city. What do you think?'

'Worth a try, sire. May I suggest putting our cavalry units to the east between our two forces? In this way, whichever side is losing, we can send them reinforcements at speed. At worst, we'll lose men...but if we're winning, it'll force the Hittites to break off and head back home. We shouldn't pursue them if that happens.'

'Right, make it happen. By the way, any news of my wayward son? Has the arrest warrant been proclaimed? Anybody found helping him will be assumed to be a traitor to the throne, is that clear? Any spies not working for *me* must therefore be working against me and are to be eliminated.'

General Ratukani frowned at this complication. A war to be dealt with *and* a palace rebellion to squash. 'Sire, the last piece of news had Prince Artatama heading towards Assyria, possibly Nineveh—and yes, sire, the arrest proclamation has been circulated. As for the spy network; the chief spy is still loyal and he's making all efforts to isolate and eliminate those who have gone over to your son.'

'He's no longer my son. As of now, I disown him and he's to be hunted down like any other criminal who's lifted his hand against my throne. *Ex* Prince Artatama,' the king added laying emphasis on the ex. The king said this with a heavy heart and much sadness. If only he could get his hands on the cause of his troubles.

His son had escaped from the dungeon, and he had no idea where the Hittite king's daughter was being held, or by whom. He'd been informed his spy network had split in two —one side still loyal to him, while the split side went over to his son. That was intolerable. His own son causing a split in *his* spy network. He had to treat his son's action as an attempted coup—there could be no other interpretation of such behaviour. His son was clearly trying to dictate the king's policy, and by default, take over the reigns of state. No king could, or should, tolerate such actions, especially not by his own son….his now *ex* son.

*   *   *

General Zidanta had been watching the distant dust cloud crossing their path from west to east and knew from experience, it was a large body of armed men on the move. They were heading towards….he estimated, Tushan.

A scout patrol came riding in to report what they'd seen. The captain in charge reported directly to Zidanta, 'General, we've come across what looks like a large army, racing in good order, back to the east, sir.'

'Thank you captain,' replied Zidanta. 'Tell me the colour of their tunics.'

'One lot had white with a dark blue sash, but the larger part of the force wore dark blue, sir. The dark blue lot brought up the rear.' The captain looked pleased he'd noted the uniforms, knowing his general's demand for details.

'Good! Yes, very good indeed. Seems you caught sight of the combined Mittani and Tushan armies. Go back and keep a watch on them. Send a scout every half a league of travel back to me to report. Is that clear? If they do anything you find strange—send back a report.'

'Yes sir, every half a league of their army's march— report back to you, sir.' The captain saluted with his right fist across his left chest, turned his horse and rode back the way he'd come.

'What did I tell you? They're racing back to the protection of their walls,' commented King Tudhaliyas when Zidanta told the king of the scout's report. 'They're not going to fight; not if they're racing away from us.'

Zidanta nodded, 'We need to speed up, sire, if we're going to catch up with them, assuming we can. I still feel the Mittani will turn and fight. It's not like them to run from a battle.'

'That may be so, but I have a feeling King Saustatar knows he's in the wrong...' said Tudhaliyas, patting his horse's neck, '...or at least his greedy son is, and having to defend his son's malicious actions by fighting us, is causing him a dilemma. We've invaded his lands, and he's bound to defend them, but he hesitates because the morality is against him. We monarchs always like to fight a moral battle for a just cause—and here, such a despicable kidnapping has put him firmly in the wrong.'

'You may have the crux of the matter, sire, Zidanta admitted, 'but I've never known the Mittani to run from a fight, not the way they're doing now.'

Later in the afternoon, scouts came racing back to inform Zidanta the enemy had split their forces. The Tushans had gone north, while the Mittani had veered south east—and more ominously, both armies had halted as if they were waiting for the Hittites to catch up. That, to the king and Zidanta, implied a battle was brewing.

'Damn them,' oathed Zidanta while reporting the latest developments to the king. 'They've split their forces —and are thus forcing us to do the same. But I'll bet as soon as one side clashes, the other side will retreat and try to join up with the one fighting. If I were Ratukani, I would put the cavalry out of sight between the two armies. That way they can race to support the ones engaged in the fighting, while one of our wings is chasing the retreating Tushans, or Mittani.'

'I have an idea,' said Tudhaliyas. 'What if we put a couple of squadrons of our cavalry into Kizzuwatna uniforms and have them appear from the south of the

Mittani. That would put a scare into Ratukani….and I'll bet he breaks off and runs for Wassukanni.'

'Sire, that's brilliant,' burst out Zidanta in a chuckle. 'Ratukani will think the whole Kizzuwatna army is upon him and it will ruin his *split* surprise tactic. He'll have no choice but to retreat and take the army back behind the safety of the capital's walls.' Zidanta stopped chuckling and looked anew at his king with a sense of admiration. 'Sire, soon I do believe you may not need my services.'

'Now, now, general—none of that. I came up with one small idea, while you've years of practical experience in commanding my army. I sincerely hope that we have many more years of mutual cooperation, to and for the benefit of our nation, and may the great Lord see fit to keep us thus.'

'Thank you for the vote of confidence, sire. I'll try to serve you to the best of my abilities. Now, let me see if we can dig up those extra scarlet Kizzuwatna uniforms for the two squadrons. We should have some spare in the baggage wagons.' Zidanta called for his aide, then explained what was needed. The aide saluted and sped off to carry out his commanders orders.

*   *   *

King Saustatar was sitting quietly at a table laid out for him by his servants, sipping a little wine and munching on some fruit, waiting for General Ratukani to report back to him on the readiness of the prepared ambush. He was uneasy, yet pleased they were preparing for battle. He didn't like running from an enemy—only a coward doesn't care. A distant noise of hooves distracted him from his dates as he popped them into his mouth, munching on them lazily.

General Ratukani came riding up and jumped from his horse, grim and resolute. 'Majesty, I have bad news.' He threw his reins at a waiting soldier.

'What?' chided the king. 'We're just readying for battle and you want to load me up with bad news? Not very comforting for me, you know.'

'My apologies, your majesty, but this *is* urgent. Scouts have returned from the south and report they've spotted a large squadron of Kizzuwatna cavalry coming this way.'

The king jumped out of his chair with a cry of anguish. '*No*! That can't be. They're supposed to be attacking Harran. They can't be approaching our position— not right now. Are you sure of your information?'

'Yes, sire. You may rely on this. If these scouts report the existence of the Kizzuwatna cavalry heading this way, then that's what's happening. My counsel is for us to move our forces as speedily as we can back to Wassukanni without delay or we'll end up done to, as we intended to do to the Hittites. Split and battling on both fronts—and we don't have the numbers for it.' The general stood waiting for the order to break their position and resume their original flight to the capital.

'Well then, give the order,' commanded the king, furious at being thwarted in his plan to ambush the Hittites. 'And send a messenger to the Tushans to abandon their positions. Tell them to go home.'

Ratukani shouted for his officers to attend him and gave the orders to make haste back to Wassukanni.

All mayhem broke lose amongst the Mittani soldiers as they reformed their marching order and resumed their journey back to their capital.

*   *   *

Both Tudhaliyas and Zidanta were chuckling and looking pleased with themselves at the success of their ruse with the scarlet uniforms.

'Sire, if you have any more of these wonderful ideas —please share them with me,' the general said between his subdued laughter. 'They fell for the subterfuge as sweetly as an over ripe medlar. My scouts report the Mittani are running for Wassukanni as fast as they can travel— abandoning any hope of an ambush. The Tushans are heading back to their capital. In one move, sire, you've split the enemy forces and sent them packing for the safety of their walls. I must congratulate you once more.'

'Don't over blow this, general,' smiled Tudhaliyas. 'We still have to take Wassukanni when we get there. I'm told it's walls are one of the strongest in existence—made of hard granite; high and virtually impregnable. They used the thick walls of Hattusas as their model. We may be in for a long siege, unless we can find a way of overcoming the protection of those walls.'

Zidanta informed the king, 'Luckily sire, we have the right engineers to deal with those walls. I made sure before we left—in case. Anyway, your majesty, we now press on to Wassukanni.'

25
Siege of Harran

The Kizzuwatna army had been on a forced march for the last three days and was now approaching the city of Harran. Harran stood a little distance back from the west bank of the Balikh River, an eastern tributary of the mighty Puranti River. Its' location was a major crossroad from the north to Babylon in the south, and as a primary trade route from the Blue Sea and Ugarit in the west, all the way through the plains of the middle Aransah River, and on to Nineveh and Assur in Assyria in the east. Nominally, it was under the suzerainty of the Mittani, but it tended to assert a great measure of independence in its own affairs.

'So tell me again, my dear general, what do we know of this city,' asked the young Crown Prince Talshura of his commanding general. 'I know you've told me once, but I was only half listening—now I can see the place, I want to make a greater effort to concentrate on what you say.'

General Tapalass, the commander of the Kizzuwatna army sighed deeply and once again tried to inform his young prince of the nature of the city they were about to invest. 'It's a major commercial, cultural, and religious centre under Mittani control. I'm even informed its name comes from *harranu*, meaning caravan road. In recent years, the Mittani have tried to reassert a stronger hold over the headstrong King of Harran, King Tupkish. According to the information supplied by our Karkamish friends, King Saustatar has stationed a couple of Mittani regiments inside the city as he did in Karkamish, to ensure King Tupkish doesn't stray in his loyalty, as is his want sometimes.

'If we could somehow get the population of Harran to revolt, together with their army, we might be able to do what we couldn't do with Karkamish—namely, take the city without having to battle for it. You remember what the High Priest said in Karkamish; if it wasn't for the Mittani in the city, they would have opened the city gates to us.

'The point of our investments upon the cities along our route is to prevent them becoming a threat to us from the rear, after we have attacked Wassukanni. We simply can't leave hostile Mittani allied cities behind us. It's unfortunate we have to deal with them in this brutal manner, but it's necessary so as not to have a dagger at our backs when we're attacking the Mittani capital. You do see, your highness, don't you?'

'Yes general, it does seem to make sense,' answered the Crown Prince. They were riding past a cluster of beehive adobe houses which appeared to be part of the outlying areas of Harran. 'All the people have disappeared from their homes,' commented the prince, as he looked at the empty beehives.

'Your highness, please concentrate on the matter at hand,' the general reprimanded his prince gently. 'We're about to go into battle again and we need to find a way of taking this town. From what our Karkamish friends have told us; this city is going to be a more difficult objective. The walls are made of solid stone and they're thick. They're high and well built. We need to find its weakness. We have a week at the utmost to take this city if we're to make Wassukanni in time.'

'King Aplahanda II of Karkamish was kind enough to supply us with some of his troops. Maybe we should involve his general in our discussion,' suggested Prince Talshura.

'Ah, yes, that's a splendid idea,' agreed General Tapalass, and told his aide to fetch the Karkamish general. 'Maybe he can suggest a weakness we've overlooked. I must admit; my first inclination is to undermine the walls.

You know; send in diggers and build a tunnel under the wall —fill it with wood and set fire to it. The wall should then collapse at that point. What do you think?' he asked the prince, not really expecting an answer.

A while later, the Karkamish general arrived on his fine white horse.

'You sent for me?' he asked of Tapalass, with barely a nod to the Crown Prince.

'Yes, General Muhar,' replied Tapalass. 'We would like your advice on Harran. Since we're going in to battle together to take this city—maybe you have an idea how we could achieve this. You know it better than we do.'

Both men looked into each other's eyes, searching for signs of sincerity. Having recently been on opposing sides, both men still had issues that muddied their relations. General Muhar sat on his horse and thought for a while, whilst the two Kizzuwatna commanders observed him.

Finally he said, 'I think I may have a solution to your problem. I brought Harupal with me, our town engineer. He's been trying to work out various ways of taking a city for the last two years. I thought he might be useful.'

Tapalass looked at his Crown Prince in puzzlement. The prince returned his puzzled glance.

'Yes, I admit it's a strange hobby for a town engineer, but he was simply trying to find counter strategies to the city being invested.' Muhar smiled in embarrassment. 'I'm aware he's failed because you succeeded in taking Karkamish. However, he might have suggestions for taking Harran you haven't thought of. Shall I send for him?'

'By all means, let's hear what this Harupal has to say.'

By this time, it was mid-afternoon and they had reached the outskirts of Harran, halting on the main road leading to the main gate of the city, four hundred cubits from the city walls. A scouting squad returned to inform Tapalass the city was closed tight and ready for siege. All the gates around the city had been closed and the surrounding area was clear of people—presumably they'd sought sanctuary inside.

'Look at it,' Tapalass pointed at the city, staring at Muhar. 'Stands on a hill, surrounded by a deep moat. But the worst of it is, the walls. Solid brick….and I'll bet they're thick as well.' He wasn't happy at all as he stared at his target.

Harupal, the chief engineer of Karkamish arrived on his horse, smiling happily, as if he had been expecting this call. 'General Muhar, I was told you wanted to see me,' said Harupal stopping short and nodding respectfully to Tapalass and the Crown Prince.

'Yes, I do,' replied Muhar brusquely. 'You keep pestering me about the defence of Karkamish, and what needs to be done to better defend it. I'm sorry I didn't listen to you more closely in the past. Now I want you to do *me* a service. Go have a look at Harran—see if you can find a weakness in *that* city. How would you take the city if you had to? Come back and report after you've analysed the problem.' Muhar turned to Tapalass and asked, 'Could you send some men with him to keep him out of trouble. He's a bit careless and likely to get himself killed if he's not watched.'

General Tapalass gave the order to his aide, allowing Harupal and his escort to leave. 'This should be interesting,' he commented as the engineer departed. 'Let me tell you, my first inclination was to starve them out, but it could take months, and we haven't got months. Battering rams on the main gate is the only other way in, and it's going to be costly. I can see from here they've reinforced the gate with bronze. Then there's tunnelling, and filling the cavity with wood. Setting fire to the wood and watch the wall collapse….but the moat prevents us.'

General Muhar coughed to get their attention, 'Ahem…I'm sorry general, but those walls won't collapse by tunnelling. They're far too well built…and then there's the moat. And yes, the battering ram will just pile up bodies. It might help if we had an idea how their water supply comes in….and we should cut it if possible. It would show we're serious.'

The Crown Prince joined the conversation, 'From here, the moat surrounding the walls is awfully wide. Someone's done a good job of protecting the city from a siege.'

Tapalass told his aide to set up his tent, come-headquarters, on the spot they stood. 'We might as well settle in—for the moment at least—till we can formulate a plan of attack. Your highness, I'm going to send a messenger to the city gate to demand the city surrenders. Who knows, it might work.'

The prince shrugged, 'Why not? It's certainly worth a try.'

Tapalass told his second in command to lock down the city tight—to station a thousand soldiers outside each city gate, light fires and begin the siege. Every postern gate was to be found and closed tight. Any tunnels leaving the city were to be blocked—and a detailed search was to be made to establish where the city got its water supply.

'Pity there's no forests around here,' Tapalass confided in Prince Talshura as he dismounted. 'We're short on timbers. We've brought the siege engines from Karkamish with us but there's no repairing them or building new ones. Once they're destroyed, that's it. I'm beginning to get a bad feeling about this city, your highness. In the time we've got, I don't think we're going to be able to take it. We may have to break off and head for Wassukanni.'

'Let's wait until tomorrow,' replied the prince, also dismounting and joining his general. 'A good night's sleep and who knows. An idea might come up which may surprise you.'

Tapalass looked sideways at his prince. He was acting as the wise counsel of caution and patience….most unlike him…and something he ought to encourage. Maybe he's growing up at last. 'I trust you're right, your highness. We'll wait till the morning before I make any final decisions.' He sighed deeply and watched the tent being raised.

Once inside the tent, sitting around a table with food and wine being served, Tapalass motioned to Muhar, 'Still no sign of your engineer? He's taking his time.'

'He's a thorough fellow,' answered Muhar. 'I'm sure he'll come up with something. You don't know the chap like I do. He's considered something of a clever person in our city.'

Just then, horses were heard outside. A rider dismounted and entered the large tent. It was Harupal, the engineer.

He looked pleased with himself and held a leather skin rolled up under his arm. 'Your highness, generals, may I?' Harupal asked for the table to be cleared and then unfurled his leather skin on the table and spread it out. There was a fine drawing of the city on the skin with a ramp at its northern end.

'What the……..?' exclaimed General Muhar.

'Well I never….!' added General Tapalass.

Crown Prince Talshura stood there and chuckled.

'What a clever idea,' said Tapalass, before anybody could say a word.

'I'm glad you appreciate it,' answered Harupal. 'I got the idea from an Assyrian engineer friend of mine. He told me one of his friends was thinking of such a way of taking a city—building a ramp all the way to the top of the ramparts.

On the leather drawing was a dirt rampart which went all the way to the top of the crenelations of the northern wall.

'Why there—why that particular spot? What's so special about this part of the wall?' asked Muhar.

243

'There's a small dirt hill nearby which can be used to build the ramp,' replied Harupal. 'No other reason. Instead of digging a hole to get at the dirt for the ramp, we use the dirt from the hill. It's more convenient. Also, there's no city towers nearby so it will be safer for the builders.'

Tapalass stood there slowly shaking his head. 'Heh, what an idea....we'll need ways to protect the builders from whatever they're intending to throw at them from those walls,' the general continued. He turned to his aide, 'Remember those wooden barricades we used in Karkamish to enter the city. Did we bring them with us?'

'I think so, sir. Let me go and check.'

'Wait...also check on the battering rams. Get them to bring all the stuff to the northern wall. Put it behind this hill so the enemy won't see them,' the general pointed at the hill on the leather map.

The aide nodded and went out to look for the equipment.

'If we're going to attempt such a thing,' said Tapalass, 'I'm sure glad it's this time of year. Later on, it would be too damp to shovel such an amount of earth. Right now, it's still dry. If we wait until it gets dark.....' He stopped and scratched his beard. 'We'll need to be careful with the noise so as not to alert the city. We'll need five thousand men digging throughout the night, all to be told to do it as silently as they can, and pile the earth against the city wall. First, we'll need to fill the moat; then go steadily up the wall bit by bit....as quickly and as quietly as we can. General Muhar....I want you to equip your men with tall wooden shields, full body length...at least two cubits high. Their task will be to cover those men who bring the earth up the ramp from enfilade fire. I'm giving you the job of protecting the workers.'

'Yes general,' replied Muhar. He turned and left the tent, aware of the urgency building up.

Tapalass continued talking to his prince, with Harupal listening in. 'We'll take the ram out of the housing and use the roof cover to protect the workers. We'll put lots of wet leather on the roofs. They'll be pouring hot oil and boulders on those workers from above. There'll be a lot of casualties to deal with.'

Tapalass called for his senior officers to attend him. When they arrived, he told one of his commanders, 'Go and make sure we've got a good few thousand soldiers outside each gate; fires lit; tell them to make a lot of noise, singing and dancing, you know the type. Beat the drums of war as well. But I don't want anybody over here,' Tapalass pointed to the ramp at the northern wall. 'Here I want complete darkness. About forty cubits to the left of this hill,' again he pointed at the hill on the map, 'I want a large encampment with small fires and lots of noise. It's to distract those on the walls from the work going on under their noses. They'll be looking at the encampment—not at the work going on. Go now, carry out my orders.'

The commander left to organise the subterfuge noise brigade.

'Now the rest of you, listen carefully. I want all those working on the ramp to be extra quiet when going about their work—but to be quick in what they're doing. We've got plenty of men, so let them work in shifts all through the night. That way they won't get too exhausted and the work will go quicker. Those on the wall will soon know what's happening, but it must only be at dawn tomorrow, and not before. I want the ramp half way up their wall by then. Tomorrow we'll continue building using the emptied battering rams as cover. By the way, how many battering rams have we got?' he asked his aide.

'Three sir,' the aide replied.

'Can't be helped. I'll want one for the main gate. We'll push the other two into place when it gets light. The builders can use them for protection. We should have full-body shield-bearers, archers, and slingers in place for the dawn shift. Any mobile barricades we have left over from Karkamish must be here by then. I want the heavy infantry helping with the digging. They'll be the first over the top.

'All of this depends on how the enemy reacts to our access ramp. We may have to attack with the ramp short of its objective, so let's have all the scaling ladders ready to go. When we're ready to assault the ramp, I want half of our army at this position—ready to go over the top. We'll have archers and slingers provide covering fire while the heavy infantry assaults the town wall up the ramp. It's good there's no wall towers nearby—means it'll limit the enfilade crossfire. Have I left anything out?' Tapalass looked at his prince with his eyebrows raised, then at the gathered officers.

'I think you've been very thorough, general,' observed his young Crown Prince, 'but what about the main gate? We must split the defenders between the ramp and the main gate. *And* we need to attack other parts of the wall just so they don't concentrate their forces at the ramp.'

'I have that in hand,' replied the wily old general. 'When we're ready to assault the ramp, I'll order an all out assault on their walls with scaling ladders, with particular emphasis on the main gate. The ram there should have made an impact by then. That'll keep them busy—and away from the ramp.'

'*Now* you've covered everything. Any thing to add,' the prince looked at Harupal.

The Karkamish engineer smiled and said, 'No, your highness. It's all up to your soldiers now.'

Tapalass looked at his officers standing around the table and said, 'Right, men, let's get to it. We haven't a moment to lose. I want this city taken by tomorrow evening and us on our way to the Mittani capital the next day. Oh, and don't forget to make a lot of noise away from the ramp —especially at the main gate.'

'*Yes sir,*' cried the officers in unison, then dispersed to carry out their duties.

'Now,' General Tapalass turned to his aide, 'How did the surrender demand go? Did you tell them they would suffer the consequences if they refused?'

'Sir, near the Harran officer our messenger was talking to, we spotted a bunch of Mittani soldiers. Our messenger didn't manage to finish his demand—when one of the Mittani arrows shot him down from his horse. Then the Mittani shouted, "*Give that to your general. That's our response*," and they loosed off more arrows at us.'

'*They'll pay for that,*' exploded the general. 'Was the messenger under a flag of truce?' he asked angrily.

'Yes sir, as per normal. I carried the flag myself. There were three of us, and one even held his shield above his head in the old sign of truce.'

'*I will have every Mittani in the city staked out,*' shouted the general furiously. 'War is war, but there are a few rules I won't allow to be violated—the flag of truce is one of them. Damned barbarians!'

By dawn of the next day, the sentries on the city walls woke to the awful sight of a huge earthen ramp reaching three-quarters of the way up the northern wall—and they raised such a fuss and alarm that soon the wall above the ramp was filled with Harran soldiers in their muddy grey uniforms. They pointed at the ramp in horror and confusion until a lot of Mittani soldiers arrived and took charge. The dark blue uniforms mixed with the grey began to set up squads of archers, slingers, and javelin throwers, ready for the attack. They began strengthening their part of the wall with barricades and more stone.

The ramp builders had stopped work while dawn broke through the darkness, but now they resumed their building, hiding behind the full body shields provided by

Muhar's soldiers in their light blue tunics. The battering rams devoid of the rams, were moving up the ramp, followed by besieging soldiers carrying baskets of earth. The nearby hill the builders were denuding was quickly disappearing onto the ramp.

By mid-morning, despite all the frantic attempts by the Harran and Mittani, to prevent the ramp getting any higher, the ramp had reached a javelin's height to the top of the wall. The enemy had thrown boulders, poured boiling oil, and turned the roof of the battering ram into a porcupine, yet the ramp kept steadily rising with each basketful of earth brought through the hell of the battering ram tunnel. Many soldiers perished building the road up the wall.

Finally, General Tapalass was satisfied his men could deal with the little left to climb of the city wall. He ordered the battering ram tunnel be cleared of debris ready for the main assault. The heavy infantry were gathered at the bottom of the ramp, eager to be at the enemy. The tunnel up the ramp would provide overhead protection. Wooden barricades were brought through, to be ready for the wall itself. Then the general ordered the thousands of heavy infantry with their scaling ladders to be fed through the battering ram tunnel towards the wall. Outside, archers and slingers provided covering fire against the mass of enemy gathered on the wall at that point.

General Tapalass gave the order for the all out assault using scaling ladders on the entire perimeter wall. The front gate was pummelled throughout the night and was beginning give, despite being reinforced. It was near to being breeched.

At the ramp site, the enemy had tried to build the wall higher to make entry more difficult for those scaling it, but they'd run out of time. Once the scaling ladders were in place, there was an overwhelming pressure of fighting men forcing their way up and over the top of the wall. The mass of heavy infantry kept charging up the ramp, through the battering ram tunnel, to assault the wall. The slaughter was immense. The bodies were piling up at the base of the wall and to each side of the ramp, both Kizzuwatna and Harran, with a smattering of Mittani dark blue among them.

Horns of alarm were heard from inside the city, causing panic. Vast portions of the city walls were abandoned as the fighting population rushed to the northern wall where the ramp was creating such an impact. Kizzuwatna and Karkamish soldiers were atop the northern wall fighting desperately to clear it of the Mittani, who now predominated in the fighting there. They were tougher fighters than the city's soldiers, and put up stiffer resistance to the breach of the city's defences.

'We seem to be getting in control of this wall,' commented Tapalass to Muhar, both standing at the bottom of the ramp, urging the soldiers on. 'We shall have to find a suitable reward for your Harupal.' They both encouraged and pushed their soldiers up the ramp, keeping a critical eye on the heavy infantry move swiftly by them into the tunnel towards the wall.

'Once our king learns of his part in this battle, I'm sure he will reward him,' replied General Muhar.

'By the way, have you seen the Crown Prince recently? I seem to have lost contact with him when the assault began.'

Muhar shrugged his shoulders, 'No, I'm afraid not. I think I saw him at the mouth of the tunnel a while ago.'

'If that young man gets himself into harm, his father will have my hide for not taking better care of him. I'd better go through the tunnel and climb the wall—see if I can find him.' Tapalass told his aide to get his bodyguards ready. They were going up the wall and into the city. 'Coming?' Tapalass asked Muhar.

'Well of course. I wouldn't miss this,' replied the Karkamish general at the head of his own escort, following Tapalass through the tunnel to the wall.

By mid-afternoon, the two Mittani regiments had been neutralised within the city of Harran and the battered gates of the city were thrown wide open. The majority of Harran's soldiers were not interested in fighting to the death, and they surrendered in droves.

King Tupkish appeared on the palace steps as the fighting died down. He had his numerous priests surrounding him, almost like a protecting escort. The sanctuary of Ehulhul, based in Harran, as was the sanctuary of the moon god Sin—had plenty of priests, and here they were in the escort. The sanctuary of Ehulhul stood next to the palace. The king, hiding in their midst, assumed he would be safer surrounded by Sin's priests, and to that extent he was correct.

Crown Prince Talshura approached King Tupkish, followed by hundreds of scarlet uniforms. He'd managed to evade Tapalass' injunction to avoid going into battle, and was at the forefront of the fighting, much to the admiration of his soldiers. He'd been in the second wave over the wall of the city and had participated in some of the fiercest fighting with the Mittani.

Talshura halted a cubit away from the city's king and stood there looking up at him as if he were a curiosity. Tupkish in his turn, waited at the top of a flight of steps, hoping to force whoever wanted to talk to him, to climb the stairs, almost as if he were still in charge of the city.

Finally, the priests descended the stairs and approached Crown Prince Talshura. At that point, General Tapalass appeared from behind a building facing the palace. He was followed by General Muhar and a host of scarlet and grey uniforms. Tapalass went to his prince with the firm intention of berating him for his foolishness of putting himself in danger. Halfway, he noticed the strange stand-off between Tupkish and Talshura.

Tapalass turned to his second in command and shouted, 'Get that king off of his steps and on his knees in front of our Crown Prince. The vanquished will bow to the victor or suffer the consequences. I won't have this nonsense going on any longer,' he pointed at Tupkish.

Kizzuwatna soldiers rushed the stairs in a bunch, knocking the small parade of priests on to their backsides. They grabbed Tupkish none too gently and marched him down to where Talshura waited, forcing him on his knees in front of the young prince. Tupkish struggled at first but then accepted the inevitable humiliation.

The chief priest of Sin came to Tapalass and said, 'My king wished me to inform you we would have opened the gates to you at the outset but we were prevented from doing so by the two Mittani regiments quartered in the city.' The priest waved his hand at the few dead Mittani bodies in the square. 'We don't have an argument with our Kizzuwatna friends and the king wishes you and your allies be treated as his guests while you are here.'

Tapalass raised his eyebrows as he heard this familiar speech. 'I've heard all this before, in Karkamish.' He looked at General Muhar and laughed. 'Have all the priesthood in this area got together and come up with a formal recitation of surrender?' he asked between guffaws. 'This would be funny if it hadn't cost us so many dead.' Tapalass drew his sword and thrust it into the chief priest's stomach, just as a gasp of shock left the priests lips. He collapsed to the ground amongst his stunned acolytes, blood spreading in a red pool where he lay. The other priests couldn't believe what had happened to their leader. The former king of the city took it as his queue to bow his head to the ground in front of Talshura, in case this mad general decided to do the same to him.

The Crown Prince asked quietly, 'General, why did you do that?'

'I've listened to too much prattle from this bunch of cowards, and I'm afraid I've reached my limit. These damned priests firstly encourage the fighting with their blessings and the like, and then hope to avoid the consequences after the battle is lost. Well there's *one* priest who now knows the consequences of war.' He threw a glance at the body at his feet.

Other priests soon picked up the body and processed it solemnly to their temple, leaving the ex monarch of the city to his fate in front of his captors. Then, a small crowd of scarlet uniforms rounded a building, leading a group of dark blue uniformed prisoners.

'Ah, what have we here?' growled Tapalass, as he saw who the prisoners were. 'Remember what I said about staking them out in the sun before the battle,' he asked Muhar, turning to his Crown Prince with a quizzical look. 'Your highness, I hope you have no objections to staking this scum out in the sun?'

'General, whatever you do is fine by me,' answered the young prince. 'I wouldn't want you to break your oath. I heard clearly you swear to do that after they'd shot our truce messenger. Please go ahead.'

Tapalass waited until the prisoners were brought before him, then he called for the messenger who'd been fired upon. 'Do you recognise any of them as having fired on you from the gate wall?' he asked of the astonished soldier when he arrived.

'Sorry sir, I can't say I do. I've been in heavy fighting and what happened earlier has gone clean out of my mind.' He looked downcast he couldn't support his general's accusation.

'Never mind—they're part of the same rotten bunch. I'm giving you the privilege of staking them out. Take some soldiers and spread these curs out on the ground outside the city wall. Put a guard over them and leave them until tomorrow. If they're still alive by then, finish them off in the morning. I don't want to cart around any prisoners with me. Tomorrow we cross the river and leave for Wassukanni.

26
Pharaoh at Terqa

Terqa stood on a hill a little distance from the banks of the mighty Puranti River. There were three massive defensive concentric, solid masonry walls forty cubits thick surrounding the city. Then there was the broad moat encircling the outer ring, forty cubits wide fed by a small canal from the Puranti. So spacious were these walls, the outer ring possessed a passageway to allow the defenders to mobilise around its long perimeter.

These monstrous fourteen cubit high walls were placed on foundation stones and aprons of solid rock which were meant to repulse both human enemies and natural disasters, especially floods. The foundation stones had been brought down with great effort from the nearby hills two leagues away and made a formidable and effective a barrier to tunnelling and undermining.

This once great city had seen better days two hundred years ago, when it was a leading power together with Mari, in what was then the Khana Kingdom. It stood on a long trade route to the eastern sub continent doing business with the great Mohenjo Daro. Now, it was reduced to being a vassal city of the Mittani who had imposed Parushtar, as the Mittani Governor on to Terqa. He was a brutal and arrogant plutocrat who wielded absolute power. All the soldiers in Terqa wore the Mittani dark blue, and the people deeply resented them. The people prayed daily to their old fertility god Dagan, for relief and freedom from their cruel governor and this Mittani oppression.

The Governor of Terqa stood on the main tower above the huge bronze gates protecting the inner city, watching the approach of the Khemet army in the noonday sun. Parushtar smiled at the dust cloud thrown up by the approaching enemy. He was entirely convinced the Pharaoh's siege would turn out to be futile and the city was utterly safe from being taken.

* * *

Pharaoh Amenhotep II peered at the city from his royal chariot and was taken aback by the size of the walls he was seeing. He'd assumed King Atalshen of Tikhsi had exaggerated the strength of its fortifications—but now he wasn't so sure.

The pharaoh's twenty thousand strong army had recuperated in Tikhsi and was now ready for combat. Atalshen had added his ten thousand soldiers to the enterprise, and this sizeable army had been confident they would make short work of such an insignificant city as Terqa. Atalshen had warned the pharaoh otherwise, citing Terqa's decline on the one hand, but emphasising its mighty past as a caution not to expect an easy siege.

'Pity we can't get them to come out into the open,' said the pharaoh to General Hatupt, the commander of his troops. 'Our charioteers would make short work of them on the field of battle.'

'With walls like those to protect them, they have no need to come out into the open, your majesty.'

'Yes, I suppose it would be foolish of them to come out—yet we must get in. I've looked at the maps King Atalshen has provided and I'm left with no way to break into the city. We're going to have to pray for a miracle to open the gates for us.'

'I'll organise the royal stockade for the night, sire.'

'Thank you general.'

King Atalshen astride his horse, joined the pharaoh and shook his head. 'I told you there would be a problem getting into the city.'

'Yes my dear king, you did, but I didn't believe you until now. Three walls—what are they afraid of?'

'A Khemetian army led by the pharaoh,' replied Atalshen with a smile.

'But how did they know two hundred years ago I would be coming?' rejoined the pharaoh with a laugh.

'Soothsayers, you majesty, soothsayers. The city's god is Dagan, and they say he's mightily protective of his city.'

Both the sovereigns laughed at this bit of banter.

Later on in the afternoon, sitting in the pharaoh's tent inside the royal stockade, eating a sumptuous meal, the two sovereigns continued their friendly conversation on how to break into the city. Each strategy proposal was rejected as being useless against the sizeable walls.

'Your majesty,' called an officer from the entrance.

'Enter,' shouted the pharaoh.

'Your majesty,' repeated the officer as he came inside, 'a messenger has arrived from the Assyrian king. He asks permission to present himself to you.'

'By all means, send him in.'

Atalshen looked at the pharaoh, 'I think you have our neighbours worried as to why you're here.'

An exhausted Assyrian officer entered the tent and prostrated himself in front of the pharaoh.

'Yes, what can I do for you?' asked Amenhotep.

The Assyrian rose to one knee and pulled out a clay tablet from his shoulder bag. 'I was asked to hand this to you by my king, King Ashur-Nirari II of Assyria.'

'Do you know the contents of the message?' asked the pharaoh.

'Yes, sire.'

'Then it would save a lot of time if you told me what the message says.'

'Felicitations from the monarch of the Aransah to the monarch of the Iteru. Why has Pharaoh wandered so far from the Iteru? Has his own river run dry and he seeks replenishment from my mighty Aransah? We are concerned as to why he is in our vicinity.'

'Is that all?' asked the pharaoh.

'Yes sire. I was ordered to wait and bring back your answer to my king.'

'Here's my answer,' smiled the pharaoh. 'I have a treaty obligation to my brother monarch, King Tudhaliyas of Hatti. I am merely fulfilling the treaty obligation and nothing more. I have no wish to take any of the waters of the Aransah and have no designs on any territory not already beholden to me. I will carry out my treaty obligations to the Hittite king and then depart back to my dear Iteru—you have my solemn word. Please convey this to my brother monarch King Ashur-Nirari II of Assyria, and wish him peace and prosperity from the Pharaoh of Khemet, Amenhotep II.'

There was a clear look of relief on the Assyrian officer's face. He had expected the worst, and instead had been given some good news. The pharaoh ordered the Assyrian officer be given food and a good horse on which he could return speedily to his king bearing his good tidings.

'After this meal, I want to convene a council of war,' ordered the pharaoh. 'We've got to find a way to get into the city.' He waved at his aide, 'I want all my senior officers and the King of Tikhsi and his senior officers present.'

'Yes you majesty,' answered the aide.

After the meal the dishes were cleared and a bigger table brought in. An army architectural engineer had already built a small replica of the city out of mud and wood, and it was brought into the meeting.

When all had assembled, the pharaoh began, 'You know why I've called you here at this time. This infernal city is all but impregnable—yet I need to find a quick way to take the city, just to show there is no such thing as an impregnable city. So…has anyone any ideas how to get inside?' Pharaoh stood and scrutinised their faces.

There was coughing, a few "hums" and "ahhs" but for the most part no one came up with anything—until the army architect-come-engineer raised his hand.

'Sire, may I speak?'

Pharaoh raised his eyebrows to this unexpected interruption. 'Well, my engineer, do *you* have an idea for us?'

'Yes sire. It's a bit devious….but it might work.'

'Well…devious is good. Let's hear it.'

'I'm proposing we built boats and cross the river….'

'What? You mean….leave the city as it is? Go round it?'

'Well…yes and no sire. I want us to be devious…and make the enemy think we're going on to Wassukanni, leaving them alone…..circumventing them. I'm proposing to use trickery to take the city.

'I'm proposing you promise the governor of the city peace terms, which includes them leaving us alone to ford the river….and we'll leave them alone...and give them something for not attacking us. Then I propose half of the army cross the river very openly, making lots of noise and such…..while we hide the other half behind those two hills….namely, your swift chariot regiments. You have four thousand men on them. We need to do this by evening…so under the cover of darkness the soldiers can get back to the city in time to help those fighting at the gate.' The architect pointed at a couple of mounds on the model. 'We hide behind those.

'I suggest General Hatupt admit to the governor his city is too strong to take and that we'll leave tribute to the cities god, Dagan...a tribute to his might and power. I'm suggesting we send as tribute, a long string of basket-laden donkeys into town....say two hundred donkeys. The donkeys will supposedly bear gifts and supplies, and should be driven by a few Tikhsi soldiers, since the Terqa are familiar with them, and it will lessen their suspicion. I'm hoping this tribute will be allowed to enter the gates. Then as they come parallel to the gates, our armed troops will spring from the baskets and secure the gates. That should be three hundred and eighty soldiers to secure the gates. They will hold the gates open for your chariot regiments to come charging through the city gates a little while later. In the baskets we should place your best fighters, sire, since they'll have to deal with the Mittani.'

One of pharaoh's senior officers took offence at the latter comment from this impudent engineer and pointed out angrily to this flippant upstart, *his* soldiers would put the Mittani in *their* place.

As the architect-engineer finished explaining all this, mouths dropped open, and eyebrows were raised—some were even openly chuckling at this mischievous plan.

The pharaoh was looking with interest at this devious engineer and was gently shaking his head. 'I'm not going to be able to hold a strategy meeting in future without your presence. This is really one of the most ingenious plans I've ever heard. Do you really think it could work?' The pharaoh was looking round the table for comments.

'It's certainly bold,' replied General Hatupt.

'I like it,' declared King Atalshen. 'It has just the right mix of boldness and cheek to succeed. But could I add, we would need to include say ten donkeys at the front of the convoy laden with proper gifts and good provisions, so if we had to, we could show them what gifts we were bringing in for them. We must be able to show them the tribute is genuine....but only in the first ten donkeys,' he added.

One of the senior Tikhsi officers said, 'Lets hope nobody decides to check the rest of the baskets, or poke spears through them.'

A Khemetian Lieutenant commander answered, 'If our army has departed, then it shouldn't happen. People are only suspicious when they're threatened. If the threat has gone, they'll relax and let the donkeys through. It's important the donkeys reach the gate when we're seen to be on the far side of the river—supposedly heading for Wassukanni.'

Another added, 'If we're on the other side of the river going away from Terqa, they'll think they're safe and let the tribute in without checking.'

Others around the table began nodding their approval…then they burst into a round of applause.

'Well there you have it my engineer…your plan has gained our approval,' commented the pharaoh. 'Our next move should be to begin building the rafts and boats to cross the river. I'm wondering why they haven't built a bridge near here already.'

'There's one at Mari,' explained Atalshen. 'The people of Terqa use that bridge.'

'General Hatupt, it's time you went and had a word with this Mittani governor.' Pharaoh winked at him conspiratorially. 'Offer him the tribute mentioned by our engineer here. Be sure to lay it on thick….how we're too exhausted to capture his city…even if we wanted to. How it's too well protected…and remember to mention their god….what's his name.'

'And the donkeys…..' reminded King Atalshen. 'If you don't mind….I'll have my people organise the string of donkeys….and the baskets….with the provisions.'

In the late afternoon, under a flag of truce, General Hatupt sat on his horse outside the huge city gates looking up at Governor Parushtar of Terqa, standing arrogantly above the gate, and spun him the agreed story. The governor didn't look at all surprised his city wasn't going to be put under siege. At the outset, he'd been convinced the city's defences were strong enough to withstand any such assault. Finally the governor condescended to fully accept what this Khemetian general was telling him....and was auto-convinced it was the truth.

'Thank your pharaoh for his kind gifts,' Parushtar shouted down to the general, 'and assure him we have no intention of attacking him while he crosses the river.'

The general waved his farewells and his thanks up at the governor, then swung his horse round and led his little group back away from the city gates at a trot. In the distance, coming towards the general from the river, heading towards the city gates, was an extremely long string of donkeys, each laden with a basket hanging on either flank. They were led by ten unarmed Tikhsi soldiers with their bared torsos.

As the general's group passed the donkeys, he gave a discreet thumbs up sign to the Tikhsi officer in charge, and then quickly left them behind, heading for the Puranti River. As had been agreed with the governor, the donkeys halted two arrow shot lengths from the city walls, waiting for their Terqa escort to guide them into the city.

General Hatupt led his small group to the river and down to the beach where a huge armada of rafts and boats were already crossing the Puranti River. Instead of joining the crossing, he led his band along the shore upriver, to where two thousand chariots, with a lot of difficulty, were hidden behind the two hills about a quarter of a league away from the city. Behind one of the hills, Pharaoh was waiting for the signal from the gates, which would be in the form of a fire arrow into the sky and a Khemetian horn blasted at full volume.

He was impatient to be off, to charge for the gate, knowing this would be a tricky moment for his charioteers. They would have to speed their chariots to the gate to support the three hundred and eighty fighting there to prevent the gates from being closed. His charioteers would then have to fight off the whole city as it awoke to the dangers until the main army could turn around their rafts and bring him reinforcements from the beach.

The fifty Mittani soldiers escorted the string of donkeys towards the moat bridge, kept looking around as if they were expecting an ambush. One of the Mittani escort thrust his sword into the basket of the fifth donkey, withdrew it and looked for blood. By the time the long convoy reached the wide open gates, the escort seem to visibly relax and they began to joke amongst themselves at the cowardice of the retreating Khemetians.

As the leading Tikhsi officer crossed the moat and came parallel with the city gate, he turned and waited for the donkey caravan to bunch up closer, then gave a shrill whistle through his teeth. The lids of the hundred and ninety baskets containing the secreted Khemetians burst off, and armed men jumped out. For a split second the Mittani were utterly dumbfounded, then they quickly drew their swords and charged the pharaoh's soldiers. A loud horn blasted from the back of the donkey convoy, still some way away from the gates. Khemetian soldiers were running frantically, rushing towards the open city gates. A blast of a Mittani horn sounded from inside the gates and the gates began to slowly close.

Orders were being shouted in Khemetian demanding those assigned to prevent the gates from closing to carry out their tasks. As more of pharaoh's soldiers arrived at the gate, they fanned out into a semi circle, pushing the defending Mittani back. Those assigned to keeping the gates open, broke down the tower's doors housing the gate mechanism situated on either side of the gates. They crashed through them, and rushed to disable the gate mechanism to prevent its closing.

Pandemonium broke out in the city as the daylight was fading, with alarm trumpets blaring, and more Mittani arriving at a run to join the battle for the gates. Civilians were shrieking, running away in terror from the clash of bronze on bronze, clogging the streets, preventing the Mittani reinforcements from reaching the gates.

The pharaoh was out in front, pushing his chariot as hard as he could, speeding ahead, leading his regiments through the ensuing darkness towards the city gate, trying to close the distance to the gates to help his men. The thunder of two thousand chariots reverberated all the way to the city and dark blue uniformed men on the city walls were pointing into the twilight with panic, at the dark dust storm raised by the hooves and wheels of the approaching enemy. More horns joined in the hub-hub of battle sounds until it seemed the Dark Earth had opened up, vomiting out Anhur, the slayer of enemies—at the head of his underworld deities.

The three hundred and eighty at the gates had diminished to half their numbers when pharaoh's chariots finally arrived, yet the cost in lives had not been in vain, for they had managed to keep the city's gates open, and pharaoh burst through them into the midst of the Mittani defenders, crashing his chariots into his opponents. The plaza before the gates was now littered with dead and dying, both Mittani and Khemetians, and the fighting was gaining in fierceness rather than diminishing. The darkness was lifted somewhat when the full moon came out of the clouds and threw its eerie light on the scene, revealing twisted bloodied bodies. More Mittani rushed into the battle through the narrow streets. Pharaoh had to abandon his beloved chariot to fight on foot. His bodyguard went about ferociously defending him from the inevitable onslaught on the leader of the enemy.

General Hatupt was in the thick of it, hacking and thrusting his sword into any Mittani foolish enough to come into striking distance. The battle went on for some time; neither side seemed to be getting the upper hand, yet the gates stayed open. Pharaoh's forces had secured the plaza in front of the gates but try as they might, they couldn't get further into the city. Arrows and slings were continuing to fall on them from the top of the gate towers and the city walls. The Mittani had climbed on to the rooftops of the nearby houses and threw everything they cold throw onto the heads of the invading enemy.

Amenhotep managed to extricate himself from the fight and went to stand on the moat bridge looking for the rest of his army. In the distant moonlight he spied the huge column rushing towards the city and he allowed himself a half smile of satisfaction. It seemed the engineers plan would come to fruition after all.

By morning, the city had been secured and the last of the Mittani ferreted out and now corralled in the plaza in front of the city gates. A ring of Khemetian special soldiers with their distinctive coats of waded leather and bronze helmets guarded the prisoners.

Governor Parushtar of Terqa had taken his own life, falling on his sword in disgrace. The invincible city of Terqa with its three concentric walls had fallen to an evil trick and he'd been the cause of it with his arrogance. He should not have taken the gifts and tribute inside the city walls without thoroughly examining the goods. He blamed himself—and knew without a shadow of doubt, so would his king in Wassukanni.

On the palace balcony, Pharaoh Amenhotep II and King Atalshen of Tikhsi watched as the priesthood of Amun began to celebrate the victory with their elaborate rituals, giving thanks to the gods of Khemet for providing their pharaoh with another triumph.

27
Siege of Wassukanni

Following the failed ambush of Tudhaliyas by the Mittani King, Saustatar was forced to lead his army back to his impregnable capital of Wassukanni, feeling angry and somewhat ashamed.

'We had a good chance there and we let it slip through our fingers,' the king grumbled to his commanding general. 'We should have called the Hittite's bluff.'

'Sire,' General Ratukani replied, 'I also think the Kizzuwatna squadron was a ruse by Zidanta...but would you take the risk...if it wasn't? We would have been in real trouble if the whole of the Kizzuwatna army had joined in the battle.'

'Hmm! I'm just angry we're going to have to endure a siege we could have prevented. The ambush would have solved one of my problems.'

'Yes sire, but Wassukanni has never been taken by siege....and I don't think it will fall this time.'

'Well then, give the order as soon as we get inside the gates. Full siege alarm—all food to be rationed. Those who want to leave for the east should do so before the gates are closed and sealed. It might reduce the mouths to feed,' the king commanded, still fuming at being thwarted in his plan to ambush the Hittites.

Ratukani shouted for his officers to attend him and gave them the king's new orders, then they made haste to get back to Wassukanni, which was now only a short distance further on.

The capital of the Mittani Empire was on the eastern bank, near the headwaters, of the western tributary of the Khabur River, which itself was the eastern tributary of the mighty Puranti. The city was well supplied with water by large underground baked-clay pipes running from the river to storage caverns below the city. Huge granaries had been built within the palace complex walls to guard against any blockade which might be attempted by a foe, and now in autumn, these were well stocked. The tall walls were made of stone and they were thick. What could go wrong?

*　　*　　*

'The Tushans are heading back to their capital…so in one move, sire, you've split the enemy forces and sent them packing for the safety of their walls. The art of deception is one of the fundamental principle in warfare, and sire, you've excelled in using it. I must congratulate you once more, sire,' General Zidanta said to King Tudhaliyas.

After they cleared the night camp, the General rode with the King in his chariot through the early dawn towards the Khabur River.

'Don't over blow this, general,' smiled Tudhaliyas. 'We still have to take Wassukanni when we get there. I'm told its walls are one of the strongest in existence—made of hard stone; high and virtually impregnable. They used the thick walls of Hattusas as their model. We may be in for a long siege, unless we can find a way of overcoming their protection of those walls.'

'Luckily sire, we have the right engineers to deal with those walls,' Zidanta told the king. 'I made sure before we left—just in case. Now, your majesty, we press on to Wassukanni and see the city for ourselves. We should be there sometime today. We've been on the march for two days now and I'm itching to get this war over with.'

'So am I my dear general, so am I. I want Saustatar to admit his wrongdoing and hand his son over to me, so I can find my daughter. I'll squeeze the information out of that scurrilous young prince. He must know where she is?'

'We'll get her, your majesty, never fear,' replied Zidanta.

Early in the morning, the Hittite army crossed the Khabur Bridge and marched west into the barren desert towards Wassukanni. At the head of the army were the standard-bearers and a number of priests from Hattusas' Great Temple; behind them came the king riding with Zidanta in his chariot. The large contingent of the king's bodyguard followed. After them came a number of chariot regiments, then came the cavalry units, the massed infantry regiments and, bringing up the rear, was the baggage train with the rearguard. Following the Hittite army was the Isuwan contingent of ten thousand in their brown tunics, led by their new sovereign, King Kanisa.

The great cavalcade of seventy thousand soldiers, swept across the barren landscape until noon, when they came within sight of the Mittani capital. The city of Wassukanni stood there in the midday sun, looking majestic. It was defended by double thick sandstone walls with strong towered gates. The fortifications included strategically placed towers built into the city walls, almost identical to Hattusas.

General Zidanta gazed at the city from afar and noted that a high citadel overlooking the distant Khabur River stood in the centre of the city. 'That must be Saustatar's palace,' he pointed out to the king.

'What do you think, how long to take it?' asked Tudhaliyas.

'I'm not sure, sire. Could be days; could be weeks. I'll defer judgement until I hear from the experts.'

'A fair assessment general,' replied the king. 'We should surround the city and set up siege camp as soon as possible.'

'My staff have the job in hand sire. Do you want to parley with the opposite king?' asked the general.

'I suppose I should offer him the chance to come to terms. I will demand he hands over Artatama for trial. I can't do less.'

'Yes sire, I understand. As soon as camp has been established I'll send out an officer with a white flag to make contact.'

'Keep me informed.'

'Yes sire. Oh, and I think I see King Kanisa coming towards you.' Zidanta went off to talk with his staff officers, to begin the siege and formulate a plan of action for the city.

Zidanta immediately ordered a tight lock down of the city—and had a thousand soldiers positioned outside each of the two city gates. Every postern gate was to be found and closed tight. Any tunnels leaving the city were to be blocked—and a detailed search was to be made to establish where the city got its water supply. The siege had begun.

Tudhaliyas came and found Zidanta in the afternoon, accompanied by King Kanisa.

'General, have one of you officers raise a white flag and go to the main gate of the city and ask those inside for a parley,' ordered Tudhaliyas.

The officer returned a little later and reported to General Zidanta, a senior Mittani general had agreed to talk to them. 'He will meet with our representative outside the city gates in a short while.'

'Good. Thank you.' He turned to the king, 'What had you in mind, sire?'

'I want to give them a chance to surrender my daughter. If they can't, then I want Artatama. This will be their last chance to avoid the destruction of their city. Send one of our generals to make that clear in the parley. If they refuse, see if you can grab their general. Am I clear?' asked the king.

'Clear, sire. The only question is how? How do I get men in behind the Mittani general at the gate?'

'Oh, I'm sure you'll find a way, general.'

Zidanta sighed a deep sigh and went off rubbing his chin.

When the time came for the parley, a Hittite colonel rode to the main gate of the city followed by four men, one of whom was holding a spear with a white flag fluttering from it.

The gates opened slowly and a man in a dark blue tunic walked out, head held erect, a shiny general's helmet on his head. Two men stood by the gate at his back.

The colonel walked forwards a short distance and beckoned the general to join him.

The general didn't move. 'I can hear you just as well from here,' he said derisively.

'Very well! I'm asked by my king to demand the return of his daughter. This is the only demand he makes,' shouted the colonel.

'My king is sorry but he has no idea where your king's daughter is. He cannot return that which he hasn't got.'

'If that's your answer; my king then demands your king send out Artatama to answer for the kidnapping of the king's daughter. The rest of the message is for your ears only. I'm not going to shout it out so all can hear. Please come closer.'

The Mittani general sneered, 'I don't mind letting everyone hear what you've got to say. Speak up now...from there.'

'What I've to say may save your city...but not out loud, sorry. If you want to know what it is, walk half way towards me and I'll meet you half way. Then I'll whisper it to you.'

The general hesitated, then nodded, and began to walk towards the colonel slowly and reluctantly. As they both drew near to touching distance, the colonel lunged at the general. The general half expecting this, tried to block with his hands and throw the colonel off, but this colonel was an expert at close quarter grappling, which is why he was chosen, and soon had swung in behind the general and had him by the throat. The colonel's four companions swiftly kicked their mounts close to their colonel and his prisoner. A rope was thrown round the prisoner's neck and he was hauled onto the colonel's mount, while the colonel nimbly jumped on behind, and the whole party rode away speedily from the city gates. Furious shouts were coming from the battlements, but no one dared to fire at the departing party in case they hit their own general.

When King Saustatar's general had been safely ensconced in General Zidanta's tent, Tudhaliyas and Kanisa joined them. Both kings stood to the side as they observed the tied up enemy general, who stared furiously at his captors.

'A despicable trick; typical deceitful Hittite behaviour,' spat out the captive.

'Now, now general. One good deed deserves another,' responded Zidanta. 'How despicable is kidnapping a young girl. Is that an honourable act? Should we play by the nice rules, while you run rings around them?'

The general just stared at them with hate.

'What? No witty answer? So, now we're no longer in view of you friends, let me ask you the same question my colonel asked...and mind your answer. Where is the king's daughter?'

Another angry stare greeted the question. 'I've no idea. I told this to your sly colonel, before he grabbed me. Nor has my king. We had no idea what the Crown Prince was up to...until it happened. Where he's holding her, no one knows.'

Tudhaliyas couldn't contain himself, '*Tell me where my daughter is and you can go free?*' he shouted.

'I can't tell you what I don't know,' retorted the general grimly.

'*Then where is Artatama?*' shouted the king again. 'Are you willing to have this city turned to rubble to save a no good kidnapper?'

'My king has disowned his own son for carrying out such an unworthy act. He's deeply sorry it happened. He would not have sanctioned such behaviour. On the other hand, he cannot permit you to invade his kingdom. He demands you leave Mittani, and only then will he talk with you.'

'Oh, I think he'll talk to me a lot sooner,' sneered Tudhaliyas. 'I'm putting an end to this despicable royal house of his. He should have made more effort to control his son while he was able to. Now we've reached this point, I'm going to teach him the same lesson he should have given his offspring. I will not put up with people attacking *my* family. King or no king. If his son is not in the city, then I'll continue to hunt him down wherever he is, after I've dealt with his no good father. This has to end.'

The captive general became quiet and sat sullenly, but some of the hatred had gone out of him. This king was right. The kidnapping should not have happened. Even his own king had condemned it by disowning his own son. He knew his own fate and accepted it. It was the fate of all soldiers in wartime. To win or lose, to live or die.

Tudhaliyas led Kanisa out of the tent in disgust and left it to Zidanta to decide what to do with the captive.

Zidanta called in the guards, 'Take him and hold him somewhere,' he pointed at the captive. 'Give him some food and drink, but make sure he's well guarded at all times. If he escapes, I will execute all those responsible. Am I clear?'

'Yes sir,' said the chief of the guards. They lifted the captive general to his feet and took him from the tent.

Then, another guard reported, 'A scarlet tunic is heading this way general.'

This was followed by an out of breath soldier wearing a scarlet uniform appearing outside, and being ushered into Zidanta's presence.

'Sir,' said the Kizzuwatna non-com. 'Compliments from my Crown Prince and my commander.'

'Relax. I assume your people are not far behind. How near are they?'

'About half a league behind me general. I've been asked to inform you the whole Kizzuwatna army is here to join you as you requested, sir.'

'Splendid. I look forward to seeing them. Now go and have some food and drink and then return my compliments to your commanders.'

'Yes sir, thank you sir.' He about faced and left the tent.

The Staff tent was close by and Zidanta marched over to it. Inside he found the staff officers working on plans to take the city. He found the initiatory attack involved them catapulting clay pots filled with scorpions into the city to sow fear and panic—the scorpions were to be fired in the early bombardment which was due shortly.

Another section was planning the mining of the walls. The demolition of the stone walls were to be attempted by placing clay pots of burning charcoal at the base of the walls, moistened with urine. The stone wall was susceptible to intense heat, which would cause it to crack and then collapse. Then there were the tunnels to undermine the battlements.

Yet another group were organising a ram against the main western gate. All the rams were brought with them from the siege of Malidiya.

'Have we identified all the postern gates? Are they secured?' asked Zidanta of his deputy, General Muttalu.

'Yes sir, and the water supply. We've cut the water but they've got caverns filled with water under the city... and food silos. We won't be able to starve them out.'

'I'm not planning to be here that long,' ejected the general angrily.

Horns outside announced the arrival of the Kizzuwatna army, and Zidanta left hurriedly, going outside to greet them.

King Tudhaliyas and King Kanisa came out of the royal tent, to welcome the reinforcements the king's closest ally was bringing.

The Kizzuwatna army marched in, almost as if they were on parade, and placed themselves to the south of Wassukanni, all the time watched with increasing alarm by those on the city battlements.

Crown Prince Talshura accompanied by General Tapalass jumped down from their chariot near to the two kings and came towards the royal tent.

'Welcome my young friend,' cried King Tudhaliyas. 'And you're most welcome too general,' he greeted Tapalass. 'May I introduce the new king of Isuwa, His Royal Majesty King Kanisa. He was kind enough to join me on this little expedition.'

'Your majesty, we've also managed to persuade an extra ally to join us. May I present General Muhar of Karkamish, who has kindly reinforced us with an extra ten thousand soldiers.'

'Welcome General Muhar,' Tudhaliyas said warmly.

'Your majesty,' responded the general.

'Shall we retire to my tent? I've sent for refreshments. We can sit and talk in comfort. Maybe even get down to a little business.'

General Tapalass excused himself for a moment to confer with his deputy. He ordered him to see to the army's disposition and encampment, then to come and join him.

Inside the royal tent, couches were laid out in a circle with low tables laden with food and drink in front of them.

'Please,' Tudhaliyas swept his hand over the couches, 'sit, relax and help yourselves.'

The six people, three royals and three generals, eased themselves onto the couches and picked at the fare before them.

'I hear good news from the Kizzuwatna campaigns so far,' Tudhaliyas said to the Crown Prince. 'You've pacified Karkamish and Harran. How many do you bring with you in support of our effort?'

'Sire, the Kizzuwatna army has fifteen thousand, and we've been joined by ten thousand from Karkamish,' replied the Crown Prince.

Tudhaliyas looked at Zidanta with a query on his face.

'Sire, that's a combined force of ninety five thousand that will be besieging this city,' replied Zidanta to the silent query.

All those present looked pleased and somewhat astonished at the figures.

'Extraordinary! It's the largest army gathered in my memory,' replied the king.

Again, the gathering nodded in agreement.

'If I were Saustatar, I would open the gates now and spare the city its inevitable grief,' said King Kanisa.

28
Siege Tightens

Any army rash enough to oppose the Hittites, faced formidable opposition. The main fighting force of the Hittite army was its infantry, wielding slings and spears, or swords and bronze battle-axes. The head was protected by a pointed bronze helmet, while carrying a leather shield on their left arm.

A minority of professional troops were especially efficient. They worked as teams of three. Two companions, one carrying a long shield and the other a spear, protected an Archer with a long bow.

The cavalry operated in pairs; one horseman used a composite bow, while his partner sheltered him with a shield. The two-wheeled chariots had a driver, an archer come-spearman, and a shield-bearer to protect the occupants.

The bow was the main weapon of the infantry. It was used in groups with a shield bearer protecting the bowman. The bow had a range of over five hundred cubits. Their quiver held fifty arrows and its captain commanded one hundred bowmen with their shield bearers, which produced formidable firepower

The Hittite's allies were now similarly organised and the combined force had become complete master of the surrounding countryside around Wassukanni. The city was sealed tight. The siege was under way.

King Saustatar, ruler of Mittani, peered at his nemesis from the battlements with his dark eyes, trying to assess his chances. General Ratukani, Saustatar's commanding general was by his side.

'This is all my own work,' said the king miserably, sweeping his hand out at the enemy. 'I made Artatama…and he presented me with this. I rue the day I begat him; yet, he was such a promising child. Keen, intelligent…and now look what he's done. He's destroyed me. I've worked hard to build up this empire, and he's brought it all down with his stupid machinations. What did he think he was doing? How could he have turned out so dumb?'

'Your majesty, we may yet withstand this siege,' Ratukani tried to sooth his anguished king. Then added, 'Although it's a pity we didn't manage to flood the moat.'

The king long locks of dark curled hair swished round in despair, 'You said yourself earlier, that you've never seen the likes of such an army. Let's not kid ourselves. No matter how long it takes, they'll eventually take the city. If not immediately, then next month, or even next year. Tudhaliyas isn't going to let it go. He's after my blood. *And*, I would do the same if I were in his place. That's the truth of it. What Artatama did was so wrong, I would strangle him with my bare hands if he were here before me.'

*   *   *

General Zidanta's nearby Staff tent was the scene of a strategy meeting, called by him to allocate the various responsibilities in this siege.

General Zidanta opened with, 'I've been made aware of someone named Harupal, a town engineer, and how Harran was taken.' Zidanta looked at the young Crown Prince, 'and I propose the Kizzuwatna army does the same here. So I would like you to concentrate on building a ramp against the eastern city wall, if that's acceptable to you your royal highness.'

'What do you say, general,' asked the prince of General Tapalass.

'I say, what we accomplished once, we can do again, your highness.'

'Good, it's settled. General Muhar! I would like your men to concentrate on the front gate. Use the covered rams we have for you and see if you can't break through them. It's a tough assignment…you'll take a lot of casualties…but someone has to do it.'

Then turning to King Kanisa, Zidanta said, 'The Isuwans I understand are expert slingers. Their job will be to make sure the people on the battlements keep their heads down so they don't interfere with our siege works….especially at the front gate and near the ramp. The other slingers, including the Hittites, will be at your disposal to help you. Maybe your people could pass on some of your slinger's techniques on to them to improve them. The rest of the city perimeter should have archers evenly spaced around it, but they're only to fire if they see a clear target. We don't have unlimited arrows. Any enemy arrows fired at us are to be collected and reused. My people will be trying to encourage them to fire arrows at us needlessly. I'll have Hittite soldiers dancing out in the open to egg them on.

'I'll have *my* men work on undermining the walls and digging tunnels under the city. That'll be particularly dangerous work with rocks and boiling liquid being throw down on them. Any comments so far?' The general stopped and looked at the faces around the map on the table. 'Each of you has open access to me or the king, and I welcome any suggestions from you at any time. Thank you for your patience so far.'

Tudhaliyas led the others from the tent, leaving his commander to deal with the disposition of the Hittite forces. Zidanta now turned to his deputy, General Muttalu, and asked, 'How's the scorpion bombardment coming along?'

'We hear a lot of screaming and shouting after each lot goes over the wall. It's doing its job sir.'

'Good, keep it up. On a separate project, I want to set your men to building four siege towers. We'll need them when we come to the high point of this siege. Have you spotted any weaknesses in their defences?'

'There's a deep ditch below the walls,' his deputy told his commander, 'and it looks like they were getting ready to flood it with water, until we came along.'

'A moat, eh? Lucky for us they didn't finish it.'

'Sir,' an aide whispered to Zidanta, 'there's a message from a sentry near the entrance flap. He says it's urgent.'

'Yes, well send the man in,' replied Zidanta, looking with mock anger at his deputy.

'Sir,' said the flustered messenger, 'The Mittani general sir…he's dead, sir.'

'*What?* How did it happen? Speak up man.'

'The guard went in to make sure he was alright and found him dead on the ground. We think he took his own life sir. There's no sign of a wound and his face is distorted with pain.'

'Damn, I wanted the man alive. He might have been useful later. Poison, eh? Get the medical man to check that? I want to be sure. Dismissed!'

When the messenger had gone, Zidanta continued his conference with Muttalu, his deputy, 'Must have brought poison with him. I never thought to search him.'

'All his weapons were removed, but if he were determined to do away with himself, sir, he'd have found a way,' replied Muttalu.

'Yes your right. What's done is done. Now, let's get on with taking this city.'

'Sir, shall we go and inspect what's being done so far?'

Zidanta smiled, 'Good idea, let's go have a look.'

Both left the tent, and were followed by the general's bodyguard. They first went to the main gate to see the progress there.

The covered rams had been strengthened, the roof covered with shields and the ram itself was made heavier to use against the mighty doors of Wassukanni's main gate. Two rams stood ready to go, just waiting for General Muhar's orders.

Muhar joined Zidanta and both commanders gazed at the two towers bearing enemy soldiers on either side of the gate.

'I'm ready to start. Would you like to give the order?' asked Muhar.

'No general, it's all yours now. You go ahead. I'll just watch for a moment, then I've the rest of the siege to inspect. I see you have the piles of sand ready to extinguish the oil if it's poured down on the ram roof.'

General Muhar nodded at Zidanta's observation, then nodded to his own deputy to push the first ram against the gate. Boulders appeared on top of the tower to the left and as the ram connected with the thick gate, the enemy dropped the boulder onto the ram. The enemy boulder was heavy enough to dent the shields atop the ram but it then rolled off to the side.

'Damned them, I think they've damaged it,' cried General Muhar.

'Pull it out and use the other one. I don't think they can have another boulder that size up there,' urged Zidanta.

The partly damaged ram was drawn back and the next ram brought in. The deep thuds of bronze against wood began their regular pounding against the massive doors. Isuwan slingers kept up a stone barrage against those on the towers, making them wary about sticking their heads above the parapet. Despite the sling shots, hot oil was poured down on to the ram roof and then set ablaze. The fire petered out quite soon as it was quenched with shovelled sand and did little damage due to the type of covering.

Zidanta and Muttalu continued their tour of the city walls. They walked round to the southern side to see Hittite tunnelling experts begin digging four evenly spaced tunnels towards the walls. The initial holes were already dug and they were just about to go horizontal. The shaft holes were carefully concealed with wattle screens and a number of false screens were put up to confuse any onlookers.

'We're going six cubits deep and then straight towards the wall batter, then through the wall to the filling,' explained the colonel in charge of the tunnelling.

'Are you shoring up the tunnels colonel?' asked Zidanta's deputy.

'Yes sir. I always do. It saves on cave-ins. Gives the men more confidence in their work.'

'How long before you're in a position to undermine the wall itself?' Muttalu continued.

'A couple of days, sir.'

'What about boring holes in the wall base and filling them with charcoal?'

'We'll do that when we're at the walls with our tunnels. It'll be easier and less dangerous.'

'Very good, keep me posted.'

'Yes sir.'

Zidanta and Muttalu continued their inspection tour. They walked round to the eastern side where the Kizzuwatna army had moved, and encamped. They had begun building the ramp, but this time made no secret of it. There were thousands of Kizzuwatna soldiers involved in the build.

'General Tapalass, how is it coming along?' asked Zidanta of the Kizzuwatna commander.

'As you can see general, we've just determined the start point of the ramp from the wall...which in turn determines the elevation.'

'Good! I see you've got the large mobile barricades in place to protect the workers.'

'Of course,' said Tapalass with pride. 'The enemy has tried to set them alight, but they're covered with hides and difficult to burn from a distance.'

There were two thousand men digging holes a good distance away from the wall. More men were transporting the earth on wooden sledge palettes, drawn by horses, to the build site. These were being protected by a large number of men hauling mobile barricades, three men high, shielding them from the enemy salvoes emanating off the wall. Others were piling earth on the ramp, again being shielded by yet more mobile barricades.

The enemy was staring at the beginnings of the ramp with alarm. Harupal, the engineer in charge, was supervising the elevation, making sure it would allow a tower to be hauled up the ramp when it was completed.

'What have you come up with so far,' demanded Muttalu of the engineer.

'Well sir, as the wall is sixty cubits high; in order to get a reasonable ramp, I'm starting the ramp three hundred cubits from the wall. I know it's a long distance away, but enemy fire is minimal at that distance so it should go quickly and smoothly until we get to within firing range.'

'You're aware that the arrows can reach five hundred cubits? You're already in their firing range,' advised Muttalu.

'In that case they're slow off the mark. There's been little firing so far. My guess, they must be waiting for us to get closer so as not to waste their arrows,' responded the unruffled engineer.

'When do you expect to be finished,' asked Zidanta of the engineer.

'With the huge manpower at my disposal, two or three days, sir,' replied Harupal.

'Will the tower be ready,' Muttalu asked Tapalass.

'It just needs assembling. We repaired it from our Harran campaign and I have my men working on it over in the shallow gully further off.'

'Most impressive,' lauded General Zidanta, looking approvingly on the work in progress. 'Well, we must press on. Keep me posted,' he told Tapalass.

'I will general.'

Zidanta and Muttalu continued round to the northern side where the catapults were still lobbing scorpions into the city.

'Ah, colonel, any reaction from inside?' Muttalu asked the colonel in charge of the catapults.

'Apart from the initial panic; all's quiet. They did send some human manure over our way initially, but it's ceased now. Worse news sir, although I've men scouring the surrounding neighbourhood for more scorpions, we're running short on the little buggers. We've enough for another four of five shots. I had my men stocking up on the way here, but we're running out.'

'Those four or five shots ought to go over the eastern wall to help the ramp builders, colonel.'

'No problem, sir. I'll reposition now,' and the colonel went off to give the necessary orders.

'As far as I can see,' said Zidanta to his deputy, 'we seem to be on schedule. At this rate, we should be in a position to have a go at taking the city in two to three days. Any thoughts?'

'Not really, other than to agree with your assessment sir,' Muttalu replied. 'I would think the ramp and the ram at the front gate will be the city's weak points. We should position our troops to break into the city at those points.'

'Yes, I think you're right,' agreed Zidanta. 'But I'll do that at the last possible moment, so we don't signal our intentions to the enemy. We don't want them reinforcing those points more than they're doing already.'

29
Fall of Wassukanni

The siege of Wassukanni had been ongoing for the last two days and nights and was finally coming to a climax. The ramp was almost ready against the eastern wall, being only a few cubits from completion. The siege tower was dragged to the base of the ramp.

The front gate had been breeched a number of times but each time the defenders managed to reinforce it with material from inside, shoring it up. Nevertheless, as the intensity of the attack increased, even this last-ditch effort was crumbling and the gate was beginning to give way.

The tunnellers on the southern wall had no success, yet had taken heavy casualties in the process. General Zidanta deemed this portion of the siege a complete failure. The charcoal attempts to crumble the stone wall was another unmitigated disaster which had cost many lives but had got nowhere. No walls had collapsed but the spots where the miners had tried to use charcoal had become swollen with bodies of those who'd perished in their attempts to carry out their given orders.

Standing, gazing in the early morning sun at the eastern ramp on the third day of the siege, Zidanta and his deputy reflected on the progress of the town engineer's work. General Tapalass stood nearby directing the assault.

The Hittite commander shook his head in a mixed emotion of anger and frustration. 'Stubborn lot these Mittani. The city's resisted mining, and our four assaults to date. In our turn, we've lost heavily in those attacks. It's now clear assault ladders are no way to take a city the likes of Wassukanni. Without this town engineer from Karkamish, we'd have had no choice but to rely on the battering ram at the gates. No wonder the king was so confident they could withstand a siege. With this ramp in the east, and the ram in the west, we've split the city's defenders in two.'

'We've had reports they're trying to put together a counter tower here which will look down on our tower,' Muttalu informed Zidanta.

Zidanta nodded at the wall, 'You mean like the one there.' He pointed at a wooden structure which had just appeared on the inside of the wall, and was coming to a point opposite the ramp.

'Well I never! Is it going to do anything?' asked Muttalu.

'It'll make life more difficult for those on *our* tower, but I doubt it'll stop us. Give the order to deploy our troops up the ramp. Use poles to help push our tower up the ramp. Reinforce the side barricades. We've got the manpower advantage…let's use it,' ordered Zidanta.

'Yes sir,' from nearby Tapalass replied.

'And make sure the troops are massed in front of the main gate. Last time I heard, it was ready to be breeched. When the ramp and the gate are ready to go, we'll try another ladder assault. It'll stop them moving their forces to the ramp and gate. This will be our final assault…I hope,' sighed Zidanta.

General Muttalu ran over and jumped on his chariot to inform those at the front gate of the impending push.

At the ramp, men began swarming up behind the rickety tower, now slowly progressing upwards. The imposing contraption was being pushed all the way up the incline. Soldiers were filing up the tower, making it heavier to move, but it continued its steady progress towards the eastern city wall.

The people in the counter tower fired salvo after salvo at the assaulting tower—and those inside returned their fire with equal ferocity. Fire arrows, slingers, javelins, and anything they could use, was thrown back and forth, yet the assault tower reached the city wall and the tower access ramps came crashing down on to the wall disgorging a surge of sword wielding soldiers on to the city wall.

The shield bearers pushed forward whilst the sword wielders hacked at the enemy opposite, pushing them steadily but surely backwards along their own wall. A mass of dark blue tunics giving way to Kizzuwatna scarlet and Hittite yellow. It was a slaughter beyond endurance, and the floor of the wall was flowing red with carnage. The Kizzuwatna soldiers had forced their way into the counter tower and were clearing it of the enemy, while the rest of the invaders began fanning out into the city.

At the front gate, the ram had broken through and punched a massive hole in the door amidst the other rubble used to shore it up. General Muhar's troops in their light blue tunics poured through the gap and fought their way into the square behind the city gates. A frantic fight ensued to contain the situation but it was beyond the defenders control. The pressure of the troops pouring through the damaged gate was overwhelming. Light blue tunics, grey tunics, and yellow Hittite tunics mingled in battle with the deep blue of the Mittani. Hittite troops began the business of clearing the rubble from behind the gate area to allow the gates to be thrown wide open.

The battle for Wassukanni lasted throughout the day, while the invaders winkled out the last defenders. Orders had been given by Tudhaliyas not to massacre the city's population. What the Mittani royal house had done was beyond the fault of the ordinary inhabitants and he saw no reason to persecute them to destruction.

The inner citadel was yet to be taken. From various prisoners, General Zidanta understood, Saustatar had retreated to his palace together with the main body of his bodyguard, and the gates closed tight. Unfortunately for the Mittani king, one of his bodyguards had been sloppy in securing the northern postern gate. A group of Hittite soldiers sent to check on all the citadel's postern gates had quickly discovered the mistake and taken speedy advantage of it. A fierce battle ensued inside the citadel courtyard and more invaders rushed to reinforce the men fighting inside. The defenders were outnumbered but the bodyguards fought to the last man for their king.

Finally the citadel had also been taken and Zidanta was informed of their final victory.

'Where's the Mittani king?' asked Zidanta of the captain sent to report the taking of the citadel.

'I know we had orders to take him alive sir, but unfortunately we couldn't,' replied the officer. 'We found him in the throne room, slumped on his throne, dead sir. His consort was by his side. The queen had also taken her own life. We don't know exactly what happened but the Mittani commander was near them with a sword in his stomach.'

'That'll be Ratukani,' said Muttalu. 'I didn't think he'd surrender quietly.'

Zidanta nodded in agreement. 'Shame it had to come to this. And a big pity. Now we can't question anybody, and we don't know where the king's daughter is.'

'I've got our spies questioning their spies,' responded Muttalu. 'We should come up with an answer.'

Kidnapping's End
30
Between the Rivers

The autumn day was fresh after the previous day's storm and the sun high in the sky, once again heating up the ground. Ammuna kept mulling over what the old fisherman had said about the nomads. Warning him to beware of them.

'Colonel, send scouts out to our flanks, and out in front, to keep a sharp eye out for nomads. I'm going to take old Harmin's warning seriously regarding these thieves of the desert. We've had one lucky escape from marauding tribesmen, but I don't think our storm god will be kind enough to provide another earth-shaker to defend us this time.'

The lanky Colonel Lawana looked disgusted with Ammuna's sacrilegious joke, but forced a smile to his face to conceal it. He wasn't very religious himself, but respected other people's need for the comfort religion gave them. He simply responded with a, 'Yes sir.'

The longer they ventured into this semi-arid region the greater the discomfort the men began to feel. In parts, there was dense shrub land, intermingled with vast tracts of straggly bushes, and bedraggled grassland struggling to rise out of the clay soil. The were bare undulating hills which sometimes broke the monotony but they also alarmed

Ammuna, as they hid gullies from where an ambush might emerge.

Late in the afternoon Lawana finally recommended they look for a suitable campsite for the night, as the light was soon to dwindle. They badly needed a source of water and in this dry land, which might be a problem, for them as well as the horses. They'd filled up with water from the river, but a day's travel in these conditions had depleted this somewhat. Another dilemma would be fodder for their animals—but Ammuna insisted the sparse intermittent scrub cover would have to do for now.

The column stopped as Lawana consulted with the other officers. Ammuna kept aloof and stared into the distance.

The only Lieutenant in the group said, 'Sir, we passed what looked like a dried out river bed a little while back, remember? The dip in the hills?'

'There's been a number of dips in the hills. Which one are you referring to?'

'It was deeper than the usual one….about a quarter of a league back.'

'Well….yes, what of it?' Lawana vaguely remembered such a deep gully.

'Well sir, if we go back there and dig down, there may be water in the ground. Sometimes there are underground water pockets trapped in the riverbed. We might be lucky and hit one if we dig around.'

'Hmm! Right! Good thinking, lieutenant. Can you remember where the riverbed was?'

'As I said, about a quarter of a league back, sir. If we turn back now, we'll be there in no time.'

'In which case lead on, lieutenant.'

Colonel Lawana informed Ammuna of what he had in mind, and the general ordered the column backtrack to the dried riverbed.

At the riverbed, men began digging deep holes in the clay soil. Two of the holes produced results and began filling slowly with brackish water. More holes were needed because of the animals. Eventually out of around twenty holes dug, five produced sufficient water for both animals and humans. The water for the humans was filtered through a number of layers of cloth before it was boiled.

Lawana ordered latrines to be constructed on the west side of the camp as the wind was coming from the east. Brushwood was gathered and fires built. When everyone was settled and the sentries posted, Lawana asked the lieutenant where he'd got the idea for the dried riverbed water.

'Sir, I come from a small village which sits out on a wide plain. Every year about this time, when the summer has dried out our river, we have to dig holes in the riverbed to get by. Once the rainy season begins, our river overflows once more, but it's the holes in the riverbed which allows us to survive the dry season.'

'Thanks to you and your village, we now have water. I mean we weren't exactly short of water, but who knows when we'll get more. We need to fill up when we can.' Lawana gently patted the lieutenants left shoulder as a sign of approval.

The lieutenant just shrugged his shoulders and smiled happily. He thought this trip was the big adventure of his life—and on top of this, he would have riches to bring back to his village when he returned.

In the middle of the night, the officer in charge of the sentries woke Lawana.

'Sir, I'm sorry to wake you but I thought you should know—we've had visitors.'

'Ahhh, what's that?' Lawana yawned. 'What visitors?' He got out of his bedroll and took the captain away from the sleeping area. 'What's all this about?' he asked again.

'One of the sentries heard a noise from the east. It must have been carried by the wind. He went to investigate and discovered a lot of footprints on the lee side of the hill. Someone's been watching us, sir. I went to have a look and it seems like around five or more people have been spying on us as we slept. The footprints headed back east. There's no sign of them now, but I thought you should know as soon as possible.'

'Thank you captain. You were right to wake me. Put extra guards around the camp until morning, then come and remind me again. The general will need to know this. Carry on.'

'Yes sir.'

Must be those damned nomads the general was on about, thought Lawana as he climbed back into his bedroll to resume his sleep.

When the dull dawn broke, fracturing the night asunder, the camp roused themselves from their slumbers, and then Lawana mentioned the visitors to Ammuna.

'Seems your nomads, general, gave us a once over last night.' Lawana informed Ammuna as he sat on his blanket spooning the porridge in to his mouth.

'Colonel, they're *not my* nomads. Thanks to the old fisherman, at least we had a warning of them. Do you know how many there were?'

'A small scouting party, by the looks of it. Around half a dozen. If it hadn't been for the wind, we may never have known. Seems the wind carried their noise and alerted one of our sentries, and he had a look…then reported to his captain…who woke me.'

'Good! That was their first mistake. Maybe they'll make more mistakes we can benefit from. Double the scouts this morning…stay alert. If they're watching us, it means they'll want to have a go at us. Might be sneak attacks or it could be a full frontal…depending on their numbers. I want us to be ready. Warn the troops…they're to come to battle readiness.'

'Are we going to have a go at them, sir?' Lawana asked.

'All depends on their numbers. I'll try to avoid a fight…but if there's no other way…I want us to be ready.…you have your orders.'

'Yes sir.' Lawana was staring into the eastern sky. 'Sir, have you seen what's coming?' he pointed at the darkening clouds approaching from the east.

Ammuna quickly glanced at the sky…then stopped. 'Hmm! I see what you mean. Think a storm's coming?'

'Yes sir, I do. It's the right season for it. We're right out in the open. We should get ready for a storm *and* a fight. If those bandits come at us using the storm as a cover, we'll be in trouble.'

'Load the animals, and cover their eyes with cloth.' Ammuna took full command now. 'We'll lead them on foot throughout the day…or until the storm subsides. Whatever happens, keep an eye out for the sun.…tell the men, always head towards the sun no matter what happens. Even if the storm gets bad, there are always indications of where the sun is coming from.…head towards it. It'll keep us going towards the Aransah River. One man to follow the one in front—always keep the man in front in sight. Make sure the brat is in the middle of the column out of harms way. Put twenty men with good bow skills out front. Anything moves out there…they're to let them have it. Let's get to it!'

'Yes sir,' Lawana was relived Ammuna had asserted his command. He rushed off to give out the orders to his three remaining junior officers.…they would pass it on to the non-coms.

The column got back under way without tidying up the campsite, which was unusual for them. Scouts went out in front, followed by the twenty bowmen. The rest led their horses as the wind picked up during the early morning, lifting the sand and debris into the air. All the men tied handkerchiefs over their noses and pulled their bronze helmets down, to give cover to their eyes. The horses were well trained and trusted the men, giving little trouble in being led blindfolded.

The column inched forward until mid-morning, all the time fighting the wind, which was pushing them westwards. About noon, the wind began to die down and a semblance of normality resumed with the sun breaking through the cloud cover.

31
Sand Storm

Following the late afternoon river crossing of the Puranti, Mokhat led his *special forces* south, two leagues further on into the open desert from the river, where they spent the night.

As dawn broke through the cloudy sky, the camp stirred, with sleepy eyed soldiers waking to a persistent nagging wind. Some had been woken by the howling and were now taking emergency measures to protect the animals. The force of the wind was picking up, throwing the sand around. Amid the flying debris, cooks were busily handing out the cold rations to the subdued huddling denizens who had taken cover underneath their blankets.

'Looks like more dark clouds coming in from the east,' Onasiyas observed to Palaiyas.

Palaiyas looked hard at the eastern sky, shielding his eyes with his hand, and finally said, 'My guess is, we're in for a right old sand storm.'

'I'm afraid you're right,' added Mokhat. 'We're in your hands now,' he looked at Onasiyas. 'What does your training suggest we do?'

'I suggest we dig in. There's no point in trying to travel in this type of weather…we'd only get lost. My training tells me to call the men together. They all know what to do…but for you my dear Generals, I suggest you find a cloth and cover the animal's eyes and noses. Make sure they can breathe. Then get them to lie down with you and hold them tight. Talk to them gently throughout the storm to keep them from panicking. You would do well to cover your own eyes and your noses and no matter what, stay calm with your horses. We'll do this in six circles of sixteen men each.'

Mokhat looked at Palaiyas and shrugged. 'Well, let's do what we've been told.' He smiled encouragingly at Onasiyas.

The whole camp was now a hive of activity with soldiers forming the six circles with their animals and busy covering their eyes and muzzles with cloths—then getting them to lie down and keep still. Pack animals in the centre held there by their handlers, surrounded by their packs. The wind had increased slowly, almost sneakily, until it became a howling spectre screaming for blood.

All through the early morning, the wind was increasingly tempestuous, causing the sand and debris to take to the air, trying to tear the blankets from the men using them as cover. By mid-morning there was a full-blown sand storm viciously throwing sharp grains at the circle of soldiers buried under their blankets.

Then just as quickly as it had begun, the sand storm finished drubbing them and the wind died down. Even the clouds parted a little, allowing the sun to peek through. Men were throwing off their sand covered blankets and helping their animals back on their feet, taking off their blindfolds. A few of the men were on their knees giving thanks to Taru, the Hittite Storm God for their salvation.

Mokhat was spitting on the ground, 'Ahgg, phew, damned sand's got everywhere,' he complained.

Almost everyone was spitting, ejecting the dust from their mouths, trying to blow their noses to clear them. People were pounding their clothes and stamping their feet.

'That wasn't that bad, was it?' asked Onasiyas, smiling to himself.

'We've lost the whole day with this cursed sand storm,' complained Palaiyas.

'Stop moaning and get some water down your gullet...and go easy on it...we don't know where the next watering hole is,' Mokhat told him, running his fingers through his hair and shaking his head. 'Rotten sand—I can feel it's got into my ears.'

Onasiyas looked around at his men to ensure they'd all made it safely through the storm. He went amongst them to encourage them, talking to the odd man here and there.

Mokhat followed Onasiyas' progress and nodded approvingly. 'He's a good commander,' he said to the nearby Palaiyas, grooming his horse.

'I've said it many a time. We're lucky to have him....and his men,' he added. 'I'm not sure how we'd have gone about rescuing the king's daughter without his help.'

'Yes, you're right.'

Onasiyas came back saying, 'We should get under way as quickly as possible. We've lost a day with this storm. The only good thing is, it must have hit Ammuna's bunch as well. Let's hope the king's daughter is alright.'

32
Brigands

'**O**ver there,' shouted Lawana to Ammuna, pointing to the distant left. They were skirting a mountainous region when from out of nowhere a solid phalanx of camels blocked their path—around a hundred of them. The horde appeared out of a dip in the hills and now sat astride the ridge just to the left of Ammuna's column.

Both sides halted, eyeing each other. One of the camels came forward with a man holding a small white flag on a spear. He seemed to want to talk.

Ammuna shouted at the bowmen to bring this bandit down. He was in no mood to talk to thieves.

As the camel came to within bow-shot, an arrow flew into the sky and the bandit on the camel fell to earth, dead, knocked off his camel.

A great shout of anger arose from his comrades. More of them appeared from the dip in the hill.

'I thought so,' said Ammuna. 'Give them a taste of their own treachery and they'll show their true colours.'

Lawana smiled at Ammuna's cunning. He trusted his commander in a fight.

'How many can you make out?' Ammuna asked his deputy.

'About three hundred, at a guess.'

'That's my estimate as well, probably around three fifty,' Ammuna replied. 'What do you think…will the wind stay down while we deal with this scum?'

'I think so,' said Lawana drawing his sword. 'We have horses to their camels, which makes us more manoeuvrable. Remember the tactic used by those Hayasa nomads? Attack, fire and retreat? I think our archers can pick them off as we approach, then we wheel around and retreat a short distance, before charging them again. We do this a few times and we'll reduce their advantage. That way, by the time we have to get in close, there'll be about the same numbers as we have…assuming they don't run away.'

'It's a good plan, colonel. Go ahead and give the orders.'

Lawana told his officers and non-coms what he'd in mind, and they quickly got ready. The bowmen remounted their steeds and around a hundred and fifty men, bows in hands, began to approach the camels at speed, guiding their horses with their knees, meantime notching arrows and drawing the strings on their bows. All the while the bandits in their turn, shouted abuse, waving swords, and moved their mounts forward towards Ammuna's men.

Hooves pounded the hard clay towards the bandits, and as the horses neared, they veered left and right at the critical moment loosing off a volley of arrows at the brigands. The horses wheeled round and retreated while the enemy fell to earth pierced by arrows. Many of the camels went wild, having been hit by the volleys of arrows. The bandit camels chased the horses once they regained control, only to have Ammuna's men wheel round again and perform the same tactic. More of the bandits fell off their two humped camels, and more camels began bucking wildly from their injuries.

This performance was repeated four more times before the bandits' ceased giving chase after the horsemen. The cost was beginning to exact an unacceptable toll on the camel riders.

Both sides stopped to inspect their positions from a distance, staring with intense hostility at each other. Ammuna hadn't lost any of his men—whilst the bandits had lost half their numbers. The thieves shouted abuse more in frustration than threat. They shook their swords, but it seemed to the robbers, the professional fighters had outmanoeuvred them, and they didn't like the experience.

'*Well*,' Ammuna shouted at Lawana. '*Have they had enough or shall we go round once again and finish them off?*' Ammuna had sat with the provision ponies on the ridge of a hill, Asmunikal and her non-com minder behind him, watching his men perform.

Lawana led a couple of the charges and felt elated at the rush of action. He was breathing deeply and wiping his forehead with the back of his hand. '*I think they've had it, sir,*' he shouted back.

The bandits, still yelling and cursing, began to disappear slowly from where they'd appeared, back into the dip behind a ridge, then heading for the low mountains to their left, their imaginary tails firmly between their legs.

Lawana joined Ammuna on the ridge, both smiling widely at each other.

'That'll teach them to attack Hittite soldiers,' chortled Ammuna, brushing down his tunic with his free hand. 'Another thing, Colonel, not one of the brigands had a bow. They all relied on getting up close to their prey and thrashing it out with swords and knives. How stupid and arrogant can you get?'

'Yes, and as a result of their foolishness, we tore them to bits,' agreed Lawana. 'We haven't lost one man, sir. Not even a fall from a horse…'

'All down to your professionalism and good training, Colonel,' commended Ammuna. 'By the way, it might be an idea to get the men to collect a couple of those dead camels for meat. Let the cooks butcher them and we'll eat well tonight…what do you think? Dry out the rest and add it to the provisions, and we'll have meat for a while on our journey to the Aransah. Might as well have some good come out of this unwarranted distraction.'

That's a new way of describing the ferocious battle they'd just been in—as a *distraction*, thought Lawana. However, to Ammuna he simply said, 'Yes sir, that's a good idea,' and Lawana proceeded to give the orders to collect the camel carcases.

Ammuna, in the mean time, went over to one of the enemy dead and stared at the robed figure lying there with an arrow through his throat and a surprised expression on his dead face. Ammuna then did something he'd never done before; he bent down, removed a gold amulet from the dead bandit's wrist, and placed it in his own pouch.

Lawana was just returning to his general, and saw from a distance, what Ammuna had done. He was utterly shocked his general had stooped so low as to rob the dead. *He's definitely a changed man since this kidnapping thing began*, thought Lawana. *The general I once knew would consider it well below his dignity to rob the dead. I'm not sure I like where this whole affair is leading.*

Ammuna caught sight of Lawana and waved him over to him. 'Look at this brigand,' he pointed at the dead bandit. 'Have a look at how he's dressed. The quality of his cloth is exceptional—fit for a lord. I would not have thought it was such a profitable business.'

'Depends on how many travellers they've come across…how many they've robbed.'

'True…true. They must've been easier to rob than us,' Ammuna continued to muse. 'I'm glad we gave them a hiding they won't forget in a hurry. Maybe next time they'll think twice about this thieving game of theirs.'

'I doubt it sir. I don't think they know anything else. They're more likely to exact a terrible revenge on the next caravan which comes through here. All we've done is made them angry and frustrated.'

'Well, that's not our concern. Our concern is keeping the brat safe and getting us to Nineveh as quickly as we can so we can get paid. We'll camp up ahead once we've moved away from this slaughter house. Have the cooks drag the dead camels to our next campsite. They can finish with the camels there,' Ammuna informed Lawana and his three officers.

The column reformed and after about a league's travel, scouts came back and reported that they were reasonably close to the main river, the mighty Aransah, which would lead them all the way down to Nineveh.

'We'll camp a little distance from the river tonight,' Ammuna announced to Lawana as the light faded from the sky. 'Give the men a rest and have some food as well. We'll follow the river in the morning. Oh! And be sure to tell the men, the general says, they did well with the bandits.'

Brushwood was again gathered and the cooks got to work with the camel meat. Large portions were roasted and handed out to the men, since in the aftermath of the earlier battle, the men were inordinately hungry.

Let's go and get our share of the meat the cooks are roasting. I can smell it from here.' Ammuna led the way in the moonlight to the campfire.

33
More Bandits

The order was given to move out and the *special forces* formed into a column, heading in the direction of the low mountains in the distance to their left.

'According to one of my men, who's been in this direction before….if we pass by those mountains and keep going south, we should reach the Aransah River in a couple of days,' Onasiyas told Mokhat.

'What about Ammuna? Any chance of catching him?' asked Mokhat in reply.

'I'm sorry sir, but the storm's made a bit of a mess with the pursuit. We'll just have to see what comes up. Ammuna's entire trail's been wiped out.'

Mokhat looked disappointed, but was forced to shrug it off as the whims of fate. After all, he could hardly insist the Storm God cease his activity, could he. He may have left the priesthood but he still had a remnant of a belief in the power of the gods. If the gods wished to throw a sand storm in their path…then so be it. He would have to accept it… and live with it. He was utterly convinced he would catch up with Ammuna and rescue Asmunikal…and it would have to do for now.

Around late afternoon, it was clear that Ammuna was not to be caught that day, and the scouts returned reporting no sight of their enemy. The sand storm had wiped out all traces of their tracks. By this time, they were not far from the low mountains and so Onasiyas suggested they call a halt for the night as the fading light made further travel pointless. Animal fodder, which was now at a premium, was shared around in feedbags, and the men laid out their blankets on the sandy ground. More cold food was distributed amongst the tired soldiers.

'I don't need to remind you to post the sentries,' Mokhat said to Onasiyas.

'No sir. I've already made the arrangements.'

'I thought I'd mention it....but I see you're on top of it as usual. It's just a force of habit,' Mokhat tried to excuse himself. 'By the way colonel, may I commend your behaviour during and after the storm? I was saying to Palaiyas...I don't think we'd have managed without you and your men. Putting this special force together was an act of pure genius....and it came just when it was needed most. I've never really thanked you for being with us...I know you're only doing your duty as an officer in the army, but you're most welcome. In fact, colonel, it's been a pleasure knowing you from the time we first met in Ivalanda three years ago. It's a shame your friend isn't here with you to share this unfortunate venture.'

Onasiyas listened to Mokhat respectfully, coming from a senior general in the Hittite army, but at the mention of his dead friend Feliyas, his eyes grew sad and he sighed. 'Yes general, I miss him a lot. We were close...but that's the life of a soldier. I think I told you how he died?'

Palaiyas joined them just then and they all sat down on their blankets.

'Yes you did, but if you'd like to tell me again, I would be honoured to hear it.'

'Yes, please do tell again,' Palaiyas encouraged.

'It's a year ago now,' Onasiyas began solemnly, 'Feliyas fell in a useless battle near the Ahhiyawan border. It was an unnecessary patrol followed by a skirmish with a larger force, and Feliyas ended up being cut off. Overwhelming numbers slaughtered his entire company. There was no way of stopping it. It was a tragic incident. If they'd been better trained they might have survived...who knows? It was this slaughter which prompted me to form the *special forces*. This lot I'm privileged to command is a tribute to Feliyas.'

'And as fine a bunch of men as I've been privileged to know. They've saved my skin twice now...'

'Don't forget my skin,' Palaiyas rebuked gently.

'And we're *both* most grateful to them,' continued Mokhat. 'I've never come across anybody who could fire arrows as quickly and as accurately as they can.'

'It's been a rigorous training,' Onasiyas smiled, 'which is paying off each time they draw their bows. If you wish, I will let you in on the secret of their accuracy...but I'm not sure you'll like it.'

Mokhat raised his eyebrows in surprise, 'What secret?'

Palaiyas was looking askance at Onasiyas.

'Well, remember, after I've finished telling you this story...you asked for it. Here goes; a time ago, I found a wandering group of Gimirri roaming along the Ahhiyawan border....and one of them was an expert archer, who amazed us with his skill. It gave me an idea...so I sent for another expert archer from...the distant Hayasa, who I'd heard were famed for their archery. It was a time when I was in the process of beginning the training of my *special force*.'

Mokhat's face grew stern at the mention of the Hayasa, while Palaiyas smiled in astonishment.

'I found the best archer in the Hittite army,' Onasiyas continued in spite of Mokhat's frown, 'and I put them into competing against each other for a whole week.'

Palaiyas interrupted, 'So when we fought that bunch of Hayasa by the riverbank, they were getting a taste of their own medicine?' He chortled at the idea.

Onasiyas nodded. 'You should have seen them. The competition amongst those three was ferocious...each trying to outdo the other. They came up with a number of new tricks to improve their firing skills...and my men have benefited from those tricks.'

Mokhat began to smile as the story unfolded. He was shaking his head in astonishment at Onasiyas' account. 'I can see the sense in what you did...and the results are magnificent, but I'm not sure I would have used your method. I'm glad you told us...it explains your men's archery skills. Also, I'm convinced recounting the story of your friend's untimely death, lifts part of the burden from your spirit—at least that's what I've found when I was working as a priest. The more you tell the story, the easier it gets to bear the loss.'

Palaiyas added, 'It's clear, you have a special flare for this type of work—and I'm glad you're here...*with us* and *not* an opponent.'

Mokhat nodded in agreement and laughed at the idea they might meet an opponent as good as Onasiyas' men. 'Fat chance...there aren't any as good as your lot,' he exclaimed.

Onasiyas looked pleased with the remark, especially coming from the commander of this special mission. He took great pride in his men and their skills.

'Right, enough of this chatter—time for some sleep,' Mokhat told them, settling into his blankets. 'Tomorrow will be a busy day.'

At dawn, Mokhat was up early, eager to get the camp moving. He was determined to continue the hunt for Ammuna—and maybe this was the day they'd catch up with the renegade general. The day was sunny and bright, almost too sharp for the eyes. It was a typical autumn dawn. More cold food was handed out, and gulped down—dried meat and biscuits.

By mid-morning as they breeched a hill, Mokhat spied a couple of men lying in the sand, almost at the same time as Onasiyas did.

'Those look like our men,' exclaimed Palaiyas.

'They *are* our men...those are *our* scouts,' shouted Onasiyas. '*Column at alert*,' he yelled back to his men.

As they came close, one of the men moved his right arm.

'One of them is still alive,' barked Palaiyas as he got off his horse to tend to him. Palaiyas leaned over the man as the injured man tried to tell him something.

'They....they jumped.....out..of..the..sand....' was all he could manage before passing away. He'd held on long enough to pass on the vital message.

Palaiyas jumped to his feet and pulled his sword from its scabbard. Mokhat looked surprised at this move by his companion, as there was no one in sight.

'*They're in the SAND*,' screeched Palaiyas at the top of his voice.

Cloaked figures were emerging from the sand all around them, swords in hand, spitting breathing reeds from their mouths. Mokhat and his special forces were being ambushed by people jumping out of the sand—one moment it was empty desert; the next they were fighting for their lives.

Then from a gully, out poured two hundred and fifty would-be-robbers shouting and whooping at them on their two humped camels, swords raised high to attack.

'*Dismount*,' screamed Onasiyas. '*Bows and arrows....and make them count.*'

A special forces prepared manoeuvre took place with some men rushing to ward off the bandits who'd jumped out of the sand, engaging them, whilst the rest unleashed volley after volley at the oncoming would-be-thieves charging towards them on their camels. The speed of the volleys fired at the bandits knocked half of them to the desert floor—it took four volleys for it to be accomplished. By the time the bandits reached Mokhat's men, there were fewer than fifty left on their camels—and they only came forward because they could no longer control their camels.

On the ground, the battle raged against the thugs. The *special forces* had slain all but one of those who'd jumped them out of the sand. He was now on his knees begging for mercy. The twenty or so of Onasiyas' men then sheathed their swords and un-shouldered their bows', letting off volley after volley of arrows at what was left of the crooks on the camels.

The battle had only lasted a short time, but it cost the brigands all their lives—some two hundred and seventy in total. It could be justifiably called—a massacre of the guilty.

Mokhat stood with Palaiyas, both their swords stuck in the sand, and both were shaking their heads in dismay.

Onasiyas came up to his commander, grim faced. 'This is atrocious!' he exclaimed. 'Worse…I've lost three men to these scoundrels. Five, if you include those two scouts they killed.'

Mokhat nodded in sympathy. 'I'm truly sorry,' he commiserated with Onasiyas, although he felt no blame for the events. It was an automatic reaction from a former priest.

'Who are they—where did they come from?' demanded Onasiyas.

'There's one still alive, over there,' Palaiyas pointed at the robed thug begging for mercy on his knees.

'Bring him over here,' ordered Onasiyas.

Two of Onasiyas' men dragged the pleading bandit to their commander.

Onasiyas looked down on their captive with contempt. 'What is he saying?' he asked. '*Does anyone understand this language?*' he shouted above the thundering quiet. Only the high-pitched bleats and bellows of the injured camels broke the silence, as an eerie calm descended after all the slaughter.

'It's Assyrian, sir,' replied one of his men as he came up behind Onasiyas. 'He's asking us to spare his life. He says he has a wife and children….and if we let him live, he'll show us where his thieving associates keep their loot.'

'Ask him why his friends attacked us? I'd like to know why he thought we had anything worth stealing.'

Onasiyas' man interrogated the prisoner, and the poor wretch couldn't say enough, hoping his replies would save his skin.

'He says they attacked a larger column yesterday just further on—but were badly beaten and were forced to retreat. The leader of the gang was upset and angry that he'd lost so many men, and he promised that he'd wipe out the next caravan he came across—not for the loot, but in a perverse rage-revenge. We happened to come along—and still overwhelmed with his anger—he decided to wipe us out.'

'It's the stupidest thing I've heard in a long time,' exclaimed an angry Mokhat. 'Clearly this bandit chief sits on his brains. Ask him where he fits into this thieving band?'

Again Onasiyas' man questioned the snivelling crook. 'He says he's only a humble follower, and holds no position in the band….and he's clearly lying.'

'Why do you think that,' asked Onasiyas.

'Well look at him, sir,' asked the interpreter. 'Look how he's dressed. Look at the knife in his belt—it's encrusted with jewels. Either he's their leader, or he's high up in the gang.'

'Tell him, that either he begins to tell us the truth, or I'll stake him out in the sand right now. He can roast in the sun while we watch him die…tell him that,' Mokhat ordered.

The interpreter conveyed this to the prisoner, who then stopped his whining and sat back on his haunches, glaring at Onasiyas.

'That's better,' said Onasiyas. He grabbed the prisoner's black turban and pulled it off his head. 'Let me have a look at that knife,' he said pointing at the jewelled blade in the bandit's belt. On being handed the knife, Onasiyas turned it over in his hand and then handed it to Mokhat. 'What do you make of it?'

'I'd say we're looking at the wily bandit chief,' spat out Mokhat. 'All his cronies are dead and he thought he'd save himself with a little play acting, begging us gullible saps for mercy. What do you say Palaiyas?'

'I agree. Let me have a go at him. I'll teach him to attack the weak and honest going about their business.'

'I'm for my original plan—stake him out in the sand,' insisted Mokhat. 'Anyone against?'

They all looked at the glaring bandit, now fuming he'd been uncovered, and daring them to do their worst.

'Right,' Onasiyas said to those guarding the crook. 'Stake him out...and make sure he can't get loose.'

Onasiyas' men quickly spread the uncomplaining thug out in the sand and gave him a few kicks for good measure. Then they looked around for stakes, but none were available. They told Onasiyas and he advised them to dig a hole, place the bandit chief inside so only his head stuck out above the surface.

Onasiyas then called his deputy, Captain Neti over, 'Listen, get the men to strip and collect some of the dead bandit's outfits, about twenty robes should do. I might want to use them later on as disguises. Pack them on the supply ponies.'

'Yes sir, right away.'

'Another thing, we can't cremate our dead as is our custom, so we'll have to bury them,' Onasiyas ordered.

'Collect our five dead men and I'll say a few words over their bodies.'

This done, the whole column now moved away from the scene of the battle and resumed their journey, leaving the villain's head above the sand, shouting obscenities at his departing enemy.

As they travelled away from the buried bandit chief in the noonday sun, Onasiyas made sure he wasn't going to be caught out twice, and put four scouts out in front to keep a sharp lookout for any more surprises.

'Remember the bandit mentioned they'd been in a battle with others the previous day?' Mokhat said to Onasiyas. 'It could only have been Ammuna's lot, surely.'

'But he also said he'd been badly beaten,' Onasiyas replied, 'which means Ammuna thrashed the living daylights out of his mob.'

'And that's without our accurate arrow volleys,' added Palaiyas.

Later in the afternoon, scouts reported not far ahead, they'd come across more bodies laying in the sand. They said it looked like the aftermath of a battle.

Mokhat's group reached the scene, and concluded it was more of the brigands who had died.

'This must be Ammuna's work,' affirmed Onasiyas. 'The other battle the bandit chief mentioned.'

'Yes I agree. Between the two of us,' Mokhat said, 'we seem to have wiped out this bandit hoard.'

'*Good*—and in doing so, made this area safer for the weary traveller,' added Palaiyas with venom.

Mokhat and Onasiyas exchanged glances at Palaiyas' pique of malice.

Both kicked their horses into a furious gallop, followed by Palaiyas and the rest of the *special forces,* intent on catching up with Ammuna's elusive bunch of thugs as soon as possible.

Only the disappearing daylight forced him to put a halt to the chase.

Mokhat had thoughts of trying to pursue Ammuna throughout the night but Palaiyas and Onasiyas counselled against it on the grounds the terrain was far too unfamiliar and uneven to make it a safe proposition. Anyway, they might run into more bandits during the night trek, and Onasiyas didn't think it was a good idea.

So night camp was established and everyone settled down to eat and rest.

'We've driven the horses hard today,' commented Palaiyas, sitting on his blanket as the cooks were again distributing cold food.

'Not half as hard as I would have liked to,' replied Mokhat. 'Do you know what I think?'

'That Ammuna isn't too far ahead,' replied Onasiyas with a smile.

'Exactly!' continued Mokhat seriously. 'It means all we need is a little extra push and we'd have him. We've been chasing him for ten days and we've never been this close. I can almost smell him in the air, and we saw traces of his handiwork with the bandits at the battle scene we passed.' Mokhat was simmering with frustration at his friend's caution.

'What if the canny general lays an ambush for us in the night…or we run into more bandits?' asked Palaiyas.

'Then we'd fight them—and I'm confident we'd win.'

'With Ammuna we'd be outnumbered two to one. I think we'd win as well but we'd lose a lot of men. I want to ambush *them*, not the other way round.' Onasiyas was calm and determined. 'For the sake of a little extra time, I still say we should act rationally and according to military sense. The last thing *I* want is to have a bloody battle in the middle of the night and have the king's daughter's death on my hands.'

It brought Mokhat to his senses. He'd forgotten Asmunikal might get hurt in a night fight. 'Well, yes.....a good point. Thank you for reminding me why we're here.' There was no hint of sarcasm in his voice—Mokhat was sincerely grateful for the reminder. In his eagerness to catch Ammuna, he'd forgotten why they were chasing him.

'Now I suggest we get some rest and we'll start again at dawn—good night.' Onasiyas climbed into his blankets and closed his eyes. The rest of the camp followed his lead.

34
Aransah River

Early next morning, at breakfast, Ammuna's men tucked into more of the roast camel meat, a leftover from the previous night's feasting. A few of the men complained about muscle aches following the other day's battle with the brigands, but they quickly stopped their moaning after a tongue-lashing from their non-coms.

Once back on their journey, Ammuna's column quickly breached the ridge of a hill and found themselves facing the mighty Aransah River, only a short distance in front of them. The waters glistened and shimmered playfully in the morning autumn sun.

'There,' Ammuna told Lawana, both riding at the head of the column. 'We're almost at our destination. A few more leagues downriver and we'll be rich beyond our dreams.' He had a satisfied smile on his face and felt vindicated for all the trouble he'd led them through. 'By the way...how's our investment holding up?' Ammuna added, meaning the princess.

'Fine, general,' Lawana replied. 'Her non-com minder told me this morning we ought to be able to deliver her in good condition. I'm estimating another five or six days before we get to Nineveh.'

'That sounds about right. As far as the brat goes, I'm glad to hear she's in good condition. It wouldn't do any other way, would it? She's the only reason we're all here. The sooner we're paid the better I'll feel. Are the scouts ahead?'

'Yes sir, four of them. I doubled their numbers now we're in Assyria....just in case.'

'Good thinking. I don't want to be caught off guard by the Assyrian army. Prince Artatama ought to have cleared us with their army, but you never know. For added security, put two more scouts out on our left flank and make sure the usual rearguard non-com and his five men are wide-awake. Give them a pep talk—tell them to stay alert. I want to know if we're being followed...I *don't* want any surprises.'

'Yes sir, I'll do it right now. I ought to have thought of the flanking scouts myself.' Lawana was surprised at his own carelessness. All morning he'd been mulling over his own part in this enterprise, and was regretting having got involved. He shook his head, trying to clear his mind of its moodiness. He'd need to stay sharp if he were to survive this venture.

The column finally reached the big river and swung left, following the riverbank throughout the morning until around midday, Ammuna finally called a halt.

'Get the cooks to hand out the remaining cooked camel meat...I assume we have some left?' Ammuna asked the captain in charge of provisions.

'Yes sir, this will be the last of it. After that...it'll be dried camel meat. The cooks have exposed it...drying it in the air as we travel, spread out on the provision ponies.'

'Good, carry on.'

Following lunch, they continued the journey, until late in the afternoon, scouts reported back there was a bridge over a river in front of them, guarded by a small contingent of Assyrian soldiers.

'Here we go, our first problem with the locals,' Lawana sighed to Ammuna.

'Don't be so pessimistic. I'm sure they'll be reasonable; at a price.' Ammuna shot back. 'Remember we're guests in this country. What we must avoid is any signs of aggression; otherwise, we'll have the whole

Assyrian army on our backs. When we get to the bridge, let me do the talking. Now go find our translator.'

Ammuna pulled out a folded leather sheet from the horse pouch, on which a map of Assyria was detailed. A gift from Artatama's spy. On it, he noted the river in front of them was called the Kalat, an eastern tributary of the Aransah, with its headwaters up in the distant Zagros Mountains. The river wasn't wide and the Assyrians had thrown a wooden bridge over it as a military highway, which the locals also used when they needed to.

'How many soldiers are we dealing with?' Ammuna asked of the non-com in charge of the waiting scouts.

'Only six from what we could see. Three at either end of the bridge.'

Turning to his deputy, Ammuna said, 'Where's the translator I asked for?'

Lawana raised his hand and beckoned an older man over to him. The man rode his horse closer to the general.

'You know Assyrian?' Ammuna asked the man.

'Yes sir,' the man responded, while restraining his horse, which was shying away.

'When we get to the bridge, watch me carefully and translate only what I say. Is that clear?'

'Yes sir.'

'Stay close to me. Have you got a square piece of white cloth?'

'Yes sir...I thought we might be needing it, so I came prepared.'

'Good man. Tie the white cloth to the tip of your spear and raise it high. Well, let's not keep them waiting.' Ammuna led his column over the next rise and down to the small bridge.'

'Well, what a bit of luck,' Lawana voiced aloud, trying to input levity into the tension. 'The bridge I mean... saves us getting our feet wet.'

Ammuna made no reply.

As they approached the bridge, the three Assyrian guards spread themselves across their route and one of them put his hand up—the other two pointed their spears at the oncoming foreign soldiers.

Ammuna halted his column fifty cubits away and came forward with his translator riding by his side. He pulled up his mount short of the Assyrian.

The Assyrian barked out some strange words.

His translator interpreted them as, 'He wants to know who we are and where we're going?'

'Tell him we're going to Nineveh to meet up with Prince Artatama of the Mittani. We're Hittite soldiers carrying a great prize for the Prince. He should have received orders from Nineveh to let us pass.'

The Assyrian thought it over for a split moment and then shook his head, barking out more strange words.

'He says he's received no orders from Nineveh to allow Hittite soldiers to cross his bridge.'

While this was going on, a number of onlookers had gathered at the southern end of the bridge, curious as to the strange ongoing at the northern end. One small man in a long light-grey robe pushed through to talk with a guard at his end, and then strode boldly across the bridge towards Ammuna.

'Tell this oaf we definitely have permission to cross this bridge, otherwise how does he expect us to get to Nineveh?'

The translator gave the Assyrian guard the gist of what Ammuna said.

The guard was still shaking his head, when he heard a shout from behind. He turned and saw a grey robed man approach him holding something out in his hand. The guard turned and met the small sturdy robed figure. They talked for a bit, and the guard kept looking at something in the stranger's hand, then both returned to Ammuna. This time the Assyrian's demeanour had change from hostility, to a smile on his face.

The small grey robe approached the surprised Ammuna, who was too experienced to show anything on his face. He merely raised his eyebrows, emphasising his dark piercing eyes.

'General Ammuna?' asked the stranger in Hittite.

'Do I know you?' Ammuna responded quizzically.

'No sir, but I'm here to smooth your passage. But so I can say I saw it, do you have anything to show me?'

Ammuna reached into his pouch, withdrew the Mittani royal seal, cupped his hands and discretely let the stranger have a quick peek at it.

'Thank you sir. I can now tell my master, I saw proof of who you are. I have shown the official *pass* to the Assyrian guard. You and your men are free to cross the bridge.'

'I must say you're a welcome sight. I thought we were going to have problems here. And what's all is this about a *pass*?'

'I have a *pass* for you, issued by the senior commander of the Nineveh garrison—arranged by my prince.'

Ammuna turned on his horse and waved to Lawana to bring his column down. He turned back to Artatama's agent, 'May I see it?'

'But of course, sir. I was asked to find you and hand it to you. It allows you to cross Assyrian territory without hindrance, courtesy of the Nineveh commander. Should you come across any other Assyrian patrols, just show them this.' He pulled out a small baked clay tablet with cuneiform writing and a seal at the bottom, and handed it to Ammuna.

Ammuna looked at the tablet closely, then handed it to his translator. 'Can you read this?' he asked.

'Yes sir. It is a short statement to whomsoever it may concern that the bearer of this tablet is under the protection of General As-belam, Commander of the Nineveh garrison.'

The translator handed the pass back to Ammuna, who popped it into the same pouch which held the Mittani seal at his waist.

Ammuna sighed deeply, as if a great weight had been lifted from him. 'Now I know we'll get to Nineveh without being forced to fight our way through.' He smiled at the robed figure. 'Do you have a name, or is it too indelicate a question?'

'Normally I keep my name to myself, but I was ordered to give you my full trust and assistance....so...I'm called Haratam,' replied Artatama's agent.

Lawana arrived with the rest of the column, and because of their numbers, the three Assyrian soldiers were again looking at them nervously. These were Hittite soldiers on Assyrian territory, and although they were not at war with each other, they were foreign soldiers—vastly outnumbering them.

As the column began to cross the wooden bridge spanning the Kalat River, Ammuna introduced Haratam to Lawana. They nodded politely at each other.

Haratam was walking by Ammuna's horse.

'Will you travel with us down to Nineveh?' he asked Haratam, looking down at the grey cowl atop the burly Mittani. 'I can supply you with a horse.'

'I think not. I will be somewhere in the vicinity but I doubt you will notice my presence. I will be of more help to you if I'm not caught up in any situation you may come across. That way I'll be *free* to help you.'

Ammuna looked again at this canny Mittani agent. He was quickly gaining the general's respect.

They had now crossed the bridge and Ammuna smiled at Lawana. 'Thanks to our friend here, we have just been given a safe ride into Nineveh.'

'Where's he gone?' asked his deputy, looking to where Haratam had been. They had reached the small crowd on the southern side, waiting to cross the river.

Ammuna looked down to where he'd last seen Haratam, and was astonished to see the agent had vanished. 'Hem, that is one resourceful undercover agent, I must say. One moment he's here, the next he vanishes. Keep an eye out for him as we head down south,' Ammuna ordered his deputy.

'I certainly will, sir.'

After their crossing of the Kalat, they galloped swiftly along the Aransah, putting distance between them and the bridge.

Up ahead Ammuna noticed a fat man in a red robe riding a camel coming towards him, followed by two carts. As the caravan came by Ammuna's men gazed on a double line of bedraggled women tied to each other at the waist, following the last cart. On either side of the women were four burly men swinging whips, urging the women forward. Such slave caravans were a common sight wherever people travelled and it made little or no impression on Ammuna. His men on the other hand hadn't seen a woman for a while and whistled at them lustfully. Only Lawana felt a pang of pity for their plight.

The day was fast disappearing when Ammuna's rearguard informed him a large Assyrian force was catching up with them, but on the other side of the river.

'How large?' Ammuna asked the non-com in charge of the rearguard.

'There's three hundred plus in the cavalry squadron, sir.'

'They're on the other side of the river, you say?'

'Yes sir.'

'What do you think,' Ammuna asked his deputy.

'They could be following us....or not. If they had word from the bridge guards, then they know we're here

under the general's protection…the one in Nineveh. If not…
then they don't know who we are. And it could be
awkward.'

Ammuna mulled this over and said, 'It's too late now
to bother with today. The light's fading and we'd better set
up camp for the night.'

'Yes sir,' Lawana raised his hand, halting the column.
He gave the order to dismount and start collecting wood. A
hundred and eighty men set up bivouac for the night,
lighting two large fires. Cooks got to work boiling up
porridge and reviving the camel meat for the evening's
meal. There was no sign of the Assyrians from the other
side of the river.

35
Slave Women

Mokhat was already on his feet, watching the encroaching dawn climb over the eastern mountains when Palaiyas rubbed his eyes in the bedroll next to him.

'Come on my lazy friend, another day is rising and the time has come to chase the rogue general and rescue our princess.'

Palaiyas groaned in mock despair, 'Must we?'

'Well, no. We can simply go back to Nerik and abandon the king's daughter. Would you rather do that?'

'Put so brutally, I suppose we must continue.'

'Rise and shine then. The cooks are already dolling out the breakfast.'

The meal was a cold and miserly affair but it put something into the men's stomachs. When the meal was finished, Onasiyas had the men climb back on their horses and continue the drawn out chase.

No sooner had they begun, when a scout rode back and reported a small slave caravan was coming their way, heading up north across the desert.

'Don't do anything to frighten them,' said Mokhat. 'We'll give them a wide road.'

The scout went back to his duties, and within a short time, along came a tubby figure riding a camel resplendent in a rich dark red robe. He was followed by a couple of two wheeled carts pulled by mules, driven by a couple of old men in each cart. Behind the carts in two bedraggled lines, all dressed in rags, came around twenty women tied to each other at the waist by ropes, walking in between four burly men either side, wielding horsewhips at them.

As the two groups passed each other, only twenty cubits apart, the women looking at Mokhat's darkly dressed riders with pleading eyes.

The pleading looks seemed to incense the burly guards and they began using their whips mercilessly on the screaming women's backs.

Mokhat watched with outrage at the brutal behaviour and finally shouted, '*Stop that.*' Mokhat then repeated his shout at the guards. He didn't really want to interfere but he could see the whips opening up wounds, causing blood to flow, and he was furious at the callous treatment of these poor unfortunate women. He assumed the women must be slaves.

The man on the camel turned and began to shout at Mokhat; although it was in Assyrian, it sounded like abuse.

On hearing Mokhat's shouting, Onasiyas nodded to his men to deal with the burly whip wielding guards.

The bearded men of the *special forces* soon jumped off their mounts and had the guards disarmed, making them stare at swords pointing at their throats, with their whips lying safely on the ground. The leader on the camel wheeled his mount round and recklessly charged his camel at Mokhat's men, clearly infuriated at this interference in what he deemed was the pursuit of his lawful business.

Onasiyas put himself and his horse in the way, grabbed the reins of the camel as it passed by, and pulled it down, tumbling the rider from his mount, and ending up tumbling off his own horse in the process. The overweight slave owner hit the ground hard, rolling to a stop near one of the wheels of the leading cart. He sat upright against the wheel, fuming and yelling, rubbing his right shoulder.

By now, bows had been drawn by Onasiyas' men and arrows pointed at all of the men in the slave caravan. The men in the caravan could do little. The women were cheering this on, while the slave guards stood there looking surly in defeat.

'Search them and disarm them,' commanded Mokhat. '*Where's the Assyrian speakers?*' he shouted aloud.

Three men astride their mounts appeared at his side.

'Sir,' said all three in unison. 'Assyrian speakers reporting.'

'Find out what's happening here. Ask the women.'

The Assyrian speakers went around and had a chat with the grateful women, while they tended to each other's wounds, then came back and reported.

'Sir,' said the non-com, 'It's as you suspected; they're all slaves bought in Nineveh. Some claim they've been kidnapped against their wills, others are wives of prisoners. All have a sob story to tell of mistreatment and what they say is illegal captivity at the hands of this slave master.'

'If we set them free what would happen to them?' Mokhat asked.

The non-com asked the women the question, and they all began to shout at him, while wailing piteously.

'What's happening now?' Palaiyas joined in, amazed the offer of freedom elicited such a response.

'No, sir, don't misunderstand,' said the non-com translator. 'They want you to set them free. They say they'll head east into the hills. There's brigands there who'll look after them, and be grateful for their company. But they're also begging you to kill the fat slave master and his thugs.'

'Tell them sorry, but I can't do that,' replied Mokhat. 'The best I can do is to tie them up, so it'll give the women a good head start. After, they're on they're own.'

The women untied themselves from the ropes holding them, and began rummaging in the slave master's carts. Finally, they kicked the old disgruntled men out of the driving seats and took over the two carts.

'It's too early in the morning for this nonsense,' complained Palaiyas in mock disgust. 'Why can't they do

323

this in the afternoon when I'm more in the mood for rascality.'

Mokhat smiled at nearby Onasiyas regarding Palaiyas' banter, yet all three watched with approval, while the slave master and his thugs were forced to stand by, while the women robbed them. The fat slave master, his face red with anger, had listened to the talk and fumed silently, all the time looking at his thugs being held at sword point. He was helpless and was having to accept it, albeit unhappily.

Onasiyas ordered his men to tie up the master and his thugs as promised, and then looked on as the women drove the two carts into the east as fast as it would go.

'What'd you think? Will the women get away?' Mokhat asked Onasiyas.

'Oh, my men made a good job of tying this lot up. It'll take them a while to get loose. It all depends on luck, sir.'

'Anyway, I wish them luck,' added Palaiyas. 'I was about to interfere, but you got there ahead of me,' he said to Mokhat.

They remounted and continued, leaving the tied slave master and his thugs struggling to untie themselves. Around mid-morning, a number of leagues further on, scouts came riding back to report the big river they were aiming for was over the next rise ahead.

36
Assyrian Patrol

The next day, early at dawn, Ammuna's column got back on the road and they continued on their way downriver. A while later, he was informed the Assyrian squadron was not far behind his rearguard.

The general's dark curly neck-length hair swished around as he searched for their presumed followers. 'How far back did you say,' he asked the non-com in charge of the rearguard.

'If you wait a short while, sir, you will see them rounding the bend in the river.'

Just then, a dust cloud announced the Assyrian's arrival. A long line of horsemen, four abreast, rode on white chargers at a canter along the other river bank. The bright sun sparkled on the river in the morning dew, reflecting from the bronze scale armoured coats they wore.

Ammuna peered keenly at them, shielding his eyes with his hand, his strong features entirely impassive. 'They're on the road earlier than us, hmm. What do you make of them,' he asked Lawana, by his side, astride his horse. 'Are they trailing us?'

What he assumed to be their commander, cantering out in front, seemed to wave at him. Ammuna waved back in a casual manner, not at all clear what it all meant.

'Doesn't seem hostile, sir,' responded Lawana.

'Yes…might be a bluff. Well we can't hang around here…let's get moving.'

And so Ammuna with his deputy by his side, continued leading their men in a canter along the Aransah.

The two columns paced each other for the whole of the day, giving Ammuna a small headache, with Lawana continually speculating as to why a large Assyrian squadron of three hundred men were dogging them on the other side of the river. Would the Assyrians follow them all the way down to Nineveh?

The trouble was—with not knowing. It was getting on their nerves. Ammuna didn't even call for a lunchtime halt as was customary—he was so absorbed by the squadron opposite. By evening, both horse and men were eager to recuperate, exhausted and desperate for the night's halt. Not stopping for breaks meant they'd outpaced the Assyrians, who had halted.

'Get the latrine squad digging—get the horses fed, then we'll eat,' Ammuna ordered gruffly, still peeved at the Assyrians.

In time as the evening drew on; they saw four large fires lit on the other side of the Aransah, meaning the Assyrians had caught up with them. As the Hittites were eating their evening meal, Ammuna's *loyal* mercenaries heard Assyrian music and song drifting over the waters towards them. Pipes and lyre accompanied by the deep sonorous sound of male voices. The wind was in the right direction.

'They seem to be enjoying themselves,' commented Lawana wistfully.

'And we're *not*? Is that what you mean?' Ammuna snapped back, still preoccupied with the Assyrian's intent. 'In a few days we'll be set up for the rest of our live—while those over there sings their way to wherever they're going. Who's better off, them or us?'

'I'm sorry general; I meant nothing by my comment. I'm tired that's all.'

'Then its time we turned in, goodnight colonel. By the way, did you post the wide ring of sentries I asked you to?'

'Yes sir, all done. Goodnight sir.'

The next morning sentries woke the camp with cries of alarm. The non-com in charge of the sentries came rushing to a half-awake Lawana and told him Assyrian soldiers in large number were coming towards them.

That brought him wide-awake, 'How many?' demanded Lawana.

'On horse…must be hundreds. They're a quarter of a league away. They'll be here shortly sir.'

'Right, wake the whole camp—everybody combat ready, get to it. Any sign of the squadron across the river?'

'No sir. They must've moved off before dawn.'

'The sentries must have seen them go—ask them when they went and report back. But first, go and wake the camp.'

'Yes sir, right away.'

Lawana climbed out of his bedroll and nudged Ammuna, who was still unusually fast asleep. Normally the general woke Lawana.

'General, sir, we have incoming Assyrians. A whole squadron….sir.'

Ammuna yawned, then abruptly sat up. 'What's all the shouting about?'

Lawana again repeated, 'Incoming Assyrians….a lot of them.'

Then Ammuna understood, and jumped to his feet. '*How soon*?' he barked.

'Almost on top of us, sir.'

Ammuna pulled on his ankle boots and straightened his attire. 'Have you got the men organised?'

'Yes sir, combat ready.'

'Be prepared, but show no offensive action. I don't want to be seen as if we want a fight…understood?'

'Yes sir.'

'Is the other squadron still in camp on the other side?'

327

'No sir. I'm told they moved off before dawn.'

'Damn! There's something fishy going on here.' Ammuna was trying to work out how their current predicament with these latest Assyrians coming up on their camp, fitted in with the Assyrian squadron on the opposite side of the river. Were they somehow trying to collude to thwart him in his attempt to reach Nineveh? He rubbed his chin. 'Hmm! Right, carry on.'

'Yes sir.' Lawana immediately went to his three officers and told them to get the men ready but on no account to show any aggressive intent. 'Don't draw your weapons.'

A couple of Assyrian scouts came to the edge of Ammuna's camp and swiftly turned their horses round to gallop back to report.

From the Assyrians they heard a horn blast. Then the Assyrian squadron came in ready for combat, stretched out three deep, in long lines of horses ready to charge.

Ammuna had got hold of his translator with the same white flag on a spear and went to meet the Assyrians on the edge of his camp, with his men behind him.

Both sides halted and stared at each other for a while. Ammuna's men in an arc from the river, out in the open with no shelter, and the Assyrians on their horses in an opposing arc steadying their mounts ready to charge. Then it would seem the Assyrians noticed the white flag, prompting an Assyrian officer to ride forward to where Ammuna was, stopping just short. He demanded the meaning of the white flag. Were they willing to surrender? Then he added gruffly, 'Who are you?'

'Tell him we're not hostile and show him this *pass* from the Nineveh commander.' Ammuna extracted the tablet from his pouch and handed it to his translator.

The translator walked ahead, holding the *pass* out in his hand, talking all the while to allay the officer.

The Assyrian looked at the tablet, then took it from the translator's hand for a closer inspection. Finally, he smiled and gave the tablet back. He then held his hand out to the translator. As the Assyrian squadron watched this scene unfold, they became visibly more relaxed on seeing the handshake. The Assyrian waved for someone to come over, and what must have been his commander rode forth accompanied by five riders.

A small conference took place amongst the Assyrians, before they came and joined the translator, who then brought them back to where Ammuna waited.

'Sir, may I present Colonel Pudil; he's in charge of this squadron. I've explained who you are.'

Both men were large and took the measure of each other slowly, then locked hands, and firmly shook them. That seemed to raise an almost audible sigh from both Hittites and Assyrians, as they understood there would be no fighting.

The translator continued to convey the Assyrian's words. 'The colonel says he's sorry for giving you a fright, but he's sure you would have done the same in his shoes. Two hundred men in Hittite helmets with Hittite shields deep inside Assyrian territory…he could not do otherwise. It would have been a dereliction of his duties had he not taken an antagonistic stand—until he knew differently.'

'Tell him he's quite right,' agreed Ammuna. 'I would have acted just as he did, and I commend him for his sensible military behaviour. We were just about to have breakfast. Would he care to join us?'

The burly Assyrian colonel was taken aback at the invitation, thought for a split moment, then told the translator he would be delighted to, assuming Ammuna could accommodate his officers.

'No problem, we have enough food and drink to go round. Anyway, we can always buy more from the locals if we need to.'

The Assyrian squadron rode closer to Ammuna's camp and dismounted, settling themselves on the ground and passing around their own food and drink.

Ammuna led the Assyrian officers to one fire, while his *loyal* soldiers huddled around the other. Both fires had been relit and barley porridge was now boiling in the pots. Ammuna invited Colonel Pudil and his men to make themselves comfortable while Ammuna's deputy, his two captains and the lieutenant sat close by. One of the Assyrian officers spoke Hittite, so he did the translating for his commander. Ammuna's translator did the talking for his own officers when they conversed with the Assyrian officers.

'Could you ask your colonel, why he's up so early?' enquired Ammuna through the translator.

The Assyrian colonel answered through his translator, 'We start well before dawn every day. That's the period when the real mischief is carried out. Anybody wanting to cause trouble along the river road always tries to do it at the end of the night...and we try to catch them and prevent them. Mainly robberies, but all sorts of other things like boat thefts, livestock theft.'

'Thank your colonel for that. Now I understand,' replied Ammuna.

The Assyrian colonel, seeing what was for breakfast spoke to one of his officers, who jumped up and raced over to where the nearby Assyrians had settled themselves.

The porridge was being handed round and the Assyrian translator said to Ammuna, 'General, would you wait one moment, my commander has something for you.'

Ammuna raised his eyebrows, and nodded.

The man who was sent off returned with an accomplice, both carrying earthenware pots.

'My colonel says, as a peace token, he would like to offer you and your men a little honey on your porridge, if it's acceptable.' the Assyrian translated.

Ammuna was startled, but then quickly said, 'That's most generous of him. Ask him if he's sure he can spare it.'

'We have plenty of the stuff,' replied the Assyrian. 'We wouldn't offer it if we couldn't afford it.'

'Then yes, with pleasure,' smiled Ammuna in answer. 'My men and I would love some,' and he held out his bowl as the pot came round, and was dolled out a large spoonful on his porridge.

The honey pot went round all the officer's porridge bowls—then more honey pots appeared, and they were then conveyed to the next fire for the ordinary men.

Hot herbal tea was brought round and dished out into bronze mugs from a large container.

Ammuna smiled and patted the Assyrian commander's right hand, as he was sitting to his left. 'Please thank your colonel for his generosity,' he told the Assyrian translator.

'My colonel says, he has plenty more where that came from. He's also curious as to your destination. He presumes it must be Nineveh, since the general in Nineveh put his seal on the *pass.*'

Ammuna confirmed it was. 'Tell you colonel we have a clandestine diplomatic mission to deliver to the Governor of Nineveh.' Then Ammuna placed his index finger to his nose, indicating it was all hush-hush.

The Assyrian colonel nodded gravely and said no more.

'Could you ask the colonel about a squadron of Assyrian cavalry that's bee trailing us on the other side of the river. Does he know anything about them?'

The Assyrian commander smiled and nodded. His translator said, 'It's his counterpart on the other side. He's says it's probably Colonel Musuri and his men.'

Ammuna looked puzzled.

The translator continued, 'There are two large patrols out of Assur which go up and down the river, policing their respective sides. The patrols make sure order is kept and the river traffic travels the river in peace. There are quite a lot of bandits about.

'We are currently going up river to Tushan and then we'll cross the bridge there and come down the other side. Colonel Musuri and his squadron are now going down, returning to Assur, having done the same. Then another squadron will take his place...and so on.'

'Ahh...thank you. That's cleared everything up,' sighed Ammuna. 'I'd got it into my head the squadron was following me.'

'No general...it's mere coincidence.'

Ammuna nodded in satisfaction. Breakfast had been finished and the chat continued.

'My colonel tells me to warn you of a large pack of feral dogs attacking people. We saw them earlier but they left us alone because of our size. They might go after a smaller party, so you should be on the look out for them. Many people have died from their bites. If they're still in the same place where we spotted them, then you might come across them around mid-afternoon today. Be careful... they're cunning.'

'Will you thank the colonel for me,' Ammuna replied. 'I'll warn my scouts to be on the lookout for them.' Then Ammuna turned to his junior officer and said, 'Lieutenant, go find some wine for us to toast our Assyrian friends with.'

The junior officer rushed off to obey his general. He came back with mugs and a number of men carrying drinking skins. From the skins, all the mugs were filled with wine.

Ammuna rose to his feet and declaimed, 'I raise my cup for a toast to our Assyrian comrades-in-arms. *Long life.*'

The translator did his job and all the officers rose and shouted in their own tongues, '***Long life.***'

The translator continued, 'My colonel thanks you for your hospitality and now he says he really must get on with his patrol.'

Ammuna and Lawana accompanied the Assyrian colonel and his officers back to his men and watched as they mounted their white horses, reformed their column four abreast, and waved as the Assyrians rode off upriver.

'Thank the Lord Taru for this meeting,' expelled Ammuna. 'That's cleared up my worries. Now I know what that squadron is up to.' As he said this, he cast his arm in the direction of the opposite bank of the river.

Lawana smiled, 'And it was such an innocent explanation.'

'It was the not knowing which ate into my thoughts,' replied Ammuna. 'I was thinking of sending one of you over there to show them the *pass*, just in case.'

'Yes, it would have been a good move. Anyway, now it's all settled, general.'

'Yes it is, isn't it?' Ammuna smiled. 'Do you know, I've got to liking this Assyrian Colonel Pudil. What with the honey and his splendid information regarding the other squadron. It's put me into good mood. Right, so let's clear the campsite and reform the column. We've wasted enough time.'

'Yes sir,' replied Lawana.

'By and by, did you know this is the fourteenth day of our journey out of Hattusas? We've been on the road with this venture now for two whole weeks.'

'Yes sir, I did know.' Then Lawana relayed Ammuna's orders to his two captains. They in turn barked their orders to the non-coms, who then shouted out as loud as they could, for the camp to be tidied and the men to get ready to move out.

The column set out and rode throughout the sunny morning, and according to the scouts, they were slowly catching up with the Assyrian squadron on the other side of the river.

The riverside road traffic up and down, was getting quite busy, even at this time of the morning. They had to slow down many times to avoid charging into various caravans with their merchandise. However, they made reasonably good headway until around lunch, when one of the non-coms rode up to Lawana and reported one of the men's horses had gone lame.

On being informed by Lawana, Ammuna called a halt to the column to inspect the problem.

After a while Ammuna asked his returning deputy, 'Well, what's the verdict?'

'Seems the horse's front hoof slipped on a large pebble he stepped on, and its gone lame.'

'And?'

'The horse is in no condition to continue. Maybe if we were back home, it could be let out to pasture to recuperate, it would probably survive, but it wouldn't last long at the pace we're going. I recommend we either let it loose, or we put it down.'

'Right, get the cooks to put it out of its misery and butcher the animal for food tonight. I'm just about getting sick of their dried camel meat. We'll have fresh roast meat tonight.'

Lawana wasn't squeamish but he still didn't like killing an injured horse. 'Yes sir.' He called one of the captains over and gave him Ammuna's command.

The captain smiled and went away to carry out the order.

'Everything else all right?' Ammuna asked.

'Yes sir. The putting down and butchering is going to take a while. As it's around lunchtime, may I recommend we call a halt here for food?'

'Yes, good idea. Give the order.'

Lawana shouted to the rest of the men to dismount, relax, and get some food down them.

After a while, a non-com, followed by a man with a bloodied apron, came to Lawana, as he sat with Ammuna chewing on a dried piece of camel meat. 'Well? Speak.'

'Sir, the butcher tells me the horse meat is not fit for human consumption.'

'What's this? Why?'

'He says the liver they removed from the horse was all speckled with disease, and so the rest of the meat must be diseased as well.'

Ammuna was listening to this and intervened, 'Fine, get rid of the meat,' he told the non-com. To Lawana he said, 'We'll just have to put up with more of this camel meat, that's all.'

'Shame about that. I wonder how many of the horses are like this?'

'We've driven them hard over the last thirteen days, but I dare say they'll do till we reach Nineveh. It's only another three more days.' With the last quip, Ammuna ordered Lawana to get the column mounted and they continued their journey downriver.

37
Crossing the Kalat

'That'll be the Aransah. I can almost smell the river air,' said Palaiyas.

'It'll be good to have fresh water again…and I enjoy the sound of flowing water, even if I don't like to get into it,' Mokhat said aloud to no one in particular.

'Might catch some fresh fish for supper,' agreed Palaiyas.

'It would be nice. Pity we didn't get a few fish from those fishermen when we left the Puranti.'

'We should fill up our water skins from the river; we're getting low, sir,' captain Neti informed Onasiyas.

'Right, get that organised, will you.'

The captain nodded and turned to his non-com and gave the necessary orders.

'Sir,' the man who had been on this route before, had ridden up to Onasiyas, 'We should be careful. A little further downriver, there's a bridge crossing the Kalat. It'll be guarded by the Assyrians.

'How far from here?' asked Onasiyas.

'Oh, only another two leagues.'

'Thanks. If you have any more information like that, come and tell me, but do it well in advance so I can take proper measures.'

'Yes sir.'

Onasiyas turned to Mokhat, 'Sir, from now on, we can't afford any campfires at night. They'll give us away. It'll have to be cold food until we rescue the princess and leave this area.'

Mokhat nodded his agreement.

Onasiyas continued, 'I've just been informed we'll reach a bridge in a short while, guarded by Assyrian soldiers. We can go left up the tributary and swim across to avoid detection, or we can force our way across this bridge. It's your decision sir.'

'I don't feel like swimming today. Can you deal with the Assyrians quietly?'

'I'll find a way, sir.'

Two leagues later, the same man who had been down this way, rode up and said, 'Sir, the bridge is over the next rise.'

At noon, the column came to a point below the small hill in front of them, and dismounted, keeping them out of view of those on the bridge. Cautiously the three commanders peered over the rise at the bridge below.

'Hm, only six guards. Three at either end,' said Onasiyas. 'I've worked out a plan; permission to carry it out,' he asked Mokhat.

'Permission granted.'

'Captain,' Onasiyas turned to his deputy, 'I have a job for you…and those three Assyrian speakers. Up to it?'

'Of course sir,' replied his deputy.

'Right, listen up. Find another couple of volunteers, and then I want the six of you to get dressed in the brigand's robes you'll find on the pack ponies. Then two groups of two men, with a limping man in the middle, are to go down on foot to the bridge. The man in the middle is to be the non-Assyrian speaker and to play at being badly injured.

'When you get to the bridge, one group is to have the middleman collapse and be at death's door. The other group is to continue to the other end of the bridge to where the other Assyrian sentries are. If you have any acting talent, this is the time to exercise it.

'Then the rest should be easy. Deal with the sentries. Disable them or kill them, but get rid of them as best you

337

can. I'll be watching from here. When I see you make your move I will come down with the rest of the column. By the time we reach you, I want to be able to cross the bridge in safety. Do I make myself clear?'

'Absolutely,' replied his deputy.

'Right, get on with it.'

Mokhat and Palaiyas had been listening to the plan and both smiled their approval.

Mokhat said, 'I say again, I'm glad you're with us, colonel.'

'I second this,' added Palaiyas.

Onasiyas' men all stayed below the rise out of sight of the bridge, while their three commanders peered over the ridge at the bridge below. They watched the two groups of robed bandits hobble their way down to the bridge, and smiled as one of the groups placed their middleman down at this side of the bridge and solicitously fussed over him as if he were in his deaths throes. Two of the sentries came over to see what was going on.

'We've been robbed,' snarled the Assyrian speaker amongst the robed men. 'About a league back up north,' he said softening his voice in mock sadness. 'Our friend here was stabbed and he's in a bad way.'

'*We're going on to the other side,*' shouted the Assyrian spokesman for the second group as they sauntered past, dragging their limping friend along. 'We'll wait for you on the other side.'

'*Right, but don't go on without us,*' the Assyrian speaker for the first group shouted in response.

'Is he badly hurt,' asked one of the sentries.

'I afraid he's had it. It's a deep wound in the back.' Since the role player was lying on his back, the so-called wound could not be inspected.

'Right,' said the other sentry. 'About a league back up there,' and he pointed up north to where the rest of the column was hiding.

'Yes, that's right. About fifteen bandits…they stripped us clean—took everything we had,' replied the group spokesman in Assyrian.

After this initial exchange with the Assyrian sentries at the northern end, the second group continued over to the far side of the bridge, laying their man down as if he was in trouble as well.

It prompted the sentries to come over and see what the matter was at their southern end; they found to their shock the men had all drawn daggers and quickly plunged them in to the sentry's stomachs. On seeing their compatriots make their move, those at the northern end of the bridge did the same. All six sentries were quickly tumbled over the bridge rail into the river.

Onasiyas ordered his men to mount and the column came galloping down the hill towards the bridge.

The column pulled up at the northern end of the bridge where the three pretend bandits were waiting.

'Was there no way to disarm them?' asked Onasiyas of the three, looking down at them from his mount.

'We'd have needed more men to do so, sir,' replied the captain, who'd waited patiently for the arrival of his commander.

'Ah, well, can't be helped,' intervened Mokhat. 'You were very convincing,' he complimented the captain.

'Thank you, sir. I tried.'

'Right you three comedians, here's your mounts, get on them and let's get going. The last thing we want is to be seen clowning around here,' urged Onasiyas.

'I thought we did a good job of acting,' complained the captain sub vocally to his two accomplices, wearing a mock smile.

The column cantered south across the Kalat River Bridge, passing a couple of people waiting to cross to the north.

'Pity about those two,' Palaiyas said pointing at the people waiting to cross. 'They must have seen what happened. They're our only witnesses.'

'We could have forced our way across this bridge,' said Onasiyas, 'but there would have been no guarantees we wouldn't inflict casualties, one's which might jump in the river to get away from us. That might have left soldiers as witnesses, and soldiers have their commanders. We'd have had a whole squadron after us in no time. Civilians; that's a different story. Most soldiers don't believe what civilians tell them.'

Mokhat smiled at the Onasiyas' cynical reasoning, but had to admit there was a kernel of truth in what he said.

'We could have killed their casualties and left no witnesses to talk,' put in Palaiyas sternly.

'I'm not in the habit of killing innocent injured men,' replied Onasiyas getting grim. 'Forcing our way across would have entailed a fight, and maybe a mess—this way, they died quickly and cleanly as soldiers should.'

Palaiyas shrugged his shoulders in resignation.

'I have another proposal for us to consider,' stated Onasiyas, changing the subject. 'We're right on the main river road at the moment, and it could spell trouble for us if we're spotted. There'll be a lot of river traffic on this road. We're here to rescue the princess, *not* to get into a fight with the Assyrian army. If we stay on this road, I'm fairly certain it's what will happen.'

'So what do you suggest, colonel,' asked Mokhat.

'Let's get off the road right now,' said Onasiyas, swinging his horse leftwards, going inland.

The entire column followed, going inland two hundred cubits, then paralleling the road from there. As they cantered along the grass, the conversation continued.

'Anything else?' asked Mokhat.

Onasiyas sighed as if his thoughts weighed him down, 'Before the bridge, I'd been mulling this over. Now we've moved away from the river, I'm a lot happier. As it is, we stick out like a sore thumb in our unusual costumes. We might have to think about changing into something less sinister. We should have taken more of those bandit robes. We could do with them. But now, we might want to find some other shirt tops just so we blend in more and stick out less. I've no idea where or how; I'm just voicing a worry which might get us into trouble with the locals, and interfere with our mission.'

'I've also been thinking on the same lines,' said Mokhat. 'So far I agree with you. Keep a sharp eye out for any source of tunic change we may come across. As for moving inland, it was a splendid idea. I suggest from now on, our forward scouts all wear those bandit robes, they're less conspicuous. Hand out the rest of the robes to various men, especially our Assyrian speakers. If we come across anybody, we can use those men as our front people, maybe bluff whoever we meet. It'll buy us time. I think we've got twenty or so robes available.'

Palaiyas was listening intently to this exchange, as was Captain Neti, Onasiyas' deputy.

'If we're to survive to rescue the princess,' Onasiyas continued, 'we'll have to be more cautious as we continue downriver. The closer we get to Nineveh, the more likely we'll run into an Assyrian patrol. But our caution cannot be at the expense of speed. The scouts need to be acutely aware of that. Our night camp will have to be off the beaten track, well inland as well. We can't afford to be seen or get involved in a confrontation.'

'I agree,' said Mokhat.

Onasiyas went on, 'When we stop off tonight, I'll give the men a pep talk on being more alert and how we should behave from now on. With a little luck and a lot of caution, we should succeed. But our biggest worry at the moment is time.'

'How do you mean?' Palaiyas asked.

'If Ammuna gets to Nineveh before we catch up with him, we've lost the princess.'

Mokhat pulled up his horse, and the whole column came to an abrupt halt.

'By Taru, you're right,' Mokhat exclaimed, turning towards Onasiyas. 'We have to overtake him before he reaches his destination. Otherwise we've failed.'

The import of what Onasiyas was saying had just sunk in. If Ammuna was allowed to reach Nineveh with Asmunikal, he would deliver the princess to Artatama and then they'd have to try to grab her from the Mittani prince. If he had a large retinue, as was likely, it would be much harder.

'I'm glad you've voiced this,' said Mokhat. 'From now on we have to combine caution with speed. We'll keep going late into the night from now on. I'm beginning to get a bad feeling about our ability to catch this rogue. I hope I'm wrong.'

Palaiyas intervened at this point, 'Let's at least be fully determined about rescuing the king's daughter—no matter who has her.' He was beginning to feel grim at this unpleasant turn in the conversation.

'Yes...that I am determined to do, no matter the cost to us,' agreed Mokhat. He kicked his mount back into motion and the column followed.

They rode on like this in a gloomy mood, putting on riding speed well into mid-afternoon, and well into early evening. As a result of their earlier conversation on time and speed, Mokhat had them continue well into the night. The moon was full and the going was relatively good in the scrubland they were travelling through. Somewhere around midnight, Mokhat called a halt. They pastured their horses, and ate a miserly meal.

Just as they were about to turn in, Onasiyas called for attention. 'I won't keep you long, I promise. I know your all tired. Now we're in Assyria, I need you all to stay extra alert. If their army, no matter how good we are, spots us here, we'll not survive the numbers they can throw at us. At the first warning of Assyrian soldiers, we need to hide. If we're spotted, we must make sure they don't get back to report our presence. Do I make myself clear?'

There were a lot of nodding heads to show they men had understood the implications of their commander's words.

'Right, thank you for listening, and good night…and captain, don't forget the sentries.'

'Yes, sir,' answered Captain Neti.

Night-time had again caught up with them. Late as it was, they all rolled up in their bedrolls and went into an exhausted sleep.

38
Feral Dogs

Around mid afternoon, one of the forward scouts came riding in fast and halted by Lawana's horse.

'Sir, we've spotted wild dogs up ahead, and they've spread themselves across the road as if they were trying to block it.'

'Ha, it must be the feral dog pack the Assyrian colonel warned us about. How many are there?' asked the colonel.

'We saw at least twenty,' replied the scout. 'It was unnerving; they behaved as if they were patiently setting a trap. Our non-com is watching them and trying to pick a few off with his bow.'

'How far ahead is this?'

'Another half a league, sir.'

'Captain! Take ten men with you and go back and use your bows on them. See if you can disperse them.'

'Yes sir,' said the younger captain riding behind Lawana.

The little troop galloped off towards the dogs while Ammuna called a short halt.

'Colonel, get your men ready for a bit of fun. We're going to have some sport. It'll be good for morale. We'll sit on our horses and use our bows. The man who gets the most dogs will get an extra hundred golden shekels from me.'

Lawana smiled at this, and turned to his remaining officers to pass the word down the line to the men.

As the column neared where their scouts were fending off attacks from the dogs, they noted the dogs seemed to sense the danger to them and avoid the arrows fired at them.

There were more dogs than initially reported. Two packs were darting around and successfully avoiding the arrows fired at them. One pack with thirty dogs was prowling around the southern route, blocking it, while another larger pack away from the river to the east, was nipping in and trying to harass the horses from the side. Both packs were managing to do this while staying out of the way of the arrows. Growling and howling, the dogs would come charging in, but zigzagging, then swerve and run back out of range, as if teasing the bowmen.

Ammuna and Lawana stared at the situation in astonishment. Ammuna smiled but his colonel had both eyebrows raised, almost in horror.

'I don't believe what I'm seeing,' burst out Lawana. 'They're behaving more like an army squadron than wild animals.'

'Colonel, they're feral not wild. And like all dogs, they work as a well coordinated group,' responded Ammuna. 'If you've ever seen a wolf pack at work rounding up and cornering deer or goats, you'd know they're intelligent and resourceful. Mind you, this pack size is big; much bigger than I've ever seen or heard of. They only gather in this size if there's a famine or a major threat. I wonder what made the pack this large? But damn it, this *is* impressive, don't you think?'

'General, what have you in mind? What are we going to do? I count only seven dead dogs from our arrows. I don't' think we should put up with *feral* dogs blocking our route.' Lawana was getting angry, but struggling to keep himself under control.

'Move the column forward. Lets see what *they* do.'

The column moved closer to the southern pack blocking their path...they in turn backed off to stay out of range of the arrows. The eastern pack then divided and one group moved north to block their exit upriver.

'Classical manoeuvre. Now we're surrounded,' complained Lawana.

'Relax colonel, I expected this. I'm trying to get them to come to us. Remember we have bows and they only have teeth. To get to us they have to come in close…there's no other way for them to eat us.'

'That's comforting,' replied Lawana.

The northern pack was beginning to close in on the back of the column, and the rearguard was picking off a few. Ammuna and Lawana could hear howls of pain as the arrows hit the dogs.

'Watch out,' yelled Ammuna, as the southern pack made a sudden charge and ran at the legs of the horses.

Ten riders moved out of the column and moved to the front to place themselves between their officers and the lead dogs. Just then, a few of the frontline horses reared up, throwing two men to the ground. The dogs made a charge at the men on the ground, managing to bite them before they swiftly scrambled to their feet. Another five more dogs were pierced with arrows….and the dogs retreated back downriver out of range.

Ammuna was watching this confrontation with amusement, then his face hardened. 'Colonel, watch the mouths of the dogs. I think I spotted a couple with what looked like froth on their muzzles.'

Lawana didn't immediately understand the significance of those instructions. 'What am I looking for?' he asked.

'Think man, think. There's a terrible disease which comes from dogs with such muzzles—have you forgotten?'

'Ah, yes…now you mention it. I think I did see one of the dogs frothing at the mouth, but I put it down to excitement.'

'If either horse or one of the men gets bitten,' continued Ammuna, 'by those types of dogs, then they're finished. I've never seen anyone recover from this kind of bite. It takes a couple of weeks to show, but it's a miserable end. Ask the Doc if you want the gory details.'

'I will,' replied Lawana gruffly while notching an arrow into a bow he'd borrowed, then letting the arrow off at the distant dogs. Somehow, a desire to kill all the dogs had arisen in the colonel and he was venting his anger by shooting arrow after arrow at the vermin.

'*Look over there*,' shouted Ammuna. 'What do you see?'

'Where?'

'Over there,' Ammuna responded irritably, 'on that hillock in the far distance.' He pointed to the south-east.

'Ah yes, you mean the dog standing on the small hill, staring at us.'

'That's the one. I'm fairly certain he's the lead dog—the pack leader. Look how he's staring at us...as if he's sizing us up.'

'Hmm, he probably is. There's another four dogs milling around him, heads down. You don't think they're his deputies?'

Ammuna was still staring, 'Probably.' Then he looked around behind him. 'Captain, over here.'

The only captain left behind him was the Doc, and he nudged his horse over to Ammuna. 'Yes sir.'

'Keep your eyes trained on that dog on the hill. Don't let him out of your sight. As soon as the dog moves from the hillock and makes to come this way, let me know immediately. It'll be the signal for their final assault. It's then, all the dogs will come charging at us. Before you settle to the job, go find the best archer we have and keep him by your side. When they come at us, I want the archer to concentrate on killing that lead dog. Do you understand? This is important.'

'Yes sir, I *do* understand. I'll go get the archer now.' And the doc moved away to seek out their expert bowman.

'Good, it takes care of their leader. Now I want all arrow fire to stop. We're just wasting them. Wait until they come in for the final assault…which I'm sure won't be long now.'

Lawana ceased his activities and shouldered the bow. 'General, shall I get the men to close up? We can form a half circle with our backs to the river, horses hobbled inside. And I suggest we get the princess inside the circle; I'll make sure the non-com guarding her has four more men to help protect her. Then it's a matter of waiting until they attack. What do you think?'

'Good, yes, do that. It'll put some order into this chaos.'

Just then, a couple of dogs ran towards them from the south, now the arrows had stopped, and one of the horses out in front reared up, throwing its rider. As the dogs swiftly nipped at the horse's hooves, the horse arched back and fell heavily on the dislodged winded rider lying on the ground, snuffing out his life in an instant.

Lawana watched helplessly as he saw the life being crushed out of the astonished young man, and he recoiled with a start at the suddenness of it.

'*Damned vermin!*' shouted Ammuna in anger at another one of his soldiers being killed.

As if this death was the awaited signal, the dog on the hillock jumped down and made a dash for the half circle of men—followed by the rest of the huge pack, coming at them from all sides. They came at Ammuna's *loyal* mercenaries from the north, from the east, and from the south. Forty or fifty dogs, howling and snarling with their teeth bared, still weaving in and out to avoid the arrows.

Lawana had ordered the men to create the half circle against the river with their mounts inside, to prevent the horses from rearing in fright. Everyman was now on foot, with his bow ready and an arrow notched in it, waiting expectantly for the dogs to get close enough to wreck some heavy damage to them with their arrows.

'*If any get through, use your knives—and try not to get bitten,*' Lawana shouted to his men.

As ordered, the doc and his expert bowman were ready and were only concentrating on the pack leader. As the dogs closed the distance, Ammuna ordered the first volley to be loosed—followed by another, and then another in quick succession. Dogs were falling dead or injured, but more got through to reach the men. A number of them leaped high to get at the men's throats; others went for the midriff and legs.

The expert archer was holding his bow loosely, fully concentrating on the lead dog, waiting for his chance at a clear shot—it came at the moment of impact when the two sides clashed. The lead dog went down without a whimper, an arrow through the front of his tan hide, roughly where his heart would have been.

No dog survived long as knives were buried in their contorting bodies—canine bodies twisting in defence beyond the natural ability of a body to contort itself. Both were experienced fighters but teeth against knives were a complete mismatch, and the carcases kept piling up. That is not to say all the men came out of the encounter unscathed. Some had been badly bitten, and when the remaining pack finally broke off and went yelping off into the east, followed by those wounded which could still manage to run or walk, there were some forty dog carcases lying around on the field of battle, both near and far.

Soldiers stood wiping their knives—others had unshouldered their bows and were firing on the remnants of the retreating pack. Men sat on the ground tending their wounds while others, the uninjured, helped the injured.

The Doctor Captain was shouting, 'Those who can, head for the river. I want every man who's been bitten to

349

wash their wounds in the river as much as they can. Wash them thoroughly at least ten times. He was limping as he was giving those instructions.

'Doc, how bad are you hurt?' asked Lawana, who had been wiping his iron knife. He now sheathed it and came over to their only medical expert.

'It's nothing, really,' replied the doc.

Lawana could see a torn rag concealing the wound. The doc had tried to administer his own remedy.

'I didn't ask you if it was something...I asked you how *badly* you've been bitten.'

The doc sighed, 'It's not the wound, sir, it's the dog which did the damage. I saw it too late, but I distinctly noticed froth on its muzzle. The wound isn't bad, really, but I'm afraid if I'm right, I'm done for.' He shook his head sadly and went to sit on a low boulder nearby.

'What about following your own orders, doc. Go and wash the wound in the river; that's a decree from your immediate superior.' Lawana helped him to his feet and led him to the river, leaving the doc to wash his wound.

Ammuna was wondering around his men, trying to comfort those needing it, and making a quick tally of the injured.

'More than I expected,' he told Lawana as his deputy joined him.

'Yes sir, I know. On the plus side, that's the end of the vermin. Most of the pack is lying here,' he swept his arm in an arc, indicating the canine carcases lying all around. 'I assume we have no dead?'

'No, but I'm afraid that's not going to be the end of the matter. I was watching carefully as they charged in, observing closely how many were frothing. I noted quiet a few. Some may have been frothing out of excitement, but others will have been diseased. There's no way of telling who got bit by whom. We'll have to wait...and we'll know in a couple of week's time. The doc was right to get them to wash the wounds in the river—it might help, but I'm not so sure. Anyway, he's the expert.'

'Sir, if you agree I'll get the men to gather and move downriver a league, and then we'll make camp for the night. The wind is from the south so the stench of these vermin won't get at us. By the way, I noticed you were counting the injured...how many?'

'I counted eight. We'll sort all that out in camp. Let's walk down there. It'll allow the injured to take their time. Give the order. But first, get men to retrieve all the arrows we used. We might need them later.'

'Yes sir.'

After a league of walking, they reached a spot which satisfied Ammuna, and the campsite sprung up in no time. A couple of fires were lit while the doc limped round the injured and had a careful look at the wounds, bandaging and making sure they'd been cleaned properly.

The latrine was dug downwind in the northern end, and the horses hobbled and left to graze.

The cooks got the staple barley porridge going while Ammuna and Lawana sat with their remaining officers and non-coms, discussing the day's events.

'Does anyone remember me talking about having a little sport before the fight?' Ammuna asked ironically. 'If so, I apologise. I feel as if we've been in a real battle.'

The gathered company nodded, but made no comment.

'So doc, how's the leg?' asked Ammuna.

'Fine sir...well the wound isn't too bad, but...we'll see.'

'You mean the dog which bit you? It was diseased?' asked Lawana.

'Yes colonel, I think it was.'

'So how are you going to know? What are the symptoms, so we can keep an eye out for them in the injured men?'

'No real symptoms show up in the first two weeks, later, anybody infected seems to get a runny nose and looks like they're suffering from a cold—after come headaches and fever—then they complain of pains and just sit around not wanting to do anything. Following this, it progresses to acute pain throughout the body with violent movements. The patient becomes uncontrollable with excitement, interspersed with bouts of depression. If you offer the patient any form of water, they cringe away from it and fear it. The water test is a good one. They produce excess saliva which looks like foam at the mouth....then death isn't far off.'

'Have you ever seen anyone die from it?' Lawana persisted.

'No colonel. What I'm quoting is what I've been taught, but I've no reason to doubt my teachers. The same symptoms occur in all animals bitten by such a dog, be it man, horse, or dog.'

Lawana looked disgusted. 'If I was Assyrian, I'd round up all the dogs and butcher them...put them out of their misery.'

Ammuna looked at his deputy with a faint smile on his face. 'Now, now, colonel, remember why we're here. Try to keep in mind what's to come in a few days time. Then if you still feel like this, you can hire your own private army and go hunt down all the dogs you want...but not until then.'

That made Lawana smile. His brow creased up and then he let go and relaxed. 'I don't know why, but this dog business got to me. You're right general, I *can* hire all the men I want and go dog hunting next week....but I think I'll give it a miss. Let the Assyrians sort out their own problems.'

Then both the general and his deputy laughed...with the others present joining in for company.

'By the way, doc, how are the wounded? What's your verdict on their bites?' asked Ammuna on a more serious note.

'Only one case is dangerous, and that's because he was out front and was attacked by a number of the dogs. Otherwise, most of the bites are superficial. I'll only be able to fully answer your question general, in a couple of weeks, if symptoms start showing.'

'Fine. You did a good job, doc. I'm sure my men will back me up. Now colonel, how is the brat? She still in good condition?' Ammuna asked finally.

'Yes sir, nothing came near her. They never broke through to the inner circle.'

'Good. Now where's the food,' Ammuna demanded, just as the cooks began to dole out the thick barley porridge.

39
Night Fright

'**S**ir, sir,' whispered the sentry urgently into Captain Neti's ear, trying to wake him.

'Awe, yea,' yawned the captain, 'what is it?'

'Sir, Assyrian scouts, heading this way.'

It brought the captain wide-awake. He jumped out of his bedroll and enquired, 'How many and how far?'

'We spotted two on horses, about three hundred cubits to the west of us, coming in slowly.'

'Are we visible to them?'

'I'm not sure…I don't think so.'

'What time of the night is it?'

'Just before dawn, sir.'

'Right, quietly, go round and wake people. Tell them what you told me, and tell them to gather on the western edge of our camp with their bows.'

'Yes sir,' answered the sentry, then went off to carry out the order.

'I'll wake the colonel.' Neti turned and shook Onasiyas' shoulder gently. His commander was in the next bedroll. 'Sir, incoming Assyrians.'

Onasiyas was awake and heard the captain. 'Captain, the horses,' his commander whispered urgently. 'They're the most visible part of us. Get people to lead them further inland. Hurry! Make sure you keep them quiet.'

'Yes sir, I should have thought of that.' The captain found people on their feet, gathered twenty or so, and went to see to the two hundred odd horses and pack ponies.

They unhobbled their mounts and led them off into the east as quickly and as quietly as they could, away from the incoming Assyrians.

Mokhat and Palaiyas joined up with Onasiyas on the western edge of the camp and found him peering into the west, listening carefully.

'What's up?' asked Palaiyas.

'Assyrian scouts, they've been spotted by my sentries. I set sentries during the night near the river road, to be warned if any Assyrians were in the vicinity. Shush! There, can you see them. Two of them coming slowly towards us.'

They all heard the steady thud of horse's feet walking in the dewy grass. The Assyrians were whispering to each other. Then they suddenly stopped.

'Have they heard us?' whispered Palaiyas.

'Hush, listen,' whispered Onasiyas.

All they could see in the low light was a couple of outlines against the darkened sky to the west. They made out the shadows of two men on horses.

'Lucky they're silhouetted against the sky,' commented Mokhat in as low a voice as he could manage.

The men were all lying down noiselessly in the grass, bows in hand ready to grab an arrow and let loose on the two individual Assyrian scouts who had strayed towards them.

A man crawled up to Onasiyas, 'Sir, I'm one of the scouts posted near the river. I've come to report a massive squadron of Assyrians are coming up river.'

'Any idea how many?'

'It's in the hundreds, sir. My guess is somewhere around four hundred.'

That alarmed Onasiyas. 'You're sure?' he whispered worriedly.

'Yes sir.' Nodding in the direction of the scouts, he continued, 'they're the forward scouts of the squadron.

Whatever you do, don't fire on them. If they hear a sound, or don't report back, we'll be in trouble.'

Onasiyas looked closer at his own scout and recognised a non-com. He was wondering who was making such bold suggestions to the commander. The non-com was right of course.

They lay in the grass and watched the dawn begin to show in the eastern sky, peeing over the eastern mountains. The two Assyrian scouts wheeled their mounts around and slowly rode back towards the river, both heading northwards, oblivious of the Hittite *special forces* he'd nearly stumbled upon hiding in the grass.

'Phew! That was close,' Onasiyas ejected. 'Four hundred! By all the demons, what are they doing along the river this early,' he demanded.

Mokhat looked at Palaiyas and both raised their eyebrows.

'Good question, colonel,' said Mokhat. 'Any ideas?'

'Must be a detachment detailed to patrol the river. That's my guess. What puzzles me is why they're up so early.'

'Why such a large detachment? It's massive...more like a squadron,' said Mokhat.

'They wont' need to call in reinforcements if they come across anyone they need to deal with, will they? It's the overkill principle. Maybe they want to catch someone?' Palaiyas suggested.

'That would imply they had prior information,' said Mokhat.

'Yes it would. Another question...how did Ammuna get by them? They must have crossed paths. Both are large groups. Did he get help from his criminal friends? Did they give him safe passage? Damn, this isn't getting us anywhere,' exclaimed Onasiyas angrily. 'Too many unknowns and too much guessing for my liking. We'd better stay here for a while until this lot's moved further upriver, and then we continue. I'll double the sentries for the moment.'

Palaiyas nodded, then patted his stomach, 'Agreed. Time to go back and have food, eh?'

'Lead on,' smiled Mokhat.

They got up from the grass and urged everyone back to the middle of the camp. The cooks dished out cold food, yet it tasted better as a result of their near encounter; as the old saying went: a little fear always encouraged the appetite.

'Where's the non-com,' called out Onasiyas as loudly as he dared.

'Here sir,' replied the elderly man, appearing from nowhere.

'Go get the captain and tell him to bring the horses back.'

'Yes sir,' he plodded off to obey the given order.

After food, the column remounted and carried on as fast as they dared, paralleling the river road downriver. The scrubland they rode through was mostly thin with the occasional clumps of thick shrubbery. The sparse tree cover was stunted as if the nearby river was reluctant and withheld its water supply. The truth was, it took more than it gave.

After a while, Onasiyas said to Mokhat, 'Sir, I've just had a thought. Sometime in the next couple of days, the squadron which passed us will come to the Kalat river bridge and find the sentries missing.'

Mokhat said, 'Well yes. Of course they will, but so what?'

'If they turn round and come back down to investigate.'

'Who's to say *this* is the direction to look for the culprits. Why not look for them up north instead? Anyway, we'll be far gone by the time they look for anyone...if they come at all?'

'I suppose,' said Onasiyas, a worried look on his face. 'You know sir, little things are beginning to niggle me...like this thought just now. I'm getting worried about our ability to rescue the king's daughter. I don't feel like we're making any headway. We've been on the road now for twelve days and we're no nearer to catching him than when we started.'

'Colonel, at this point in the journey, there are only two alternatives,' said Mokhat sternly. 'We go on, or we turn back. It's that simple. There is no other choice. What would you have me do? And don't forget, we've gained a day on Ammuna.'

Onasiyas sighed, 'Yes, we *have* gained a day. Putting the alternatives so starkly, I'll curb my despondency and press ahead more enthusiastically, sir. And thank you. I needed that. Your clarity is as good as a kick up the backside, sir.' Onasiyas then smiled a broad smile to show he'd overcome his mood swing and proceeded to kick his horse to go faster.

Mokhat joined him in the increased speed, followed by Palaiyas and the rest of the men.

Throughout the day, scouts brought back reports of various travellers going up and down the river road, mostly small groups of people going about their daily business. Some on horse, others in carts, and one small caravan composed entirely of ambling camels. Around noon, they reported a flotilla of three boats they'd sighted going down river, probably from Tushan, and likely heading for the capital. There was little wind to speak of, and the day was bright and sunny.

The column continued throughout the rest of the day with one stop for a break and a bite, all the way into late evening, when Mokhat called a halt to set up camp for the night.

The routine was the usual; cold food and no campfire, but the men were hardened soldiers and able to put up with it as part of army life. Onasiyas promised he would make it up to the men when they got back home. He insisted he'd throw them a celebratory banquet, especially in honour of them succeeding in rescuing the princess. The positive note went down well with the men and they settled into their bedrolls more convinced of their mission.

Mokhat took note of Onasiyas changed mood and upbeat outlook and felt satisfied the proverbial kick up the backside had worked.

40
Fisherman's Festival

For Ammuna's men, the next morning was another early start. What was unusual was the air of suppressed excitement pervading through the camp as the men realised their journey was coming to a close. The dawn showed a clear sky with a hot autumnal sun rising overhead. A sparse gentle mist drifted over the nearby river, glistening and sparkling in the early sun as the sheen broke through and fell on the water.

Non-coms were shouting at the men to rise-and-shine and get their lazy bodies out of their blankets. Ammuna was on his feet watching Lawana put his boots on.

'Up and at them colonel, let's get this show on the road.'

'Yes sir,' Lawana replied, jumping to his feet. 'Have we got time for breakfast,' he asked teasingly.

'Only just,' responded the general. 'Only just.'

'More porridge I suppose,' asked his deputy.

'Unless you can cook up something different.'

'Porridge it is then,' smiled his deputy.

'I quiet enjoy the stuff,' smiled Ammuna. 'It's filling and sits comfortably in the stomach; apart from being good for the bowels.'

'Yes sir. On a more solemn note sir, we're almost running out of the stuff, so the cooks informed me last night. We'll have to try to find a place to re-provision our stock.'

'You mean for the return journey?'

'Yes sir. Those who head back after being paid, will need to have provisions to get them home.'

'Remind me to have a word with the men about returning home tonight when we make camp. It's not going to be a simple journey. The border guards will be on the lookout for all of us. I've got a little advice for them.'

'You're not coming with us?'

'No. I think I'll try out the Assyrian hospitality in Nineveh for a few months, until I decide what to do. That's if they'll let me.'

'Oh, I think if they're paid enough, anything is possible.' Lawana meant it cynically but thought it wise to utter it neutrally.

'That's what I'm hoping. Now let's get some of the famous porridge you mentioned.' Ammuna led his deputy to the fire where the cooks were busy.

Following a quick breakfast, the column got back on the river road to Nineveh. After a pleasant ride, around mid-morning, one of the scouts rode back and reported they were coming up on to a small fishing village, but it was on the other side of the river. The scout told Lawana the Assyrian squadron they'd seen on the other side of the river seemed to have stopped off and was resting there.

'I've an idea,' Ammuna told Lawana. 'When we get to the spot opposite the village, I want you to signal for them to send a boat over to our side. I want to send over Colonel Pudil's compliments and I want to show the other colonel our *pass*. The colonel in charge there must be as puzzled by our presence as I was of theirs.'

'Colonel Musuri, sir,' replied Lawana.

'What?'

'Colonel Musuri sir, it's the name of the other Assyrian colonel leading the squadron.'

'Oh yes, thank you colonel. Anyway, send our *pass* across and satisfy his curiosity.'

'Yes sir.'

It wasn't long before the fishing village came into view round a small bend in the river.

The column stopped and were ordered to dismount.

Ammuna planted himself to face the fishing village, and watched a couple of Assyrian sentries ogle them from across the water. 'We'll make this a short rest stop. Let the men relax and get something to drink and eat. This shouldn't take too long.'

'Yes sir.'

'See those two sentries?' demanded Ammuna. 'Have the lieutenant signal them to send a boat. They can't miss our signals. Make it simple.'

The lieutenant faced the other shore and shouted at the two Assyrian sentries to get their attention. One of the sentries immediately ran off to get his superior. A bunch of Assyrians came out of a hut and joined the other sentry.

The lieutenant pointed at one of the boats on the shore and made motions towards his side of the shore. He had to repeat the signal a number of times before it was understood. Then a couple of fishermen were called for, and they climbed into the boat with an Assyrian and began rowing towards Ammuna's men.

'Get the Assyrian translator to come to me,' Ammuna told his deputy.

'Right away sir.'

When the boat beached below Ammuna, he handed the *pass* to Lawana and told him to go and talk to the Assyrian.

Lawana, accompanied by the translator and lieutenant, went down to the boat and gave the Assyrian officer Colonel Pudil's compliments and asked if his lieutenant and translator could be taken over to see Colonel Musuri.

The Assyrian was startled to find these people knew the name of their commander, and readily agreed to ferry the lieutenant and his companion to the other side.

It took a while but both lieutenant and translator eventually returned beaming with smiles and were met by Lawana on the shoreline as the boat landed.

'Well, what happened?' Lawana asked impatiently.

'Nothing sir, really. It went very smoothly.'

Lawana led both of them back up the riverbank to where the general waited.

The lieutenant saluted his general and reported. 'Colonel Musuri sends the general his compliments and thanks him for his thoughtfulness in satisfying his curiosity. He says he wasn't worried because he knew his counterpart, Colonel Pudil would sort things out. He says they're good pals. He also says if he can be of any assistance, then the general shouldn't hesitate to ask. Finally, Colonel Musuri says he'll see us shortly. There's a bridge across the Aransah at Nineveh and he'd like to meet you in a couple of days and shake you by the hand.'

Ammuna held out his hand, and the lieutenant stared at it before realising the general was requesting the return of the clay *pass* tablet.

'Sorry sir,' replied the lieutenant as he handed the *pass* back to Ammuna.

'Good, well done. You may resume your duties.'

'Funnily enough, I feel safer after this exchange of formalities,' said Lawana.

'That's why I did it. I needn't have done it, but it's cleared the air between the two sides of the river. Now he knows who we are and why we're here. There can be no more misunderstandings—and he's offered his help to us should we need it. I know it's only a couple of days before we reach the end, but it's safer this way.'

'Yes sir.'

'Right, let's get the men mounted. We've got to get on.'

The column reformed and continued their journey, leaving the Assyrian squadron behind on the other side.

363

Sometime in the middle of the afternoon, scouts reported a large fishing village up ahead.

Lawana spotted smoke rising up in the distance, clearly coming from a settlement of some size.

'Yes colonel, I can see it,' pre-empted Ammuna as his deputy pointed to the smoke.

'Half a league, I would guess sir.'

'I want to see if we can buy flour and other provisions there. It'll be cheaper than buying it in Nineveh. Make sure the men behave themselves.'

'I'll pass the word along,' replied his deputy.

As the Hittite column neared the village, a small welcoming party came forward from the village.

'Bring me the translator,' Ammuna commanded.

Once again, the translator was brought and he accompanied Ammuna to the meeting with the village head.

'Tell the headman we wish to buy flour and I'll pay him in golden shekels, if he's willing.'

Having given the head fisherman this news, the translator told Ammuna, 'He's more than happy to sell you the flour, and the shekels will be most welcome. He's also inviting us to join him and his people in the feast of the House of Akitu in honour of the high god Ashur. He wants us to be his guests. They're about to celebrate the end of the productive year. He says their fish feast will involve *the best fish on the river.*'

'Tell him we'd be delighted to honour his god with much needed fresh food.' Ammuna's thought of the dried camel meat waiting for him, and it prompted a speedy acceptance of the chief's invitation.

Being told this, the headman first smiled broadly at the general, then turned to his own fellow fishermen, indicating to Ammuna he should follow him.

In the middle of the village, the small party approached the side of a small hut which had been elaborately decorated and hung with various fruit, flowers and branches.

The translator continued, pointing at the hut, 'The headman says it is the House of Akitu in honour of the high god Ashur. I think he means it's a simulation of the House of Akitu in Assur. The headman says this is their New Year feast on the first day of Tasritu, the beginning of the agricultural year.'

When they came round to the front, Ammuna saw a small altar had been erected at the front of the hut. There was an elaborate drawing on door of the hut, which illustrated a circle representing the sun, suspended from wings, and enclosing a warrior holding a fishing rod in his left hand while the right hand was uplifted as if to bless his worshippers.

Pointing at the hut, Ammuna said, 'Ask the headman if this didn't offend Ishtar, the patron goddess of nearby Nineveh.'

When the fisherman heard this, he smiled and said something in Assyrian.

'He says their mighty king, Ashur-Nirari II in Assur, insists we celebrate the Feast of Ashur as it has always been celebrated from time immemorial. He says they are only obeying the wishes of their king, and...enjoying the festivities.'

Ammuna looked at the smiling headman and said, 'Tell him it is most reasonable, and we hope to enjoy the festivities with him. Thank him once more for including us in the celebrations.'

The headman led the group to another larger hut off the main village square, clearly his home. Just before they entered the hut, Ammuna told Lawana, 'Colonel, we left the men outside the village. Go tell them to hobble their horses and put them to pasture for the night. Then make sure you give them another lecture on good behaviour before bringing them into the village. Let them wait over there out of the way, opposite this hut, then come inside and join me.'

'Yes sir.' Lawana hurried off to carry out the orders.

Inside the hut, there was a strong smell of cooked fish. After all the dried camel meat, Ammuna's stomach rumbled to the waft of fresh food.

The translator said, 'The headman says to make ourselves comfortable. His wife will bring us something to drink.'

No sooner had they sat down, when a middle-aged woman came in carrying clay cups and a large clay pot of drink. She poured a measure out in each cup and handed them to Ammuna and the translator, then the headman lifted his in a toast.

'The headman says *to new friendships* on this first day of Tasritu.'

Ammuna lifted his cup in salute and then took a gulp and smiled in pleasant surprise, then gulped more of the liquid down. The translator was more cautious and sniffed at it first before taking a sip.

'Sir,' he exclaimed in surprise, 'this is an excellent barley brew.' He quickly began gulping the beer down as if in the throes of a mighty thirst.

'Steady on there, boy,' Ammuna counselled. 'There's a whole evening to go. You'll be out cold in no time. There's a kick to this stuff...not I'm complaining, but go steady or you won't enjoy the evening. Ask the village headman if it's alright with him if we make camp outside the village for the night.'

A little Assyrian talk ensued and then the translator said, 'The headman says he'd be delighted. It means you'll be able to stay for the whole of the festivities.'

The hut door was gently pushed in and Lawana sidled through the door.

Ammuna put his palm out to Lawana, 'Colonel, I'm sorry but I need you to go and get the men to make camp outside the village to the south. Find a nice spot and get the latrines dug; get a fire going, then bring the men back here. Make sure you leave the wounded comfortable. By the way, how are they?'

'Last I heard from the doc, the bites are not too bad. The one who was more badly bitten, seems to be recovering. I'll make sure I leave someone to look after him; the others can join us at the festivities. Don't worry sir, I'll keep an eye on them.'

'Good…right, off you go and set up camp.'

Lawana gave an inner sigh, 'Yes sir.' He left to carry out his new orders.

More of the beer was consumed before Lawana reappeared.

'Ah, colonel, come and have some of this wonderful beer.' Ammuna shoved a cup into his deputy's hand and indicated for the waiting woman to fill it, which she did.

Lawana took a swig and his face lit up. 'Why this really good stuff,' he said in wonder.

'Ask the village headman if I can buy a couple of barrels from him for my men,' Ammuna told his translator.

'I don't think you'll need to do that, sir,' interrupted Lawana. 'As I came inside I saw a bunch of women bringing large clay pots over to the men. I think they're already enjoying the beer.'

'Oh, good. After all our long ride, I want them to let go and enjoy themselves tonight…well not entirely let go, but certainly to enjoy the evening's festivities.' Ammuna turned to his translator and said, 'Ask him how many bags of flour he can spare,' and as he said this, he pulled his money pouch off from his belt and placed it on the table.

The headman's eyes immediately settled on the pouch, as Ammuna knew they would. The general opened the pouch and poured all the golden shekel coins on the table. There were some twenty odd coins there, a magnificent sum to a poor fisherman. 'Tell the headman it's all his,' and Ammuna pushed the coins towards the headman.

The headman's eye bulged wide at this stroke of unexpected luck. He slowly shook his head, while watching the general push the coins towards him. Ammuna's head was nodding to contradict the fisherman's head shaking.

'Tell him very firmly it's all his, and I won't take *no* for an answer,' Ammuna insisted.

The fisherman's wife was ogling the money on the table with unashamed greed….and began quickly to fill the cups with more beer.

Finally the headman talked to the translator, who told Ammuna, 'He says not to worry. He'll supply all the flour we'll need…and throw in more. Now he would like us to go outside and join the rest of the village in their festivities.'

Ammuna nodded his agreement and got up from the table, picking up his empty pouch but leaving the shekels in place.

The headman nodded to his wife and the golden shekels, and she quickly swept them into her apron and rushed off into another room to hide them.

Outside they faced a gilded vision of the western sky as the golden sun eased gently over the horizon. Then they joined a solemn procession waiting for the headman. The village chief directed Ammuna to join him, and they both headed for the small altar in front of the decorated hut in the middle of the village.

A priest stood behind the altar ready to go into the hut. Both the headman and Ammuna turned before the altar to face the people and waited, then it seemed, the whole village filed past them, arms lifted in supplication towards the altar and hut, all the time chanting and invoking the god, past the hut, acting as the surrogate House of Akitu. The procession carried a small fishing boat filled with the year's produce as an offering to invoke further fertility from the god Ashur and placed it before the altar, in front of the priest.

The headman laid an arm on Ammuna's arm and led him round the altar into the hut, following in the footsteps of the village priest. Those outside heard a gong being hit seven times, and a little while later Ammuna reappeared with the headman. The crowd cheered them, and the headman led Ammuna to the far side of the village where a huge number of tables were laid out with food. Ammuna's men were already there, seated and waiting for their commander.

Laid out on the table was baked fish, fried fish, fish pie, fish stew, fish rolled in flour and fried, fish turned on a spit. There were many types of bread, pancakes and dumplings to go with the fish. Large clay pots of beer stood on side tables ready to fill the cups of the seated drinkers.

The headman led Ammuna and his officers to a separate table where a number of the village dignitaries sat. Ammuna was seated at one end while the headman sat at another end. When all were seated, the headman called for quiet and rose to his feet. He gave a long speech in Assyrian, which passed over the heads of the Hittites. Only Ammuna's translator whispered the gist of it in Ammuna's ear. Then a toast was pronounced and the cups were raised…and emptied.

By this time, the light had faded and the darkened heaven was flooded with a plurality of stars, sparkling brightly, each seeming to outshine the other.

As the evening progressed, Lawana, who was sitting to Ammuna's right, looked up and said wistfully, with a slight slur to his voice from the drink, 'My, what a glorious night.'

The food had gone and people were getting up from the tables. Two lyres, three flutes, and drums began to make music. Men began slowly, dancing clockwise with a net in the middle, going round and round, bumping it up and down on the ground as if there were fish in it. This continued in a mesmerising tempo for a time, and then the tempo changed and women joined them. Because women weren't allowed to fish, they danced in a circle behind the men, going round them counter clockwise to the men's circle. Another circle of men formed near the first, with another net in the middle...and in a short while...more women joined them dancing behind their men. A third circle formed and a few of Ammuna's men were dragged in to join the dance. The music went on like this well into the night—drink and dancing, until it finally came to an exhausted halt.

Ammuna then thanked his host for allowing them to join in the festivities, and he led his wobbly men off south to their campsite outside the village proper.

41
Dead Dogs

Nearby howling woke the whole camp just before dawn with a sentry reporting a small pack of prowling dogs in the vicinity, or they could be wolves. He couldn't tell the difference in the dark.

'It's time to get up anyway. They did us a favour,' said Onasiyas, climbing out of his bedroll.

'Do you know how many dogs there are?' Palaiyas asked the departing sentry.

'No sir. I can hear them but I can't see them.'

'Right, carry on.'

'Cursed pests!' exploded Mokhat. 'If I could see them, I'd use my bow on them.'

'If it's dogs?' reproached Onasiyas. 'Could be wolves for all we know. They sound much the same.'

'It would still be good bow practice, whichever they are. Anyway, another day, another chase,' said Palaiyas switching the talk to the order of the looming day.

'Pity we're so far from the river. Otherwise we could have a proper wash,' Onasiyas complained, then began to do a small workout.

'Look at this,' said Palaiyas pointing at Onasiyas. 'Where does he get the energy from this early?'

Mokhat's reaction was to join Onasiyas in doing the same exercises. At the display of outrageous prowess, as Palaiyas saw it, he walked off in mock disgust, looking for the cooks to dish out food from the provisions.

The light finally climbed over the distant eastern mountains lighting up the heavens in an arc to the west. A red half disk of the sun crept over the mountain ridge, indicating it would be a fine sunny day.

Breakfast was handed out and eaten quietly. Water was poured from the heavy water skins into bronze cups. The biscuits and dried meat was repetitious but filling.

'Right, let's clear the camp and get mounted,' ordered Onasiyas.

They continued and tried to hurry through the scrubland, but it was hard going, especially for the pack ponies.

'This is impossible,' Onasiyas complained finally as the scrubland became thicker. 'We can't continue like this. I'm loathed to leave this route but the going is impossible.'

'Any ideas?' asked Mokhat.

'What if I send scouts out far in front dressed in those robes we have. We might take a chance and use the river road, else we can abandon any chance of catching up with Ammuna. I know it's a risk, but we have to take it. What's your opinion general,' Onasiyas asked Mokhat.

'I'm afraid your right, colonel,' Mokhat replied. 'We have to put on more speed than this. We'll never catch Ammuna this way. We have to get back on the main road.'

It being agreed, Onasiyas sent more scouts dressed in the bandit outfits to join and inform the other lookouts to scout further downriver than they'd been doing. He ordered them to report back more often and had a rota drawn up to rotate the eight scouts out front, four times during the day. The rearguard was equally ordered to keep a sharp eye out for anyone following them.

The *special forces* then swung to the right, heading back towards the main river road, galloping along it at a furious pace. Seeing them coming, other road traffic quickly removed themselves from the road to allow the speeding column to go by.

Later in the day, around mid-afternoon, scouts returned to report a strange scene along the river road. A large number of dog carcasses lay over a wide area.

'It looks like the scene of a battle, said the baffled scout. 'They were definitely killed, sir,' he reported.

Mokhat's men arrived at the scene of the carnage and stopped to look around.

'Must have been the large Assyrian squadron clearing out wild dogs,' suggested Palaiyas. 'See, they would need a large contingent to deal with this pack size. Dogs in such packs can be a bit of a nuisance to people and road traffic, especially if the pack gets this big.'

'Keep an eye out for any of the stray dogs,' Onasiyas told his scouts. Then to Mokhat he said, 'Remember the howling this morning? I think we might have had a visit from them just before dawn. It was probably what's left of them howling at us.'

'Yes, I was just thinking the same,' Mokhat replied.

'Anyway, let's get moving, we're losing valuable travelling time,' urged Mokhat.

The detachment kicked their mounts back into motion and they sped once more along the road in pursuit of Ammuna.

During the rest of what was left of the day, Mokhat's men galloped as if their lives depended on it, switching mounts every now and again to keep their speed up. They travelled like this until well past the light fading, until finally Mokhat raised his hand and halted the men.

'Time to make camp,' announced Mokhat. 'Colonel, we'll follow your idea of staying off the beaten track and move inland again to make camp. It worked with the large Assyrian squadron yesterday.'

They swung inland to the left and found a secluded spot for the camp. More cold rations were handed out and consumed. Horses were bedded down and sentries posted in a wide circle round the night camp. Everyone was far too

tired for any chitchat and all who could, climbed exhausted
into their bedrolls and fell asleep.

42
Att Tuk River

In the grey dawn of the morning after, Ammuna's camp awoke from the night's festivities, with many suffering from hangovers. The sentries reported to their superiors the village fishermen were already hard at it on the river.

'They're even earlier risers than we are,' commented Lawana to his commander as they washed themselves in the nearby river, all the while looking at the disappearing fishermen rowing hard upriver.

'You're lucky to be in the army colonel,' quipped Ammuna. 'Apart from a little fighting, there's no softer job.'

'You forgot the dying, general, that part isn't so soft. The fishermen's lot may be hard but it has its compensations, like a wife and children to come home to. What has a soldier to look forward to? Training, discipline, and more fighting.'

'And rewards, colonel...don't forget the rewards. We're just on our way to collect ours, or had you forgot?'

'Yes, there's that. Thanks to *you*, general, we're going to be more fortunate than the rest; but we're the exception, not the rule.'

A smile fluttered across Ammuna's face in acknowledgement of the side compliment. 'This time I can't argue with you...you're right of course. Just be happy fortune has smiled on us. Make the most of it...and leave the fishermen to their own fate. Now let's go get some breakfast.'

Both men returned to the camp and had their porridge ladled out into a bowl. After the food, the campsite was tidied up and the column reformed.

'Captain, pop across into the village and give my compliments to the village headman, if he's there, and thank him for last night's hospitality. Tell him it was much appreciated. If he's not there, leave the same message with his wife. You'd better take the translator with you. You can catch us up.'

'Yes sir,' the captain responded and went off to search out the translator.

To his deputy, Ammuna said, 'Did we get the promised provisions?'

'Yes sir. Twenty bags of flour, a lot of fruit, and various types of fish. Some preserved in oil, others dried, some smoked. The headman was as good as his word, sir. We'll be eating fish for a while.'

'Fish is good for you,' answered Ammuna. 'Are the scouts deployed?'

'Four out front and two on the left flank, sir.'

'Then let's get on with it. Tomorrow we should be in Nineveh.'

With Ammuna leading his mounted *loyal* mercenaries, was on with the journey downriver.

As they rode Ammuna commented, 'What do you think, colonel, will it keep off?' He was peering at the sky into the east.

'You mean the rain sir?'

'The clouds look ominous, especially far to the east.'

'We shall have to see, sir. But I'll lay my bet on it the weather is stirring up another storm.'

'Only this time I don't think we'll have any tree cover. We'll have to make camp at the first sign of rain; rapidly put the bivouacs up, otherwise we'll get soaked. Tell the men to be ready.'

'Yes sir.' Lawana turned round on his horse to his officers to pass on the order. He noticed two riders coming up fast on the outside of the column. 'The captain's back,' he told Ammuna.

As he said this, the captain rode up to his commander and said, 'Sir, the headman wasn't in but I did as you asked and left the message with his wife.'

'Good, thank you. Rejoin the column.'

Throughout the whole day's riding, the heavens threatened them with a soaking. The clouds continued to darken and the wind blew up from the east. In the afternoon, following the midday lunch break, Ammuna had enough and ordered the bivouacs to be erected. He called the scouts back and had the men crowd into the few leather tents they had put up…and then the camp waited. As the last tent went up, large drops of rain began to descend. Unlike the previous storm, this was a steady downpour and lasted only a short time.

'Is this all?' asked Ammuna as he cautiously looked outside of the officer's tent at the sky. Then he said, 'The sun's come out. I don't believe it. Well, so much for the storm…let's get going.'

The tents were shaken out and repacked, and the column reformed. It was late afternoon by the time the scouts went on their errand out front and to the sides, and the column settled down to more riding until the evening's camp.

A while later, one of the scouts came back to report there was another bridge crossing a river in front of them.

'How many guarding it?' Lawana asked the scouts.

'About twenty—ten at either end, sir.'

Ammuna extracted his leather map of Assyria from his horse pouch, and looked for the river. 'Ah, there it is,' he told Lawana. 'It's the Att Tuk River. Should be no problem now we have this *pass*.'

Rounding a bend in the river, they came in sight of the bridge.

Ammuna called for the translator to join him. When the elderly soldier arrived, Ammuna said, 'Right, as before. Tie the white cloth to the tip of your spear and raise it high.' To Lawana he said, 'Colonel, go have a chat with their commander. Here, take the *pass* with you.' Ammuna gave his deputy the cherished *pass* from his pouch.

'Yes sir. When you see me wave, it'll mean it's all right to bring the men forward to the bridge.'

The Assyrians had brought all their men to the northern end of the bridge to face the oncoming soldiers and had readied their bows in anticipation.

Seeing the Assyrians stance, Lawana went forward cautiously with the translator by his side. On reaching the Assyrian soldier, the translator told the man they had permission to be in Assyria, and permission to cross this bridge by order of their commanding general in Nineveh. He held out the *pass* in his hand as proof.

'Sir, this officer says he knows nothing of this. He doesn't want to look at the pass, and says we cannot come across.'

Lawana looked angry at the news. 'Tell him to read the *pass* or I will be forced to make him read it...and he will regret making me do that.'

The Assyrian looked startled at this unpleasant turn in the talks. He shouted something, which Lawana's translator interpreted as, 'Sir, he says if we want to cross, we have to leave all our arms on this side of the river. We can have them back when we return. He won't let armed men across his bridge.'

'Tell this oaf this *pass* allows us free passage across his bridge, and we certainly have *no* intention of disarming.' Lawana waved the clay tablet at the Assyrian.

In response, the Assyrian shouted to his men, and they notched arrows into their bows getting ready to fire at the two Hittites before them.

Lawana took the hint, turned his horse around, and went back to Ammuna, followed by the translator and the white flag.

'Well? What's the matter. Are we going across or not?' A vexed Ammuna asked.

'Something's not right here,' answered Lawana. 'The officer in charge is refusing to look at the *pass* and is intent on denying us access to his bridge.'

Ammuna stopped, puzzled. Then said, 'Is he after a bribe? Does he want money? What's the matter with the man? Why's he acting this way?'

'I've no idea sir. But he's refusing to budge....unless we all disarm and leave our weapons on this side of the bridge. Sir, I suggest we force our way across. We outnumber them ten to one.'

'If we have to fight our way across we'll lose more men. No colonel, that will be my last resort. What's this about disarming?'

'He says he'll let us across if we all disarm and leave our weapons with him. He says we can collect them on our return journey.'

'Is he out of his mind? Why does he want us disarmed? Something's very fishy about all this. Who's pulling his chain?' Ammuna was staring at the bridge and noticed a commotion at the southern end.

A robed man was shouting and shaking his fist at the two soldiers who had been left on guard there. The robed figure then forced his way past the soldiers and dared them to cut him down. He was waving it seemed, at Ammuna.

Ammuna said, 'Look, over there on the bridge. Is that Artatama's man coming across?'

'Could be. Shall I go and see?'

'Yes, do so. Take the translator with you…and the truce flag. We've got to get to the bottom of this.'

Lawana nudged his horse forward and beckoned the translator to follow him. Both men headed back to where the Assyrian officer stood, but he now had his back to them, looking at his own bridge, staring at the robed figure purposefully striding across towards him. He noted the two horses coming up behind, but chose to ignored them. His men kept their bows trained on the approaching horses.

'Colonel,' shouted the robed figure, waving at Lawana. 'I'll try to see what's going on here. Be patient.' Artatama's agent reached the Assyrian officer and began talking to him.

The Assyrian's face turned red and he went to strike the robed figure.

Haratam jumped back out of reach and shouted angrily, yelling in Assyrian at him. Whatever he said, it stopped the officer in his tracks. They stood there fiercely staring confronting each other. Then the officer laughed aloud, went to Haratam, clasped Artatama's agent by the shoulders, and gently shook him. Both began to laugh and the atmosphere relaxed.

Haratam waved to Lawana to come down and join them. The Assyrian soldiers lowered their bows on their officer's command, and the tension dissipated.

'What on earth is going on?' asked a bewildered Lawana, as he joined the agent and officer.

There was another exchange between the agent and the officer, and Haratam told Lawana urgently, 'I'll explain later. Now go and get your men and let's cross this damned bridge quickly, before this dolt of an officer changes his mind again.'

Lawana waved to Ammuna to bring his column to the bridge. The Assyrian soldiers moved aside to allow the Hittites to cross, and Haratam led Ammuna and his men across the Att Tuk River. They quickly skirted the small village sitting on the southern side of the bridge, and followed the riverbank road south towards Nineveh.

Once back on the road, with Haratam now riding a horse by Ammuna's side, Ammuna asked, 'Now pray tell, what the demons was all the fuss about. Why did he refuse to look at our *pass*.'

'General, I'm frankly not sure. He claimed he wasn't interested in looking at a forgery. He didn't like the look of your men, and he said he wasn't going to let any dammed Hittites across his bridge without a fight. It might have been personal...but I'm still a little stumped by what's happened.'

'So what changed his mind?'

'I told him I'd see him stripped of his uniform and I quoted a number of names of the senior officers in Nineveh at him. That's when he realised I had high connections and he might be in real trouble. He may have thought he could have a bit of a fight with you and blame it all on you...but then he realised others were aware of this situation and he'd better behave, or else. I told him the officers I quoted at him were expecting you in Nineveh...and if anything happened to you and your men, he would pay for it.'

'Why did he insist we disarm?' asked Lawana.

'Yes, it puzzles me as well?' Ammuna added.

'Now that, I don't know,' replied the agent. 'Maybe he thought you'd be silly enough to comply and then he could deal with you a lot easier. With no weapons, you'd be an easy target.'

'I smell something more in this,' Ammuna replied, but then fell silent.

'Sir, we'll have to make camp soon,' shouted the captain behind Lawana. 'It's late in the afternoon and we'll have to find a place for the night.'

'I know of a good spot a bout a league ahead,' Haratam informed them.

'Good, lead on,' Ammuna told him. 'Oh, and by the way, thanks for intervening once again. You seem to appear when we need you.'

'I'll be with you till we reach Nineveh now, if you don't object.'

'How can I object? You've saved me having to battle across the bridge. You're most welcome.'

After a couple of leagues more, Haratam said, 'General, over there...see the gentle slope leading down to the river; round the slope there's a good place to camp. There's easy access to the river from there, and the wind can't get at you because of the hill at your back. We'll be facing open country. The hills are behind us from now on, general.'

The column rounded the slope in the river and came to an open landscape spread before them. From there, in the fading light, they could see the long vast Nineveh Plains stretching into the far distance. A lush fertile pastoral, agricultural land which was the breadbasket of the two mighty cities it fed.

'How far is Nineveh from here?' Lawana asked the agent.

'We should be there after noon tomorrow,' replied Haratam.

'That's assuming we don't come across any more Assyrian officers trying to disarm us,' mocked Ammuna.

'Yes, I don't know why,' repeated Haratam.

'Right, let's set up the camp. You know the drill, colonel. Get them to it.'

'Yes sir.'

The pasture was excellent and the hobbled horses set to munching the lush grass with enthusiasm. The normal latrine holes were dug and firewood was gathered from the shrubs lining the riverbank.

'Sir, you asked me to jog your memory about talking to the men regarding their return journey,' Lawana reminded Ammuna.

'Ah, yes. Thank you colonel. I'll do that after we eat. I'm looking forward to more of the fish from the village.'

'So am I,' replied Lawana.

Later, sitting satiated round the cosy fire, Ammuna yawned and then stood and stretched his legs. '*Right men, give me your attention,*' he said in a loud commanding tone, looking to the second fire where Asmunikal sat with her non-com, as far away from Ammuna as possible. 'Keep you seats and let me have your ears. Tomorrow we reach Nineveh...you know...the place we're going to be paid. Now I know most of you will want to return to your Hittite homes. That is where you will have to be exceptionally careful. All along the border areas, the army will be on the lookout for you...so I counsel you head across the bridge at Nineveh and make for north of Karkamish, and then on to Kizzuwatna. Try to go for the area around thirty leagues from the Hittite border with Kizzuwatna. It'll be the least guarded.

'When you get home, don't make a great show of having money or you'll arouse envy and attention. It'll get you noticed and you'll be asked where you got your sudden wealth. If they connect you with me...you're in trouble. Spend carefully and don't let your family or friends know you have money. This advice is for your own safety. Those who don't have family; find a new town as far to the west as you can. Best place I can think of is Ahhiyawa. There, no one will question your money. You can live in style. Nice house, servants, slaves...the lot. There'll be many people involved in this business tomorrow, which is why I'm saying goodbye to you tonight.

'Tomorrow, we'll find a secluded spot somewhere and share out the reward as we agreed, and then those going back can take the horses with the provisions and go across the Nineveh bridge. That, sadly, will be the last time we'll meet. Good luck to all of you and thank you for your loyal service.' Ammuna sat back down, while a gentle applause came to his ears from his men. He raised his hand in acknowledgement and then resumed his conversation with Lawana and Haratam.

Artatama's agent said, 'That was a fine speech, sir.'

'Yes it was,' agreed Lawana.

Ammuna bowed his head in polite recognition. 'That as may be, but its time we hit the blankets. We have a heavy day tomorrow.'

43
Pretend Merchants

Next morning after another lacklustre breakfast of cold rations, Onasiyas shouted angrily, 'Come on men, get mounted and let's get moving; we're losing time.'

Everyone sensed the urgency Onasiyas had put into his voice, knowing they had to reach Ammuna before he made it to Nineveh if the rescue mission was to succeed.

Mokhat led them back to the river road, and as they paused to look at the river, he said, 'Have you seen the sky?'

Only then did Onasiyas look at the heavens. 'Oh, I see. Looks like a storm is brewing. What can we do about it? If it comes, it comes.' Onasiyas shrugged and gave his horse a nudge to move forward.

'We can keep an eye out for when it reaches us,' replied Mokhat.

'Yes sir. I'll keep my eye on the clouds, but we can't stop because of a little water. Ammuna is almost at Nineveh.' There was a pleading look to Onasiyas. He was worried the rogue general would get to the city before they could stop him. Then their troubles would double in any rescue attempt.

'Yes colonel, I'm not disagreeing with you. I'm simply saying we should expect a storm, that's all.' Mokhat had the same sense of urgency but past experience had taught him to keep his mind focused on the bigger picture. A storm could pose a problem if it developed into something bigger.

Onasiyas simply said, 'Shall we,' and pointed downriver.

Mokhat nodded and then began another day's galloping which had other travellers rushing to get out of their way of their furious charge along the river road.

The first drops of rain began to hit them in the afternoon, but the galloping column tried to ignore them and hastened on further, until the rain became a deluge. Then Mokhat finally called a halt and made an effort to find cover. They slowed to a canter, then wheeled their horses inland where there was a small clump of trees ahead, which they took shelter under. The horses were left out in the open as there wasn't enough room for them and the ninety four men huddled under the branches, although it made little difference. They were all soaked to the skin.

'Army life,' joked Palaiyas, as he stood against a tree, dripping wet. 'Everyone should be forced to try it. Maybe then they'd appreciate it more.'

As suddenly as it had started, the rain ceased.

'Look, the sun's come out,' Mokhat said in astonishment. 'What kind of weather is this?'

'Typical autumn weather,' replied Onasiyas, shaking himself. 'Come, let's get moving. The wind will dry us off.'

More galloping commenced into the late afternoon, then one of the scouts returned and reported a large fishing village ahead. 'Seems all quiet, sir,' he said.

'How big is it?' asked Onasiyas.

'About a hundred huts,' replied the scout.

'Right, resume your duties.'

The scout rode off again to resume his forward position.

'Hey, the scout's robe just reminded me. Remember what you said about acquiring some different clothing?' said Palaiyas. 'Now's our chance.'

'What'd you think?' Mokhat asked Onasiyas.

'Worth a try. As long as it doesn't take too long. The village seems big enough. Even if they don't have exactly what we want, we could buy more robes so we can cover these dark tunics of ours.'

'That settles it,' said Mokhat. 'We'll send ten men into the village, dressed in the brigands robes, leading eight pack ponies. The cover story will be we promised our business partner in Nineveh to deliver some robes and shirts but our usual source ran out. He claimed someone bought his whole stock a couple of days before. Now we've been trying to buy up any robes we can get our hands on, just to fulfil our end of the contract with our man in Nineveh. What'd you think?'

'Sounds plausible,' responded Onasiyas, stroking his beard.

Palaiyas nodded in agreement. 'Should be all right. If we pay in golden shekels, they'll leap at the business.'

'That's settled then. Can you organise it colonel?'

'With pleasure sir.'

The bend in the river was to the right and the fishing village could be seen from a long way off.

Mokhat halted the men and led them inland out of view of the main road. There, Onasiyas organised the ten men, including the three Assyrian speakers, who were to do all the talking. Finally the little group of pretend merchants rode off on their horses, leading the ten half empty pack ponies, towards the village.

'We'll skirt well around the village and meet our so-called merchants south of it as arranged,' said Onasiyas.

While the robed group headed for the village, Mokhat led his men through the scrubland to the south of the hamlet. There they waited for the men to return.

The non-com Assyrian speaker in charge led the little group of pretend merchants to the edge of the fishing village and halted. He was waiting to be noticed but no one came to investigate.

Curious, he thought. He could see a couple of men in the distance doing something to the nets at the far end of what looked like the main square. He dismounted and walked into the village to the largest hut, paused, and then gave three loud knocks on the door.

After a time the door opened and a woman peeked her head round the corner. 'What do you want,' she said gruffly.

'Is the master at home? I want a word with him. I have some money for him.'

At the mention of money, the door opened wider and a middle-aged woman stood in the doorway. 'What money?' she asked suspiciously.

'I would like to do some business with the headman of the village. If I'm at the wrong house, please excuse me. Maybe you could point out the right place for me.'

'No, this hut belongs to the chief of the village. I'm his wife. What kind of business?'

'If you don't mind, it's between me and your husband.'

'He's out back doing some carpentry. Wait a moment, I'll go get him.'

She closed the door and was gone. A while later, the door opened wide and an old sturdy man stood where his wife had been.

'What can I do for you,' said the village chief.

'Good day to you. Sorry to disturb you. Me and my men are travelling from Tushan,' said the non-com leading the group. 'I've come to see if you can sell me some robes you may have to spare. My usual supplier wasn't able to fill my order and I'm trying to pick up what I can en-route to fill a business deal I've got in Nineveh. I'll pay you well. In golden shekels if you can find as many robes as possible in your village. They don't have to be new. I'm looking for around a hundred of them. Can you help?'

The chieftain looked surprised at the request. 'We're only a poor fishing village. Let me think. I could probably find some robes, but I don't know how many. Let me get the people together and ask them. We might be able to dig up a few robes for you. You say they don't have to be new?'

'That's right. Any condition will do.'

'Wait a moment.' The chief turned to shout inside his hut, '*Laina*, go fetch the rest of the village, quickly now. Tell them to come here. Tell them there may be money for them.' He turned back to the non-com and said with a grin, 'That should bring them all out.'

Both men smiled at each other conspiratorially. Money was always a magic word in a poor land.

The villagers gathered in no time. The non-com was surprised at the size of the gathered crowd. When he'd come to the hut initially, there seemed to be no one in the village.

The village headman explained to the crowd what was wanted...and by implication, the fact they could exchange their old robes for money and buy some new ones and still be in profit.

No sooner had the chief finished, than people rushed off home and brought back their old robes and piled it in a heap where the headman indicated.

The other nine men of the group sorted through the pile, counted them.

That makes seventy eight robes the non-com was informed.

'We make seventy eight robes. Does this agree with you?'

'Yes, I agree.' He stood there expectantly.

'I'll pay you a half a golden shekel for each robe. I estimate it's about ten times their worth. Is it all right with you?'

'More than generous.' He turned to the villagers, and saw a sea of nodding faces.

The ones at the front had heard the figure and the news spread throughout the crowd like wildfire.

'Can my men pack them while we two settle the deal?'

The village headman nodded enthusiastically.

The non-com detached the money pouch from his belt and held it out. 'Where do you want to do this? Out here?'

'Bring a table,' he said to a man nearby.

A table appeared together with two chairs.

The non-com sat on one chair, while the headman took the other.

The shekels were upturned on the table and thirty nine shekels counted out to one side in front of the headman.

'Please count them, and then we'll be off.'

The count was made while people looked on with barely concealed greed. They'd got rid of their old clothes at a ridiculously inflated price and they simply couldn't believe their luck.

'Thank you. You've made a lot of people happy today,' said the village chief. 'I was hoping you would stay and have some food with us. We have some marvellous fresh fish from today's catch. At least stay and let us offer you a drink with us.'

'I'm sorry,' said the non-com, trying to end the transaction. 'We're already late. People are waiting for us in Nineveh.'

The non-com saw his companions had packed the robes on the ponies and he shook hands with the village chief before climbing back on his horse and cantering slowly out of the fishing village, heading south to where his colonel was waiting for them.

'Well? How did it go?' asked Onasiyas, when the non-com reached him about half a league south of the village.

'It went well sir,' he answered. 'Some of the garments are old and bug-ridden, but most just need a wash and ought to do just fine for what we want.'

'Good man. Well done!' complimented Onasiyas. 'We'll see to their laundry when we stop for the night. They'll dry out overnight and I'll hand them out in the morning. Now join the column.'

'Yes sir,' answered the non-com, and kicked his ride to join his companions.

With the replacement dress taken care of, Mokhat's men continued their charge along the river road well into darkness, until Mokhat swung his horse inland to set up camp for the night. Men were immediately set to launder the newly acquired robes in the nearby river. Doing it in the dark was a bit risky and one of the men fell in the river ending up wetter than the cloak he was attempting to wash.

44
Nineveh Plain

The next day when dawn broke, the sky was resplendent with deep blues in the west, all the way through to orange and red, as the sun began to rise in the eastern sky.

Ammuna was on his feet staring up at the changing colours. 'Up you get you lazy rich people,' he shouted at the sleeping Lawana and the others. 'Time to go and collect our money.'

Following a hurried breakfast, the column reformed and began to make its way into the Nineveh Plains, through the lush fertile lands that fed the large populations of the two great cities of Nineveh and Assur. The plain had a favourable climate resulting from the abundance of water from all the rainfall and the various natural springs. They didn't need to build complex canals to irrigate their fields. The long river valley, through which the Aransah flowed, was well suited for intensive agriculture, while in the hills to the east were kept the large herds of livestock at higher altitudes. Moreover, the mountains up there, possessed rich deposits of copper that was mined from time immemorial. Their informative Haratam explained all this to Ammuna and Lawana as they rode towards their journey's end.

There was only one stop, about mid-morning, when they rested and feasted on more delectable fish, so expertly prepared by the fishwives of the fishing village. Then the journey continued in the heat of the autumnal sun.

Finally, on the far distant horizon, the agent pointed out the outlines of a city rising out of the Nineveh Plains.

'There, good sirs, is our journey's end. I give you the mighty city of Nineveh.'

The column stopped and all those present gazed at the distant metropolis. A sudden loud cheer arose from the soldiers, venting exhilaration at the end of their long trek.

'I second that,' Lawana added when the cheering had subsided.

Ammuna had been thoughtful all through the morning, and now simply smiled at his deputy.

They rode on throughout the rest of the morning until noon, all the time watching the big city walls loom closer, until finally, they were only a league away from their destination.

Ammuna halted the column and turned his horse to face them. '*Listen up!* I want strict discipline when we enter the city...and watch me closely. I don't want to have to repeat any of my orders. Don't do *anything* without my orders. Anything to add, colonel?'

'No sir, I think you've said it all.'

To Haratam Ammuna said, 'Do you know where the prince will meet us?'

'I was told it would be at the Nergal Gate. It's the main gate into the city from the north.'

'And you're leading us there?'

'Yes general.'

'Right, lead on.'

45
Over the Bridge

The night went without incident until dawn crept in on their sleep and a further day brought an added day's chase.

After another hurried breakfast, the new robes were shared out amongst Onasiyas' men, giving the whole outfit a less sinister appearance. Some were still a little damp but Onasiyas insisted they would dry in the wind, once they resumed their journey.

'With these old robes and the ones from the brigands, all our men are now disguised as civilians,' Onasiyas announced to Mokhat. 'We're less likely to be challenged by the Assyrians.'

'Except for the size of our group,' replied Mokhat. 'And I accept colonel, there's nothing we can do about it.'

Onasiyas nodded and they rode on into the morning until around noon.

Mid morning, Onasiyas decided to take pity on his men and he pulled them off the river highway inland and gave them a short break.

'Sir,' said the man who'd been down this way before, coming up to Onasiyas. 'We're coming up to another bridge.'

'Eh? Damn it! Know what the river's called?'

'Yes sir. It's called the Att Tuk. Last time it was heavily guarded, not like the Kalat. We may have a problem with these sentries.'

'Any idea how many?'

'I seem to remember around twenty men guarding it the last time.'

'That's all we needed,' spat out Mokhat. 'Another forced crossing this near the city. I assume we're close to the city by now?' he looked at the soldier who knew the route.

'Another day at the outside, sir. If we can get over the bridge quickly, and then put speed on, we might make it today. Over the bridge, and we enter the Nineveh Plain, then a bit further on, and we'll be in sight of the city sir.'

'And still no sign of Ammuna. What do the scouts report? Have they seen the general's column up ahead?' Mokhat asked Onasiyas.

'No. Not so far sir,' Onasiyas responded.

'I'm really not happy how this chase has gone,' said Mokhat with a touch of anger. He held his palm out at Onasiyas and said, 'And before you get defensive colonel, I'm not blaming you or your men. The blame is squarely on Ammuna's shoulders. He's set a cracking pace and no matter how hard we've chased him, he's still outpaced us. I fear we're going to have to come up with a plan to snatch the princess from Artatama if we're to rescue her.'

Palaiyas proposed a plan, 'If we can catch the Mittani just after they cross the bridge at Nineveh, before they reach Mittani territory, we might be able to ambush them.'

Mokhat's head went from side to side as he contemplated such a move. 'This won't do. We'd better get going or we'll never catch him.' He swung himself back on his mount while the rest of the men did the same, and then the galloping continued downriver for the rest of the morning.

Soon afterwards, the scouts reported the bridge round the next bend in the river.

Mokhat halted the men and began a short conference with Palaiyas, Onasiyas and his deputy. 'Any ideas how we cross this?' he asked his companions.

'Surely, the same problem applies as last time. Either we force our way across the bridge, or we go upstream and swim across higher up,' Palaiyas responded.

'The time factor would militate against the swim,' Onasiyas pointed out.

'Yes, I agree colonel,' said Mokhat. 'Any other ideas?'

'Look at us. We're not now the sinister group we were. Any chance of pretending to be a merchant's caravan?' asked Onasiyas.

'Could we pull it off, that's the question?' said Mokhat.

'Let's try,' suggested Palaiyas. 'If we're challenged, then we deal with the sentries. Otherwise, we might just get away with it. We've nothing to lose if we try it this way, as merchants. The alternative is, we go to the bridge in a big charge, and then I'm sure we'll lose men to their bows. If we're challenged close up, I think our men will deal with the Assyrians without any casualties. It's a neater solution, don't you think.'

Onasiyas nodded. 'Either way it's risky. I think my men will be better off close up to the Assyrians.'

'Right then, close up it is.'

Without further ado, the company rode off towards the Att Tuk bridge river crossing.

Everyone now had civilian robes over their dark blue tunics. Onasiyas led the column, with Mokhat and Palaiyas riding behind. He claimed it was a safety precaution. However, the Assyrian speaking non-com and his two Assyrian speaking friends were out front.

Ninety-four mounted men, each leading a spare horse, slowly made their way to the northern side of the bridge, followed by forty pack ponies. There they met an Assyrian officer holding his hand up to stop them.

'Before I let you across,' said the Assyrian, 'I need to know what the purpose of your travel is and what you're carrying on the pack ponies.'

The Assyrian speaking non-com, promoted to leader and spokesman, responded, 'We're merchants on our way to Nineveh to sell a few items and pick up a cargo of slaves. All the slaves are men and so that's why there's so many of us. We don't want any trouble from the slaves on our return journey.'

'And what's in the packs?' asked the officer.

'Spare clothing, robes to sell, food stuff for the journey, camping gear and such,' answered the non-com, keeping a serious face.

'And you're coming from where?'

'Tushan. It's been a long ride. Can we go on?'

'I suppose. You've no contraband in those packs?'

'Certainly not,' the non-com replied seeming offended at such a question. 'We're law abiding honest business men.'

'All right, all right, I have to ask. That's my job.' The Assyrian officer ushered them onwards across the bridge. He waved to his counterparts at the other end to indicate the party coming was cleared.

Once clear of the bridge and riding along the river road again, Onasiyas turned to his Assyrian speaking non-com and patted him on the back, 'That went as well as I could have expected. You put just the right tone into your voice. You even had me believing in your story. Good work! You're heading for a promotion when we get back.'

'Thank you sir, but I'm not sure I want that,' replied the non-com.

That raised Onasiyas' eyebrows, 'And why not? Right, you don't have to answer right now…think it over. There's plenty of time.'

The non-com went back to his place in the column. The gallop continued until they rounded a slope, and then they were met by the vista of a huge plain spread before them.

The man who'd travelled the route already, explained that this was the Nineveh Plain they were entering, and it was flat county from there on until they came to the city itself.

'How far from here?' asked Mokhat.

'If we hurry; sometime this afternoon. Slower, and it'll be late this evening.'

'Sir,' came a call from one of the men who'd wandered over to a spot near the slope and dismounted. 'I think I've found a large campsite that fits Ammuna's men.'

Onasiyas and Mokhat rode over to where the man was prowling around. They both looked at the site and agreed with the soldier's assessment.

'I think you're right. From the state of it, I'd say they left this morning,' announced Onasiyas. 'They can't be that far ahead.'

The information animated Mokhat into action. 'Well? What are you waiting for. I want speed from everyone until the horses drop. I can smell Ammuna in front of me,' barked Mokhat at those present.

The whole company set off at a rapid pace towards the distant city, each one trying to outdo the other. They raced like this along the river road until the scouts reported they'd sighted a long column of riders far ahead in front of them.

46
Nineveh

Ammuna's column continued towards the city, passing a small number of huts banking onto the river with a number of boats beached on the river shore.

Haratam noticed Lawana's questioning look at the huts and explained, 'They're a small bunch of fishermen taking advantage of the nearby marketplace. They take their early catch to the village market outside the city wall, beating all the other fishing boats arriving later. There's only around ten huts here, so they're too small to be a proper threat to the bigger fishing village further up, but because they're the first fish to arrive, they get a good price.'

'Thank you. I was wondering what they were doing here,' replied Lawana.

They continued riding until they came in sight of a large village which had spread outside the city gate. Being outside the city, the village wasn't under the restrictive rules governing the inner walled city itself.

On riding closer, Ammuna noted, they would have to ride through the village centre to get to the gate. He looked questioningly at Artatama's agent.

In return, Haratam nodded towards the city, implying they should go on towards the gate.

'Sir, I think the stable over there to the right, the one with the big corral attached to it, might be useful,' Lawana pointed it out to his commander.

On the outskirts of the main road leading into the village, Ammuna was staring at a group of men in dark robes lounging around as if they were waiting for something. He felt an itch at the back of his neck and he didn't like it. The business of being asked to disarm still bothered him.

Haratam waved to the robed figures, and one of them waved back.

'General, I think my prince is waiting for you,' said the agent.

Ammuna peered at the hooded men in dark robes and smiled. 'Yes, I recognise one of them. The tall burly one with the black beard. He's the merchant I met in Adaniya... the one who negotiated all this.'

'That's Napat, the prince's trusted agent,' replied Haratam.

'So that's his name,' said Ammuna. 'He was never mannered enough to introduce himself.'

The column stopped a short distance from the robed figures and the agent and Ammuna dismounted. They strolled over to where the hooded men stood.

'General,' said the burly merchant, 'we've been expecting you. My prince is waiting for you in the market square. If you'll put your horses in there,' he pointed at the nearby corral, 'and then follow me; I'll lead you to my prince.'

'Colonel,' Ammuna called out loudly back to his deputy. 'Be so good as to have the men dismount, and then put all our horses in the corral here. Leave four men to guard them...then join me and we'll *all* go to see the prince. Oh, and don't forget to bring the brat with you.'

Ammuna and the robed group waited until Lawana had organised the stabling of their horses, and when all Ammuna's men were with him, the robed merchant and his group led Ammuna and his hundred and seventy nine men into the market square. Asmunikal was held in the centre of this crowd of Hittite soldiers.

The square was large but virtually empty, apart from three mules in the middle weighed down with heavy bags across their haunches. Waiting with the mules were four more dark robed figures. Around the rim of the square, people were peering out of their houses, staring at the mules in the centre, curious as to what was going on. At the southern end of the square, the area leading to the city gate, a group of Assyrian soldiers were milling around, but keeping back out of the square itself.

Burly Napat and small Haratam now led Ammuna and his men over to where the mules waited. One man quietly uncovered his cowl, and it was immediately clear this was the Mittani Crown Prince. Artatama's dark long locks flowed over his shoulders; his dark piercing eyes ate into Ammuna from an angular face, which sat on a muscular frame.

Ammuna's dark piercing eyes returned the stare with equal intensity. Both men were unashamedly sizing each other up, looking for weaknesses.

Artatama's hand shot out at Ammuna as they closed to touching distance. 'General,' said the prince in an ingratiating tone. 'It's a pleasure to finally meet you again. I haven't seen you for how long?'

'Since the civil war, your highness,' answered Ammuna, matching the prince's worming tone of voice. 'How have you been keeping? Is your father well?'

A deep anger fluttered momentarily across the prince's face, before he regained control, but it shook Ammuna.

'Your highness, what's happened?' Ammuna asked warily.

'Haven't you heard; Wassukanni has been taken by *your* Hittites and my father is dead. *My father is dead,*' snarled the Mittani prince. 'Wassukanni fell to the Hittite army two days ago.' Now the prince didn't bother hiding his anger. 'Unfortunately, I am now the king…but with no

401

capital to call my own,' he said furiously. 'Damn that king of yours.'

'Two days ago? Then how do you know? It takes at least three days from here to Wassukanni,' asked Ammuna suspiciously. He was thinking this was a ruse by this prince to avoid paying him.

'Pigeons my dear general. I assume you've heard of them? The message was, "Your father's dead; Wassukanni about to fall." *Does that satisfy you*?' Artatama shouted.

Lawana listened to this and was flabbergasted at the revelation. The conversation was in Hittite, and all those near enough, heard the stunning news.

Ammuna stood erect and said loudly, 'Sire, the Hittite king is *no* king of mine...as witness what I've done against him...for *you*.' Ammuna motioned for Asmunikal to be brought to the front so Artatama could inspect his merchandise.

The reluctant Hittite princess was pushed to the front, but Artatama made to motion her away. 'Listen general, I'll hold up my part of our agreement, but in return...get rid of her for me. She's useless to me now with the changed circumstances. Send her head or something to the Hittite king. Tell him one good turn deserves another. My father for his daughter.'

Ammuna said with suppressed anger, 'I suppose I can do that for you. No extra charge. But I still need paying for this,' he motioned at the princess.

'Of course, I said I would....as agreed. There it is,' Artatama pointed at the mules. Then he neared Ammuna's ear and said quietly, 'One and a half million golden shekels as arranged.'

Ammuna motioned to his deputy to come near, 'Colonel, take the brat out of here and wait for me with the horses. I'll deal with her later.'

Lawana's emotions were up now, but he fought desperately to maintain control. He'd clearly heard what the

402

Mittani prince wanted Ammuna to do with the king's daughter—and he would not permit it. He refused to be a part of her murder. The first thing was to get Asmunikal out of the square, as far away from Ammuna as possible. The general had unwittingly made it feasible by putting Asmunikal in his charge, and so he pushed his way out of the throng and led the small girl down to the stable at the northern end of the market square. Once inside, he took a fresh horse and put a blanket over it, then he squatted down to talk to the girl.

'Listen carefully princess, we're leaving this foul place and I'm taking you back to your mother. Don't be afraid, but we must hurry, so please be quiet and do as I ask. I'm going to put you on this horse and lead the horse through the herd in the corral. Bend your head down on the horse's neck so we won't be noticed. When we're through the herd, I'm going to jump on the horse behind you, and we'll ride as fast as we can back to Hattusas. Nod if you agree.'

Asmunikal looked deeply into the eyes of her captor and saw a gentleness in them missing from the other soldiers up to now…apart from her non-com minder. She was still confused by everything going on around her, but she nodded and patted Lawana's cheek to show she trusted him.

Lawana sat Asmunikal on the horse and told her to lean forward against its mane, then opened the other doors at the back of the stable leading out into the corral, and he led the horse quietly through their resting herd to the outer gate, which he opened. He then jumped up behind Asmunikal and kicked it into a gallop away from the village, and as he headed out of the village he looked back at the road and made out four bodies lying in their own blood. Those were the men he'd left to guard the horses. Lawana then understood Ammuna's reward was a mere illusion, and he'd walked into a trap devised by Artatama.

The colonel rode swiftly away from the village and Ammuna, heading back upriver as fast as the horse could carry them. Asmunikal was holding on to the mane of the horse as hard as her small finger could, while Lawana held her round her shoulders with one hand, making sure she was safe.

Back in the square the tensions had first risen when Artatama had mentioned the death of his father, and then subsided, as Ammuna realised they were going to be paid after all.

'Well sire,' Ammuna continued, 'are we all settled? Shall I have my men take charge of the mules,' he swept his hand in their direction.

'By all means, the mules are all yours.' Artatama stood back and told the four men holding the mule's reins to hand them over to Ammuna's men.

Ammuna's men took charge of the three mules.

The four Mittani men sauntered casually backwards towards the nearby houses round the square. They were slowly followed by the rest of the robed figures who had led the Hittites into the square. Only Haratam and Napat remained with the young Mittani king.

'Sir,' said the doc captain urgently, 'over there.'

Ammuna looked to where he nodded, and discovered a large number of Assyrian soldiers had appeared from nowhere. They had their bows at the ready. As Ammuna stared at them, more appeared from the direction of the city.

'What's going on?' Ammuna demanded of Artatama.

'What? Oh, I see them.' The new Mittani king looked over to where the Assyrians were, and stroked his chin as if surprised. 'What on earth are they up to? I didn't ask them for any help. Let me go have a word with them. I'll be back shortly.'

404

What appeared to be the Assyrian commander was shouting something in Ammuna's direction.

Ammuna stood in Artatama's way. 'Something's not right here. No one is going anywhere until I know what's going on.'

'And how are you going to find out? Do you speak Assyrian?' demanded Artatama. 'Don't be foolish; let me go and speak to their commander, find out why all these soldiers have appeared. I promise I have nothing to do with this.'

Ammuna still barred the young king's way. He hesitated to release what he took to be his only worthwhile hostage.

'Look, I'll leave my two agents with you if you don't trust me. I'll be back as soon as I've found out why the Assyrians are here. I promise. Maybe their commander has it in his head he can force us to give him a bribe?'

Ammuna looked at Artatama's two agents and then stood aside, nodding at the Assyrian soldiers. 'I'm sorry, sire, I'm just on edge. Of course you must go and see why they've appeared.'

All of Ammuna's men now stood facing outwards, looking to where this large number of Assyrian warriors were surrounding them in the entire village square—with bows at the ready. A number of Ammuna's men had reached for their bows and were readying them to fire back should they be attacked.

As Artatama walked over to the city end of the village square, Ammuna's translator appeared and said, 'Sir, the Assyrian commander is demanding our surrender. He insists we lay down our arms and move away from them.'

'Is that what all the shouting is about?' Ammuna asked.

'Yes sir. He insists we surrender.'

'Now I'm beginning to understand why those at the bridge wanted us to leave our arms there,' Ammuna exploded. 'I don't know if this young Mittani scoundrel is behind all this, but it has the hallmark of treachery written all over it.' Ammuna looked to where Artatama was now talking to the Assyrian commander, and he made a decision. '*Men, get ready for the fight of your lives*. It's the only way we're going to get out of here.'

The Assyrian commander greeted Artatama with a smile and said, 'How's it going your majesty. Are you sure you want us to kill them all? Shall we mow them down now?'

'Not just yet. I want to be seen to be trying to convince you to let them go. In a little while, tell your men to use their bows, and remember, as we agreed, no one is to be left alive. I want Ammuna's head. Our agreement was you get half of the money and I take the rest with me. Not bad for you, eh? A mornings work and you've earned a quarter of a million golden shekels.'

'What about your two men?' the Assyrian commander asked, pointing at Napat and Haratam.

'What about them. Both have failed me and they know the penalty for failure. Kill them all,' snarled Artatama callously.

When Artatama failed to return, Ammuna was absolutely certain this was a premeditated trap. He had his men prepare to defend themselves. Ammuna looked to where Artatama was, and saw him turn and smile at the Assyrian commander. It confirmed without a shadow of a doubt, he'd been betrayed by this snotty nosed prince.

Suddenly Ammuna had the most bizarre sensation of chickens coming home to roost. He'd betrayed his trust to his lawful king, and ventured onto the betrayal roundabout. Now he'd been betrayed in turn, and this would probably be his last time, seeing the number of Assyrian soldiers his men were facing.

Ammuna shouted at his men, loud enough for Artatama to hear, '*You and I have been betrayed by that no good Mittani scoundrel who calls himself a prince.* Put those mules in front of you; use them as a barricade. If you have your shields, put them out in front of you and get rid of these traitors.' Ammuna pointed at Napat and Haratam.

Before his men could do anything, a sudden massive volley of arrows came cascading down on their heads. In the blink of an eye, Ammuna noticed an arrow sticking out of Napat's eye, and the tall bearded merchant buckled to his knees. Then it seemed, the heavens opened up and was showering them with deadly arrows. Volley after volley fell on Ammuna's *loyal* Hittites, leaving them looking more like porcupines than people. Napat, Haratam, and everyone packed tightly in the middle of the market square were pierced with arrows. The mules went mad with pain, jumping and kicking, shedding their loads, as they tried to avoid the deadly projectiles.

Men moaned pleadingly, falling on the dry clay earth, their life ebbing out of them. Ammuna had an arrow through his throat and a couple protruded from his chest. Still he held tenaciously to life, staring with bitter hatred at his betrayer, before succumbing to more arrows. He drew his last breath with a curse on his lips, and breathed out, '*May you join me soon you bastard.*'

The three Assyrians nearest, rushed forward after the arrows stopped, and were getting ready to cut Ammuna's head off. All were looking for a trophy. Artatama rushed after them, shouting for them to stop. He reached Ammuna and drew his dagger intending to slit Ammuna's throat himself, but then saw Ammuna was no more, and he stomped his foot in frustration. On Ammuna's face, as he died, was an angry quizzical expression painted on with venom.

Artatama clearly heard Ammuna's cry of betrayal and the part about him being a *scoundrel*. This had infuriated him and made him determined to kill the Hittite general personally. Now it had been taken out of his hands and he was left angry and frustrated.

The Assyrian commander arrived on the scene and said, 'Satisfied?'

'No, but it'll have to do,' spat out Artatama. 'Those two sacks over there with red scarves tied to them, they're the one you want. There's a quarter of a million in each bag. The others are full of stones. Take one of them, and let me have some more mules to carry the rest away.' Artatama hoped this Assyrian wouldn't bother checking the rest of the mule's bags since they all contained gold.

The Assyrian commander shrugged his shoulders and shouted to his men to bring some mules from the stables.

I've an army to raise and a capital to regain, mouthed the new Mittani king to himself. *I'll need the two million from the Treasury if I'm to regain Wassukanni.*

47
The Princess

Mokhat urged his poor horse to go even faster on hearing the news that Ammuna had been sighted. A little later, he switched horses in mid gallop to let the one he'd been riding, rest from carrying his burden. Seeing their commander switch mounts, they all followed suit.

The pace picked up, but only marginally. After a long time of hard riding, Palaiyas shouted he could see Ammuna ahead of him. He was certain of it.

Riding by Mokhat, he called out, 'It looks like he's just coming up to a large village near the city.

About then, they came to within sight of a small village to their right and Mokhat pulled up and halted the column. He sat dumbfounded as he clearly watched Ammuna and his men far up ahead, stationary near the outside of the big village.

'*Curses, we've lost him*. He's almost in the city,' cried Mokhat in anguish. 'Damn! Damn! Damn!'

Onasiyas was shaking his head in despair. Palaiyas' attention was focused on the village they'd stopped in.

Palaiyas shouted to Captain Neti, 'Get your men to secure this village. Round everyone up and put them in one hut. We're probably going to be here awhile. There can't be many of them, not with so few huts.'

Onasiyas deputy gave the order after an exchange of glances with his boss. Onasiyas had nodded his accord.

Mokhat continued to watch as Ammuna and his men disappeared into the village far ahead of them.

'He's gone into the village,' he griped in despair, pointing in its direction.

Palaiyas joined him and peered at where Mokhat was pointing. 'Yes, I see them. There's nothing we can do.' He shrugged his shoulders in downcast state. 'I've secured this village. We might want to use those boats.' He pointed at the shoreline.

All three stood watching for a while, unwilling to accept fate had willed against them.

The protesting villagers were found and locked into the largest hut in the village. Men were posted round it to keep it secure.

'Sir,' Captain Neti reported, 'There's around thirty people, all locked up and safe.'

'Thank you captain,' replied Palaiyas, still staring at the distant village where Ammuna and his men had vanished. After a time, Palaiyas suddenly shouted, 'Look, over there. There's a horse coming this way from the village. I can't make it our clearly. Has he got a small child sitting on the horse in front of him?'

'I believe he has,' agreed Onasiyas. 'I wonder what he's up to.'

'Looks like he's running from something,' speculated Mokhat. 'He's got the horse going as fast as it can go.'

'Wait a moment,' shouted Onasiyas. 'I think its one of Ammuna's men. He hit his forehead with his hand and shouted, 'You lot,' indicating a group of his men holding their horses, 'Stop that horse at all cost,' he pointed at the fast approaching rider. 'Whatever you do don't let him get away. I want the child he's got sitting in front of him. Make sure she's safe.'

Suddenly Mokhat understood, 'You don't think that's her, do you?' he asked anxiously, looking for his own horse.

Palaiyas didn't wait as he grasped what they were implying. He found his tethered horse and jumped astride in one leap, swinging the horse round to face the oncoming rider, he kicked his horse in pursuit of Onasiyas' men who were already blocking the road.

The rider in a white tunic, saw people in robes trying to block him, and swerved inland to get by them, but Palaiyas had anticipated the move and sped his horse in the same direction, catching up with the frantic rider.

'*Stop you fool or I'll have you off your horse,*' shouted Palaiyas in Hittite.

Hearing Hittite, the rider looked even more frenzied but with a baffled expression replacing the crazed look he'd wore up until then.

All of a sudden Palaiyas lunged at the rider's reins and grabbed them from him, bringing the horse to a canter then a halt. By this time, the other ten robed men arrived and surrounded the befuddled rider.

'Who are you,' demanded the rider in Hittite. 'What do you want?'

Palaiyas looked closely at this rider, then switched his attention on the girl in front of him. The rider was holding her with his right arm across her chest, and the girl was hanging onto his arm, looking alarmed.

'Princess? Princess Asmunikal?' asked Palaiyas calmly but with a soft voice, trying not to frighten the girl any more.

The girl still looked frightened, but was now curious as well.

'*Who are you,*' shouted Lawana in desperation.

'We've been sent by the king to rescue his daughter. Is that her?' asked Palaiyas aggressively.

'How do I know you're here to rescue her,' said Lawana, now on the defensive.

By this time Palaiyas and the group of ten had led Lawana's horse back to where Mokhat and Onasiyas waited.

'I think it's the princess,' shouted Palaiyas as they neared. 'This oaf here won't confirm it yet, but I'm pretty sure it's her.'

'Get them both down from the horse,' ordered Mokhat.

Lawana was pulled off the horse roughly by four men and held tightly, whilst the girl was gently removed from Lawana's grasp.

'Princess Asmunikal,' said Mokhat quietly, 'Do you remember me? I'm your godfather; Prince Mokhat of the Kaska. I was at your birthday party three years ago. Your mother, the queen, sent me to fetch you back home.'

The girl burst into tears, went up to Mokhat, and put her arms round his neck. Lawana stared at the scene and began to understand whose hands he'd fallen into.

'Uncle Mokhat,' is all the girl could say, and quietly cried on his shoulder.

'I'm Colonel Lawana, formerly of the Hittite army,' Lawana told Palaiyas. 'I was trying to rescue the girl from Ammuna's murdering hands.'

Onasiyas eyes narrowed as he looked at Lawana. 'Your Ammuna's right hand, aren't you? What happened? Had a falling out? Not enough gold for you?'

Lawana looked shocked at the sarcastic venom in the voice. 'Believe it or not; I was trying to prevent Ammuna from murdering the princess.'

'Really? I find it hard to believe,' replied Onasiyas.

'Artatama didn't want her after all,' continued Lawana ignoring the malice towards him, 'and asked Ammuna to get rid of her; send her head to her father.'

That caused alarmed looks among the listeners.

'Why on earth spend all this effort to drag the poor girl all this way and then murder her. My dear ex-colonel, it's obvious you're trying to spin us a bunch of lies to save your own neck, isn't it?' said Onasiyas with disgust.

'No it isn't,' persisted Ammuna's deputy. 'Artatama blurted out Tudhaliyas has taken Wassukanni and killed Artatama's father, that's why he wanted the princess's head sent to the king. I couldn't be any part of such a deed. I was already uneasy by my role in this affair, and this was the last straw. I wanted no part of this murder. Ammuna told me to take her away and look after her until he could deal with her; I took her to the stable, and instead keeping her there for him, I jumped on a horse with the princess and rode upriver as fast as I could to get out of there. I also think Ammuna's dead.'

This last bit of news was another revelation which stunned those listening. The strange news was piling up. They intended to murder the princess, Wassukanni had fallen, Saustatar dead, and now Ammuna's supposed death.

'How do you know he's dead? Did you see it happen?' asked Mokhat, still trying to soothe the young girl.

'No, but the men guarding our horses were lying in a pool of blood as I rode away, and the Assyrians were surrounding our group in the square as I left. I think we walked into Artatama's trap. He had no intention of paying out the money for the girl. Not after the loss of his father and Wassukanni.'

'I'm afraid it makes sense, assuming what you say is true,' said Palaiyas.

'Sir, we've got to get out of here, fast,' said Onasiyas. 'We have the princess, and so we've succeeded in the mission, but if we don't move fast, we still might find ourselves in trouble with the locals.'

'If Wassukanni's really fallen, then what about heading there,' suggested Palaiyas. 'That's where the king will be...*and* all the Hittite army.'

'That a good plan,' answered Mokhat. 'What do you suggest?'

'Those nine boats down there on the beach,' Palaiyas pointed at the river. 'We can use them to ferry the men across the river, and get the horses to swim behind the boats as we did with the Puranti. Then it's three to four days ride to Wassukanni.'

'I'm in favour,' Onasiyas looked at Mokhat's sharp face. 'Tie this ex-colonel up, we'll take him with us. Let the king sort this out.'

Mokhat nodded, 'Right, let's do it. I'm still left with the stink of treachery burning in my nostrils. That Artatama *needs* killing; but that's a job I'm content to leave to Tudhaliyas. That rogue prince is going to be a pain in the gut until he's gotten rid of, mark my words.'

With those prophetic words ringing in the ears of all those listening, they hurried down to the river to organise the river crossing. Horses were stripped of blankets and pack ponies unburdened.

The first batch of men reached the other side without incident. The boats came back for the next, and so on until all the *special forces* were on the western side of the Aransah.

Mokhat was the last to cross and as he sat in the boat, he listened to the music of the water flowing downriver and relaxed, wallowing in, and being cradled by the sound of nature, and he pondered. His mission was a success and he was on his way home to his wife and children. He'd badly missed them. True it would take some time to get back to Nerik, but now he had all the time in the world.

48
The King

Mokhat's group reached the outskirts of Wassukanni after a four day trek east across the open desert. The horses were tired and in a bad state, as were its riders. The first view of Wassukanni gave them a shock as they came in sight of it over a sand dune. There was a huge ramp leaning against the city wall facing them. Atop the ramp was a massive tower. Everything was absolutely quiet, but for the screech of the carrion crows and the vultures feasting on the many dead lying around the city. Soldiers were collecting the dead onto carts, but the carrion feeders kept up their persistence.

Mokhat and his men went round to the western city gates and found them in an utter shambles. Hittite soldiers stood guard outside, trying to ignore the huge hole in the right gate.

'I'm looking for the king,' Mokhat said to the officer in charge.

The man looked at Mokhat's dark dusty robes and said mockingly, 'And who may I ask is seeking an audience with the new king of Wassukanni?'

'Prince Mokhat of the Kaska and this is a group of *special* Hittite *forces* returning with the king's daughter.'

The man seemed to have been hit in the face with the news. Everyone in the Hittite army knew why they had wrecked such savage havoc on this city—and here was a man claiming to have the king's daughter.

'I'm sorry sir…your highness, sir,' blurted out the officer. 'The king is in the palace. I'll escort you there myself.' The officer was staring at the little girl tightly holding Mokhat's hand.

Asmunikal had clung to Mokhat all the way, holding his hand when she could, refusing to let it go. She slept close to him during the nights, and during the day, insisted on riding all the way to Wassukanni with him on his horse. The poor girl was traumatised and badly needed her mother. Mokhat understood this.

The tired *special forces* dismounted and walking their horses, followed the officer leading Mokhat towards the centre of the damaged city to where the citadel stood.

The gates to the citadel stood wide open and Hittite soldiers milled around outside. The arrival of these people in dark robes caused a stir and a lot of staring. Tudhaliyas' bodyguard were guarding the citadel and one of the officers in charge recognised Onasiyas.

'Colonel, where have you been?' asked the officer, as Onasiyas came close. 'I hardly realised it was you. You missed all the fun here.'

'Oh we've had our own fun,' he nodded at Mokhat and the girl.

The officer immediately recognised Asmunikal, and his face dropped in amazement. He shook his head as if to clear his eyes, not believing them, then turned and rushed inside the palace at a frantic pace.

'I assume he's gone to inform the king we're here,' smiled Mokhat at Palaiyas.

There was uproar from the first floor as if a huge cheer had suddenly burst out from those inside. The sound of running feet came from inside, and then Tudhaliyas came running down the stairs into the courtyard, tears unashamedly flowing down his face. He rushed over to where Mokhat was holding Asmunikal and grabbed the smiling girl off her feet and into his arms. She in turn buried her head in her father's shoulder and cried with joy.

Those near, watching, were overcome with their own emotions at the happy reunion.

Mokhat stood there beaming at Palaiyas and Onasiyas. All the soldiers present smiled and patted each other on their backs at the successful conclusion to this unhappy incident.

Tudhaliyas looked into Mokhat's eyes with such deep gratitude as to make Mokhat wince.

'My Kaska friend,' said the king, 'there are no words to thank you enough for what you've done. You and Palaiyas have....' the king choked. 'I now feel, the same I felt when she was first born. This is the second miracle. I know her mother will feel as I do when we return to Hattusas. She will want to thank you personally.'

Epilogue

After another week and a half on the road back to Hattusas, Mokhat and Palaiyas, both finally rested in a proper bed. They were then invited to a *thank-you-feast* with the king and queen, and with Asmunikal seated back where she belonged, between her parents. They said their farewells to a grateful King Tudhaliyas, to Queen Nikal, and to the little princess, now once more her normal smiling self.

Mokhat and Palaiyas paid particular thanks to Onasiyas and his *special forces* at a special informal banquet, where they said their goodbyes to their recent comrade-in-arms. Eventually they left Hattusas, and managed to return to Nerik, and into the arms of their own families.

In a quiet moment later, while the two friends were alone together in the Grand Hall of the castle in Nerik, Mokhat turned to Palaiyas and said, 'This is positively the last time I help the Hittite King get out of a fix. He's become far too dependent on us to get him out of sticky situations. It's not as if the Hittites had a small empire. He has *all* his other subjects to choose from to carry out these special tasks; why do I have to be the one he picks on? This is the last time *ever*, I mean it. Here am I putting myself at risk with every episode for a foreign king, and it's not going to happen again—not after this. My family comes first.'

Murder in Hattusas

Sasha Garrydeb

Murder in Hattusas is the 1st Volume of the Hittite Trilogy.

At the close of the Old Kingdom in 1420 BC, the realm of the ancient Hittite Empire is in chaos. Muwatallis, the king has been assassinated in the capital, Hattusas, by the feared Kaska Assassin's Guild. Muwas, the dead king's brother blames the two sons of the previous king, Huzziyas, and he insists he be the one to succeed his brother. The two sons of Huzziyas, Kantuzzili and Himuili, insist the next king be Tudhaliyas, son of Himuili, since rewarding Muwatallis' previous assassination of Huzziyas, is unthinkable. Neither side is prepared to give way, and the scene is set for civil war. Tagrama, the High Priest of the temple of the Storm God Taru, tries to broker a peace, but is up against outright stubbornness.

Muwas then hires Harep, of the same Assassin's Guild, to kill Tudhaliyas. Only Mokhat, the former spiritual adviser to the Assassin's Guild, knows what Harep looks like, and he is determined to stop all the damnable assassinations. He's had enough of the Guild's murdering ways.

Muwas calls upon his Mittani allies, the Mittani King Saustatar, who sends his son Artatama with an army to Muwas' aid. The Kizzuwatna King Shunashura changes allegiance and abandons the Mittani in favour of Kantuzzili's faction, sending an army to help Tudhaliyas.

The Pharaoh Amenhotep II threatens to invade Mittani unless they pull their army out of Hatti. Saustatar refuses.

When Tudhaliyas meets Nikal, he falls for this daughter of the Kizzuwatna king. They announce their engagement. Harep, the hired assassin, makes a number of attempts on Tudhaliyas' life, but is foiled. The major Battle of the Wide Plateau settles the civil war but in the mean time, Harap manages to kidnap Nikal.

The protagonist, Mokhat, is in search of himself after his sordid ministrations to a bunch of murderers. It is a bronze-age thriller, which includes a romp through the Hittite landscape, a civil war, and chariots in battle. This is a tale of love and adventure set in the most fascinating recently discovered culture of the ancient world. Volume 2 is due for publication in February 2011.

A must for all fans of the Hittite civilisation.

Madduwatta's Rebellion

Sasha Garrydeb

This is the second volume of the Hittite Trilogy.

It has been three years since the Battle of the Plateau put Tudhaliyas on the throne in the Hittite Empire, yet instead of feeling secure, he feels menaced. His chief spy, Satipilli, has vanished, and trouble is brewing in the west, possibly from Ahhiyawa. The Mittani are threatening Isuwa on the eastern border, seeking revenge for their humiliation in the civil war. All this requires reliable intelligence reports. Tudhaliyas is forced to turn to the unknown faces of Mokhat and Palaiyas and asks them to go to the west, to Millawanda, and discover what has happened to Satipilli, the chief spy of the Hittites.

On their journey, they are followed and someone keeps trying to kill them; with each failure, their attempts become more desperate. The assassins follow Mokhat and Palaiyas but are finally dissuaded; then they suddenly reappear in Khemet (Egypt). Somebody doesn't want them to complete their mission.

At the close of the Old Kingdom in 1417 BC, Madduwatta, the Governor of Lukka, a nominal vassal of Tudhaliyas, has plans of his own. How is he implicated in all this? He has his eyes on Arzawa. He badly needs friends, and will ally himself with anyone prepared to help him achieve his goal. But who has stirred him up? Who has gone to all these lengths to create a rebellion for the Hittites?

Meanwhile, Ahhiyawa is in the grip of a Civil War, with two brothers fighting it out for the throne in Millawanda. The outcome of the conflict will impact on their neighbours, Arzawa, the Hittites, and the Governor of Lukka.

Palaiyas, a Prince of Tiryns, decides to go home to make peace with his father, the king. While in Tiryns, he's abducted by his uncle, Elektryon, the king of Mycenae, and brought to account for his desertion; then forced to complete his tour of duty on Keftiu (Crete). Mokhat follows him and rescues him. After Khemet (Egypt), Ugarit, and Lukka, they finally discover the truth. Mokhat falls in love in this romp through the ancient Med, all in a search for Satipilli.

The Wizard of Kálar

Sasha Garrydeb

On the distant planet of Kálar the two hundred year old life cycle of the Schánda once again menace the idyllic lives of the Bólani, a small tribal village of forest dwellers living in their hollowed Lándo trees.

The schánda stand half a cubit high, have a two hundred year life-cycle and normally live up on the northern edges of the tundra of the planet of Kálar. They are an insect, something like a cross between a spider and a scorpion. The adult form has no poisonous stinger and isn't carnivorous. Then the mating urge mutates the schánda into a massive swarm of ferocious carnivores. It doubles in size, grows the stinger and large claws in its fourth and final moult, then begins its long march from its home-ground in the North of Kálar, south to its mating grounds on the shores of the Golden Sea.

In its path live the small peaceful Bólani tribe who make their homes in living Lándo trees in the forest. Around the same time as the schánda begin their journey, the Bólani's collective unconscious, an imbedded memory of these carnivorous insects, triggers nightmares. They dream of an unstoppable carnivorous procession intent on eating their way to their mating grounds, heading their way.

The Bólani must gather their possessions and flee ahead of the encroaching swarm. They escape south to the shores of the Golden Sea just ahead of the voracious insects. Their long march to the shores of the Golden Sea takes them through a series of adventures with small blood sucking insects, vicious storms, predatory birds, unfriendly villages, lakes of volcanic lava, and desert worms. Only the skill of their apprentice wizard, Morác, saves them from disaster—transforming his powers in the process. Even when they

425

reach the Golden Sea their problems are not at an end. Imprisoned by a coastal tribe and then buffeted by storms on their flimsy rafts the dynamics of the tribe are changed forever before they finally manage to return to their small forest village back up in the far North.

This is an eco-fantasy tale stretching the imagination beyond the solar system.

Worlds Beyond Ours

Sasha Garrydeb

In the fourth millennium humans finally invent the warp-drive and set out to explore the Galaxy. The first mission is sent to our nearest star, Alpha Centauri, and the starship returns to a stormy acclaim by earth's population. It then comes as a shock to our planet when aliens visit earth and announce that the Galactic Federation intends to lift its quarantine around the Solar System. Since humans now have warp drive capability, would they like to join the Galactic Federation?

This story brings humanity for the first time into contact with a variety of alien life-forms: elfin-like creatures, dinosauroids, insectoids, and many more, when Earth's Embassies are sent to other worlds. As the humans fan out from their home world they encounter a number of adventures which shape humanity's future for generations to come. Wonders like floating cities in the sky, terraforming other planets and genetic advertising.

The story at the end comes full circle when it culminates in another first contact, but this time from our neighbouring galaxy for this Galactic Federation.